continued . . .

"If you're looking for smart, upbeat fiction with snappy dialogue and a fun peek into ethnic traditions, *Happy Any Day Now* is perfect. A lively read that offers an interesting behind-the-scenes look at a symphony orchestra and a midlife heroine who is all grown-up but still capable of being comically and poignantly bewildered by life."

—Nancy Martin, author of the Blackbird Sisters Mysteries

"Judith Raphael is half-Korean and half-Jewish, and full-on fabulous! Toby Devens's novel is warm, witty, and wonderful."

—Wendy Wax, author of *The House on Mermaid Point*

"Never has a midlife crisis—or actually a perfect storm of them—been treated with such charm, insight, and smart, sardonic humor. Judith Soo Jin Raphael, the heroine of Toby Devens's engaging new novel, is half-Korean, half-Jewish, and facing her fiftieth birthday; she is carrying enough emotional baggage and family history to last several additional lifetimes. With a deft touch, Devens spins a tale of lost opportunities and rediscovered romance, second chances and second thoughts, family secrets and lasting friendships. Set in the fascinating world of classical music—with all its pressures, rivalries, passions, and loyalties—Devens's *Happy Any Day Now* is a virtuoso performance that is bound to win Devens a host of new fans."   —Liza Gyllenhaal, author of *Bleeding Heart*

barefoot beach

TOBY DEVENS

NAL ACCENT

NEW AMERICAN LIBRARY
Published by New American Library,
an imprint of Penguin Random House LLC
375 Hudson Street, New York, New York 10014

This book is an original publication of New American Library.

First NAL Accent Printing, July 2016

For more information about Penguin Random House, visit penguin.com.

LIBRARY OF CONGRESS CATALOGING-IN-PUBLICATION DATA:

Names: Devens, Toby, author.
Title: Barefoot beach/Toby Devens.
Description: New York, New York: New American Library, [2016]
Identifiers: LCCN 2015041940 (print) | LCCN 2015045294 (ebook) | ISBN 9780451418999 (softcover) | ISBN 9781101616246 (ebook)
Subjects: LCSH: Female friendship—Fiction. | Vacation homes—Maryland—Fiction. | Domestic fiction. | BISAC: FICTION/Contemporary Women. | FICTION/Family Life. | FICTION/Humorous. | GSAFD: Humorous fiction.
Classification: LCC PS3604.E885 B37 2016 (print) | LCC PS3604.E885 (ebook) | DDC 813/.6—dc23
LC record available at http://lccn.loc.gov/2015041940

Printed in the United States of America
10 9 8 7 6 5 4 3 2 1

Designed by Kristin del Rosario

Penguin
Random
House

chapter one

The summer house on Surf Avenue carried some kind of spell, concocted of—I don't know—salt air, sea grass, and Old Bay Seasoning, that over the years had permeated its walls and floorboards. Whatever it was, the place cast fabulous magic. For a while, anyway.

The drive from Baltimore to Tuckahoe had taken me two hours and ten minutes, which was good for mid-June. I pulled into the garage but left the few suitcases and boxes in the trunk; first things first. The sky was in motion. I walked around back through the Indian grass and wild geranium and down the path to the beach.

At the bottom of three weathered-to-silver wooden steps, I slipped out of my flip-flops. The stretch of sand behind my house that some equally besotted Victorian had named Barefoot Beach invited its guests to kick off their shoes. The fine-grained sand, paler and silkier than the grittier stuff up the strand, was pure bliss. As I buried my toes in its warmth, I felt my tense muscles slacken, my shoulders relax, and my rib cage expand to hold my suddenly larger but lighter heart. I exhaled a breath of release. I was here! It was summer! I had nearly three months to look forward to! Everything in me but my knees wanted to cartwheel.

I made my way through scattered blankets and striped umbrellas, skirting sand dollars and half-buried scallop shells, inhaling the coconut scent of suntan lotion that was eau de summer for me. Up the beach, in the shadows cast by the towering hotels, the crowds were beginning to thin. The childless would probably spend the next few hours in dry clothes with a drink and the breathtaking view from the Crow's Nest bar atop the Boardwalk Hilton or Rick's on the roof of the Hotel Casablanca. The kids, of course, wanted to play until the last shred of light vanished. I nearly got mowed down by a sextet of preteens racing to the surf, the boys clamping boogie boards to their hairless chests. The girls, whose bikini tops displayed them in all stages of flowering, held their boards high, shrieking as they ran.

Downwind, kites were up, swaying on gentle drafts. A fish kite, puffed with air, swam in the wind. An origami bird rode the currents.

Nearby, a little girl danced around, clutching the string of a large yellow smiley-faced balloon as she chanted, "I want to let it go. I want to see it fly." She stopped and faced her mother. "Mommy, please."

"Okay, but if you let it go, it won't be coming back. You know it will be gone forever, right?" the mother answered.

"I know. It's okay."

"Then it's up to you."

Yelling, "Wooo!" the girl flung the string. The three of us followed the balloon lofting past the horizon, becoming a speck of yellow as it reached cloud altitude.

When it disappeared, the girl said, "I think it's in heaven."

She skipped off, swinging her plastic pail. Children move to a faster rhythm than grown-ups. The mom and I exchanged smiles.

Now it *was* sunset. Beams of rose gold made fuchsia glitter trails on the water. And as I stood there basking in the warmth, the sky brightened to flamingo.

I turned to take in the silhouette of the Surf Avenue house against the shimmering sky. With my sunglasses on, I could make out its details: white trim against cedar shake shingles; the second-floor widow's walk, my refuge when things got really bad; and the deck where I'd spent luxurious afternoons napping in the hammock or stretched out on a canvas lounge chair, reading and sipping lemonade or, once upon a time, sharing coffee or wine and easy conversation with my husband.

Lon had brought me here to propose. Smart move. I'd met him at a book signing, an event so mobbed that his adoring fans had to take a number to queue up. I drew lucky seven and approached his table carrying my well-worn copy of his first book, *Canyon of Time.* (Twenty-three weeks on the *New York Times* bestseller list. "Brilliant, epic debut novel."—*Publishers Weekly.* "Brings the rugged mountains of California to life with unforgettable characters and thrilling plot twists."—*The New Yorker.*) He looked up at the redheaded grad student, twelve years his junior, and turned on the Irish charm. As the crowd behind me rumbled with impatience, Lon and I chatted. Finally, he wrote, "To Nora and great first chapters," on the flyleaf of his newly released *Banshee River.* I wrote my phone number on the back of the business card he'd nudged toward me and we traded. So, I suppose, I'd fallen for him hard at first sight, and he supposed I'd fall that way for the house and say yes to both of them. He'd been right.

We were married on that deck overlooking the beach. A small, just-about-secret ceremony for the media darling and his young bride, one designed to duck the potential for paparazzi lurking behind the dunes. We were wed at dawn, when only the best of friends, the most devoted family, would show up, Lon said. Thirty of them had come and tossed bread crumbs instead of rice, so the gulls wouldn't choke.

When I settled in that first summer, it was as if I'd lived there forever. And now twenty-some years later, it *had* been almost forever. The house stood dune-high to watch over the tides that counted as much as clocks this close to the water. Within its walls or in its giant shadow, life happened: the conception of a child, the creation of a book, the ambushing loss of a husband in his prime. I always felt that as long as a hurricane didn't thrash it to bits and sweep it out to sea, the house would be in our family for generations.

As of today, I wasn't so sure.

No time for worrying about things that might never happen, I thought as I made my way along the path. Live in the moment. Isn't that what Margo liked to say? Not that my best friend's advice was always sound. But this bit I tried to believe. So, better unpack and get things in shape before my son got in from college. Haul the cushions out and hang the hammock. I climbed the steps to the deck. Give the planks a good sweeping. Citronella candles. Need to find those and . . . Someone was moving around my kitchen. Beyond the glass I saw flashes of pink and blond. That gave it away. Also the music filtering from—I peered in—the iPad she'd propped on the counter. "Shall We Dance?" from *The King and I.* Of course. The local rep theater was putting on the musical this summer, and Margo was going to be its director.

I stood watching for a moment as she fussed around in the kitchen in a halter dress that displayed too much cleavage for a forty-seven-year-old woman. But Margo was not your average forty-seven-year-old. She was not your average anything, this Welcome Wagon lady sporting DKNY sunglasses as a headband and two-carat diamond stud earrings.

She was larger than life and had been making mine crazier and more fun since we'd found each other back in college. I had no sisters, but I loved her like one, consistently but ambiguously. There were times when I wanted to smack her. More times when I wanted to hug her. *Like now,* I thought, smiling as I watched her lay out her annual thanksgiving-for-summer-and-my-arrival gift.

I tapped the glass. No response. I pounded on it, sending her spinning. Eyes afire, she strode over to click the lock and nudge the sliding glass door open just wide enough so I could edge myself in.

"Brilliant, Nora." She flared her surgically narrowed nostrils at me. "Sneaking around out there. You almost gave me a heart attack. And you're late. I had to let myself in and the key jammed in the lock. I was jiggling out there on your porch for at least three minutes."

She stretched an arm to turn down the volume on the music. Then she kissed me on both cheeks, one of her affectations that used to drive Lon crazy. "She's from Brooklyn, for God's sake," he'd said. "Who kisses on both cheeks in Brooklyn?" When she released me, she murmured— already into a new, forgiving role—"I've missed you."

"Missed you too," I said.

Which sounded as if it had been forever, as if we hadn't caught up by phone on Wednesday or seen each other two weeks ago in Baltimore.

During the colder seasons, I lived in a row house in the city's Charles Village neighborhood, a hive of academics not far from Johns Hopkins University, where Lon had taught. Margo and her husband, Pete, former star second baseman for the Baltimore Orioles, resided half an hour, and half a world, away in the tony suburb of Greenspring Valley, where their towering Tudor sat on a sward of lawn large enough to graze a flock of sheep. Their place up the highway in Rehoboth, Delaware, was twice the size of mine, but I had the fabulous ocean view.

The Manolises always arrived in early June so Margo could get a head start at the Driftwood Playhouse, where she chaired its board, sometimes directed, and frequently acted, and which she generously funded.

Now she flourished a hand toward the granite-topped island where she'd parked the yeasty part of her annual welcome-back gift. In a special see-through bag designed to keep them fresh were a dozen bagels. Also a babka coffee cake, a package of black-and-white cookies, which were to New Yorkers what madeleines were to Proust, and a tin of rugelach, the sweet-cinnamon-and-raisin-studded pastries my son, Jack, relished.

I'd eaten last at eleven a.m., a cupcake at an assisted living center. I was starved. I swiped a rugala and bit into the rich dough.

"Hands off. Those are for Jack." Margo slipped the tin away after I'd grabbed two more.

She loved my son, had played his aunt throughout his childhood. "When does he arrive?"

I shrugged. Midafternoon, Jack had called to tell me that his plans had changed and he wasn't going to be leaving Duke until eight or so, and, "Please, Mom, don't wait up. Promise me." His voice had been ragged, which made me think the delayed start was due to the latest episode in the soap opera featuring his off-again-on-again girlfriend, Tiffanie. So, of course, I added a layer of agita about that to my garden-variety fears of him dozing off at the wheel or getting hijacked at a gas station in some hick Carolina town.

I was a mother. I worried. Maybe more than most because we'd gone through so much to bring him into the world and I didn't trust the fates. Fickle broads. They could smile on you one day and backhand you the next.

"Jack will be fine," Margo assured me. "Whatever time he gets in, there's all kinds of stuff for a late-night snack. Check out the fridge. Come on," she urged, trying to distract me.

She'd stocked it with her idea of staples: smoked salmon, sliced sturgeon, a container of organic cream cheese, a wedge of Fontina from Italy, an obscenely expensive jar of caviar, and two pounds of hand-carved Jewish deli meat.

"A feast," I agreed. "But, really, you don't have to do this every year."

"Yeah, yeah. Didn't Mamma-mia teach you manners? The correct response to a gift is a simple thank-you."

She'd also brought flowers from her garden—rugosa roses, blue-flag iris, and a cloud of moonbeam coreopsis—and had arranged them in a vase on the center island.

"Beautiful," I said. "Thank you, Margo."

She looked around, nodding with pleasure. "I love this kitchen." Of course she did. She'd taken charge of renovating it the summer before.

When she'd first suggested the makeover, I'd countered, "I'm in no hurry."

"That's a major understatement. You, my dear, are stuck. It's been seven years since Lon died. To put it bluntly"—and no one was better at blunt than Margo—"he's moved on." She pointed upward. "Now it's time for you to do the same, though in a different direction. May I suggest forward? And I'll bet brighter, more open surroundings will do wonders for your mood. The entire downstairs needs an update and I've got ideas for turning that dreary living room into a gorgeous great room. But, in deference to your aversion to change, we'll start with the kitchen."

She'd always hated the dark, cramped bachelor's cave of a kitchen, which Lon had refused to renovate. With him gone seven years and a few twitches signaling restlessness from me, she'd seen her opportunity. "We're ripping the whole freakin' thing out. If it's not a supporting wall, it goes. And I'll introduce you to my appliance man."

Margo had a faucet man, a trim man, a grout man, a man for every job except, you know . . . Well, she had her husband for that, but she'd been whining about the quality of the service lately. Pete Manolis was courteous enough, and she used to brag that he was a master of technique, but he wasn't showing up on time these days, and his performance was not as high-end as she expected from one of her experts.

I'd let her go to town with her "refreshment," as she called it, of the décor. With a few exceptions. As in, I'd never part with the kitchen table. Too many good memories. Family dinners, birthday parties. Lon had signed an unexpected contract for his last novel on its well-worn surface, chortling at the craziness of it all as he flourished "Henry London Farrell" on the last page.

"I never thought this would happen," he'd said. And, of course, as things turned out, it hadn't. But who could have known back then? And we were delirious. Our seven-year-old, still in his jammies, wandered into the kitchen, and Lon swept him up and swung him high. "Daddy's book is going to be published," he exclaimed, which Jack, as the child of an author, understood was a big deal. "Yay!" he shouted. A minute later, we were dancing, hands linked, around the totem of our good luck.

What did Margo say? Men plan; God laughs. Or smites. He's an emotional All-Knowing. Not big on subtlety.

As far as I was concerned, the table would stay through hell and high water. In spite of my loss of faith at the time, it wasn't God's fault Lon had died. It was mine.

"Don't frown like that; it makes lines," Margo said, interrupting my reverie. She stared at me for longer than her customary attention span. "You could use a little refreshing yourself, Nora. You really do look like shit."

"Thanks," I said. "Kind of you to say."

"I'm not supposed to be kind. I'm your best friend. I'm supposed to be honest. You've got dark circles around the eyes. And they're puffy. Not enough sleep? Hairy drive over the Bay Bridge? Something else, then, because you're giving off fireworks of negative energy." She peered at me questioningly. "Aunt Tillie hasn't come to call, has she?"

Margo's coy euphemism was one her prude of a mother had used for menstruation. Margo took every chance she could to mock Paulette, a brilliant woman but one cut out to save lives, not raise them. I shook my head, trying to reflect on the absurdity of the question. I was forty-six. Aunt Tillie hadn't paid a visit since before Christmas, and even then she'd only hung around for a weekend.

"You're obviously dragging." Margo checked her Cartier watch. "You're usually here by midafternoon. And you're late because?"

I explained that my Movement to Music session at Vintage House had given me my annual going-away party before I left for my three-month summer hiatus. I didn't tell her that I'd been summoned to a surprise post-party meeting with the corporate administrator, which was what had screwed up my schedule.

"Old people. So depressing," Margo said. She had issues left over from childhood she kept reheating. Her narrow shoulders shuddered. "All those potbellies and liver spots. And the poor souls who can't remember their own names. I don't know how you do it."

"It's what I was trained for. And I love doing it," I said. What I didn't say was that I might not be doing it for much longer. The decision hadn't been made yet, but Kimberly Kline thought she ought to alert me to the possibility that my contract would not be renewed for the coming year.

I'd swallowed hard against the first wave of panic. Vintage House was one of several Baltimore-area locations under the Vintage Health and Resource Inc. umbrella. I was a certified movement-and-dance therapist and my work at its nursing home and assisted-living residences provided my major income stream. The trickles—six hours a week working with patients at a private psychiatric hospital and a shift at the veterans' medical center getting the healing wounded on their feet and moving smoothly— wouldn't cover even the basics. As for We Got Rhythm, the dance school I ran in downtown Tuckahoe, I loved it, but it had been turning a profit, and not a big one, for only the last year. So losing the Vintage contract would be a catastrophe.

"Both locations? House and Manor?" I'd asked Kimberly that morning.

"Afraid so. It's all about the bottom line. Mind you, the final decision hasn't been made. It's between you, art therapy, and twice-weekly meat on the menu."

Great. I'd be up against pottery and prime rib. Not a fair fight.

"I'll be pulling for you," she promised. "I'm going to emphasize the health aspects of your work. How it prevents blood clots and depression. Maybe even staves off dementia. But just in case, since this is your last day on the premises before your summer break, I wanted to prepare you in person."

The budget would be released on July first, and either way she'd phone as soon as she knew something. "In the meantime, try not to worry."

She might as well have said, "Try not to breathe." Slightly dizzy, I'd sucked up oxygen, a lungful that pierced the kind of pain under my ribs that I hadn't felt since Lon's death. I'd pressed spread fingers against it. And as I stood in my kitchen reliving the meeting, an echoing stab drew my hand to my chest. Margo stared at me. "You okay? Something's definitely up."

I bit my lip to keep from saying what. If my actress friend got even a whiff of the possibility that Vintage might not pick up my contract, she'd have me weaving through Saratoga Street traffic holding a "Homeless—Hungry—Help" placard.

When I didn't answer, Margo twitched an eyebrow and switched tactics. "Well, in case you need to blur the edges, I tucked a bottle of merlot in the fridge. Not plonk, either. This is from Pete's stock."

Pete had bought into a winery in Napa. His face—captured twenty years ago for a baseball card—beamed from the label.

"I'd love to stay and have a glass and get to the bottom of whatever is bothering you." Margo drew a quavering breath. "I've got my own troubles. Big ones. I'm at the point where I could really use your advice." *No, no staying. No bottoms. No advice in either direction.* "But I'm afraid this visit's a hit-and-run. Your fault. I thought we'd have more time except you were a slowpoke getting here, and I'm due at the theater, so not tonight. But we'll talk." Of course we would. We had since college. "Hopefully tomorrow. I need to sort this through."

She'd taken my hand. "You know you're like the sister I never had," she said, then ruined the moment by murmuring, "and, frankly, never wanted. My parents had little enough attention to spare on one kid, let alone more. But at this age, a sister is a good thing."

She patted my cheek and said, "Speaking of age, you're getting a little hollow there. Nothing major, but you want to get ahead of the early signs of wear and tear. Women in their twenties are doing it now. Dr. Marx could take care of that in one appointment. Seriously, you might want to think about it. Pete's been rambling on about some new business contact, last name Cassidy, single, very rich, very sharp. Could be a dating prospect. You know, it really is time for you to get back in the game. But you're not thirty anymore and you need to do all you can to level the playing field."

That's when I swiveled her around, placed my hand squarely on her back, and pushed her toward the door.

"Sorry to leave you by your lonesome, darling," she said as I opened it. *Not lonesome. Alone. And, oh God, I wanted to be alone.*

I gave her a final shove onto the porch, closed the door, and leaned against it. I was *home.* My home. But the question loomed: For how long?

chapter two

That night, after a supper of bagels and smoked salmon, too much of Pete's wine, and three hours of mind-candy TV, I wound my way through the house to the master bedroom. We'd had an unusually cold winter and a drenching spring in Baltimore, made more depressing by the solitary life I led, with Jack away for his freshman year at Duke. But as I forced myself to walk slowly, taking inventory of the treasures and pleasures of the house, I felt the lush joy of summer begin to seep into my soul.

The great room stopped me with its beauty. After she'd redone the kitchen and I'd fallen in love with its whitewashed cabinets and the reproduction of a happy painting of Coney Island that her tile expert had fashioned into a backsplash, I'd let her go full tilt on redoing the living room. Her original vision had been for all white, but I'd protested it was going to look sterile, so she'd added pops of color. A chair in lemon yellow. An orange-striped chaise. A wall gallery of seascapes and photographs of local birds and wildflowers. With his permission and to his delight, she'd appropriated Jack's collection of artifacts he'd found on the beach over the years—strangely beautiful shells and stunning coral, some old coins and an antique spoon he was sure had washed up from a shipwreck—and artfully arranged them atop a driftwood-based coffee table. Picture frames, odd boxes, and what she called tchotchkes in gold, silver, and the copper shade of my hair added just the right touch of sparkle. On the August afternoon that she'd pronounced it finished, we had stood back to take it in, leaned against each other (as we'd been doing one way or another for decades), and cried, each in her own way. Margo had stifled sobs, sniffed, and blotted with a real lace-edged handkerchief. I'd nodded and let the tears roll silently.

"It's beautiful. Perfect," I'd rasped when I managed to dig up my voice. "I love it. Lon would have loved . . ."

She'd held up a hand that halted the sentence and the sentiment. Lon had been evicted from the room. And to be honest, he probably would have hated it. Too cheerful and distracting for a serious novelist who'd struggled with writer's block toward the end.

Margo had also wanted to tackle his office, which she'd disparagingly called "the shrine."

The dancer in me had balked. My girlfriend had my rhythm all wrong. She wanted me to merengue into the future. Lots of quick steps and no looking back. For me it was two steps forward, one reverse, and an occasional glance over the shoulder.

She'd trailed a finger over the desk and displayed her gray fingertip. "At least let the cleaning service dust in here. The room looks like it's covered with the poor man's ashes. Really, Nora, it's unhealthy emotionally and physically."

So the dust shifted, but I made sure nothing else did. All was as Lon had left it before he'd headed to San Francisco and never come back. All was as it would be.

I saw as I entered the lavender master bedroom that the cleaning service had been by earlier in the day to get the house ready for our arrival. A silver-wrapped chocolate kiss had been left on my pillow, Meryem Haydar's personal touch. Merry worked for Clean on Board whenever school was out—and when she wasn't giving her mother grief by getting into some kind of trouble. Emine, my friend and off-season manager at We Got Rhythm, worried endlessly about her fifteen-year-old rebel, but

I thought that behind Merry's pink-tipped spiked hair, the eyebrow ring, the fake tattoos, the fresh mouth, the curfew breaking and smoking on the sly, the tantrums at home, the bad behavior at school, the acting up and acting out, there was a kid with a good heart.

Merry had left the balcony window open to let the sea air freshen the room. I moved to it and slid back the sheers to allow the moonlight to flood in. And maybe thoughts of Lon.

The first time he'd wafted through that window was a week after his memorial service. Dressed in his favorite seersucker suit and striped bow tie, he'd stood silently—for a minute? an hour?—before blowing me a kiss and evaporating. A few nights later, he'd wakened me by stroking my back from his perch on my—*our* bed. That rattled me so hard I'd called a shrink friend at Poplar Grove, the psychiatric hospital where I worked part-time. Was I losing it?

"You were probably in that fugue state between sleep and wakefulness where the mind plays tricks," Josh Zimmerman had calmly stated. "You needed comfort—it gave you comfort. The literature is full of such benign hallucinations. These self-designed spirits take off when they're no longer relevant. Not to worry."

My husband's silent apparition dropped in three more times. On the last visit he wore his ratty tartan robe and scuffed slippers. There had been no command performance since, so maybe he'd been absorbed into eternity, which made me sad. Though sometimes I caught the unmistakable scent of the aftershave he'd said smelled like California at dawn—woodsy-citrusy.

Tonight I was hoping for a visit or at least a little telepathic advice about what to do if the financial roof at Vintage caved in. Lon had been one of that rare breed, a writer with his feet on the ground. I was the dancer who stepped on her own toes moving forward. I said a prayer in my best New York accent to Saint Anthony, finder of lost things. "Yo, Tony! Looking for Lon down here." And when that didn't work, I sent out a personal invitation. "So come on in already, sweetheart."

I imagined Henry London Farrell riding the fragrant sea breeze from the balcony to the bed, where I lay against two pillows, drifting, drifting.

A strong draft of night air suddenly whipped through the window, perfuming the room with beach plum and wild lilac and turning the white sheers to dancing ghosts.

But they were the only ghosts. Lon was a no-show.

Our son was conceived in that airy master bedroom. Or at least the idea for him was hatched there during a night of moonlit marital passion. As Lon rolled me to my knees, the preferred position for success according to a handout from my gynecologist, he whispered from behind me, "I want us to have a baby."

"I know, my love," I said. But I'd known that far too long. Through a year and a half of tests, promising surgeries, and disappointing outcomes. Through the mea culpas or, as Lon put it, "It's not youa—it's mea culpa."

It *was* him.

His confidence was already at a low ebb, sapped by the experience with *Banshee River*. Initial sales had been strong, but as the reviews came in ("Disappointing second act."—*The New Yorker*), they dropped precipitously. He was struggling with his third novel, *Wild Mountain*, when the doctors' grim report came in.

"Abnormal sperm motility and morphology" was the medical term for a lethal combination that defied the best efforts of science to correct. Lousy swimmers, was Lon's diagnosis.

"I'm fucking sterile in every way. Well, the hell with the little buggers. We'll find a way."

On that night, on that bed, as he lifted my hair to nuzzle my neck, he'd murmured, "You're going to have our baby, I promise you. You're going to get pregnant and have morning sickness and throw up on my Harris Tweed jacket. You're going to get waddlingly fat and weighed down with a pair of double D knockers, and you'll need to pee all the time and knit booties or whatever it is they knit these days. And at the end, you'll pop out a red-headed girl or a blue-eyed boy, smart and funny and a royal pain in the ass, just like Mom."

"Ah, you say the most romantic things. Tell me more," I shot back, and heard his gruff laugh go lusty as he growled from behind, "Show, not tell. The writer's credo," and we made the kind of frenzied love that under normal circumstances would have, *should* have produced something more than sweaty sheets.

Afterward, with me nestled in the crook of his arm, as our breathing slowed, we stared at the filmy curtains billowing in the light breeze, thinking the same thing, I was sure. Wonderful sex but fruitless, in the truest biological sense of the word.

After a few minutes, I felt him gently shift me aside. Before Lon had given up cigarettes because smoking inhibited sperm production, this would have been the moment he'd flick on the bedside light and rummage in the night table drawer for his pack of Marlboros. Now he extracted a clipped sheaf of papers. "Take a look at these," he said. "You floated using a sperm bank as an option a while back and I wasn't all that receptive. But you know me; ideas have to churn. I've been thinking about it and I decided to follow up. Did a little research. Made a few calls. Stopped by to pick up some printouts." He glanced at me, his eyes registering concern that he might have overstepped some female-drawn invisible boundary. "Just a possibility. No pressure."

As he handed over the papers, he said, "The quality of the donors is surprisingly impressive. Three look particularly good. But check out number 1659. I really like the sound of him."

I read aloud, "'Six feet two inches. One hundred seventy-five pounds.' Your build. 'Ethnic background: Dutch.'"

"Close enough," Lon said. "Irish, Dutch, same continent."

"'Skin: light. Hair: dark blond. Eyes: Hazel. Religion: Protestant slash agnostic.' Whatever that means." As a cafeteria Catholic, who was I to judge?

Lon read over my shoulder, "'Likes hiking and fishing.' That's a match. 'Enjoys Beethoven.' A man of good taste. Bonus: he's a medical student, on his way to a noble profession, unlike mine. And he's an Open ID Donor. That means when the kid's eighteen, number 1659's willing to meet with the product of his . . . uh . . . ten minutes with a *Penthouse* magazine in a small white room."

"You're okay with that? The meeting part?" I wasn't sure how I felt about laying out the welcome mat for some nameless number who liked Beethoven.

But Lon was. "Absolutely. Everyone has the right to know where they come from. If our child is interested, I'll invite the guy over for a beer. We'll do some backslapping and I'll brag about how well John London Farrell or Maureen London Farrell turned out."

"Let's call him Jack. It's a strong name. But Maureen *Quinn* Farrell, please," I said. "I'm a person too."

"That you are, Nora Farrell née Quinn," he said. "And a fine figure of a lass, indeed."

I reached for his hand. It was warm and I brushed the back of it with my lips. "You really think this will work out?"

His fingers unfolded to stroke my cheek. "Yup, it's going to be good," Lon said.

And he was right; it was very good. For quite some time. Until something or someone screwed with the magic, and it wasn't.

chapter three

Jack's car pulled in at three twenty-six a.m. I knew the time precisely because at the sound of the garage door grinding up, I roused from a restless half sleep to check the neon green numbers on my bedside clock. I heard the garage door go down, an assortment of thumps and creaks, then Jack's tread mounting the stairs. For the child of a dancer, he was not light on his feet. *Clump, clump, clump.* On that reassuring music, I floated off until dawn.

In the new light, I peeked in his room, and, frankly, I didn't like the look of him. His normally ruddy complexion was washed out. He was curled on his bed in jeans and an old golf shirt of Lon's, probably the same clothes he'd worn on the drive. His fists were clenched, and his eyelids, fringed with thick blond lashes, twitched. He'd propped his iPhone on the pillow next to him so I figured he was waiting or hoping for a morning call from Tiffanie, the sophomore, the older woman, the mean-mouthed girl. Even in the sexy-pouty, too-much-cleavage-revealed glamour shot he'd passed around at Christmas, she'd looked narrow and pinched. The camera didn't lie and Photoshop couldn't blur her essential skinniness. The picture told the story: there wasn't enough of her to share.

She'd been jerking Jack around since February and had administered the coup de grace during finals week. Finals week! How cold was that? My nineteen-year-old, in the throes of first crazy love, accent on the crazy, had decided to stay on at Duke for an extra month to try to salvage the relationship while Tiffanie started summer school. I wondered how that had turned out.

The room was cold, over-air-conditioned, thanks to Jack's heavy hand with the thermostat. I pulled the top sheet up to cover him. Even that light touch caused him to stir. He flinched and turned his head so his cheek rested smack on the iPhone. Not a good move.

I smiled at a memory. When Jack was eight, he and Lon had worked together over a two-week stretch of August twilights to build a model of the Wright Brothers' first flier. It turned out to be a delicate wonder of struts and strings that set off a frenzy of high-fiving between them. Exactly how it happened Jack couldn't tell us, but after spending a few days on his bookshelf, the model had found its way to my boy's pillow and sometime during the night it got crushed. Lon repaired the damage, but you could see where it had been patched. That was Jack's first lesson in how bad stuff happens and afterward things might never be the same.

Thinking of the splintered airplane, I moved in to rescue the iPhone, sliding it out from under the weight of his head, slowly, carefully, but not carefully enough, because he gave me a slitted stare and mumbled a cottony, "Hey, Mamma-mia."

That was what I'd called my mother, whom Jack had never met. Born Maria Bellangelo, Italian through and through, Mimi Quinn died when I was seventeen, but I'd told Jack about Mamma-mia and he'd picked up on it.

"Hi, Bambino," I said. But he wasn't my baby anymore, I thought with a catch in my inner voice. It all goes so fast. From tentative baby steps to giant strides—all that moving away in less than two decades. That was the natural order of things and, yes, it was right, but sometimes the yearning for the scent of baby lotion or the desire to nuzzle toddler-smooth skin melted me to just short of tears. I consoled myself with the hope that though the maternal gravity would weaken, the power of love would always be strong enough to keep him at least at the edge of my orbit.

The hand splayed on his chest was a man-sized paw with fuzz on the knuckles. He stirred and his fist opened. I planted the iPhone in his palm, brushed a kiss on his forehead, and watched him lapse back into sleep. Then I went back to bed and tossed and turned for the next two hours.

I came down to the kitchen a little after eight to find Jack sipping orange juice, chomping on a bagel draped with lox, and thumbing through the *Coast Post*, the resort strip's newspaper. From the glint of his blond-streaked hair I could tell he'd showered, but he hadn't shaved. Or maybe it was the style again, the all-day five-o'clock shadow.

He'd dressed in khaki shorts and a shirt I recognized from last summer, the Duke Lacrosse Blue Devils tee that was too small for him now—my son had built muscles over the school year. His eyes, a startling amber—Lon had called them golden eyes and said he'd never seen them in a human before, though some eagles, owls, and domestic cats had that color—brightened as they lit on me.

They flicked back to the paper and he read aloud: "'Get moving, get happy, and get dancing. Zumba and belly dancing at all levels. Ballroom lessons, group and private. Sign up now for summer classes.'" I moved to look over his shoulder. The ad for We Got Rhythm had landed on page four of the newspaper. Good placement for the first advertisement of the season. I needed to thank Emine, who'd negotiated the spot. She had the touch for driving a hard bargain.

"That's one of my favorite pictures of you," my son said.

The head shot had been taken just before I'd opened the studio. My hair had been longer then, and what the woman at the Clinique counter at Nordstrom euphemistically called laugh lines hadn't begun to sprout around my eyes. I looked five years younger, which of course I had been.

When I sighed, Jack said, "There's also a page-one story about someone you know. That army guy who was in your class a few years ago, the one with the fake leg?"

Scott Goddard. The lieutenant colonel wore a prosthesis that replaced the half a limb he'd lost during an insurgent attack in Iraq.

Jack handed me the paper. I flipped pages and my heart did its own flip as I got my first look at Scott's photo. It wasn't recent either, this portrait of an active-duty officer. He was wearing dress blues, his chest decorated with stars and bars and badges. His face, shaved to a gloss, was a ruddy, healthy color. His hair was buzzed to half an inch of his scalp.

"Combat Hero to Lead July Fourth Parade," the headline announced. I tried to focus on the copy, fighting the tug back to his photo.

"Army Colonel Wounded in Iraq Chosen Grand Marshal." Scott Goddard was currently residing in Tuckahoe, according to the lead paragraph. When they were in my Tuesday night ballroom class, Scott and Bunny had lived a few miles up the coast. Her mom had terminal cancer and they'd moved into her Rehoboth house to care for her. Maybe Mrs. Gleason had passed on and they'd found a place here in town. "It's an honor and a privilege to preside over this event," the article quoted Scott. His eyes were very blue, the irises outlined in black. My glance stalled out. His smile, warm and confident, exposed even white teeth. Colonel Goddard was my definition of handsome.

"Earth to Mom," Jack said. "Hel-lo up there."

I tossed the paper on the table and shook my head to clear the last image and the accompanying guilt. The man was married, after all.

"You must be beat," I said, rushing to change the subject. "You didn't get much sleep."

"I learned during finals that I can operate on fumes. Anyway, I'll catch up. As long as I'm here, I'm fine."

Did that mean if he wasn't here, he wouldn't be fine? I heard the tremulous echo of my meeting yesterday, the one that put my job on the line. I had a son in an expensive college, rent due monthly for the house in Baltimore, taxes on the beach house, rent and salaries at We Got Rhythm . . . I grabbed a sesame seed bagel and bit into it to keep from gritting my teeth.

Jack slugged the rest of his orange juice and enfolded me in a bear hug, temporarily wiping away all thoughts of disaster. Before letting me go, he bent down and pecked the top of my head, the way I used to kiss him when he was a baby.

His father had nicknamed him Jacko early on, but after we saw the writing on the wall (the penciled height marks were still visible in his closet), he became Big Guy. By twelve, he'd already topped me by three inches. Now he towered over my measly five foot six, the shortcoming that was my mother's greatest disappointment. She'd danced for nearly a decade in the line at Radio City Music Hall and she yearned for me to follow in her tap shoes. But I didn't make the Rockettes' minimum height requirement. On her deathbed, she forgave me. "Not your fault, Nora. I should have married a taller man. But I loved your father." She would have adored Jack. Maybe the chromosome for tall had jetéd over a generation, or more likely he'd inherited it from #1659.

Jack backed off, grinned, and rolled his glance across the kitchen and its view to the sea. "Oh man, I have been so looking forward to this." We took in the scene for a moment. Then he made his way to the fridge, calling behind him, "The drive in was okay?"

"Fine," I said. "Except there was hardly any traffic on the bridge and the sky was clear so you could see the scary part." A kink in the Chesapeake Bay Bridge created the optical illusion that you were about to drive off the end of the world. "But I sang my way across. To 'Surfin' USA.'"

Lon had suffered from bridge phobia, and the Bay Bridge was his worst nightmare. He'd discovered that singing along with the Beach Boys worked as a distraction from the fear. At the beginning it was just him and me pounding out, "If everybody had an ocean, across the USA." After

Jack was old enough to chime in, we were a trio. Then, without Lon, we became a duet again. That was until this year. Yesterday, I'd sung solo. Felt solo.

"And I'll bet you also yelled, 'Is this where summer begins?' at the Coastal Highway," Jack said. He'd asked that question for the first time when he was five, and from then on, when we hit the final route to the beach, we shouted it in unison to mark the official start of the season. I nodded.

"Tradition," he said. "You're really big on that." He was rummaging around deep in the refrigerator, but he looked over his shoulder to smile at me. Indulgently, the way adult children smile at their parents. "I thought all that tradition stuff was Dad's thing, but you're as bad as he was."

As bad? My ears pricked up. Jack had adored everything about his father. Up till now, even Lon's memory could do no wrong.

"You got a problem with tradition?" I countered, half joking, half defensive.

"Just saying. You don't want to get hung up in the past, right?"

He pulled out the jar of osetra caviar. "Whoa, fishberry jam for you, and look at this, corned beef *and* pastrami. Thank you, Aunt Margo. You really outdid yourself this year. But no coffee, huh?" Jack asked. Margo hadn't included coffee because she figured I'd be stopping by the Turquoise Café, the Haydars' coffee shop, on my first day in town to pick up fresh ground.

"Only instant."

"Slumming." Jack laughed.

I fixed two mugs and carried them out to the deck, and he followed, balancing a second bagel piled with cheese and lox for him and two black-and-whites. He handed over a cookie and we stood together at the railing, munching and marveling silently at the stunning stripes of sky, ocean, beach. God, I loved Tuckahoe, the house, the view, the waves breaking with a calming *shushh-shushh.* I felt my breathing slow to their rhythm as I lost myself, or maybe *found myself,* in the scene. No other place had this effect on me. No other place ever would, I suspected. For a few minutes, Jack and I stood mesmerized.

"So, what are you up to today?" he asked finally.

As I talked though my schedule, Jack pulled his iPhone from his pocket and stared at it as if he could summon up what he wanted to see. A message from Tiffanie, I guessed, which, from the sudden slump of his shoulders, I figured hadn't arrived.

His stare was still fixed on the screen when he said, "Okay, coffee with Mrs. Haydar; then you're teaching class. That takes you to midafternoon. What's on tap for the rest of the day?" Odd, this sudden interest in my calendar.

"Heading back here to spend the afternoon reading on the beach. I'm halfway through a pretty good mystery." The heat and the rhythm of the waves would probably lull me into a nap after a chapter or two. I'd wake up hot and sweaty. "If the water's warm enough, maybe I'll take a quick dip. By then, it will be time to start dinner."

Jack grunted, but to me it sounded like thunder on the horizon. Mothers read their kids like a weather map and I could feel his barometer drop.

"Don't bother with anything for me," he said. "It's my first night back at Coneheads and I'm meeting a couple of friends at the Burger Shack before work."

Jack had signed on again for the weekend evening shift, scooping the best ice cream on the Delmarva resort coast. "I haven't seen most of my Coney buds since last summer. And this morning I've got two first-timers for Sea Spot Run." The dog-walking service he'd launched when he was sixteen was paying for his books at Duke. "I'm thinking of adding an extra half-hour session late afternoon." He turned to me, his amber eyes clouded. Sunshine beat down on the deck, but I picked up electricity in the air. "The summer's really going to be jammed, like, killer busy," he said. Then lightning struck. "Mom. We need to talk."

Oh God, one of the most ominous phrases in the English language. I'd never known anything good to come of it.

"Sure," I said. But the crop of goose bumps sprouting on my arms showed just how unsure I was.

"The thing is," he began, but got stopped immediately by the ring of his iPhone. I looked over to see if Tiffanie's photo had surfaced, but he'd turned away to scan the screen. "Gotta take this."

Instead of his usual casual greeting, I heard a serious, "Yes," before he swung around to take the deck steps double time. Obviously a private call. I could only watch, wonder, and worry as he trotted down the path to the beach.

Throughout Jack's childhood, I'd played a game with him. With myself, really, because he didn't even know about it. What if my sweet child wasn't the biological offspring of donor #1659? What if, this one time, against all odds, the passionate coupling of Henry London Farrell and Nora Quinn Farrell had produced a pregnancy? Jack hadn't been test-tube generated, after all. My gynecologist had used a modern variation of the old turkey baster to introduce donor sperm to egg, so it was on the outer edge of possibility that Lon's feeble swimmers had suddenly and unaccountably turned into Olympic champions, beating out #1659 for the gold.

Could be, I'd told myself. Lon and I certainly had sex around the time I conceived. And anything could have happened within the deep, dark recesses of my inner passages and chambers. Who was to say we hadn't hit the lottery that one time? Maybe a miracle occurred, part of a divine plan to lure me back into the folds of the Mother Church. Stranger things had happened. People prayed to grilled cheese sandwiches embossed with the image of the Virgin Mary before selling them on eBay. Maybe, just maybe, Jack was *Lon's* genetic offspring.

For a long time—because it didn't seem fair that a love as potent as

Lon's and mine wouldn't create a fusion of the two of us—I wanted that to be true. Also, as the daughter of a biology teacher, I gave nature more power over nurture than it probably deserved.

So all through Jack's early childhood years, I looked for evidence of a genetic link between my husband and my son. And found none. Lon was black Irish: hair the color of coal, eyes green, complexion fair. Jack had been born bald, and when his hair finally arrived around his first birthday, it came in corn-silk blond. By adolescence, his hair and skin color almost matched, in summer a tawny gold. Jack didn't have Lon's dimpled hands or his square jaw, his big feet, or the cleft in his chin. Nothing. But I continued to hope.

Jack was six the first time we took him to the circus, and in the lobby we ran into a high school friend of mine. She backed off from our reunion hug, scanned the three of us, and said, "Oh my gosh, Nora, the child is your clone. Except for the hair, he's your total clone, down to the crazy arch of your eyebrows." She glanced at Lon, back at Jack, and laughed. "I mean, you're sure he's not the Immaculate Conception?"

That night, after Jack was tucked in bed with his new stuffed elephant, Lon took a slug of Jameson and asked, "Your friend's comment today, that bothered you, didn't it?"

"No," I lied.

"Please," he said. "I saw your face."

"Okay, but only because I didn't want you to be hurt."

He slammed down his glass. "Now, you listen to me, Nora. I don't give a crap about his genes, designer or otherwise. In every way that counts, that boy is mine. If I weren't shooting blanks, if that DNA had been Farrell—handed down through a long line of drunks, mogs, chancers, wastrels, and highway robbers, by the way—I couldn't have made a better son or one I love more. In a couple of years, we're going to let Jack know how he was conceived. And you better get good with that before we tell him, because I'll be damned if I'll have him thinking he doesn't measure up for any reason. Especially not a bullshit one."

The next morning, when Lon wasn't around, I opened the #1659 file on my laptop. Our fertility bank hadn't shared pictures of our donor as an adult, but we'd been able to look at him as a kid. I hadn't checked out the photo for a while. There he was at seven, the contributor of half my son's genetic material. And it showed. The hair as pale as buttercream, the light eyes, the pigeon-toed stance that had made my toddler trip over his own feet. And I got good with that.

Here's where the miracle really happened. Within a year, Jack's walk had taken on Lon's California cowboy swagger. By the time he was eight, he'd developed a beautiful singing voice that my mother-in-law swore was identical to Lon's when he'd been a choirboy at Saint Dominic's. For Jack's tenth birthday we went on a fishing trip to Lake Tahoe, and one night, under an ink black sky sprayed with stars, Lon spun the story, in ways only a man brilliant with words could, of a most-wanted son and how he came to be. When he was finished, Jack said, "No kidding. Wow. That is so cool."

The questions came later. Mostly for me, because within the year, Lon was dead.

What reminded me of this, after more than a decade, was seeing Jack pace the beach as he talked into his iPhone that Friday morning in June. Lon had done that. Back and forth, back and forth, on the conversations with his editor when sales of his last book were flagging and he'd begun to refer to himself as Henrik Hasbeen. Back and forth, when his mother called to say his dad had been diagnosed with cancer.

As I watched from the deck, Jack walked his endless loop, his free hand slapping a quick tattoo against his thigh the way Lon's had done. And after Jack jammed the phone in his pocket, he sat down on the flat of Mooncussers Rock and sank his head in his hands. I'd never seen that before. From Lon, yes, during what he called "the bog times." But not from Jack.

My instinct was to make it better, whatever *it* was. Kids grow up, but parents don't outgrow the need to chase monsters, soothe nightmares. The desire to rush to my son was almost irresistible.

No. Let him fall. The phrase was one I'd learned from a pioneering movement-analysis professor in grad school. It was the mantra I repeated silently when one of my clients swayed wildly on a damaged leg or a new prosthesis. *Steady him if you can. But if he's out of control, don't try to catch him. You're no good to him if you go down. And, worst case, even if he hits the floor, it won't be as hard as his fear of the fall. And he'll get up stronger and wiser.*

I made myself wait on the deck until I saw Jack raise his head. Then I took the stairs slowly and, forcing a measured tempo, walked along the path to the beach. When I reached him, he was staring at the ocean, his arms wrapped around his knees. And he was laughing.

chapter four

Walking on sand in bare feet makes no sound and Jack hadn't heard me approach, but when my shadow merged with his, he looked over at me and that single glance switched off his laughter.

I gulped a relieved breath. I thought he'd been bent over in anguish, but he'd been laughing. *See,* I told myself. *See, Nora. You worry too much.*

"Good phone call?" I asked brightly.

"A funny call," he said, gazing again at the ocean. "Not as in stand-up funny. Surprising funny. Good? I guess we'll see."

"Tiffanie?"

That slipped out. I tried to be Switzerland when it came to her. Neutral. At least with Jack, because (a) I got more information that way and (b) she might, God forbid, be my daughter-in-law one day. But he had to have known what I thought of her. When he'd dated that sweet Carrie back in tenth grade, the one who made it to the semifinals of the *Jeopardy!* Teen Tournament, I sent the girl a congratulatory e-card and posted a photo of her with Alex Trebek on my Facebook page. With Tiffanie, I just listened and lost sleep.

"The call wasn't from Tiffanie. But yeah, she's involved in a way. You and I were going to talk," he said. "We really have to, Mom. Now."

My heart flipped. It bounced so high on the rebound it nudged a cough from my throat.

There was space next to Jack on Mooncussers Rock and I fervently hoped he'd pat an invitation to sit down, because my legs were suddenly too weak to hold me. But he stood up. "I've got pins and needles in my ass from this rock." Wry smile. "Let's walk."

It was going to be bad. He'd said Tiffanie was involved. He wanted us to be on the beach, among people, because he knew I wouldn't make a scene in public and he was afraid I'd scream and froth at the mouth when he told me she was pregnant and he was going to quit college and live with her and the triplets over her parents' garage. Or she'd written a sequel to *Fifty Shades of Grey*, only it wasn't fiction—it was autobiographical, and she'd named names and devices. Or she . . .

"This goes way back," Jack was saying. Somehow I was walking. Alongside him. One bare foot in front of the other. I'd gotten a pedicure before leaving Baltimore, and on a whim I'd had my toenails painted blue. What had I been thinking? Beach equals carefree; that's what. Not this.

Jack took my arm as if I were an old lady in danger of toppling over. "The phone call was from the Baltimore Fertility Bank."

It took me a moment to recognize a name that had once sounded like poetry.

"I called there yesterday before I left Durham. I asked them to start the process for me to contact my Donor Dad. My DD."

Donor Dad! DD! Freshly minted phrases I didn't like the sound of.

It wasn't long after we told Jack about the circumstances surrounding his conception that he'd nicknamed #1659 "Sixteen." For a while, after he'd helped scatter his dad's ashes on the ocean behind the Surf Avenue house, he didn't talk about Sixteen. Maybe he thought it would be disrespectful to Lon's memory. Then, a few years later, he did ask some questions. What state did Sixteen live in? I didn't know, I told him. I could only assume he'd been living in Maryland when he'd donated. The sperm bank wanted you close by. But the donation was immediately frozen to last for a long time, so by now he could be anywhere. What did he look like? I stalled on that one, trying to decide what Lon would have done, then showed him the photo of the blond kid. "Cute," he'd said, and printed out a copy that I never saw again. The bar mitzvah of his best friend set off a round of questions. What religion was Sixteen? Which led to: Was he athletic? Good in math?

I consulted my shrink friend. "Tell him everything you know," Josh advised. So I did. And that seemed to satisfy Jack. But on his sixteenth birthday, after an impromptu party at a friend's house, he came home laughing-jag drunk on Goldschläger, cocked a finger at me, and said, "Here's a riddle for you. I'm sixteen, right? And my donor is Sixteen, right? So what's sixteen from sixteen? Zero, right? Oh boy, I am so shit-faced." He got grounded for a week; I agonized for months.

"Does that mean he thinks he's a zero?" I'd asked the same psychiatrist.

"Every adolescent boy has self-esteem issues, Nora," he said. "But soon they grow out of the acne and into their egos. Your son sounds pretty clever, by the way. The sixteen-from-sixteen riff. He was just showing off. I wouldn't make a big deal of it."

Last year, after guzzling too many beers at a family cookout, my brother had taken Jack aside for a private conversation. Mick had been a nasty, snotty little kid and an out-of-control teen, and now he was a troubled man, probably alcoholic, thrice divorced, still ignorant and arrogant, a toxic mix. That afternoon, his decibel level had been magnified by the Guinness.

"So, Johnny-boy, you're eighteen next month. You gonna try to meet your . . . you know?" I'd be damned if he hadn't patted his crotch.

"Nah." Jack had shrugged. "Not interested. Don't see the point. I've got family."

"That you have," Mick had slurred. "And we all love you."

I'd followed up when we got home. "Jack, you know it's okay with me if you want to get in touch with Sixteen. I'd understand." I'd meant it then.

"Sure. Thanks, but no, thanks."

And now Sixteen was Donor Dad and Jack was hunting him down.

"What changed?" I asked him as we walked the beach with his hand gripping my arm.

"I did, I guess. A whole bunch of stuff got me thinking. I finally read Dad's second book over spring break." *Banshee River*, which had received a lukewarm reception from the critics. "You know how the kid inherits his father's love for bears? The inherited part screwed with my brain. Dad writing about it. And we studied genetics in biology last semester. Plus in my psychology class, we covered Freud. Biology is destiny and all that."

"A misquote," I said. "Freud actually said *anatomy* is destiny. And he was wrong about that too."

"Whatever." Jack scowled at me. "You're missing the big picture. *You* have your total history. Grandma and Grandpa Quinn. How their grandparents survived the Irish potato famine. And the big Italian migration of the 1900s when Grandma Mimi's family came over. You've got both sides covered.

"And Dad had his connection to Jack London, how his greatgrandfather was this famous guy's doctor and close friend back in Glen Ellen, what, a hundred years ago? I mean, look how even the name got passed on, which—don't get me wrong; I like my name—but I find that a little creepy. And Dad thought what he did, writing novels about mountains and rivers and the great outdoors, was some kind of legacy."

"But not genetic," I countered.

"Kind of, through Great-grandfather Farrell. The point is," he insisted, "I've got missing pieces, big ones. I look in the mirror every morning and I wonder what parts came from where."

Was that why the scruff of beard? Had he given up shaving to avoid the mirror?

"Anyway, it all piled up and started to bother me. Then yesterday in the midst of a . . . uh . . . discussion, Tiffanie said, 'You know what your problem is? You don't know who you are.'"

I stopped short to face him while a furious flush washed over me. "That's ridiculous. Of course you know who you are."

"Look, Mom, I get that you think Tiffanie's a bitch—"

"Did I ever say—?"

"Hold on. No, you've never said it. But you think it because we're always fighting and you want to protect me and all. But Tiffanie's smart. Really. She's dean's list. More than that, she thinks things through. She's deep." *As deep as her cleavage in the glamour shot?* I wondered snarkily. But I forced myself to give her a Swiss-neutral passport. "Okay."

"And she was right this time. I knew it in my gut. So"—deep breath—"I called the fertility bank. And they just called back. That was the call." He let go of my arm, so I guessed I was on my own. "They're emailing me a form that I have to fill out and get notarized. And then they'll contact my DD and let him know I'm interested. And we'll see what happens from there."

I kept nodding like the gulls at the water's edge. Gulls have brains the size of walnuts.

Jack stooped to pick up a shell, a pearlized abalone sculpted with an open spiral that ended in a curl. Like a wave. Something else to marvel at. "What was so funny was that I've been thinking about doing this for months and it took them less than a day to get back to me. How crazy is that?"

He started to laugh again. I didn't feel like laughing, but Jack's laugh had always been infectious, and I couldn't help myself. When we rumbled to a stop, he backed away to peer at me. "So you're cool with this?"

"I just want you to be happy," I said. Which wasn't the worst answer on the fly, even if it wasn't the entire answer. The whole truth was that I wasn't cool with it; I was cold with it, shiveringly, shockingly cold, as if I'd been swamped by a splash of that frigid June ocean out there. I tried to hide my gulp for air. I needed oxygen to process what effect Sixteen's entrance, if he chose to make one, would have on Jack, on me, on Jack-and-me. If he chose not to, that was another issue.

"Thanks," my son said, as if he hadn't just dropped me into deep water with a potential shark circling beneath the opaque surface.

I thanked God for the diversion as a swell of voices and laughter came surging at us. We turned to stare at a quartet of runners racing by. In their twenties, they had no idea what they were doing to their arches by pounding away on damp sand, no idea of how little Medicare would eventually cover for podiatric services.

"They're trying to get their run in before this afternoon," Jack said. "It's supposed to go up to ninety with the humidity off the charts. Look where the sun is already. Crap! The time!" He checked his watch, Lon's TAG Heuer, handed down from *his* father. "Oh great. First run of the summer and I'm going to be late picking up the dogs. I don't even have the damn Frisbee with me." And he sprinted off, calling behind him, "We'll touch base later."

I stood for a moment, trying to take everything in. Everything.

In my direct line of sight, a ponytailed woman in a maternity swimsuit led a tow-haired toddler into the shallow lip of ocean, laced with foam. She pointed to a pod of dolphins, not far out, arcing and diving as if they were auditioning for Disney. The little boy followed her finger and, when he spotted the show, jumped up and down with excitement. *Enjoy it now,* I sent a telepathic message to the mom, *and memorize these simply wonderful moments. It gets complicated later.*

Just then, a purple sandpiper swooped down to land near my left foot, ambled around it on short yellow legs, and deposited a white spatter on my new blue pedicure. And I was only halfway through my colorful morning. I washed off the bird poop in the surf, took a final look at the sky shimmering even this early in the heat, and told myself, *Pull yourself together.* It was time to get on with my day. As my business card noted under my name and "Board-Certified Dance Movement Therapist," my slogan was "One Step at a Time." That's the way I'd take this new revelation of Jack's: one slow, tentative, faltering, probably stumbling step at a time. *But you're a movement therapist, so move!* I ordered myself.

After the undrinkable instant coffee, and then the conversation with Jack that left me—I suddenly realized—drained, I craved a cup of Emine and Adnan's brew. "Black as hell, strong as death, sweet as love," the Turkish proverb went. All that caffeine would perk me up, I told myself, and groaned at my own pun. More than coffee, though, I craved time with Em. She had a problem child. Maybe she could serve me a side of advice with the coffee.

chapter five

The Turquoise Café was located in the Tuckahoe Mews, a twisting alley off the main drag lined with high-end artsy-craftsy shops and specialty women's boutiques. I trotted by Neptune's Sister, which carried shell and coral necklaces—not my style—and silver bracelets, beautiful but pricey. I moved on past the lemon-and-lavender facade of Time and Tide Books, then ducked through the bougainvillea-draped arches of Rainbow's End, a restaurant with a largely gay male clientele who congregated in the half-walled front garden at sunset to drink and laugh and sometimes dance to Cole Porter on the sound system.

I made a left turn, then followed the aroma of brewing coffee and freshly baked muffins, and there I was at the Turquoise Café, a vibrant blue-green jewel set among the paler pastel shops. Through the glass storefront, I saw Emine behind the marble counter serving a customer. I rapped on the window and she looked toward me, smiled a greeting, and motioned me in.

The café was flooded with morning light. One pale aqua wall was decorated with photographs of the Turquoise Coast, the Turkish Riviera. The opposite wall was a backdrop for an arrangement of rugs, a red-and-yellow Oushak, a Kayseri silk, and some smaller hangings. Across the ceiling, Emine had hung banners of gauzy yellow fabric that billowed with each air-conditioned draft. Under this gossamer tent, the customers sat back and slipped into slow gear, sipped coffee, and nibbled pastry or *simit*, the Turkish bagel. You could almost see them shed their tight winter skins.

I headed toward one of the smaller tables against the window to drop my gym bag before placing my order at the service counter. I watched as Em exchanged a few words with her husband, waved me back, and met me halfway across the floor. She wrapped me in a hug and I felt the crispness of her white apron appliquéd with a rendition of the *nazar boncuğu*, the blue anti–evil eye talisman, which reputedly brought good luck or at least warded off bad. Maybe the crush of her embrace pressed into me some of its power to deflect calamity. I could hope.

She nodded at my choice of seating. "Here is good. I am taking my break."

The early breakfast rush was over; the counter line had thinned. Adnan and his cousin Volkan, who helped out at peak times, had the front of the house under control and Em could sit for a while, she said. We lowered ourselves into chairs cushioned in turquoise fabric and automatically extended hands across the table so we could interlace our fingers.

"Cold," she commented on my skin's chill. "On such a warm day, your fingers are ice."

Lon used to say that my blood literally ran cold when I was frightened, sad, or worried.

The aroma of toasted spices had given me a taste for a mug of the traditional rich Turkish coffee, or maybe for one of Em's inventions, bicultural cardamom lattes or cinnamon and clove macchiatos. But Emine had preempted my coffee order by telling Adnan to bring us both tea. He materialized on his silent tread with a tray holding two tulip-shaped glass cups, steam rising from them, and a plate of baklava still warm from the oven.

The atmosphere cooled in his presence. While he and I exchanged polite greetings, his wife turned her back on him and stared out the window at the Friday morning shoppers strolling by, the gulls pecking at crumbs on the cobblestones. Tension prickled the air. I knew the Haydars were going through a rough patch, something to do with Merry, because it was always something about their daughter. In her weekly phone calls from Tuckahoe to Baltimore to brief me on the off-season happenings at We Got Rhythm, Em's end of the conversation eventually slid from business to personal and invariably to her wayward daughter. How helpless my friend felt. How alone, despite the parade of therapists with their contradictory theories and recommendations. How she and Adnan disagreed on how to handle their difficult child.

Handsome and slim, his crisp unstained apron wrapped from chest to knee like armor, he bent stiffly to remove the items from the tray and arrange them in front of us. Traditional black tea for Emine, the apple tea I loved at my place, the plate of pastries centered.

"You are well?" he asked me.

"Fine," I said. "You?"

"Thanks God, yes." He cleared his throat and said, "This baklava is with chocolate. I know you like chocolate, Nora. But we also have—"

"Tell me when you need me back there," Em interrupted him without shifting her gaze from the gulls. It was a dismissal.

"For now, it is quiet," he replied. "I will let you two have your talking time together."

"You will *let?*" Emine whipped around. This was a new version of my gentle friend. "You will *let?* Very kind of you."

"All I meant . . ." He shrugged, raised an eyebrow to me as if we were conspirators in some plot. Then he clipped an old-school bow toward me, turned on his heel, and strode away.

Em stared into her cup. I cradled mine to warm my hands. Before sipping, I inhaled the apple scent and felt the steam soften the grip of my anxiety about my own kid.

Emine pushed the plate of baklava toward me. I pushed it back, but it was a symbolic gesture. An extra inch away wouldn't stop me from polishing off at least two pieces of the syrup-drenched pastry she made from scratch.

At that moment, Erol, the Haydars' ten-year-old son, dashed by with a pink backpack slung from one finger. He called out a hi to me.

"Again Merry left her lunch behind." Em shook her head in frustration. "She's so mean to her brother, and he tries hard to be kind. Him, she hates all the time. Me, one day she hates—one day she hugs. The doctor says the hormones of puberty are giving her the ups and downs. Like the roller coaster in Ocean City."

"Sounds like a typical teenager," I responded.

"I wish so. Meryem is not typical." She gave me a smile made crooked by pain.

When I'd first met Emine six years before, I thought she resembled a woman on an ancient Turkish mosaic with her elegantly carved features and deeply waved brown hair loosely gathered back from an oval face. Now the grout between the tiles was showing as a fretwork of wrinkles, and her hair was wisped with silver. She was still beautiful, but less vivid, more faded than her forty-one years warranted. The last few with Merry had aged her.

She went on. "So now we have new things to be concerned with. Makeup, too much. Adnan will not allow it when she works at the café. Even so we keep her in the back, not serving the customers. But as soon as her shift is over she goes to the bathroom and piles it on. Then she usually slips out the back door to sneak past us."

Em rubbed her eyes with her palms as if she could erase her daughter's image. "We grounded her for a week after she gave herself that awful haircut. Adnan pulled her cell phone when she broke curfew. A friend loaned her another one. We can't keep up. Her final grades were high. She's very smart and, I am ashamed to say, very cunning. Also stubborn. Like her father. Adnan is . . . Well, there is an Arab saying 'Stubborn as a

Turk.' He is best example." She shook her head. "Wrong—best example is his mother."

The legendary Mrs. Haydar senior still ruled what was left of the roost in Istanbul, but Emine lived in terror of her random visits. At seventy-eight, Selda Haydar was a powerhouse, as crammed with opinions, advice, and directives as her *imam bayildi*, stuffed eggplant, was crammed with onions and garlic. Selda had insisted on cooking the dish for me during her last stay, although I told her eggplant made my tongue fuzzy. "Not *my* recipe," she'd insisted, looming over me as I ventured to take a forkful. One of the reasons for the family's relocation to the States was her daughter-in-law's refusal to live under Selda's thumb.

Emine sent a sharp look toward her husband as if he'd made the choice of a mother. Misinterpreting, he lifted a kettle questioningly. More tea? She shook her head no.

She sighed. "Every day it's something new with Merry. Boys now. She's crazy for them. She winks to them. They look at . . ." Her hands made a silhouette of breasts. "Thanks God, so far I think mostly it is fantasy. But I worry that she'll step over the line. Do they have judgment at that age?"

I thought of Jack's love or lust or whatever drove his need to hang on to mean-girl Tiffanie. At nineteen, my son was no Solomon.

Emine played with a sugar packet, folding and refolding it until it sprung a leak. "Thinking about her keeps me awake at night. If she's like this now—and she just had the fifteenth birthday last month—what do we have to look forward to at sixteen and"—she shuddered—"eighteen? What college would even consider her with the way she presents herself?"

"Sometimes the future takes care of itself," I said. Kismet wasn't a particularly consoling concept at the moment, but it was all I had. Maybe I should try to believe it myself.

Em darted a look to the line beginning to form at the counter. "I'd better go help up front."

If I was going to teach the morning Zumba class, I'd better get moving, too. Em walked me to the door and stopped to tuck a pound of her finest ground coffee into my gym bag, along with a package of the sour-cherry baklava Jack loved.

We hadn't talked about him. On my way to town, I'd thought I wanted to. I'd hoped Em, a wise and caring soul, could help me sort out my conflicted feelings. But as she anguished over Merry, I thought how trifling my situation would sound compared to hers. I was worried because my son was elated at the prospect of locating his sperm donor? I should have been thrilled for Jack. I was. And I wasn't. I was scared. I'd been ambushed too many times before not to see danger lurking around every dark corner. Besides, hearing myself talk about his quest would make it real. And bottom line, what was there to say? So far nothing had happened. Not actually. Just possibly, and possibly didn't count.

Em kissed me on one cheek, then the other. "Say hello to Margo for me."

Oh God. Margo. I'd forgotten. She attended the eleven a.m. Zumba class.

"Tell her we'll be there early to set up the coffee and pastries on Sunday." The Manolises' annual Father's Day cookout. "I spoke to her yesterday about it, but you know how anxious she gets before the party. Sixty people on your lawn is a big deal. And they're predicting thunderstorms in the afternoon. She said she would try to make it to class, but she wasn't sure. She has the pool man coming sometime this morning and the tent people this afternoon."

The pool man, I got. One of her many minions. But the tent people? It sounded like a *Star Trek* episode.

"Summer begins. You are now officially in charge of the studio," Em said. "Now, go Zumba. And, oh yes, while you're there, take a look at the sign-in list for Tuesday nights. We're set with Larissa and Bobby." She meant my assistants, who would cover anyone lacking a partner for the ballroom class. "We close out registration tomorrow."

"Any surprises so far?" I asked.

We had our share of perennial students, especially among the older folks. Dancing exercised the body and mind. Music was good for the soul, and it was nice to be in a partner's embrace. For me now, having a man's arms around me was business. But once it hadn't been, and I missed that.

I hadn't thought about a man's arms wrapped around me for a long time after Lon's death. A man's body? Just the phrase had sent chills through me. The wrong kind. I replayed countless times the police officer's reporting, "Your husband's body was found . . . ," and the conference chairwoman telling me, between sobs, how and where they'd found him.

The next time I could think of a man's body with pleasure wasn't until I was in the arms of Scott Goddard. Just dancing, nothing else. Of course nothing else. His wife, Bunny, was cracking her gum only feet away. And if that wasn't enough of a deterrent, the mind-reading admonition of Sister Loretta, principal back at Our Lady of Peace Academy, came in loud and clear. "The impure thought is, at the very least, a venial sin. It is also the devil's temptation to the act, which is a mortal sin."

Those impure thoughts were addictive over that summer two years back. Scott's eyes, so very blue and usually cool, warmed when he strode over to claim me for the next dance. His arms were well muscled, his lead strong. One hand in mine was dry and warm; the other shaped a sure-fingered curve at my waist. Of course, what had sprung from those innocent gestures was an adolescent crush, and the sad truth was, I was old enough to know better.

Then one night that summer, on my deck, under the influence of jasmine-scented darkness and too much wine, I confessed to the worst possible priestess. Margo and I had already worked through a bottle of cabernet and opened a second, and I was relating the latest transgression of Bunnicula, as my girlfriend had named Scott's wife. The witch refused to socialize with the other students during breaks and went outside to smoke and yammer into her cell phone. She treated Scott with barely concealed contempt and sneered when he stumbled trying to follow my demonstration of a step.

"Ugh. He deserves better," Margo had said.

I nodded.

"After all, a war hero who gave a leg for his country. Smart, handsome, and Em says he's very charming."

I nodded.

"And sexy." She leaned forward into the glow of the citronella candle.

I nodded. It was that last nod that outed me. Margo pounced on it with her catty claws. Her smile lit up the darkness.

"So you *do* find him sexy."

That launched me into a stammer. "I mean, he's attractive. I . . . uh . . . don't know about sexy. And he's married, for heaven's sake."

"Like that eliminates him? Oh, puh-leeze."

I knew she was thinking of Pete, who had a history Margo couldn't forgive or even forget. "Never. Scott wouldn't . . . I wouldn't . . ."

But the damage had been done. From then on, at so much as the mention of Scott's name, I could see her internal wink. She knew my secret. Which by no means did she keep, as revealed by Em saying—though only once and at the end of that summer—"I can understand why you think the colonel's attractive. There's something very masculine about him."

So yes, with my two closest friends onto me, my reaction when the Goddards didn't show up for the ballroom class last year was mixed. I was disappointed, sure, but also relieved. Life resumed and I persuaded myself that I was happy being alone and, except for one or two regrettable exceptions, chaste.

Still, when Em, standing with me at the door of the Turquoise Café, murmured, "There is an interesting name on the registration list," I thought, *The Goddards are back*, and my pulse went staccato. "A Lynn Brevard," she said, and my pulse slowed. "In her thirties. She seemed nice. I will email to you the intake notes. The rest are repeaters. Dr. Whitman also signed up for private lessons with Larissa. No other surprises."

Thank you, Jesus, I thought. I'd already used up my quotient of surprises for the week.

chapter six

We Got Rhythm was listed last on the plastic placard that hung under the huge Hot Bods sign facing the boardwalk at Tuckahoe Beach. Carmella's Pilates, Cloud Yoga, We Got Rhythm, in strictly alphabetical order, according to my landlord, Sal Zito, and not, he swore, because he had a little sneaky for Carmella. The three small businesses rented studio space and time from Hot Bods, a full-service workout facility for the hard-core gym rats. My clients were generally older, softer, and, to my mind, wiser.

It was five of eleven when I skidded into the studio for my Zumba group. The bird-chirp chatter of the women quieted only slightly at my entrance. I was a familiar figure around Hot Bods in the summer and knew most of these students by name. Waves and a chorus of hi's greeted me.

When I announced, "I'll be teaching this session, and for those of you used to Larissa who haven't danced with me before, you'll get a sample today. I'm tough!" A few hoots punctuated the responding laughter. My class was demanding, but these gals figured that compared to the Moscow Marauder I was a cream puff. Well, not today, first day back.

I kicked off my sandals, pulled on socks, and laced up the very expensive Zumba shoes I wouldn't sully on the cobbled streets of the Tuckahoe

Mews. I switched on the sound system to play an Afro-Cuban beat and, as the women gathered around, handed out the brilliantly colored sashes hemmed with coins or woven with tiny bells that Emine had bought for her belly-dancing classes. These women had appropriated them for Zumba, thinking it was a hoot to jingle exotically while they were on the move.

When everyone was in place I turned the music up, and an exuberant Latin-accented baritone boomed, "Zumba!" followed by a wild burst of percussion from conga drums. Marimbas pulsed, the guiro rasped, a trumpet blared, and in front of me two rows of smiling women—soon they'd be gritting their teeth, I promised myself—launched into a frenzied salsa.

I shouted against the irresistible beat, "Let's get those heart rates climbing. Now, isn't this a fun way to burn a thousand calories? Hands up, who thinks this is better than sex?"

As if I had a clue.

The rumble of laughter faded as they had to conserve their breath. After the salsa, a merengue followed. Then a cumbia, and a mambo with soul. My energy seemed to be contagious. "Bring it on," one of the more zaftig women shouted. And I did. My pride was at stake.

"Keep hydrated," I shouted over the music. A few dancers broke from the pack and boogied over to the cubbies to grab their water bottles and swig as they jogged in place. "Don't stop moving. Never stop moving." Which was my personal credo, and God knows, there had been times over the last eight years when it was the only incentive that prodded me out of bed in the morning.

"Eyes on me, not on your feet, or you'll trip over them."

There was a flurry at the door and all heads turned as Margo Manolis breezed through, only half an hour late for a forty-five-minute class. My dear friend, who'd been a drama major at New York University and had polished her skills at Manhattan's New School theater arts program,

knew how to make an entrance. She stuffed her Gucci gym bag into one
of the cubbies and slipped into her spot front and center. Even late, even
if she had to crowd the previous occupants, she claimed her place. You
didn't mess with Margo over territory.

She sent me a shrug, her version of an apology, and followed that by
knocking herself out for the final fifteen minutes. Last off the floor after
the cooldown, she strolled over, snatched up her tote, and fell into step
with me.

"What the hell was that all about?" she demanded. "You teaching
Russian army Zumba?"

"The Larissa special," I agreed. My heart was still beating hard. I relished the rhythm and the power surge I hadn't felt for a while. "They're
used to being pushed. They loved it." I gave her a measuring glance. She
swiped her blond bangs, wet with perspiration. Her cheeks were flushed.
"Too much for you?" I taunted.

"You can be such a bitch," she growled. But fondly. "Actually, it was
great. You know I love a challenge." She paused and the next voice I
heard had deepened to a sonorous Lady Macbeth tone. "But there are
challenges, and then there are *challenges*." Her Botoxed brow tried, but
failed, to wrinkle. "You have time to talk now?"

She meant listen, but that was okay too. My brain was warning my
mouth into temporary silence about Jack's morning revelation.

"Sit outside?" I asked, hoping for a boardwalk bench facing the ocean,
a view with a calming effect.

She patted the Gucci gym bag on its monogram. "This is show-and-
tell. X-rated. It's probably better in your office."

It wasn't exactly *my* office. I shared it with Carmella, the Pilates princess, who could execute twenty one-legged push-ups without flinching,
but couldn't manage to toss a dirty napkin in the trash or blow the crumbs
from her PowerBar off the computer keyboard. Margo surveyed the
disheveled room as if it were a crack house and cast a disgusted look at

the scarred orange plastic bucket chair meant for guests before gingerly lowering herself into it. She arranged the Gucci bag in her lap and began with a few token niceties. Margo's mother, the world-renowned Holocaust scholar Paulette Wirth, for all her maternal deficits, had taught little Margo manners.

"Jack in?" she asked.

"He got in late last night. Or, more precisely, early this morning."

"Squeezing out every last minute with the crazy girlfriend? What does he see in her?"

I shrugged. "First love, I guess. It will work out. I'm not really worried about him."

She read me like *Vogue*, saw through the smooth fabric of my pretense to the places where the stitches were unraveling. "Bullshit, Norrie. You've been worried about Jack since the day he was born."

"Before that," I admitted.

"I still think I made the right decision not to have kids of my own," Margo said. Another choice driven by her bizarre childhood. "Pete's two were enough for me. Every other weekend and a month in the summer was just the right dose. And now they're all grown-up and moved on." She fidgeted with her wedding ring, a thick band of platinum paved in diamonds. "Maybe that's what's triggered this. The kids are out and now Pete thinks it's his time."

After twenty-five years of dealing with an actress, I knew a cue when I heard one. "For what? What's going on?"

Her eyes filled with tears. No one did tragedy better than Margo. Or farce. Now she sniffed, swallowed hard, and said in a tremulous voice, "Pete's having an affair."

I'd learned that you waited a beat before responding to any of her major pronouncements. You didn't want to step on her lines. And a good thing, too, because she shifted a warning gaze to me. "I know what you're going to say. That I've had these suspicions before and they only panned out that one time, and the past is past. 'It's been eighteen years since Alicia, so move on, Margo.' Well, I did. But you can't erase history."

There had been precedent in the then Yankee player's affair with a stunning New York City TV sports reporter, a liaison that almost destroyed the Manolis marriage. Pete's trade to the Orioles had ended that extramarital adventure, but the memory still haunted Margo.

I leaned back in my chair and said with all the sincerity I could muster, "Go on."

"Okay. He hasn't been himself for a while. Remember I mentioned I thought it was because of him hitting the big five-oh? But it's become clear, especially here at the beach, where I can keep an eye on him all day, three days a week, that it's much more serious."

I must have hoisted a skeptical eyebrow, because she added, nostrils flaring, "I can see it in your face. You're thinking, there she goes again, Margo the drama queen. But I've got the goods. First, he's on his cell phone almost constantly, whispering conversations, or he ducks into another room. Then, get this—Pete the Luddite is texting. The man doesn't know how to forward an email and suddenly he's tapping away with his Shrek-sized fingers on this tiny keyboard. When I asked him who taught him how to text, he told me Janet Buxbaum, the secretary at the Orioles' front office." The O's front office was Pete's home base for some kind of public relations job that Margo couldn't exactly define.

"So you think this Buxbaum person could be the girlfriend?" I asked.

"She'd better not be. She's pushing sixty, with kinky gray hair, and she stinks from the two packs a day she smokes. I will not accept that quality of competition." When I gave a half laugh, she said, "I'm trying to make light of this, Norrie, but it's no joke." She paused for effect. "He bought new underwear."

Not good. But no need to panic either. "People do occasionally purchase replacement underwear, Margo. Even happily married ones."

"He switched from boxers to briefs." *Uh-oh.* "I found these in the laundry basket this morning." She reached down into her gym bag and pulled out, dear God, what looked like . . .

"Black jockeys. So I checked his dresser drawer. Three pairs in black. Three in royal purple. What man wears royal purple briefs unless he thinks he's got the king in his pants? And quite honestly, lately, it's been just the oppo—"

My hand flew up in deflection, signaling TMI, then waved at her to get that underwear out of my sight.

In the East Village apartment Margo and I had shared in grad school, we'd talked about our dates in snorting, graphic detail. But when Lon and Pete came along, we stopped discussing the intimate particulars because in both cases we knew almost immediately that these men were for keeps and that kind of gossip seemed like a betrayal.

"Black and purple," I said. "Ravens' colors. Pete's a gung ho Ravens fan. And they had a great season. Maybe he's just celebrating."

"He's celebrating all right, but not with me. With her."

"Wait. Who's her?"

"I'm thinking some young thing, big boobs, a fan whose father probably collected Pete's baseball cards. Don't know her name yet, but I'll find out. I have my ways. All I can tell you for sure is Pete the Cheat is at it again. He's exhibiting the same symptoms as the first time. Almost. The texting is new."

"And when you asked him about the texting, the phone calls, he said what?"

She flicked me a look that let me know I was the village idiot. "Oh, please. I haven't asked him."

"Well, this may seem simple and therefore inconsistent with your script, but if you think something's going on, why not?"

"Because he'd be furious that I was going through his things the way I did in New York. And he'd deny it like he did before with that Alicia creature. Said I was insecure. I was imagining things. Like the charges for a St. Regis suite on our Visa card were a mirage. If I hadn't confronted him with that, he never would have come clean. I take care of all the bills now. Nothing so far, but they probably do it at her place."

"Pete adores you. I can't imagine after all the counseling—"

"You know what Peter Manolis adores? He adores being adored. Do you remember the Yankee Hanky-Pankies? That's what he called the women who mailed him their thongs. And what about the groupies who followed him from game to game, even out of town? He laughed about all that drooling over him, but the truth is, he reveled in it."

She dropped her head to her chest as if some master puppeteer had let go of the string. Then, after a whimper, she raised it slowly to tell me, "Look, I'm his wife. I love him. God knows, I wish I loved him less. But I know too much to *adore* him. I see his dribble on the pillow. I get boomed awake when he's forgotten to take his Gas-X. And men like Pete, the stars, they become raptors, with the fans feeding their egos. When the adoration runs out, they crave it. And now, after a famine longer than in the Bible, he's got fresh meat. What's tastier than that?"

A genuine look of pain swept across her face. Under the Botox, the collagen fillers, the plumped-up, pulled-tight skin, she looked stripped down to herself. And scared. She said in a whisper, "The thing is, even after all these years and what we've been through, I don't want to lose him."

I stretched my arm across the desk to squeeze her hand. She leaned in to meet me halfway, surveyed Carmella's chaotic landscape, and thought better of it. She checked her watch. "I've got to get home. The caterers are coming for a final consult. Pete wants to change the menu. Add more fish and veggies. And that's another thing; he's switched from steak to fish. He used to hate fish. But these days everything has to have omega-3 fatty oils. He's getting himself in shape for her."

She pulled a tissue from a box half buried on my desk and dabbed her eyes.

"Oh, Margo," I said. "Sweetie. This is all still speculation. Very premature. Don't do this to yourself." Which was all she really needed from me, a little sympathy.

She gave me a wan smile. Then her eyes lit. "Come to dinner. Pete's grilling salmon and, believe it or not, veggie kebabs." Evidence on a skewer.

Under the circumstances, I couldn't imagine a less attractive invitation. "Sounds wonderful," I fibbed, "but it's my first full day here, and you know what? I just want to let the beach seep in. Plus, Jack brought two bags of dirty laundry back from Durham so I thought I'd do a few loads and surprise him with some clean clothes."

"Jack. Damn, that reminds me. Pete sent Jack a new team T-shirt he wants him to wear Sunday." The softball game on the lawn of their summer house was a highlight of the Manolises' annual cookout. "I left the freaking shirt in the car. Walk with me and I'll hand it over."

I was leaving anyway. And I felt she needed me. She hadn't since her crisis back in New York, and she'd been there for me more recently, more times. Now it was my turn.

Margo kept up rare-for-her nervous chatter all the way to her car, a pious Prius, though there was a Mercedes in the garage and Pete's red Porsche convertible, which we'd thought *was* his midlife crisis.

"Listen," I interrupted, as she beeped her door remote, "you know Pete's a good man. And he was so contrite the last time. The marriage counseling worked. It held for eighteen years. I suggest that before you go running off—"

"Don't you dare say half-cocked," Margo shot back. But she'd made herself giggle.

At that moment, her iPhone rang. The tent people. She leaned against one of the old beech trees that cast pools of cool shade on King Charles Street. To pass the time, I picked up a copy of the morning's *Coast Post* that someone had tossed toward the trash bin and missed. While Margo talked, I unfolded the paper to get a second look at the We Got Rhythm ad with the five-year-old photo of me. My girlfriend peered over my shoulder, mouthed, "Neck," and fluttered the back of her hand under my chin like an evil moth. "Dr. Marx," she formed with her plumped lips.

I inched away against the smooth bark before turning back a few pages, but Margo's antennae were out and quivering and she spotted the two-column photo.

"Scott Goddard," she mouthed, her nostrils flaring an exclamation.

That had her speeding through the rest of her conversation. After she clicked off, she swiped the newspaper from me, stared, and let out a long whistle followed by, "Wow! I haven't heard about him since the Goddards took your ballroom class. The wounded warrior leading the parade. Your heart goes out. He's a good guy."

"Yup," was all I said. Maybe that would end the conversation. As if.

"But the wife, ugh," Margo powered on. "Bunnicula. Now, there's a woman who can suck the life out of a room. How did he wind up with her? Okay, I suppose she's pretty in a clichéd kind of way. Yeah, I can see him falling for her back in high school before her prom queen looks faded. Voted girl most likely to give a blow job in the backseat. Every teenage boy's dream. But imagine thirty years of living with that witch with a capital *B*. Scott Goddard deserves better."

That's how I felt, but I averted my eyes. Margo knew me much too well.

After she slid behind the wheel and handed over the Blue Herons T-shirt for Jack, Margo said, "Do me a favor, will you? At the party, play private eye with Pete. You love the big cheater so you're an impartial witness. Watch his moves and tell me if I'm being paranoid about the girl-on-the-side thing. Oh God, I want to be paranoid."

She took off and I began walking in the opposite direction, the T-shirt crammed into my Vera Bradley bag. I wasn't looking forward to the combination of Jack and Father's Day. The holiday hadn't been easy for him over the last eight years. This one, with #1659 hovering on the horizon, was extra complicated. Then there was Pete texting in closets. And afternoon thunderstorms predicted.

Right, Sunday was going to be fun.

chapter seven

Friday had been hot. Saturday was steaming. It was one of those days you wanted to camp in with the air-conditioning turned up high, but at the Surf Avenue house we were awake and out early. We both had errands to do. Jack left for his first dog walk of the day, whistling, still high on the possibility that #1659 was out there somewhere jumping for joy over the possibility of connecting with his bio boy. For Jack's sake, I hoped Dr. Who was doing just that. For my sake, well, I wasn't so sure.

By nine, I was looking over the produce at the farmers' market, trying to stay cool under a wide-brimmed straw hat with every curl tucked in. My auburn hair was a legacy from my father's gene pool. These days my copper tone was helped out by a colorist. But the sun was hell on dyed red and I'd be damned if I'd let my hundred-buck investment go orange.

"Well, I do declare, Miss Scarlett, all you need is the parasol," drawled Peg Lanahan, after we'd hugged hello. Peg operated Farmer Joe's produce stand. I'd known Peg and Joe since my first summer in Tuckahoe. They were good, solid people.

Peg tipped a quart basket of strawberries toward me and tumbled a few of the plumpest into my palm. "These beauties were picked this morning."

I savored them and nodded, confirming sweet and juicy.

"I'll take two baskets. How are your blueberries today?"

"Good, maybe not as sweet as later in the season, but cooked with sugar for your Father's Day cobbler, they'll be fine."

She knew the destiny of the fruit I was buying, the reason I was out in this heat. I needed the best of her berries for the one tradition I was sure Jack would never scoff at. On birthdays, Mother's Day, and Father's Day, the honoree had the privilege of choosing dessert. Lon's rice pudding, his mother's recipe, which he cooked slowly on top of the range, was what I'd always asked for. Jack chose packaged Berger cookies, a Baltimore specialty, with swirls of chocolate frosting half an inch tall. Lon had wanted my summer fruit cobbler in June and then again for his August birthday, with the addition of peaches at the luscious height of their season. When the Manolises began holding their Father's Day cookout in the afternoon, so that we all came home too late and stuffed for dinner, we moved the cobbler to the night before.

I thought Jack might find it creepy to keep up the Father's Day ritual without his dad, but he'd been good with it. "Hey, any excuse for pie" was his motto. So I'd bake the dessert this afternoon and he could have some when he finished his shift at Coneheads. Last year, when I got to the kitchen the following morning, I'd seen that he'd scooped up nearly half the cobbler before heading to bed.

Peg said, "The cucumbers are in. And the Swiss chard and most of the greens. The lettuce is pretty."

"Cucumbers," I said. "Two, please."

"How's life treating you?" she asked as she sorted through the produce.

"Happy to be back here. We had a snowy winter in Baltimore. You?"

"Record cold here. My nephew, the four-year-old, got the bronchitis that went around in December. But the doctor gave him some new medicine and he bounced back in a snap. Amazing what science can do these days. They've got a little girl who had a heart transplant at the organ-donor booth this year. She's going great guns."

The farmers' market gave free space to all kinds of nonprofits and charities. You could register as an organ donor at the Red Cross tent, drink green tea at Hug the Trees, and pick up samples of crab seasoning at the Save the Bay Foundation station.

Peg was focused on her calculator so she could avert her eyes when she asked, too casually, "And you? How's your bounce?"

"Just the standard speed bumps. I love my work."

I was hoping to sidestep questions about my nonexistent love life.

A few years before, Peg had fixed me up with her cousin. Don lived in a condo near my Charles Village house, and we had a lot in common, she'd promised. He liked sushi; I liked sushi. His wife had walked out on him. My husband had left me. Not voluntarily, of course, but wasn't the fallout almost the same?

I'd tried. Don and I had gone out twice. It wasn't awful and he wasn't awful, just ordinary, which sounds horribly condescending, but the poor man had an impossible act to follow.

"Jack's good?" Peg asked.

"Great. He made dean's list. He's back at Coneheads and doing his dog walking."

Enough information for our kind of friendship.

"Have you seen the corn?" Peg asked. "We had a lot of rain this spring and the first crop is in early."

She pointed to a bin at the very end of her awning. I wandered over to a pile of Sunglow. Their fragrance was sugary, their husks a healthy green, their tassels palest yellow.

I'd just begun stripping them halfway down, looking for kernels in soldier rows, when a dog's bark, sharp and loud, raised my head. Big dog, I thought, before I saw a massive German Shepherd prowling five aisles up.

"Sarge," a voice commanded. The leash tightened and I followed the taut trail of the strap. The funny thing was, I knew who was at the other end before I saw his face. I don't think the voice gave him away. The last

time I'd heard it had been two years before, and never snapping an order.
What I remembered were his frustrated groans when he took a beat or two
to catch up with the music. And his triumphant laugh when he'd con-
quered a new boundary, like mastering a running turn in the meringue.

Scott Goddard had put on a little weight and grown out his buzz cut
so his dark hair, salted with gray, was fuller. But if I'd had any doubts as
to his identity, which I didn't, he was wearing camo pants and an "Army
Proud" T-shirt. I felt my heart accelerate slightly, absurdly. I sucked in a
breath of heavy, humid air. Exiting, it vibrated. Idiot! If I were any more
the teenager, I would have broken out in acne on the spot. It was just the
shock of seeing him after so long, I told myself.

Still, against my will, I stared at the man as if he were something juicy
in season. Which he was definitely not. Though I did notice that Bunnicula—Bunny, I guiltily self-corrected—was not at his side.

He'd been bagging string beans, but now he rested the bag on the
wooden bin and looked at me.

I smiled. It was just a hi to someone you'd only walk over to if he
smiled in return and waved beckoningly at you. Scott smiled and nodded,
but there was not even a twitch of beckoning. No come-hither wave or
head bob to signal he was eager for a let's-catch-up-we-haven't-seen-each-
other-in-two-years conversation. He went back to picking through string
beans.

Odd, but not off-the-charts strange if Bunny was around. She hadn't
liked me. I'd rubbed her the wrong way with my demos of fancy steps
that she couldn't and (she'd literally dug in her heels) wouldn't follow. So
maybe Scott was acting like an ass to keep the peace with his wife.

I scanned the shoulder of the road, where she might have skulked off
for a cigarette. Ran a quick check of the nearby stalls. Nope, no sign of
the evil Bunny. When I turned back, there was Scott walking toward me,
the German Shepherd trotting by his side. It had been a while since I'd

last seen the man, and the air was rippling with heat and so it could have been a mirage. But the lurch of my heart told me it was the real thing. That and the dog's gruff bark.

"It *is* you," Scott said as they pulled up next to me. "For a moment there, I didn't recognize you with your hair all—what would you call it?—tucked in. I'm used to you with your hair down. The reddish color."

Typical man-speak. Reddish.

I swept off the straw hat so vigorously that its pink satin ribbon whipped me in the face.

He laughed. "You okay?" I nodded yes and shook out my hair. Copper curls tumbled over my shoulders. Okay, so I was hair-proud. It was my best feature.

"That's better. Now I know you."

A few uncomfortable beats went by. The colonel had been a marksman in Iraq and he was staring, eyes narrowed. In the shimmering sun, I shivered, feeling he had me in his sights.

Finally, he said, "You look good, Nora."

"Thanks, you too. And you too, whatever your name is, fella. He is a fella, right?" I bent down to the dog, which was nuzzling my knees.

"He is definitely a he. Of course, you haven't been formally introduced. Nora, Sarge. Sarge, Nora."

"Nice to meet you, Sarge." I offered the dog the back of my hand. Sarge sniffed, licked, and rubbed his ear against my arm.

"I think you just found yourself a new friend. He likes you and he's got great instincts. He hasn't steered me wrong yet, and we've been through some tough times together."

Speaking of tough times, I was about to ask after Bunny and her mother when his cell phone rang. He slipped it from his pocket and eyed the screen. "Sorry. Have to take this." He said, "Goddard," while Sarge, now that we were pals, allowed me to scratch his ruff and thanked me with a low growl of pleasure. Thirty seconds later, Scott signed off with, "On my way."

He tugged the leash and gave me an apologetic half smile. "Duty calls. They need me at the VFW booth. Someone's asking questions the old guy covering can't answer." He rested a hand just above my wrist, raising fresh goose bumps. "Hey, Nora, I'm really glad we ran into each other. It was good seeing you. Two years. Time . . . Actually, I was going to say time flies, but sometimes it doesn't—you know what I mean?"

I did and thought, *But now it's whizzing by too fast.* I managed, "Good seeing you too. Maybe . . ." We both blurted "maybe" at the same time. His hand flew off my wrist.

When I flourished a "You first," he laughed.

"Right. I was going to say, it's a small town and a long summer, so maybe we'll catch up again. I know Sarge would like that."

Sarge would. I gave my canine fan a final pat on the head. "Sure," I said. "Well, send my best to Bunny."

That seemed to give the colonel a jolt, snap him to attention. "Right, I'll send it." And then, in a display of more Tuckahoe magic—beach woo-woo, Margo would have called it—Scott Goddard and his huge German Shepherd disappeared. Vanished. Into thick air.

That night I baked the fruit cobbler. Not for Lon. I wasn't that delusional, although a truly sane person might have wondered if I'd conjured up Colonel Goddard and his string beans, given how he'd evaporated so thoroughly, so inexplicably, after we'd exchanged good-byes. Totally irrational, I'd gone looking for him, not having the slightest idea what I'd do if I found him. I passed the VFW tent twice, checking out a couple of eighty-somethings holding down the fort. I walked the entire market, telling myself I was searching for the perfect blackberries, though I'd never used them in the cobbler.

In fact, the events of the day had dulled my taste for dessert. I left the cobbler, still warm, crust intact, on the kitchen counter with a serving spoon propped against the baking pan for Jack.

When I got down to the kitchen Sunday morning, it was exactly where it had been the night before, untouched.

chapter eight

I was worried about Jack. He'd left for the Coneheads reunion Friday night in high spirits and was still buoyant Saturday morning, downing a whoppingly big breakfast from what was left of Margo's welcome gift before heading off to the first dog run of the day. But by midafternoon I noticed his mood had flagged, and when he'd left for his evening shift at the ice-cream shop, he was as grumpy as a four-year-old who'd skipped his nap. When I asked if he was okay, he said, "Hanging." I wasn't up when he got home, but he'd slept behind a firmly closed door and when he emerged at nine on Sunday, he had to hustle to get to the dogs.

"See you at the Manolises'. Party starts at two," I'd reminded him as he rushed around grabbing the Frisbee, the ball chucker, and plastic puppy poop bags.

"Maybe."

"What do you mean, maybe?" I dodged into his path as he moved toward the front door. I was his mother, for God's sake. He was living under my roof, for God's sake. He wasn't yet twenty-one and I didn't like his tone.

"I mean I may show or I may not. Depends."

"On what, Jack?"

"Mom, stop busting my chops, okay? And don't give me that line about hurting the Manolises' feelings. They'll have a hundred people swarming over their place and thirty guys lined up to play in the game. They won't miss me, believe me. And please"—his deep voice was not begging; it was commanding—"spare me the lecture about tradition. I am so freaking fed up with tradition, the thought of it makes me gag."

The gag reference cut awfully close to the Father's Day cobbler, which sat on the counter uncut, as pristine as a virgin. That part really hurt.

"I'm late already. Really, I've gotta get going."

So I moved out of his way. Which was, I told myself, what moms have to do sometimes. Except most moms didn't have another pseudo parent, an unknown quantity, waiting in the wings.

I turned to watch him leave as he patted his pocket to make sure the iPhone was in place to receive the call or the text or the email that obviously hadn't been dispatched by DD at the first notice from the donor bank. I didn't know whether to be grateful for that respite or protectively angry. Jack had hurried by me, shaking his head as if I were a mosquito buzzing by his ear.

Now it was past three, the Manolises' Father's Day party was in full swing, and he hadn't shown up yet. At least, I hadn't spotted him.

Margo's stare was trained on another target and she was wearing an expression I'd first seen when she'd played Shaw's Saint Joan off-off-Broadway—self-righteous and ready to go to war.

"Look at him. Ugh, my husband is such a putz!" she said as she whipped out an arm to hook a glass of pinot grigio off a passing waiter's tray.

She continued to scowl at the copse of trees at the far end of their lawn, where Pete, half hidden behind a loblolly pine, was doing something nefarious with his cell phone. It looked like texting to me.

Emine, at my elbow, gave me a nudge.

"See, this is what I mean. Something's going on," Margo said. Her gaze shifted toward a circle of laughing middle-aged men. "Half the Oriole lineup from his glory days are here trading war stories. Nothing makes Pete hotter than reliving his prime-time past. So where is he? Off playing with his damn cell phone." An even darker emotion passed like a thundercloud over her face as she gazed at Pete pacing in the trees. "Maybe he's found something hotter. Maybe it's sex on the cell. I'll bet he's sexting." She slugged her wine.

"Sexting. Only teenagers do that, yes?" Em said. "And politicians who think they can get away with anything."

"I rest my case on both counts." Margo drained her glass and was scanning for a waiter with fresh drinks when a woman all in pink wedged herself between Emine and me. Her voice, gravelly enough to pave a driveway, croaked, "Divine party, Margo." She kissed the air around my friend's cheek. "So thrilled to be invited." She allowed a brief, indifferent smile at our introduction. Then, with a neat twist of her grip, Lily Something tugged Margo into a one-on-one out of hearing distance. Which left me with Emine, happy enough to sip our drinks in silence and watch the party in action.

Sixty-some guests milled around the back lawn studded with green-and-white-striped awnings sheltering tables loaded with Maryland seafood and Jewish delicacies flown in from New York. At Pete's insistence, there was a vegetarian tent. Two bars were busy keeping the finest flowing, and next to a barbecue station, a huge grill turned out burgers and hot dogs. On a stage erected in front of the Manolises' wraparound screen porch, a quartet called Summer Breeze played show tunes and light rock. The temperature hovered in the low eighties; the skies, for the moment, showed a milky sun with a drift of thin clouds. The predicted thundershowers hadn't panned out, and there was no sign of them on the horizon. A perfect day. An *almost* perfect day.

As I was considering my next step—possibly texting Jack; better not—our hostess reappeared. "This you've got to hear. You'll never guess where Lily, that awful gossip, saw my husband, that sneaky bastard."

Her hand flew to her mouth to gnaw on her perfect manicure. I couldn't imagine what Pete had done to make her chew her gel tips.

"Let's see. On The Block making a deal with a hooker? Staggering out of a Cherry Hill crack house?" I suggested.

"Not funny, Nora. Just as bad. Lily was sitting in Montgomery Wu's waiting room when she saw Pete exiting the examining suite."

"This is bad?" Emine asked.

Margo explained, "Montgomery Wu is a plastic surgeon, famous for his 'never leave slack or crack' face-lifts. The Full Monty."

She was seething, pacing. "Another secret Pete's keeping from me. A full face-lift. Incredible! Even I haven't had a full. And that Montgomery Wu is a butcher. His patients look like they got caught in a wind tunnel. But I suppose that's what Pete's after. The fountain of youth." She placed a palm against each cheek and pulled the skin as tight as a quarter-bouncing bedsheet. "Translation: much older man/much younger woman affair." When she peeled her hands away, and not a lot of skin drooped, she inhaled a deep, obviously noncleansing breath and flashed Pete-in-the-pines a fiery glance. "Okay, that does it. Now I'm gonna go kill Captain Underpants."

Peter Constantine Manolis had earned a different nickname in his prime. The Greek Icon, the press had dubbed him. But he was no haloed icon, if you were to believe his wife, and no match for her in her role as Saint Joan. He was still walking and talking into his cell phone, oblivious. And Margo, gripping the glass of merlot she'd hijacked from me, glossy blond hair swinging, was marching into battle.

Pete had been a foregone conclusion for Margo from the day he'd sidled up to her at a fund-raiser for Broadway Battles AIDS. She'd been waiting for him ever since she'd fallen in love with a Greek statue in the Brooklyn Museum. She had told me that story on one of those snowy city afternoons that elicits reflection (we were sitting cross-legged on her bed at the

NYU dorm, passing a pint bottle of gin back and forth) in a way that sounded as predestined as a prophecy issued by the Oracle at Delphi.

It had all started with her gloomy parents: Paulette, the Holocaust researcher, and Bernard—"Bernie the Attorney," in Margo's shorthand—who'd spent his career wresting back property from the inheritors of Nazi plunder. "They were freaking Batman and Robin in orthopedic shoes," their only child said. "Partners in righting wrongs and reversing injustice."

Their brownstone on Prospect Park South was airless, joyless, and not designed for an exuberant, essentially happy child whose genes had leapt generations from a great-great-grandmother who'd coupled with a fiery Gypsy boy on a moonlit night in the Carpathian Mountains. This was Margo's fantasy explanation for being so misplaced in her parents' world.

The family's weekly visits to the Brooklyn Museum for concerts in the atrium provided the opportunity for escape. One day, she'd slipped away from the music and wandered off. What stopped her was a hall lined with larger-than-life Greek statues. All naked.

She skipped the women. She knew basically what they looked like from her own body with its budding breasts. Plus the Greeks sculpted females totally smooth down there, with all the interesting parts tucked in, so they were a major yawn. But she was amazed, fixated on the statues of the naked men with humongous wieners hanging between their colossal legs, and their testicles looking like onions in the net bags her mother brought home from Gristedes. Did men really carry all that around between their thighs? How did they walk without smacking themselves black-and-blue?

When her mother found her staring up at the stone crotch of some marble guy from the fifth century BCE, Paulette whisked her away to the boring Impressionists room. From then on, Margo hated the wishy-washy passionless Monet, but, boy, did she like Greek statues. On school trips and on her parents' Sunday afternoon concert outings at the museum, she'd excuse herself to go to the restroom and wind up standing in front of some marble Greek, his gigantic schlong at half-mast. Until she was fifteen and saw the real thing, pink, vermicular, and disappointingly small, attached to her first boyfriend, she thought all men were constructed like the statues.

When she finally found one who was, and Greek to boot, she didn't let go. Her mother had been appalled. Margo wanting to marry a non-Jewish boy was disappointing enough, but a baseball player? Heresy.

Margo had been secretly thrilled by their response, and when her parents wondered aloud how they could ever accept a son-in-law who played his life away, she knew she'd hit the jackpot.

As she stood by Pete's side in the judge's chambers and repeated "for better, for worse," she prayed, *Please, God, let me play my life away. And let there be light.*

Pete *was* the living embodiment of light, and for that alone Margo adored him. So when, five years into her marriage, she was confronted with the eye-opening truth that he wasn't a statue of perfect marble but a man made of flawed flesh and dark secrets, she was almost destroyed.

Back in Manhattan, I'd listened to her daily lamentations in the aftermath of his original sin. The hotel charges on the Visa bills, the condoms she'd dug out of his briefcase, the trips to the shrink and to the lawyers. Margo loved her lawyers.

I'd been in my twenties then. I was forty-six now—I didn't have the strength to go through it again. That's what I said to Emine between bites of grilled sausage, as we sat at a table on the lawn while the party throbbed around us.

Em said, "With Margo always she jumps to the conclusion. Love and tragedy. Romeo and Juliet. I hope she doesn't poison Pete."

Margo's problems must have seemed puny to Emine, who had real trouble on her hands. I looked around for Merry.

"Ahh. She is helping Adnan out at the dessert tent this afternoon. Not as family; as an employee. She will be paid so he can order her to cover that awful haircut with a Herons baseball cap. He agreed to a little eye makeup and lipstick. It will only be three hours she needs to obey him. She calls him Boss, with a little bow. This is sarcasm, but he doesn't understand that."

She speared a mushroom and took a sip of orange juice. "Anyway, let him deal with her. I am off duty for the complete weekend. Yesterday, I didn't go in to work. I had my hair colored. I shopped. These are new shoes. I had the whole day for myself. It was a luxury."

"Good for you," I said. "You needed it. And you look gorgeous."

She didn't bother with cosmetics at the café, but now her dark eyes, lined with kohl and smudged with shadow, were huge and shining. She'd brushed on a summer glow with bronzer. Dark curls in exotic spirals dusted her bare shoulders. She wore a thin-strapped frock of . . . what else? Turquoise gauze, filmy leaves of it as delicate as the layers of her baklava. Its scoop neckline laid bare a smooth background for a curve of silver necklace set with turquoise stones. She looked stunning.

"I needed some time away. Meryem and I are like chalk and cheese, oil and water. I get on her nerves by breathing the same air she does."

"That's the mother-daughter thing," I said. "I hear it all the time from my sister-in-law. My niece is adorable, but she's thirteen, with the fresh mouth and the slammed doors, and her mother says she understands why some animals eat their young." What came next slipped through my censor. I'd planned on sharing with her and Margo. But later. Eventually. Not now.

I said, "The mother-son thing is no picnic either."

Emine gave me a quizzical look. She'd gone to boarding school in England, but sometimes the American idioms escaped her.

"Picnic. Not easy," I said. It lost something in the translation.

"Where *is* Jack? I haven't seen him. He is usually with Pete and the baseball players."

Just then a train of clouds began to chug across the sun. Not poetically. One minute we were sitting in a pool of yellow light, the next in blue shadow. Which cast the perfect mood for telling Em everything, starting with Jack contacting the fertility clinic and ending with our face-off in the hall that morning.

"Margo knows?" she asked when I'd finished unloading.

"You're the first. I wasn't sure if this was anything to worry about. Because it's possible Sixteen fifty-nine"—I fumbled, unable to bring myself to say "DD"—"won't get back to him. I still don't know how this will turn out. But now I've decided that's not the point. The point"—the one that stabbed me in the heart—"is how eagerly Jack's going after this. Him."

"But you seemed fine with it last year," Emine said. "And suddenly you are so concerned. Why is this?"

I had to push the words past my reluctance to say them because saying them would give them life. "I guess because now it's happening. I didn't know that it would feel like Jack is leapfrogging Lon's memory to get to this new guy. And I'm scared. Who knows what this Donor Dude has in mind for my son? He could turn Jack's life upside down. Kidnap him emotionally." I felt myself beginning to lose it. Quivering lip, moistening mascara, the works. I swallowed back tears.

Emine reached over, propped a finger under my chin, and lifted it so I couldn't help but stare into her eyes. "Now who's jumping to the conclusions?" she asked. "Take it day by day. You may like this man. Jack has his genes, so how bad can he be?"

We'd been following Margo as she bobbed and weaved her way to Pete, waving hellos here, squeezing hands there, but never losing track of her mission to yank Pete the ultimate wedgie with his new underpants. But now, finally, she'd been stopped by an irresistible force—the press. On hand to cover the softball game, they always featured the children's inning, in which retired Orioles players pitched to the kids.

In a semicircle of reporters, photographers, and videographers, the star of the show, apparently unharmed and fully clothed, was shining his media smile, extra-wide and super-bright. Pete loved the camera and the camera loved him back, Margo used to say during his highest-earning phase, when he was king of the endorsements. That earnest, trust-me visage had shilled for shaving cream, designer cologne, hot dogs—no beer; he didn't want to tarnish the image—and later, only because the hair dye company made him an offer that bought the Tuckahoe house, he starred in "Batter Up for Color-Up," an ad campaign so wildly successful that it landed him a spot on *Letterman*, where he was surprisingly witty in the bantering exchange. Margo, the actress without her name in lights, had been a little jealous.

As the photographers moved in for the requisite grip-and-grin, my attention shifted to the field beyond, where some guy in a Blue Herons T-shirt was laying down bases. "They're getting ready for the game," I said, and Emine put down her fork.

"Dessert," she said. "They'll be descending like locusts on the dessert tables. I should see how Adnan is doing." Also Merry, was the unspoken tag.

"I'm coming with you." My minor meltdown over the Donor Dude's intentions had to have messed around with my makeup. "I could use a little freshening up."

On the Manolises' endless multifanned screen porch, where he'd laid out desserts, Adnan was plugging in an espresso machine. A table was covered with an array of Emine's pastries and cakes and, center stage, her fabulous Turkish Delight torte, layers of pistachio sponge cake and rosewater buttercream.

I exclaimed to Adnan, "You've outdone yourself. More pastries than last year?"

"Yes, every year more." He smiled a proud acknowledgment.

"More, but not everything." Emine's sharp eye had picked up a missing tray of cherry baklava and the absence of her child. "Where is Meryem?"

"I sent her in for the baklava."

"I'll check," she told him.

She led and I followed her into the Manolises' back hall. Its peach walls with white scallop molding and a vaulted ceiling made it feel like the inside of a seashell. I'd planned on detouring to my handbag, tucked behind one of the sofas in the massive living room, but on the way we heard, faintly at first, then as we moved down the hall louder and louder until we were bombarded with it, a barrage of laughter, hooting, and the rhythmical banging of metal on metal. Em and I traded panicked looks and she said, "The kitchen. Merry!"

chapter nine

I landed, breathing hard, at the entrance to Margo's cavernous kitchen, and it was a few seconds before I took in the scene. Merry Haydar, with a freshly applied slash of almost-black lipstick, and her skirt rolled at the waistband to hike the hem way above the knees, was dancing down and dirty with one of the catering company's help, who looked to be high school age from the mustache and the overmuscled arms. Off to one side, the pot banger spotted me and halted his spoon midair. Emine caught up and froze at my side. The hooting stopped. The room fell silent except for the gush of water from the faucets of the double sink. Her partner had backed off, but Merry, unaware, continued to move her hips in a sexy spiral.

Em and I were shoulder to shoulder so I could feel her shaking. "Merry! *Hayır! Dur!*" Then in English, "Stop that!" She rocked on the new shoes but couldn't seem to step into the scene.

Merry looked our way and her smile vanished. "Oh shit!" she said. "The cops are here." She stretched her arms, wrist against wrist, toward us. "Cuff me, Danno." Then she backed up and the boy slipped the trap.

He looked at us, grabbed his towel, and said to Emine, "She came on to me. Not the other way around. I swear."

"Come here, Meryem." I could hear the quaver behind Em's barely controlled command. *"Şimdi!"*

"That means 'pronto' in Turkish," Merry said to the backs of the boys, who were already swiping dishes or, eyelids lowered, sliding trash from trays into plastic trash cans.

"Okay, coming." Merry waved a bye to no one. When she got to her mother and me, her face was all fake innocence, her tone sarcastic. "Yes, Emine?"

For a moment, I thought I'd misheard. Emine, not Mom?

Breathing fire, Em clasped her daughter's wrist and tugged her a few steps down the hall, where Merry stopped short. "Don't . . . pull . . . me." The girl flung her arm out of Em's grip and faced her. "You're mad at me. What did I do wrong? I was just being friendly. You tell me"—here she switched to singsong—"'Merry, Americans are friendly. Always be friendly.'"

Emine pressed her fingers to her eyelids. *Tanrı bana yardım edin.* The phrase wasn't new to me. She uttered it frequently when dealing with her daughter. God help me.

"Let's go," I said. Merry allowed me to steer her down the hall, one hand on her shoulder.

"Please don't tell Margo about this," Em said, trying to keep up. "We cater so many of her parties and our reputation is good. I want to keep it so. And I don't think the boys will tell."

"Of course."

"Like it's such a big deal." Merry yawned extravagantly. I tightened my grip on her shoulder, maybe a little too hard. I navigated so we avoided the screened porch and Adnan. "Now what?" I asked.

"I will call Adnan and tell him to get the baklava. For her, I will make some excuse." Emine flashed her daughter a furious glance. "She's not coming back."

As we exited the front door, a scratchy old recording, an organist's rendition of "Take Me Out to the Ball Game," filtered over from the side lawn. That signaled Pete was about to take to the stage for the welcoming speech that preceded the migration to the field.

We were on the fringes of the gathering crowd when ten-year-old Erol rushed up to us. Emine said a few final brusque words into her cell and clicked off the conversation, all in Turkish, with her husband.

"Guess who's pitching to me. I just found out." Erol was hopping from foot to foot with excitement. "Cal Ripken Jr. The most famous Oriole of all time. Can you believe it? Can you, Mer?"

Merry wiggled under my grip and nodded.

"Cal Ripken, you love him, Erol. This is good." Emine turned to me, her dark eyes flashing joy. Her young son was a never-fail source of happiness.

"Will Dad be there watching? Not cleaning up or something?"

"He will be there," Em said. From the fire in her eyes, I knew she'd make sure he would.

"Yesssss! Go, Birds! We rock!" Erol shouted as he bounded away.

The band played a drumroll, and Pete took center stage, looking a good—a really good—decade younger than his fifty-three years. You couldn't blame Margo for feeling her husband was still fem-bait.

"Welcome to the tenth annual Father's Day cookout and softball game," he boomed into the mike. "A decade, which makes this game a tradition." Now, there was a word that had become an obscenity in my household. At least in Jack's lexicon.

Jack. At some point midafternoon, after my first mimosa, I'd decided it was unhealthy to obsess over whether my son would show up at the party. Occasionally, I'd skim the crowd, but after a second drink and no sightings, I'd almost stopped caring. Almost.

All I could make out of the players gathered near the stage were the backs of Oystercatcher and Heron T-shirts and a jumble of gray-and-blue baseball caps. "Ladies and gentlemen," Pete announced, "I give you the Oystercatchers. They're ready and eager for their first win in five years and this may be their year to break the Dreaded Father's Day Curse."

After the challengers lined up, Pete called the Herons by position. I startled out of my fog only when he announced, "On second base, Jack Farrell."

Em wagged a finger at me. "You see, he showed up."

Of course he had. *Never had a doubt,* I told myself as I swallowed the last little lump of it that had lodged in my throat all afternoon.

Jack took his place. No bounding or bow for him, though he did tip his hat and then held it against his heart as the Summer Breeze Quartet launched into "The Star-Spangled Banner."

Everyone joined in singing the national anthem, the way Marylanders did at Camden Yards, roaring the "Ohhhhh" for Orioles in the line "Ohhhhh, say does tha-at star-spangled, ba-a-nne-er yeh-et wave." When the last note faded, Pete called out, "Play ball!"

Jack stopped by on his way to the field. Maybe he'd noticed me from the stage, or maybe he'd spotted Merry at the end of the row, and my son, the thoughtful one I used to know as late as yesterday, jogged down our aisle to land in front of Merry, who'd been sulking until she saw him. Then she lit up.

"Yo, Jack. Hi-five me, bro." They spanked palms. She doffed her cap, skimming a daring glance at her mother.

"What's with the hair, Mer?" Jack said. "Lawn mower run you over?"

"Creep," she answered, but she beamed, obviously pleased by the attention. She'd always looked up to Jack, who treated her as the classic pest of a little sister, one he teased but actually liked.

"I thought punk had peaked. I gotta tell you, you're looking very last year, Mer."

"And you're looking half jock, half geek and all bullsh—"

"Hey," he cut her off. "Watch your mouth. You want to save it to cheer for the Herons."

"Go, Herons!" Merry hollered.

"What a pain. Okay, you're hired." He snatched the Herons cap from her hand and slapped it over her bizarre hairdo. Shaking his head, he jerked the bill low on her forehead. "Now you're presentable."

She grinned.

He said hello to Em, added, "Need to borrow my mom for a sec," and pulled me a little aside.

Eyeing the rush to the softball field, he said, "Apologize for this morning. For, like, the attitude. You didn't deserve it. What's going on isn't your fault. I'm just wound up, you know, with everything happening and"—he patted his back pocket, where I assumed his iPhone sat dormant—"not happening. And then Father's Day on top of all this other father stuff, well, I'm sorry."

I didn't say it was okay, because it wasn't, and I didn't reach to nudge back a hank of blond hair that had drifted over his left eye, because he was nineteen and I was forty-six and I'd learned my lesson with Tiffanie and debating his choice of a major and tiptoeing around more issues than I cared to remember. But, oh, I wanted to smooth the hair back and roll up the cuffs on the sleeves of his T-shirt and look down to see if his sneaker laces were tied tightly and, if they weren't, crouch down and double knot them. What I did was nod. What I said was, "I understand."

"Appreciate it." And because keeping your selfish anxiety under wraps is sometimes rewarded, he leaned over and planted a kiss on my cheek.

Then he raced off, one shoelace trailing—I knew it, I knew it—and his iPhone sticking out of his back pocket.

The kids' game lasted twenty chaotic, hilarious minutes so everyone could have a chance at the plate, and when Erol smacked a two-bagger off Cal Ripken Jr., who'd deliberately sweet-pitched to the boy, I thought Adnan was going to scream himself hoarse, in a very dignified way of course. Merry did an Orioles' bird dance to celebrate.

She had insisted we stand close to the action so she could lead the cheering for the Herons in the adults' game, especially for Jack, who hit a disappointing pop fly in his first at bat, a "can of corn" easily caught by an aging Hall of Famer in center field.

Heading out of the eighth inning, the reputation of the Blue Herons, undefeated for half a decade, was on the line. The score was 4–3 Oyster-catchers.

It was when Jack was trudging in from the field, eyes downcast, mouth locked in a lip-biting twist, that I saw something set off his startle reflex. His head snapped up; he came to a full stop and whipped the iPhone from his rear pocket. Not a call. He stared at that screen as if the words were alive and dancing. This had to be even bigger than a message from the hot, mean girlfriend. As he read, Jack bobbed a series of small yeses. And from the bliss that bloomed on his face, you would have thought that Moses had emailed him the Ten Commandments or Jesus had texted him the Sermon on the Mount. Sixteen, aka #1659, aka Donor Dad and Dude, had arrived for the big reveal. I was sure of it.

As Margo would have said, "Oy." *No, this is good news,* I corrected myself, *good news. Good news.* Hoping that if I hammered it home hard enough, I'd actually believe it.

As he passed me, Jack whammed a triumphant air-punch with such force that I was afraid he'd dislocated a shoulder. I gave him a "Mom gets it, Mom's okay with it" thumbs-up in return.

In the final inning, with a man on first base, he was up at bat. Pulsing with energy, he blasted a two-run homer that decapitated one of the Manolises' loblolly pines at the fringe of their property and captured a delirious win for the Blue Herons.

chapter ten

"His name is what?" Margo choked out a spritz of her caramel macchiato and Emine reached for the napkin dispenser.

At four thirty on Monday afternoon, the three of us were gathered at the Turquoise Café to perform a postmortem on the Manolises' party. We all agreed it had been fabulous. But now I reported on the email Jack had received as he walked off the softball field the day before. I wasn't sure how fabulous *it* was.

"Dr. Dirk DeHaven, Donor Dad," I repeated, adding sugar to my already sweetened chai. I needed an antidote to the sour taste on my tongue, the residue from pronouncing his name aloud.

"Try saying that fast three times in a row." Margo snorted.

"Jack thinks it's some kind of sign from above. That's what he said this morning." I didn't know whether to laugh or cry.

"The D-D-D-D-D, like a stutter. This is a sign?" Emine looked puzzled. Also tired. Her eyes were haloed, not with kohl but with the dark smudges of a sleepless night. I wasn't looking so hot either. I'd slept fitfully, pummeling the pillow, then awakened fully and finally around three a.m. from a dream about treading water. My subconscious was ridiculously transparent.

"Jack said it's amazing that he's been calling this man DD and he turns out to have the initials DD. Jack thinks it's a good omen."

Margo blotted coffee from her chin. She'd been all wound up since my disclosure a few minutes prior that Jack had been searching for Sixteen. I'd shot an eyebrow warning to Em and she'd awkwardly pretended to be surprised, playing along because neither of us wanted to hurt Margo's feelings.

"Jack told you about the email when?" Margo leaned in, green eyes glittering. Oh, the drama of it all.

"Actually, he didn't tell me much of anything. When we got home after the party, he grabbed a soda from the fridge, futzed around with his iPhone, pulled up the email, and handed the phone over. I read it."

"He showed it to you?"

"Yes." I stirred my chai into a whirlpool. "DD's first line was, 'Your note was a welcome surprise.'"

Margo had been tracing her index finger over a plate that had recently held baklava to pick up every last crumb and smidgen of syrup. "Surprise. Oh, I'll bet he was surprised. No sign of Jack when he turned eighteen, and now here's sonny boy come to call at nineteen. Quintuple D must have wet his pants." Then she added, "The welcome part was a nice touch, though."

I put her in time-out while I explained exclusively to Em, "He wanted to know all about Jack. The fertility clinic had emailed him the essentials. Jack's birthday, Lon's and my names, our contact information. But he was eager to learn more. Where did Jack go to college? What was his major? His interests? That kind of thing. He asked Jack for a photo. His was attached."

"You lie." Margo's sticky finger shot out to poke me, but I retreated into the booth's cushiony back and she missed. "The DD sent a photo with the first email?"

"A recent portrait that he said was from the staff page of the website of his hospital. In color."

Jack had peered at it for a very long minute in our kitchen while I wondered how many times and for how long he'd stared at it since its arrival.

"There's a resemblance," he'd said. "Especially the eyes." He handed over the iPhone. "What do you think?"

I'd thought that seeing DD in the flesh even in pixels was too much, too soon. But I made myself look.

Dirk DeHaven was more than presentable, posed, arms folded, in his white medical coat, pale blue shirt with monogrammed cuffs and navy tie. His hair had a just-trimmed look. Its platinum color was too light for a middle-aged man, so the blond was probably laced with white. No teeth on display in the smile, a modest, confident curve that would reassure a patient's family after he'd performed tricky, death-defying surgery on their loved one. His eyes were large, maybe magnified by the rimless eyeglasses he hadn't removed for the photo, which said to me he wasn't particularly vain. That was a point in his favor. The irises were the same bald-eagle gold as Jack's, which clawed at me inside. I'd searched Jack's face throughout his childhood for something, *anything* that would link him genetically to Lon and had come up with zip. Here the connection to DD was blatantly obvious.

"What do you think?" Jack had pressed.

"The eyes are yours," I'd agreed.

"And maybe the chin," he said. "Okay. I'm forwarding the photo so you can look whenever." He'd been sure I'd want to and he'd been right. I'd found myself mildly obsessed. By now, I'd given up counting how many times I'd opened the attachment.

"You have it on your phone? Oh dear God, why didn't you say so in the first place?" Margo was frothing, or that white mustache above her upper lip was the last of the foam on her macchiato. "Give it here," she commanded.

She and Emine leaned in so their heads touched, blond to brown. A hand from each shared a grip on the rim of the screen. After a moment of peering silence, Em pronounced, "He looks kind."

"He looks rich," Margo said. "Check this out." She turned the image toward me and tapped DD's wrist. "The watch is a Mont Heurigné. Older model. Collector's item." Margo knew her jewelry. "I'd tag it at thirty thousand dollars. Maybe more. He either inherited it or he makes a ton of money. I assume he's in private practice?"

I shrugged my ignorance. "What I know is Dirk M. DeHaven, MD, FACS, is a department head at Gilbreth Medical Center. Cardiology." A heart surgeon, which carried its own freight of irony.

"You Googled him, of course."

"He's one of the top docs in his field. Pediatric cardiology. Much published. Of international repute. He treated a prince in the Dutch royal family and operated on the nephew of the emir of Qatar. Consults occasionally on medical issues for CNN."

"So he's a *macher.*"

I knew what that meant. Back in college Margo had taught me some Yiddish. Hell, I was probably the only half-Irish, half-Italian American woman with a house on the ocean who could tell someone, in beautifully articulated Yiddish, to go shit in it. *Gay cocken offen yom.* So *macher* was a snap. Maker. A major player.

"And the personal life of this jet-setting healer?"

"Divorced. Didn't say how long. That's from the email. He also wrote, 'There's lots more, Jack, but I don't want to overwhelm you with information in our first exchange.' Something like that."

"I like him already." That was from Emine, of course. "And how old did you say he is?"

"Forty-eight," I muttered reluctantly.

Muttered and reluctantly because I'd predicted what was coming next and from what source. Margo was shooting sparks from every pore.

"Single and couldn't be more in your age range, the bio progenitor of your only child. If Shakespeare had been born in the twenty-first century, he would have written this play." I didn't ask, tragedy or comedy? "Oh God, I feel a heat wave coming on."

"Order an iced macchiato," I snapped.

"No more coffee for me. All the caffeine is sending my bladder into spasms." She slid out of the booth and onto her feet. "I'm heading up to pee."

Margo had a thing about public restrooms, which she declared were germ-infested cesspools, even the one offered at the Vatican when she and Pete had had an audience with the pope. Who knew what cardinal had committed what sins before planting his behind on what seat? She generally insisted on using a bathroom in the Haydars' apartment above the store.

Em said, "I cleaned the ones down here myself half an hour ago. Nobody's used the ladies' room since then."

"Fine. But don't you dare discuss anything important until I get back. CNN announced a comet coming on a path so close to earth it could wipe out the human race. Chat about that."

As she sashayed across the room, I figured we were safe.

I turned back to Emine. "Did you have your talk with Adnan after the party?" I noticed the tremor in her hands and laid mine over hers.

"I gave him bloody hell for letting Merry out of his sight. What was he thinking?"

The sun in the café was splintering into shadows. It was nearly five, slow time at a coffee shop. The crowd would pick up again for dessert after dinner. Adnan was lettering the menu board for the evening's special, pomegranate cheesecake. When he saw me look his way, he waved with the marking pen. I waved back, wondering if he knew we were talking about him.

Emine's voice lowered as she replayed her telling him about the scene in Margo's kitchen. "The skirt rolled up. How the boys were clapping and laughing. You know what he said?" She turned a pinch of index finger and thumb against her lips as if she were twisting a key. "Nothing. For half an hour, nothing. He sits in front of the computer, staring at a soccer game from Turkey. Then he follows me into the bedroom and he tells me he has the answer. Definitely the answer for the problems with Meryem."

Margo had peed fast, not wanting to miss anything. Em, across from me, was facing in the opposite direction and didn't see her trotting on the return. I gave my head a quick, subtle shake, but Em missed it. She was saying, "And then he tells me that—"

"Who tells you what?" Margo loomed over us.

I intervened. "Wolf Blitzer tells her that if the comet does hit the earth, he hopes it lands on your back lawn."

"Very funny." Margo plunked herself down across from Em, eyes narrowed. "So, what's the big secret?"

Emine knew it was useless to resist, and she was up to the part she was eager to share. "Adnan wants to bring his mother here." She paused to let that sink in. "For the summer, at least." Another pause. "To keep an eye on Meryem."

Margo said, "Oh shit. Selda's coming to Tuckahoe? But she was here just three years ago and you haven't recovered from that invasion yet."

"This visit has a purpose, Adnan says. Meryem has become more difficult over the past months." Em dashed a look at me that I knew was a reminder to keep the secret of the events in the kitchen. My head bobbed my guarantee. "He believes Selda can guide Meryem away from trouble. She has a strong hand, he says."

"And a big mouth, did he also say?" Margo snapped.

"To him, his mother is an expert at setting limits. At setting fires, I answered back."

Margo grabbed a handful of pistachios from a bowl on the table. "So Selda would apply some Turkish muscle, huh?" She cracked a shell between her perfectly aligned, brilliantly capped teeth. "Well, think about it, Em. It might not be the worst idea in the world."

"It is the worst in the universe." Emine bristled. "You know my mother-in-law plays the queen, wanting everyone to bow to her. Me first. She hates women. She never had a daughter. Four spoiled sons but not one daughter."

"She really does have the people skills of a boa constrictor," I added.

"She'll drive me crazy. Meryem will go—what does she call it? Ballistic. My mother-in-law is always seeing problems. Merry eats too much sugar. Her face will break out. Her feet are too big. Her voice is too loud. And Selda hasn't seen her in three years. She will be shocked at what she finds. Everything will be my fault, of course. It always is." She pulled a sigh. "I know she will only add to the trouble. I have told Adnan absolutely not, but he refuses to give up. He wants me to think it through. Then we will talk about it calmly and I will see his side. This is what he tells me. He doesn't realize I am putting my foot down on this."

We all lapsed into a moment's silence in honor of Em's foot.

"I've come to a conclusion," Margo finally drawled. "Men are idiots. Irresistible idiots, but idiots. Or maybe we're the idiots, because we don't understand the entire gender and we still give them so much power."

At which point, as if to underline her theory, Emine's iPhone sounded, playing a sweet Turkish melody that signaled an incoming email.

She looked at the screen curiously at first. When she gave me a sly smile I had the feeling it was something more than an ad from Zappos.

"We just had a new online sign-up for tomorrow night's class," she said, her voice singing a light melody.

"I thought you already closed class," I said. "We're only twenty-four hours away."

Em said, "I removed the sign-up sheet from the front desk, but with all that is going on at home, I forgot to pull it off online. But I don't say I'm sorry. Take a look." She handed me her phone.

"What? Who?" Margo leaned so close we brushed shoulders, blending our vapors of Poison and Eternity. "Oh . . . my . . . God." She swept the fringe of bangs back from her eyebrows and squinted as if she hadn't read it right the first time. She inhaled theatrically and on the exhale murmured, "Scott Goddard." She turned to me. "Scott—the handsome hero—Goddard. Well, well, well. Now, what do we make of this, Nora?"

My skin, the perpetual traitor, gave away that I made something of it. Redheads wear their emotions on their faces in neon pink.

Margo took in the splash of color and pounced. "For two years no one sees hide nor hair of him and suddenly he pops up without warning. What's that all about? I wonder."

I hadn't told her about the brief encounter at the farmers' market. The last thing I needed was Margo analyzing green beans as if they were tea leaves. She knew, or suspected, too much already.

But it had to be more than a coincidence, I told myself, my running into Scott on Saturday and him enrolling in my ballroom class on Monday.

"Also, notice please," Margo was barreling on, munching pistachios for fuel, "he didn't sign up as the Goddards. Or as Mr. and Mrs. Goddard. Or as Scott and Bunny Goddard. Just him."

I *had* noticed. Immediately.

"We've got a mystery," Margo exulted. "Scott solo. No Bunny."

"No mystery." I tried to put the skids on her. "Bunny hated that class."

I remembered my conversation with Scott at the intake interview. He was there because one of his docs at the VA hospital had recommended ballroom dancing to improve his balance and coordination on his new leg. His wife had agreed to come along, he'd told me, but she wasn't thrilled about it. She might change her mind, I'd responded. It was fun. And from my experience, dancing together was good for a marriage. Leading, following, anticipating moves made you sensitive to your partner's feelings. Scott had shrugged. "I suppose anything's possible."

Margo said now, "Didn't she tell Bobby that dancing with her own husband was bad enough, but the idea of partnering with the other students made her skin crawl?"

"Her exact words." I paused, stopped by the weirdness of what I was about to say. "And she hates music."

"She hates music? Which kind? Opera? The rap?" Emine asked.

"All music."

Em's jaw dropped to the rim of her glass. "What person hates all music?"

"Someone with no soul," Margo said.

I shrugged. "Of course, she also hates me, probably more than music."

"I wonder why." Margo again, using her most slithery tone.

I ignored all her pointed wondering. "She probably said to Scott, 'You want to go to that crap class, you go. But count me out.'" I took a sip of water to calm the pounding of my heart and pronounced with more confidence than I felt, "Mystery solved."

"Maybe it's that simple." Margo raised a skeptical eyebrow. "Maybe not." She grinned devilishly as she added, "I hope not." Then she turned to Em. "As for you, missy, don't let Adnan steamroll you into two months in hell with that bitch. How do you say 'bitch' in Turkish?"

Em choked out, *"Kaltak."*

"With that *kaltak*, then. Don't you dare cave."

A slow smile curled Emine's beautiful lips. "Yes, I think of her that way in my mind. But to say it aloud"—she released a puff of air—"feels good. Thank you, Margo. I will not cave in on this. You give me courage."

"That's what I'm here for," Margo said. "We," she corrected. "That's what *we're* here for. Right, Nora? For each other."

Oh, for heaven's sake. As if I couldn't see the setup. Next she was going to ask me for my take on Pete's behavior at the party yesterday. Had I seen signs of his cheating? No. Not definitive ones, anyway.

"That we are," I said, reaching for something and landing in the pistachios. "For better or for worse. Till death do us part."

Margo shot me a nasty look as she drained her glass. *"Kaltak,"* she said.

chapter eleven

Maybe he'd accidentally left off the *s* in "Goddard" when he registered, I told my reflection in the locker room mirror five minutes before the start of the summer's first Tuesday night class. Should I steel myself for two hours with Bunny, her pink nose twitching distain for me, or with Scott on his own? As I slipped into my Capezio dancer's heels, I couldn't make up my mind which possibility was more nerve-racking.

To the point that I'd worked myself into something akin to stage fright. My palms were sweaty, a condition not recommended for a sport conducted hand in hand. *Deep breath, slow breath,* I instructed myself as I pasted a smile on my face and entered the studio, already milling with a chattering, laughing crowd.

All that agita for nothing, I thought as I made the rounds. Welcoming everyone personally, oohing and aahing over photos of the newest grandchild, or boat, or remodeled deck, I silently ticked off seven of my eight registrants present and accounted for. Scott Goddard was AWOL.

Tom Hepburn had been a helicopter pilot in Vietnam, and as the father of five daughters not much got past him. He must have caught my fascination with the door.

"Nora," he said, as he moved in to clasp my hand. "You get prettier every year. Black becomes you. Sexy but classy."

I always wore a dress to teach ballroom, one with a skirt that swirled, but not too high, on the turns. Observing my positioning from the knee down helped my students mimic my steps. Besides, I had good legs and I liked to show them off.

Yes, I'd made an extra effort to select something special for the first night of class. *Your first impression is the lasting impression,* I'd quoted Sister Loretta to myself as I'd combed through my closet. That was the reason for the pile of rejects on my bed. Not Scott Goddard, the married man. And not searching for sexy, despite Tom Hepburn's cheeky compliment.

Did I hear a snort emanate from the far side of heaven, where the vigilant nun was keeping God's ledger and a wary eye on me?

"Like the new hairstyle, too," Tom said.

I'd drawn it away from my face into a chignon of curls at the back of my neck, but left a few coppery wisps to frame my face.

"With your hair pulled back that way, you look a lot like my second wife, and she was a knockout. Really, she almost knocked me out. Permanently. I had two heart attacks during her reign of terror. But she *was* beautiful."

Single at seventy-five, with a fan following of widows, he liked to practice his flirting on me.

"Tom," I said, "charming as always."

"Okay, we can put the shovels away now," he replied, eyes twinkling.

For a moment, I was distracted by noises coming from the hall. When the footsteps faded, I turned back to Tom, who said, "I wouldn't hold up the proceedings for Colonel Goddard. He phoned me this afternoon to tell me he was running late."

Ah, right. Tom and Scott both hung out at Tuckahoe's VFW hall. There was a three-decade span between their ages, but the country had been entangled in enough wars, military interventions, and skirmishes over the last half century to land the two vets in the same place at the same time. I'd heard they were buddies. I just didn't know how close.

"He asked me to make his apologies, in case he doesn't make it."

"He's okay? I mean the leg is?"

"Leg is fine," Tom said. "There was some kind of adjustment last winter, but that's working out. No, he had some appointment near D.C. today. Drove up this morning with the best intentions of making it back in time. But you can never predict traffic on the Bay Bridge from June on. He wouldn't want you to hold things up for him."

Him, I said to myself, just him. Remembering my manners, I asked, "And Bunny, she's all right?"

"I expect so. You do know her mother passed? In January at the Coastal Hospice."

"I didn't know," I said. "But I am sorry. I heard she was a nice lady."

"Very. The mom." Tom made the distinction clear. We exchanged knowing smiles.

"So, I guess she's still in mourning. That could be why she's not taking the class. Bunny, I mean."

Tom threw me a puzzled look. "Taking the class? Under the circumstances, I'd doubt it, wouldn't you?"

"Right. Dancing was like torture to her." And I was the torturer with the leg irons and the thumbscrews.

"Oh my, you *are* out of the loop," he said. "I thought you would have at least—"

He never got to finish the sentence, because at that moment my assistant Bobby DeCarlo glided up and slid between us tapping his watch. "At ease, Major," he barked at Tom. To me: "It's twenty past, sweetheart. This chatty little crowd will schmooze forever if you let them. Another five minutes, they're going to want coffee and Danish."

"I'm ready."

"Then let's herd the cats." And he was off, clapping for attention.

"Save me a foxtrot, my dear," Tom Hepburn said.

I squeezed his hand. "Consider it saved."

He stared at me, eyes narrowing, mouth a cryptic curl. "Then again, he could show up," he said. "You never know."

I stretched my hands in a wide air embrace of the lineup in front of me. "Hello, brave souls," I said. My glance skipped from face to face, almost all of them familiar.

The Powells, who'd been in my very first class and had re-upped for every session since, were beaming. "Some of you are old hands at this," I said.

"And old feet," Morty Felcher rang out. "Four years and counting for us and we love it more every year. Right, Marsha?" His wife nodded.

"Next year Morty's going to take over teaching the Latin dances," I joked. "And then we'll all join him and Marsha on a cruise to the Bahamas."

A few years back, their turns polished by twice-a-week private lessons, the Felchers had won a rumba trophy on the *Princess of the Seas*. The story of their triumph made the *Coast Post*. It was a big deal for them.

"Glad to have our sophomore back." I bobbed a bow to Edgar Whitman. Painfully shy at first, the pediatric dentist had turned out to be surprisingly nimble once we'd countered his inclination to take baby steps.

"And standing next to him is our only freshman. Freshwoman," I corrected as I pointed out Lynn Brevard, nervously tapping a foot. "Say hello to Lynn, gang." At the chorus of "Hi, Lynns," she fanned a small, tentative wave. Emine, who'd done her intake interview, had reported that Lynn was worried about being the only newbie in a class of repeaters.

I gave a nod to Tom. "And what would class be without Tuckahoe's own Fred Astaire."

"Except Fred's dead and I'm not," Tom quipped. "Yet."

"You all know Larissa from last year." I flourished in the direction of my female assistant. "All you lucky men will get the chance to dance with her. But don't get any ideas. She's taken and her boyfriend is, by the way, a member of the Ukrainian men's wrestling team." True. And Yuri was in Rehoboth making a ton of money waiting tables at Sir Neptune's Grill.

I turned the program over to Bobby.

"Okay, ladies and gents, here's tonight's menu. We'll brush up on the swing, first. *That* should get everybody's circulation going. We've been over the difference between East Coast classic, California, and the Lindy Hop. Handouts are on the side desk with links to YouTube samples of each. Nora and I will demonstrate the steps to refresh your memory. Then we'll practice. Second half will be foxtrot. Find a partner for the first dance. After that, we'll call out, 'Switch,' and you'll need to move on to someone else."

I saw the color drain from Lynn's face.

With a final darting glance at the door—no action there—I placed my hand in Bobby's and we launched into a demo. The group followed as we broke down the moves. With that over, I said, "Larissa, music please. Ladies and gentlemen, choose your partners." Bobby trotted off to claim Lynn for a nerve-calming first dance.

Sinatra crooned and Ella swung and Count Basie played "The Sugar Hill Shuffle." I heard Morty Felcher shout, "Go, Mama!" as his wife flew into a free spin, and I saw Yolanda Powell execute a perfect tuck turn. For the last song, the married couples reconciled, Lynn and Edgar found each other, and Bobby and I were a pair.

As Frankie Lymon sang, "Why do fools fall in love?" Bobby drawled, "Beats me." Then, "You okay, Nora? You look a little ragged round the edges."

"I'm fine. I always get a few butterflies first night."

The Teenagers doo-wopped that love was a losing game, but their rockin' upbeat didn't convince me.

Right foot forward, left cross back.

Frankie was into falsetto with his why-ohs when Bobby spun me out and I saw the door crack open.

On the return, Scott Goddard was walking through it. Alone.

Heads turned and I knew I wasn't the only one ready to interrupt a swing turn with a jump for joy.

He swept a panoramic scan of the room, found me, and mouthed, "Sorry," followed by a sheepish grin.

I gave him a nod that was more an acknowledgment than a welcome. He'd been absent from last year's class, and, dammit, he needed to see the demo to get him up to speed on the steps. He should have allowed for extra drive time to be here when we started. If he thought he could just waltz in here twenty minutes behind schedule and . . . Anger filled the space disappointment had just vacated. A part of me was aware that I was pushing back against the pure pleasure of seeing him. The other part was pissed at the first part.

Swing time over, Bobby and Larissa charted a new step, the outside swivel, in the foxtrot. The crowd moved close to watch. Scott was standing with Tom Hepburn and the Felchers, but his eyes, even during the demo, were trained on me.

"First foxtrot. Everyone take your places," Bobby announced. "Remember, you're moving around the room counterclockwise." He leaned over to me. "Scott without Bunny. I'm good with that. Oh, look. Larissa just tagged Edgar, which leaves Lynn free. I guess I'm up."

Policy called for a teacher to partner with a student at least once for each dance of the evening. It was the only way we could smooth out the rough spots and pick up bad moves that could become bad habits. But before Bobby could reach her, Lynn made a beeline for Scott, handsomely rumpled in a tieless white shirt, its sleeves rolled to the elbow, and what looked like suit trousers. I saw him brighten at the sight of the new girl in the attractive, figure-flattering red dress. Her eyes were sparkling.

"Nora," Morty Felcher bellowed, and for the next four minutes while Scott and Lynn wheeled past us in the promenade, Morty propelled me around the floor as if he were steering a cruise ship.

"Switch," Bobby called out, thank God, and I found myself with George Powell, a burly middle-aged man whose handsome features looked as if they had been carved from ebony. His ancestors had deep roots in the area and he was currently deputy police chief of the city of Tuckahoe. He led me through Ella's version of "The Way You Look Tonight," and as the last bars faded, I swirled to a stop to see Tom Hepburn heading our way, moving very briskly for a senior citizen.

"Nice style, George." Then he fixed me with questioning eyes. "Nora, that foxtrot you promised?"

"I always make good on my promises. In this case, delighted to."

"Oh, listen to that blarney. Irish through and through."

"Actually, half Italian. My mother was a Bellangelo."

"Beautiful angel," he said. "Considering her daughter, I'm not surprised."

We were in position, waiting for the downbeat, as Scott approached. He looked tired, not nearly as juicy as when I'd seen him at the farmers' market Saturday.

Scott tapped Tom on the shoulder. "Excuse me, sir," he said, "but with the lady's permission, I'm cutting in."

Tom turned to growl, but it was good-natured. "The hell you are. What about my permission? And you can't cut in before we start dancing. That's protocol. The rules, Colonel."

"Yes, well, I'm pulling rank, Major."

Tom let out a deflated sigh. Not quite believable. With exaggerated gallantry, he bowed off. "She's all yours. Lucky man."

"Damn right," Scott said.

Was this his version of charming? I was unimpressed.

He placed his hand on my back, I rested my hand on his upper arm, and we were off.

"Amazing," he said as we found our rhythm. "I thought I'd forget everything I learned. It's good to be back, Nora."

I was generating my own weather front. Cool with a chance of thunderstorms. He picked up on it, I decided, because he seemed to want to warm me up.

"Apologies again for not getting here on time," he said. "I had two job interviews and the second took longer than expected, so I got a late start on the return trip. And here I circled the meters for fifteen minutes because there were no spots open in the garage."

Sal Zito had spaces reserved for the gym in the garage attached to the Boardwalk Hilton. I'd seen Scott's Honda parked there, and not in a handicap spot. In one of our infrequent conversations, Bunny had whined that he refused to apply for the tags. He wasn't handicapped, he'd told her, and he wasn't going to pretend he was. Besides, there were other people who needed those spaces more than he did.

"But say I'm wearing heels," she'd said to me. "Really high ones, which I like. And it would be great to park closer. But no, because he's sensitive about his leg. I mean, I understand, but still, that's so inconsiderate."

My Bunny memory detoured me into different territory. She might not have been the brightest rabbit in the hutch, or the fluffiest emotionally, but she'd lost her mother and I remembered too clearly what that was like.

"Well, I'm glad you made it," I said, my attitude softened by the realization that Scott had also lost a loved one, a mother-in-law he'd been close to, cared for, cared about. "The gang was happy to see you." Marsha Felcher had planted a smacking kiss on his forehead. Morty had given him a backslap that would have sent a lesser man flying. The Powells had hugged him.

"Sorry that Bunny"—at the mention of her name, Scott's biceps tensed—"wasn't able to join us," I said, feeling my mouth dry up with the effort of spewing out that huge lie.

I wasn't sorry. Not at all. And to be fair to myself, the lack of regret had less to do with my admiration or whatever for her husband than with the fact that she was an equal-opportunity pain in the ass, nasty to all. Bad for business.

The next sentiment *was* true. "Tom just told me that her mom passed away. Sad news. I know you were fond of your mother-in-law. My condolences."

Professional dancers keep distance between them, which creates a lovely, almost balletic pattern as they move in synch. But at the studio, I taught folks who'd be dancing at weddings and bar mitzvahs and maybe, in the case of Edgar and Lynn, singles get-togethers. My students danced socially, not competitively, which meant I cut them a lot of slack. Couples could get snug if they wanted to, and there was always a buzz of talk to counterpoint the music.

The space between Scott and me was appropriate for teacher and student. Far enough apart so we kept the limits clear. Close enough so I could see the scruff of eight-o'clock shadow on his jaw and catch a whiff of something piney that could have been cologne or car deodorizer, the latter more likely after all those hours on the road. He reared back, though, when I said, "Please give Bunny my sympathies."

He cocked his head, bit his lip, and narrowed his focus, as if he were trying to figure out the origin of the universe. "Yes, of course. Your sympathies. I'll convey them."

It was only after he'd moved back into position that he said, "Tom suggested you and I needed to get current. He's right." Scott inhaled a deep breath. Then: "How about we get a cup of coffee after class?"

I blurted, "Tonight?"

"On second thought, not coffee. The Powells and the Felchers go to the Turquoise Café after class, right? Then how about ice cream to celebrate the first class of summer?" When I hesitated, he added a bonus to tempt me: "Sarge will be with us."

Oddly unsteady on my feet, I managed a nod.

"A friend has been watching him for me all day and I really should pick him up. It's on the way. We could meet at Coneheads."

"Uh, well . . ." That was my brilliant response, but I was trying to calculate the ethics here. Married man. Student. Butter pecan. Canine chaperone. Did that add up to Sister Loretta playing a drumroll as I got shoved into the fiery pits of hell? Nah.

"Sure," I said. *I mean, really, what was the harm?*

chapter twelve

Coneheads, famous for its "out of this world" triple dips and rocket sundaes, started out as "Cohen's Ice Cream—Best on the Beach" in 1957 in a clapboard shack on a two-lane road. When Nathan Cohen, son of the founder, took over in 1978, he renamed it for the *Saturday Night Live* skit. Now flanked by Lighthouse Miniature Golf and a municipal dog park, it occupied a sprawling white brick building, its flat roof topped by a forty-foot waffle cone that was a landmark for miles on the Coastal Highway.

There was inside seating for the faint of heart and sweet of blood, but most customers opted to battle the lines at the six ordering windows and the mosquitoes and humidity at one of twenty tables under the sun or stars. Coneheads had given generations of college students summer employment, and half an hour after class ended, I found myself walking the crushed-shell surround and checking out the staff for signs of Jack. He normally worked weekend shifts, but on nights when one of the counter help or cashiers was out, he had to be available to fill in on short notice. Not tonight, which was a relief, because the idea of juggling two situations in which I didn't know what I was facing held all the appeal of a migraine.

Jack's friend Stewie, back from Purdue, a kid who'd been in and out of my refrigerator for years, spotted me and said, "They're leaving over there," pointing to a table at the far end of the patio under a magnolia tree. "You solo?" he asked. Solos taking up space that could seat four provoked a fusillade of glares.

"Waiting for someone," I said. I checked my watch. "Any minute." Nervous.

It was a little more than that when Scott's maroon Honda crunched up the driveway into the parking lot. By that time, I'd claimed the table, and he made an A-OK finger circle as he walked over, his gait stable on the gravel, then the crushed shells. Trotting beside him, tail wagging, was Sarge.

"Nice," Scott said, as he slid into the seat across from me and tweaked the leash. The dog immediately sat. "Who'd you have to bribe for this table?"

"I have friends in high places," I said, and winked. Winked! When was the last time I'd winked at a man? Probably at Lon over Jack's head when our toddler son did something remarkably adorable. But here, the lowered eyelid and bantering tone could have added up to flirting. Unintended, and I felt my ever-ready redhead's blush bloom. Oh, the hell with it. I wasn't wearing my heart on my sleeve. I wasn't even wearing sleeves. I'd changed in the locker room at Hot Bods into something more appropriate for dripping ice-cream cones and Jimmy Buffett music. Off with the dress designed with enough coverage so I kept my flesh to myself, and on with the lacy top and capri pants hanging in my locker. I'd traded my heels for sandals. Scott, I saw, had also switched to more casual: cargo chinos and golf shirt. Silhouetted against giant pictures of towering, creamy swirls of soft serve and crisp, glistening french fries, he looked like the most delectable item on the menu. A thought I hustled past my dozing censor.

Drawing the dog to him, he bent down to stroke its coat. "And I have friends in low places. This fellow's a beauty, isn't he?"

The animal did have a particular elegance about him. You could tell he wasn't a slobberer, or a suck-up. He followed Scott's moves on alert, but when he settled in, the eyes were calm and wise. "A real champ, aren't you, boy?" Scott smiled at me. "We'd better put some ice cream in front of us or we'll be evicted. Hot fudge sundae for me. With vanilla. I know

I look rocky road, but I'm strictly vanilla. Freezy Paws for Sarge"—whose ears perked at the mention of the treat. "What can I get for you, Nora?"

"Kiddy cone, low-fat."

"You've got to kidding."

I gave him my best wry smile. "Same as your order. But with extra whipped cream."

"Ah, a woman after my own heart."

Oh, come on—it was just a phrase. All it meant was we shared a predilection for vanilla, but it made *my* idiot heart pick up the beat.

Tending to Sarge first, Scott stripped the lid off the cup of Freezy Paws and laid it on the pavement in front of him. With a nod from his master, the dog went at it tongue and snout.

"You like that? Oh yeah," Scott said. Then he straightened up, unfolded a napkin, spread the square at my place, and centered my sundae on it. He positioned a folded napkin to its left and a cup of water to the right of the makeshift place mat, everything arranged with military precision.

He sat and took a long slug from his water cup, all the while keeping a careful eye on me as I scooped a spoonful of ice cream. You would have thought he'd churned it himself from the way he hunched forward, waiting for a critique.

"Oh God, I'd forgotten how good this is. My first Coneheads of the season." I licked my lips and Scott laughed at my pleasure, then dipped a rosette of napkin into his water and leaned over to wipe off my chocolate fudge mustache. Which could have been an intimate gesture or just neighborly. I prodded myself toward the latter.

"Well, timing is everything. Here we are June twenty-first, first day of summer." He cleared his throat. "Lots of firsts." When I let that go by, he jabbed his spoon into his sundae and ate half of it in four bites, emitting a soft, appreciative hum between them.

The sun had gone down while we were having our dance back at the studio, but now a glimmering violet lingered, as if the light couldn't quite let go of the longest day of the year. I'd forgotten it was the summer solstice until he mentioned it.

He leaned down to scratch Sarge's ears. I had the feeling he was trying to figure out how to get started on the catch-up conversation. I gave him a push.

"Is Sarge a new member of the family? I don't remember your mentioning him when you were with us last time."

"Didn't have him then. He was still in Iraq recovering from his own injury. He got hit by gunfire in an insurgent attack, the same one that killed his handler back in Mosul."

"You weren't his handler?"

"No, his handler was a corporal under my command. Wally Gibson. He and Sarge were our elite team. The day they got ambushed, they were out front leading a patrol to clear IEDs. Corporal Gibson got hit in the chest, a fatal wound."

Scott's expression tightened and he stopped for a moment. Ice cream is supposed to melt in your mouth, but a lump of vanilla got stuck in my throat. Scott and I swallowed, hard, simultaneously.

He resumed, "Sarge took a bullet in his flank. It tore through him. The army rated him not fit for combat, so he got retired. With honors. I have no doubt that if he'd been on active duty a couple of months later, he would have sniffed out the bomb that took part of my leg."

I'd reviewed the colonel's medical report during his intake interview for class two years before. His injuries had been described in detail. The circumstances that caused them were only sketched out. A convoy in which he was riding was hit by an IED.

"Corporal Gibson and Sarge were close as brothers. These hero dogs bond with their handlers and I know for certain that if the corporal had made it through there would have been no question about Sarge's future.

But we never leave a buddy behind, and I was his best chance for a good life, so when I got on my feet, I went full throttle into bringing him over here. It took a while but we got him home. That's the way I think of it—home. And now he's living the good life—aren't you, fella?"

I'd have sworn that dog's muzzle stretched into a smile.

A drift of cigarette smoke from the next table reminded me there was someone else who hadn't yet entered the conversation. I imagined Bunny at the edge of it, slouched against the magnolia tree, wearing her ridiculous hooker heels and shooting death rays my way. So far she'd been persona non grata at our little table. Scott hadn't brought up her failure to show for class, a lapse I suddenly felt a compelling need to fill.

"I thought Bunny was allergic to dogs."

At the mention of her name, a muscle in his cheek twitched. "She's allergic to a whole list of things."

A sensitive soul, Bunnicula. Who woulda thunk it? And then the light that was dimming around us began to dawn inside me. My father used to say, mimicking an Irish brogue, "For a smart girl, sometimes you're thick as a plank, Nora." He was right. Sometimes it took fireworks to make me see the sparks.

As in Scott leaning in and for a brief, breathtaking moment laying his hand on mine. "A lot has changed since we've seen each other, Nora." His hand lifted, hovered, and went for his spoon. "It's been a long couple of years. I missed being in class. I really did. The people, the music, the dancing. You all helped me get my head on straight. And my leg, too, of course. Can't forget the leg." He gave a dry laugh. "But life kind of took over and squeezed out most of the best stuff."

Now he was nervously stirring what was left of his ice cream into pale chocolate soup. There was some kid in him. I liked that.

"You know my mother-in-law had cancer and we moved down here full-time to take care of her. I love this place, but not in winter. Then"—he caught his breath—"maybe part of it was the tension in the house, but Mom decided to enter hospice. That opened up a lot of possibilities. And yes, I'll extend your sympathies to Bunny—actually, Belinda is the name she currently goes by—but it will have to be by email." He chugged on, like a train trying to make it through a dark tunnel as quickly as possible. "She lives in Florida now. We're divorced."

For a split second—or maybe it wasn't split because it felt like an eternity—I felt a rush of pure connection to Scott Goddard. Not something censored by my thirteen years in Catholic schools, or adulterated by his situation, his marriage, his wife. To my credit, the worst curse I'd ever wished on Bunny was that she'd break a leg, not two, and a simple fracture, not compound—just enough damage so she'd have to be casted for a while and have the excuse she itched for to skip class. I'd never wished her gone in the long term, not from her marriage, not to Florida.

Scott was rapping his knuckles on the table. The beat was a march. "It will be two years in December." He wiggled his left hand to show me the fourth finger stripped of the thick gold band that had announced to the world: taken. I'd felt that ring, a cold, metallic warning brushing my skin when we'd held hands to foxtrot two years back. "Unattached," he emphasized now, his sharpshooter eyes seeming to measure my reaction.

I didn't know what to say to that. Sorry? Past due? Congratulations? Nothing, is what I chose. Because I didn't know what I *thought* about it. Him. All those fantasies starring the unattainable married man, and now he was free and there was a possibility of something real and . . . I felt a surge of panic. The way I'd felt when Lon and I went camping in Death Valley and I stood shivering and quiet among the salt flats—too much space and no landmarks to mark the way. None for me, at least. Lost without a compass. Sister Loretta had lapsed into a contemplative silence.

Maybe Scott mistook my confusion for pity, because he added, "Hey, it's okay. I'm good with it. It was a long time coming, the breakup. Our problems go way back." He toyed with a straw. "When she was in high school my daughter said it was a bad marriage and asked me why we were holding on.

For me, it was because of her and her brother. Well, they're out of the house now and some new problems surfaced between Belinda and me. The timing was right. We never told my mother-in-law about the divorce. Spared her that. So"—he reached for the cup of water and gulped—"you didn't ask me to revise my intake form when I re-upped for class. Now you can consider it current."

I was as ready as he was to change the subject, and for the next half hour, as the last light faded and we walked Sarge in the lantern-lit dog park, we talked books, new movies, nothing that would accelerate anyone's heartbeat. Scott usually walked briskly, perhaps his message to himself and the world that he could. But I slowed us down, wanting to stay and stretch the moment even as I strained to repress the opposing desire to hurry home so I could pace the balcony outside my bedroom or perch on Mooncussers Rock and wonder why I wasn't breaking out the champagne at the announcement that, ding-dong, the wicked witch had fled.

We spent our final moments leaning side by side against my car, so close that his arm grazed my sleeve.

Then, because I heard him groan as he bent to pick up a trashed beer bottle rolling toward my tire, I murmured, "Long day for you."

"It has been. All that travel. And Sarge here . . ." The dog barked recognition of his name. "I know, buddy. Mrs. Lynch did a good job watching you, but you're ready to go home, aren't you?" Scott said to the sharpening moon, "I don't really want to, though. Dancing and ice cream. A good combination. You know, we could make this a Tuesday night tradition. After class."

An alarm buzzed in my brain and kicked me into my default, which was to deflect. "I don't think the others will go for that. They're regulars at the Turquoise Café. Morty has high cholesterol and Marsha doesn't let him get near ice cream."

Margo would have my head on a platter for that response. I could hear her script. "I mean, really, darling, how could you squander such a fabulous straight line?" But that was Margo. She went for the laugh, the big payoff, and my style was lower key. "Yes, so low that only dogs can hear it," as she would say. "Which is why you haven't gotten laid since that slimy stockbroker nailed you after plying you with drink at your twenty-fifth high school reunion. But this is different, Nora. This is Scott. He's as far from slime as you can get. Pay attention to the man."

Yes, Margo.

He was saying, "I was talking about us, not everyone. Keep it in mind, anyway. And if not ice cream, a glass of wine?"

"Sounds interesting," I said, going for noncommittal until I could ponder the question, and plumb it for every bit of meaning and non-meaning.

I clicked the remote to unlock my car, but he opened the door for me and, before closing it, said offhandedly, "I meant to ask you, all I have for contact data is the Hot Bods phone number and the email listed on the We Got Rhythm website. In case of emergency, if I'm running late like tonight, I'd like to have some better way of reaching you."

So, sitting there behind the wheel, one foot swinging symbolically between the accelerator and the brake, I sent him an email with my cell phone number. Just in case of emergency.

chapter thirteen

Lon and I had wanted a sibling for Jack.

"You don't want Jack to be a lonely only," he'd urged.

Easy for him to say. He had a younger sister living in Bangkok with her diplomat husband and her three overachieving, excruciatingly polite kids. Lon saw Kate only once a year, but they shared memories of a blissful childhood spent camping with their parents in the Sierra Madres and fishing on the San Gabriel River. Even separated by half a world, they stayed in touch, emailing weekly. Kate was a great gal.

On the other hand, my brother, Mick, had been the bogey boy who popped out of closets and snapped rubber bands under my chin. He'd grown into a full-fledged wiseass of whom Lon had said, "Mick knows the name of the unknown soldier."

So I might not have been as enthusiastic about the value of the sibling bond as Lon had been, but I'd loved being pregnant and even more being a mom, and I'd watched *The Waltons* Christmas special enough times to buy into the fantasy. Jack was such a great kid I figured we'd hit the jackpot in the genetic gamble the first time, so why not try to double our luck?

When our son was three, we went back to the Baltimore Fertility Bank to get another shot of #1659. But we were told our DD had done a single run of six months—the minimum—and gone inactive. "Unavailable," was what they told us, and that, "From a legal standpoint, frozen semen remains the property of the donor and its use for insemination can be withdrawn by said donor at any time." The cupboard was empty. And Lon hadn't been keen on pressing our luck with a different donor.

Still hoping Jack might have a half brother or sister somewhere out there, I checked a national donor sibling registry online, punched in the name of the cryobank and #1659, and came up empty. There might have been other kids conceived with DD's donor material, but they weren't signed on. Over the years, I'd checked occasionally, but I never found any sibs.

And then there were two.

It was now officially summer and it felt like the height of it, searingly hot. The thermometer on the widow's walk read ninety-four degrees and the radio threatened record-breaking heat for the day. I wriggled into a year-old bathing suit. It still fit, which brightened my mood. I grabbed a hat, sunscreen, and a beach towel and followed the gulls cawing their siren song. At Mooncussers Rock, I tossed my stuff and ran for the ocean the way a lover runs to a lover, anticipating bliss.

Up to my shoulders in water that looked like velvet but felt like satin—cool and luxurious as it wrapped around me—I glided in. Fully submerged, I felt the shock of its June chill and surfaced to gasp. After a moment, though, my happiness at being where I was, exactly where I wanted to be, warmed me, and I swam easy strokes, feeling half human, half fish, tasting salt, thinking I hadn't had a margarita in almost a year and remembering every other delicious thing I hadn't done for ten months that waited for me on the horizon.

Jack, on his iPhone, caught me smiling as I emerged. He smiled back from his perch on Mooncussers Rock and, as I approached, tossed me a towel.

"Water warm?"

"Let's say refreshing." Goose bumps rising from the breeze against my skin, I toweled off. "What's up?" I asked. From my son's expanding grin, I knew something was.

"More news from Dirk," he said, glancing at the screen. "Well, not really new news. He mentioned it in our call yesterday."

Yesterday? I felt my mood plummet. I'd overheard a conversation between them two days before and caught Jack's easy, intimate tone and intermittent laughter. Were they phoning back and forth every day now in addition to the emails? My stomach clenched, a cramp of fear, a spasm of envy. During the school year, Jack and I connected once a week, and it was almost always a call from me to him. Occasionally, I'd forward a joke or a link to a newspaper article. Once in a blue moon, we'd Skype. He was so busy with classes and lacrosse and Tiffanie, whose name, by the way, hadn't come up much since DD got into the picture. Okay, I'd add that to the Dude's plus column.

"Just FYI, Dirk's pretty careful about feeding me stuff slowly. He told me there's a lot I'll want to know but we'll take it a little bit at a time so I'll have a chance to process it."

Very sensitive, I thought with a twinge. What next? The Dude's criminal record?

Jack handed over the iPhone, displaying a square of color photo. "My half sisters," he murmured, as soft as a prayer, and for a few seconds the screen dissolved to a blur.

Dirk was right. The brain can absorb only so much at a time. "What?" I said stupidly, so that Jack repeated it louder and more distinctly, as if he were talking to someone without hearing, or to a foreigner. I did feel, had felt since Jack first told me he'd started his search, as if I'd wandered into an alien country. Not France, Italy, or Spain, where if you knew one romance language you could get by. More like Hungary or Finland, where everything is unintelligible. In Helsinki, Lon and I had walked backstreets, gripping hands for balance, strangers in a strange land.

"I . . . have . . . two . . . biological half sisters. From Dirk and his ex-wife," my son pronounced.

I bobbed my head to let him know it was filtering through. I held the iPhone up and blinked until the picture cleared.

"I'll send the file on to you so you can open it on your laptop. But wait a sec." He magnified the iPhone image and peered at it over my shoulder.

Two girls were posed with their arms around each other's shoulders. Their smiles were wide and orthodontically perfect. Not a lot of makeup on either, but more on the younger one. Both wore sweaters and jeans. Behind them, flames licked a stone fireplace.

"Sara's fourteen. Jen—Jennifer—is seventeen. Sara's in middle school. A social butterfly, Dirk says. Jen's really smart, like a math whiz." Math was Jack's strong suit. "She jumped a year in high school and she's starting Berkeley in the fall."

He gave me a moment to exhale. "The picture was taken at the Tahoe house. They have a second home on the lake."

Oh God.

"Everyone likes to ski."

Jack's favorite sport. Lon's too, I reminded myself.

"So what do you think?"

Thankfully, I could get away with a shallow response. Deep down, I was churning. We hadn't given our son a sib. But Sixteen, converted to Donor Dad, now Dude, had done that times two.

Jack's brow knitted as he waited for my answer. What did I *think*? I made myself not think. Just stared at the girls' photos and ached, even as I was happy for my son.

Sara was elfin, with close-cropped brown hair, huge dark eyes, and small, sharp features, except for the nose, which she'd grow into. I predicted an exotic beauty in five years.

"She must resemble her mom," I said carefully.

The older girl was California blond, tall, with a springiness about her, an energy that two dimensions could barely contain. Her shoulder-length hair was carelessly streaked with sun and shadow and she carried the golden-eyed gene. I said, "Jennifer looks like her dad, who looks like you, so . . ."

"He was here first, Mom. I look like him."

"Of course. I got it backward."

My son regarded me thoughtfully. "If it weren't for him, I wouldn't be here. Try to remember that, okay?"

"Yes, I'll try to keep that in mind." I tuned my voice to slightly sarcastic. He needed to hear the old me. The one who had spirit, who wasn't going to fold in the face of all these goodies from Dirk DeHaven Donor Dad. The sisters. Lake house. Skiing. Father figure.

Jack picked up the tone and a spiral nautilus shell at his feet. He pitched the shell toward the ocean. It was a hard pitch. When he turned back to me, his eyes had darkened to a tarnished brass. "Mom, listen. I'm getting the feeling you're going off the deep end here. Dirk's made it really clear. He knows he's not my father. And I know it. Maybe he can be a mentor, maybe a friend. But whatever he is, he's in my life to stay."

"Are you so sure, Jack? Because he may not . . ."

"Yeah, I *am* sure. So chill, please, will you? I'm not a kid anymore; I can handle this, however it turns out."

Maybe, I thought, *but I'm not so sure I can.*

My son hadn't put his arm around me since we'd walked back together from the fringe of the ocean after salting it from Lon's cremation urn, but now he gave me a side hug. "Dad would be good with this."

What had Lon said about #1659? "If our child is interested in meeting him, I'll invite the guy over for a beer."

"Really, he would, Mom."

All I could manage was a series of nods, like the birdbrained seagulls strutting the shore.

That night, alone in the house, I entered what Margo had christened "the shrine."

Against the far wall was the sacred desk, Great-grandfather Farrell's, which we'd inherited. Legend had it, and Lon had absolutely believed, that Jack London had written "The Law of Life" at that desk. A guest of the Farrells, he'd drunk too much at dinner and Dr. Farrell had insisted he stay overnight. The next morning, struggling through a hangover and smoking through a pack of Lucky Strikes, London had knocked out the short story in four hours.

My husband had written his first and second books at that desk. The third, *Wild Mountain*, had been written in the Baltimore house on an IKEA table, a lapse that accounted for its failure, he'd been sure.

On the left, in front of the built-in bookshelves, stood two ancient wooden file cabinets I'd first seen in his New York apartment. There was also a round glass-topped table on which he'd arranged framed photographs of his departed family and friends. The Circle of Death, he'd called it. The only picture that breached the Circle of Death had been the one that showed him at eight, along with his father and grandfather, all three lined up on horseback at the Glen Ellen ranch. Remarkably straight backed, standing next to the boy's horse and holding its reins, was the iconic ninety-year-old great-grandfather, the doctor who'd treated and befriended Jack London.

Lon, you're one of them, a link in the circle. For the first time in eight years, I slipped into the chair behind the desk. When I'd been there last, a week after the memorial service, it was to search for the file folder in which my husband had kept records of household bills paid. I found it and never opened a drawer again.

Now I did.

Lon had never allowed anyone—not his agent, not his editor, not me—to read one of his books in progress. And I'd never been tempted. Not even when, after Lon's death, his agent suggested I send him the unfinished manuscript. Nate Greenberg and Lon had worked together for years. He wasn't Lon's agent when the blazing comet of *Canyon of Time* burst upon the scene, but he was already something of a phenomenon himself when he took on *Banshee River*. A combination adviser, negotiator, therapist, and cheerleader, he never lost faith, not in Lon's talent or his prospects for a triumphant comeback. He was overjoyed that Lon was writing again after a long dry spell.

At the memorial service he told me, "At first, he'd been excited about how the writing was going. But half or maybe three-quarters in, he hit a wall. Until then, he said it was the best he'd written. My feeling is he'd have jumped that wall eventually. So sad."

Nate, who had the chops to drive a hard bargain, had always been sweet with me. He'd waited a seemly time before asking to see the manuscript.

"If it's as good as he thought it was, it deserves to see the light of day."

"You mean it should be published?" I'd asked.

"Possibly."

"It's not finished, Nate. And he was struggling terribly with it."

"Lon always outlined in detail. I'm sure there were notes. Get a fresh pair of eyes to review them, someone objective and talented, and I'll bet we could work it through. Finish a book Lon would be proud of."

"So you're saying that someone else, like a ghostwriter, would take over?"

"I'm not saying, Nora; I'm asking, and all I'm asking"—his voice was actually on the edge of begging—"is for you to let me take a look at it. Let's start there and see where we go."

No way. There was no way I was going to send the manuscript on to

Nate without reading it first myself. Lon had been confident enough in his third book to let it be published. He'd been too close to see the flaws. It was my responsibility as his widow to protect him and his reputation, and that meant reading it, and I couldn't.

Just looking at his final photograph—the one sent to me by the conference organizer, taken as Lon stood at the podium speaking about savagery in *White Fang*—was almost too much to bear.

Now I reached into the desk's bottom drawer for the strongbox he never bothered to lock, slid my hand under its only tenant, a rubber-banded stack of paper, and shifted it to my lap. Was it a betrayal to read it? I wondered as I scanned the cover page. And the book itself, was it his last gasp? Or a stroke of genius?

What I was hoping was that Lon would come back to me through the words and after that maybe I'd be able to keep him close and at the same time set him free.

The working title, *Thunder Hill Road*, was underlined and centered on the cover. I read the first sentence: "At the end of the path that led down to the beach, the boy found a veined boulder, polished by wind and carved by tidal water into a chair of stone, perfect for a seven-year-old who perched on it as if he were captaining a pirate ship."

Beach, not mountain. Here, not there. Oh, Mother of God, could I get through it? And was it good enough for what I knew at that moment I wanted to do? *Needed* to do.

I took it up to the bedroom, slipped it under the quilt when I heard Jack's tread on the stairs; then, after he said good night, I began to read.

chapter fourteen

"The younger one—what's her name, Sara—is a tad Hobbity, but give her a few more years and three inches in height and I see Audrey Hepburn in *Sabrina*," Margo said.

We were at the Driftwood Playhouse, dead center in the last row of orchestra seats, and she was peering at my iPhone photo of Jack's half sisters. Onstage, the set blazed with the colors of Siam—scarlet, cobalt, and gold. The actress playing the "I" in *The King and I*—the role of tutor to the children of the ruler of Siam—was running through "Getting to Know You" with piano accompaniment for the fourth time. Margo had zoomed the photo and now she edged her reading glasses higher on her nose. "The older one, Jessica?"

"Jennifer. Jen," I corrected.

"Jen looks like Jack in drag." When I sniffed, she said, "Oh, don't get your knickers in a twist. Jack's good-looking. I meant it as a compliment. I assume the boy is thrilled, and you are . . . ?" She flashed me an appraising look. "You don't know yet. Right. Too early. You'll figure it out in a few years."

She handed me back my iPhone and called out in her director's voice, "Lydia, a touch more sweetness in the voice when you squat down for the eye-to-eye with the kids." She scribbled some words on her clipboard and turned back to me. "You haven't told me how the Scott situation panned out Tuesday night."

I'd avoided phoning Margo over the last two days, deciding I'd deal with the subject of Scott in person after Friday morning Zumba, when she'd be too wrung out to be on top of her gossip game. But she hadn't shown up that morning, and when I checked I'd discovered Margo had dropped the summer class. She'd told Em that with so much going on at the theater and some personal issues to deal with, she didn't have the time or, frankly, the inclination to dance. But for a woman who thought "private" started with "pry" for a reason, there was always time for inappropriate questions.

"The handsome colonel still make your heart go pitty-pat?" she asked now. When I gave her nothing with a warning glance, she switched gears. "And Bunny? Cackle, cackle. Did she fly over for the occasion or did she leave her broom at home?"

So I spilled the divorce story, a highly condensed version, filling in the source but leaving out the location where I heard it, skipping the entire "Scott and Nora at Coneheads" episode. Why give her more ways to torture me? In fact, at the mention of the Goddards' split, her pupils dilated to black caviar beads. "Well, well, he broke the spell," she chanted. "Finally. And now the door is open for the beautiful princess to sweep through, dance off with the handsome prince, and live happily ever after. Mazel tov!"

My face must have registered skepticism, because she added, "Oh, I get it. Now that the moral coast is clear, and the bitchy ship has sailed, you're what . . . scared your daydreams, wet dreams, or whatever will come true?" Her tone flipped to soothing. "Ah, this is about Lon, of course. The blithe spirit."

That was close enough to the truth to make me shiver. The ghost in the wings.

"Lon's gone, Norrie. And that's a damn shame. But you're here. You've been through the seven or twenty-seven phases of grief, and I know I'm not supposed to tell you"—as if she hadn't a hundred times over—"but you're past due to let it go. Let the poor man's spirit rest in peace and get on with your life. Please. Do that."

An arpeggio resounded through the hall. There was a flurry up front and Margo let me go to announce, "Okay. Owen, Lydia, we're going to run through the 'Shall We Dance?' number. Let's try"—she cast a meaningful glance at me—"not to trip ourselves up this time."

Emine Haydar slipped into the seat next to me as Anna and the King of Siam swung into their waltz. Once a week, Margo's largesse extended to providing a catered midday meal for the cast and crew, and Em had just laid out lunch. The café was less than a five-minute drive from the playhouse so the gyro sandwiches—filled with heavenly spiced meatballs called *kofte*, succulent lamb, and chicken—were still warm and their fragrance drifted into the theater from the greenroom.

Em had been around for two previous rehearsals, but this was the first time she'd seen the players in costume.

"I was twelve when I saw the film in Turkey," she whispered, watching the dancers take their positions. "We got the American movies late, sometimes decades later. *The King and I* was my favorite. I had a mad crush on Yul Brynner and clipped photos of him from the fan magazines." I could feel her glowing in the semidarkness. "Oh, look at her hoop skirt when she turns. Beautiful." Em's applause after they twirled to a perfect finish echoed through the nearly empty theater. She stopped clapping when a call vibrated on her cell phone.

It was from Adnan, and it wasn't good news.

Merry had been fired from her job at Clean on Board. What had begun as an argument between her and a coworker, angry words flung across the bed they were making, had turned into a shoving match. According to the only eyewitness, Merry shoved first and the other girl pushed back. By the time a supervisor intervened, he was dealing with a slap fight. After he separated the two, Merry took off. Grabbed her backpack and dashed out the door of the house in the Surfside Villas development west of town. "They have no idea where she went," Emine said. "But she was wild when she ran away. They used that word, Adnan said. Wild."

I didn't have to close my eyes to imagine. I'd witnessed a few of her tantrums.

"She didn't answer when they called to tell her they would mail her the last check for working, so they called the café. Two hours ago this happened, and they only contact the parents now. Adnan is out in the streets looking for her."

"Of course he tried her cell."

"No answer." Em punched in the speed dial, then speakerphone.

I heard, "Yo, it's Merry. Say what you have to say and if it's interesting I'll get back to you. Maybe." A giggle at the end.

Em shook her head in frustration. Then she said, "Meryem, I just heard from the cleaning people about the trouble and I am worried where you are. Please call me as soon as possible."

She mumbled to me, "Most of the times she doesn't. I'm not interesting enough."

"Maybe *I* am."

I held out my hand for the phone. I wanted to shake the girl, but I muted my voice to a purr. "Merry, it's Aunt Norrie. Sweetheart, we need to know you're safe. That you weren't injured. We want you to tell us what happened. Your side of the story. I'm with your mom at the Driftwood, Aunt Margo's theater. If you'd rather talk to me, you have my number. Get back to one of us. Soon, Merry. Please.

"Does she have a special place to go when she wants to calm herself?" I asked Em, thinking about Jack and Mooncussers Rock.

Emine frowned. "She used to visit the crazy cat lady."

Merry was obsessed with cats—Adnan wouldn't allow her to keep one so close to where food was prepared—and she'd liked to visit the informal refuge for strays Miss Hazel Henlopen had maintained in her large, dilapidated house surrounded by woods. After Miss Hazel died in April, apparently while trying to heft a fifty-pound bag of kitty litter, the place had been locked up, scheduled for demolition in the fall.

"Some of the cats ran off. Some were taken away. Without the cats, there is no reason for Merry to go there anymore," Em said.

"Can you think of other places she'd hang out?"

"Where she goes these days, she doesn't tell me. She could be hitch-hiking home." Em's voice rose perilously. "Or walking on the side of the road, and if the cars swerve . . ."

I squeezed her hand and ground out a smile. "I'll bet right now she's drinking a milkshake in McDonald's and bragging to her friends about how she decked some girl who dissed her. Maybe if you checked around with some of them . . ."

Em stared at me as if I'd just discovered a new planet. "So smart, Nora. Her friends. Yes, I'll call the ones I have numbers for."

None of them had seen or heard from Merry, knew anything, had any idea about where she might be, and, yeah, sure they'd get back in touch if . . .

"They keep their chums' secrets, teenagers," Em said after she'd exhausted her address book and we were in the lobby heading toward the greenroom and life-giving caffeine. "You know she makes me a dragon in their eyes. So they will think it is snitching. Is nothing worse than a snitch, Meryem tells me. When she finds out I spoke to her friends, she will be furious."

"She has no right to be anything but sorry," I griped.

A boom of thunder rolled through the building, followed by a flash of lightning that lit the sky beyond the lobby's glass doors, which were etched with a stylized depiction of driftwood. Within seconds, the rain swelled from a shower to a battering deluge.

"She'll be caught in this." Em was rocking back and forth, worry propelling her.

"Merry's in McDonald's or Starbucks or she'll duck into one. Damn! My car windows are down." I grabbed an umbrella from a stand near the box office and called behind me to Em as I dashed out, "Margo keeps brandy in the greenroom. Pour yourself a shot. I'll be back in a sec."

The umbrella was wind whipped to uselessness, so I was soaked when five minutes later I pushed open the lobby door and came face-to-face with Meryem Haydar. Her hair was drenched and flattened and her mascara streaked dark blue rivulets down her cheeks.

"Aunt Norrie," she said, "oh my God." She made for my arms, then backed off. "Sorry. I'm a mess. I don't want to get you wet . . ." We stared at each other, dripping, grotesque, then both started laughing. *Inappropriate,* I thought. *I should be livid.* What she had put her mother through! But the relief at seeing her safe flooded out my anger for the moment. I couldn't tell if she was wiping rain or tears from her eyes before I moved to enfold her. Against my neck, she whimpered, "I am so in trouble, right?"

"Yup," I answered. "*So* in trouble."

"She called me a dirty Arab. She said all Muslims should be put in jail. I said (a) I wasn't an Arab. I was American, and my parents are Turkish, which is different. And (b) that she was a racist and an idiot. She said I would burn in hell and that I stunk because Turkish people ate so much garlic and never showered. I said she was a bitch, and that's when she tugged the sheet so hard it snapped and ripped off my acrylic." She held up a raggedy fingernail. "So much for Clean on Board's policy of zero tolerance for physical violence." She singsonged the line. "Then she came around the bed and got really into my face, so I pushed her away. I was just protecting myself. The kid Jason who said I started it? He's her boyfriend, so of course he'd back her up."

Merry shivered in the sweater and jeans I'd swiped from the Driftwood's costume rack to replace her wet clothes. She took a sip of the hot cocoa Em had made for her.

"I mean, it's not fair. Like I was supposed to just stand there and take it?" She blew a frustrated breath through lips stained plum by recently applied lipstick. "So now *I'm* the bad guy." She swiveled to face her mother. "And Dad's what? Off the wall about this?" She pinched an Oreo off the paper plate, slid the chocolate cookies apart, and licked the cream filling off one side, then the other. Still a child. "Consequences. Dr. Shrink or whatever his stupid name was loved that word. Con-se-quences." Dr. Barton had been my recommendation, a friend of Josh's who specialized in adolescent issues. He was the latest of three therapists who had attempted to escort Merry through her rebellion. "And please don't tell me that cutting me off from Facebook for a century means Dad loves me, because that's just bullshit."

Her mother's sigh was loud enough to drown out the music filtering in from the stage, "I Whistle a Happy Tune."

We were sitting around the table in the greenroom. Merry had used the hair dryer and reapplied too much makeup from a basket of liners, shadows, lipsticks, and blushes while her mother made the call to Adnan to inform him that his wayward daughter had turned up. He'd been strangely silent on the phone, she'd reported, saying only, "Bring her home."

"Soon," she'd replied. Then to me, after clicking off, "I want to give him time to calm down."

"Well, he'd better not threaten to send me to Turkey." The girl wiped cookie crumbs from her mouth. "I won't go. I swear to God I'll run away. For good this time. Turkey, ugh. Like I even remember it. I was only, like, a baby, the last time we were there. And let's be honest here. You know, Mom"—ah, Em was back to being Mom—"Nene Selda is a crazy-assed b—"

"Meryem!" As much as she shared her child's opinion of Adnan's mother, Emine couldn't let that pass without comment. "Your grandmother is your grandmother. Whatever you think of her, you show respect."

Merry rolled her eyes.

"Come," Em said to her daughter. "Before your father wonders if we've both run away, we're going home."

"Great." Merry dragged herself from the chair. "I am so looking forward to that."

"I was wondering if you'd left without saying good-bye, which would have been incredibly rude," Margo said, giving me the googly eye when I ran into her on the way out. "Where have you been hiding ou—" She never got to finish the question, because Emine with Merry in tow was ten steps behind me and the sight of them stopped her short. She hadn't seen Merry since the summer before, and what she had under her microscopic vision now was an entirely different specimen. The long ponytail and the pink lip gloss had been replaced with spiked hair and over-the-top makeup.

Margo put on her best blank, nonjudgmental face as she gave us the thrice-over. The woman did have very sensitive antennae, especially for things amiss, which was why I didn't altogether discount her suspicions about Pete wandering off the straight and narrow. She must have picked up from Em's stark white face, Merry's sullen slump, and my subtle head-shake the cue for her next line.

"Merry, darling." She moved on her like a tank in heels. "Look at you. So grown-up. I haven't seen you in ages. Oh"—she reached out and ran a hand over Merry's hair, gelled as stiff as porcupine needles—"I love the brush cut. So avant-garde. Now, that shows real courage and a sense of style. But the eye shadow has to go. Too much and too blue. Only old ladies wear blue eye shadow. Blue rinses on their hair and blue on their eyelids. With your coloring, I'd say a smoky, subtle eye. I'll show you how to do it."

Merry seemed transfixed.

"We'll make a date if it's okay with your mom. Lunch at the Breakers." The most expensive restaurant in Tuckahoe. "And we'll play with makeup after that. I've got all kinds of stuff here to experiment with. How does that sound?"

"Cool," Merry said. She skipped a bewildered glance from Margo to her mother to me, then said, "My dad's waiting."

"Call me. Your mom has my number. Or better yet, drop by here and we'll set something up."

Margo waited until the door closed behind them before saying, "What the hell happened to that darling child?"

chapter fifteen

I decided Margo was right about getting on with my life.

When I finally told her about my semi-date with Scott at Coneheads and my waffling on a future one, she'd lashed out. "Oh, for chrissake, Nora—and forgive the blasphemy if you've decided to return to the Mother Church, which is the only possible explanation for your self-imposed chastity—what next? Entering the convent? The Sisters of Insanity? Really, what are you waiting for? Are you expecting Lon to float through the window and give you permission to live your life? To quote some rabbi, if not now, when? If not you, who?"

Margo and her Jewish wise guy swung my vote. When Scott and I were next in each other's arms on Tuesday—swaying to some romantic slow dance—I'd say, "Your suggestion that we have a glass of wine after class tonight? I'd like that." There. I had a plan. But first there was Lon's legacy and that particular sputtering flame I did need to tend.

For eight years, I'd been wary of approaching his fourth book, but *Thunder Hill Road* was brilliant. I fell in love with the characters, which included two strong and vulnerable women, one of them a redhead, and was totally caught up in the story line when it ended abruptly, cut off by writer's block and then the tragedy in San Francisco.

Jack spotted me reading the manuscript and lifted a page from the pile on the table next to me. He screwed up his forehead. "This some of Dad's stuff?"

"Yup. The book he was working on when he died. He never got to finish it."

"Damn shame. Maybe I'll read it someday."

Which could have led to an interesting conversation, but we got interrupted by my son's phone beeping. Cellular ringing and singing surrounded him almost constantly these days. Dirk, I figured. Maybe Tiffanie, though he hadn't mentioned her lately and in the past he'd peppered his conversation with quotes from her as if she were the Dalai Lama or Ellen DeGeneres. I hoped some of the calls were from the female coworker at Coneheads whose gift of home-baked chocolate chip cookies sat on our kitchen counter along with its note, "Enjoy!," a tiny heart subbing for the dot above the *i* in "Claire." God bless whoever was making him happy, even Tiffanie if she was the cause. And I was counting down until Tuesday, when I'd see Scott again. That was my current flirtation with happiness.

On Monday morning, I called Nate Greenberg, Lon's agent, and asked, "How do we find the right person to finish *Thunder Hill Road*?"

"My God, you finally read it! And it's *that* good?" He laughed boisterously and didn't wait for an answer. "Email it as an attachment. Flag it for my eyes only. And then leave it to me. I know two writers I'd trust to bring this off. Let me approach them confidentially."

"I want a say in the final choice."

"Of course. You'll have approval of everything. Writer, material, publisher because I'm not sure we want to go with the previous one after the last experience. If you send me the manuscript ASAP, I'll get back to you quickly. Not too quickly, though. I want to make sure we do this right." A long pause; then, after he cleared his throat: "This isn't all business for me. You know that, right, Nora? I loved the man. He was a mensch—a man of honor. And as close to genius as anyone I'm ever going to represent. Frankly, his last novel wasn't my favorite. But this gives us a chance to redeem his legacy."

His legacy. Ah, yes. I felt the flood of relief. Nate and I were on the same page.

That afternoon, I received my own interesting email. Return address: dmdh@gilbrethmed.com. That's what my eye took in first. Then the header: From Dirk DeHaven, MD. So there was no possibility of mistaken identity and exile to my spam file.

My first reaction was a jumble of emotions. Could be he'd had second thoughts about shaking up the status quo and was enlisting me to prepare Jack for the bad news. For me, the doc's change of heart might be a relief. But my son would be devastated. I opened the note, aware that my head had begun to ache—collateral damage, I supposed, from the war of feelings being waged inside.

Dear Mrs. Farrell,

Perhaps in the not too distant future I'll have your permission to address you as Nora. I hope so, but that will be your determination, as will be the subject of this email. I'll be attending a conference in Baltimore at Johns Hopkins Hospital, which would place me within a few hours' driving distance of Tuckahoe Beach. I could easily extend my Maryland visit to Saturday the ninth, which would allow me to meet and spend some time with Jack. I haven't mentioned the possibility to him yet, thinking it best to clear it with you.

I look forward to hearing from you and, if and when you're willing, to meeting you.

My best wishes,
Dirk

I read it three times before I walked off the deck and into a very dry martini. Okay, I thought, as the vodka worked its numbing magic, it looked as if I'd been too hard on the dude. The truth was he and Jack didn't need my consent for any of this. Dirk's request was a courtesy, though if I was cynical, possibly a clever man's way of ingratiating himself with the mom, sending the coded message, "You're still in charge, Mrs. Farrell. Nothing to fear from me."

Play nice, Nora, I told myself. I waited until the martini buzz ebbed and sent a response thanking him for soliciting my input and said that, of course, the final decision was up to Jack. The tone of my answer was slightly warmer than a lawyer's letter and included no response to his suggestion that he and I might, at some time in the future, have contact.

I signed it, "Best, Nora." Which settled the name issue, at least.

I was stretched out on the living room sofa, watching the eleven o'clock news, when Jack just about bounced in from the kitchen, two of Claire-with-a-heart's cookies in hand. His smile was high wattage. He bent nearly in half to kiss the top of my head, straightened, took a giant bite of a cookie, and handed me the other one.

Mouth crammed, amber eyes sparkling, he looked like himself as a kid on Christmas morning. The big gift—the scooter, the bike, the set of beginner skis—covered by the biggest green plastic trash bag Home Depot carried, or sometimes two sacks Lon had taped together, the awkward package topped with a gigantic red ribbon, was always opened last. The dream-come-true present. How long had Jack been dreaming about this one? Since Lon broke the news about his beginnings on the Lake Tahoe camping trip? Or since my boy's father came home to Tuckahoe as ashes in an urn? Or did it start on the night Tiffanie ragged my handsome, tentative son about not knowing who he was?

"Dirk just emailed me about his visit." Jack's baritone reminded me how far he was from a kid. "He said you were okay with it. So, thanks, Mom."

"No problem."

"He said you sound like a great mother." I gave my son an eye roll. "Hey, you *are.* Anyway, he's driving in on the eighth after a dinner meeting at Hopkins, so he'll get in late. He's staying at the Boardwalk Hilton." The hotel that abutted We Got Rhythm.

"That hotel was your idea?"

"I figured he'd like it. It has a gym—he works out—and the best rooms have the ocean view. And he has Hilton points. We're meeting Saturday morning and then we'll have lunch. If you want to join us . . ."

"I think it should be just the two of you this time, Jack."

"I guess." But he looked relieved. "So, we'll hang out on Saturday, then dinner I don't know where yet. And he needs to leave early Sunday to make his noon flight back to Frisco."

"I don't think people from San Francisco like it to be called Frisco."

"Didn't know that. Glad you told me." Jack bit his lip. "Maybe you ought to be there so I won't screw this up."

"Hey, he's the one who has to watch screwing up. You'll be fine. Just be yourself."

Which was enough, I thought. More than.

chapter sixteen

Scott Goddard played it cool as we gathered for the Tuesday night ball-room class. He positioned himself at the end of the line next to Lynn Bre-vard and partnered with her for two of the six practice dances. I'd gotten a wave from across the room when he entered and not much more. I finally landed him for the last foxtrot to what I thought was going to be "Cheek to Cheek," the Sinatra version. Brave or foolhardy, I'd chosen that as back-ground music for the first step in getting on with my life—my, as Margo had reminded me that morning, "emotionally stunted and stalled-out life."

"Some tips for the new and improved you," she'd said. "Be open, warm, toss your damn Giorgio perfume, which is *très* cliché and *très* passé. I recommend Prada's scent called Candy, which makes you, well, edible. Wear those shoes I forced you to buy at the Coach outlet. They make your legs look fabulous. And, for God's sake, show the man a little cleavage. He's a war hero; he's earned it."

I followed three of her four suggestions, though Candy, the quickly purchased Prada perfume, smelled fattening to me. But no cleavage. Not with Tom Hepburn, his cataracts recently removed, on the prowl.

When I finally landed Scott—outmaneuvering Mrs. Powell, who was also headed his way—he seemed unimpressed with my efforts. His leg had been working fine with Lynn during the tango. She'd only just learned the basics, but Scott had mastered some pretty fancy steps two years back and led her with confidence. Positioned properly, upper body against upper body, he spiraled her flawlessly on the turn. As I watched both of them laugh at the smooth perfection of the move, I felt a sting of jealousy. An exotic feeling for me, jealousy.

Lynn had gotten the relaxed version of Scott. As he and I began to dance, I got what he'd once called "post posture," ramrod-straight spine and stiff arms, which I didn't correct because I concluded—pulse picking up—that he knew better and was sending me a message. Maybe that his invitation for an after-class drink had expired due to my silence, my cowardice. In spite of which, and in spite of Bobby's unannounced switching from "Cheek to Cheek" to "Strangers in the Night," which I should have taken for a stop sign, I plunged ahead, wanting to get it over with, not wanting to answer to Margo.

So I blurted into what was essentially empty space, "That glass of wine after class? I'd like to take you up on it. How about tonight?" There. Done. Margo would be proud.

Or not. Because as I finished my blurt with a hard swallow, Scott missed a step, and although I gripped his hand and shifted my weight to help him balance, he floundered before he was able to right himself. He muttered, "Sorry, Nora. Don't know what happened there. I'm a little unsteady."

Me too, I thought.

"I swear I haven't been drinking." Then he smiled. The smile expanded to a grin. "Absolutely yes to the wine. I missed dinner too. But let's see if we can remedy that on both counts. Have you been to the Flying Jib yet? It's only been open a month."

Okay, here we go. It should have been an easy response. A sprightly, "No, but friends of mine have"—Margo and Pete, who never missed the newest, trendiest restaurants—"and they liked it a lot." Simple. Instead, his question translated for me as "On your mark, get set . . . !" and I choked at the starting line. *Come on, Nora!* I coached myself into a negative shake of the head.

"No? Me either. But it's got a great view of Teal Duck Creek, I hear the calamari is fantastic, and one of my VFW buddies is the manager. Sound good to you?"

My head bob elicited a hand squeeze from Scott.

Margo might have been right. Saying yes to him was like hitting the ocean in June when the water was still cold. The icy first wave paralyzed you. But if you dipped deeper and stayed in longer, you got used to the temperature and soon you were bathed in something warm and wonderful. I'd already lost my shivers. The apprehensive ones, anyway.

"Did you drive into town?' he asked.

I'd walked, to discharge some nervous energy, to see how the hibiscus and the magnolia trees were blooming in the yards along the residential stretch and the geraniums were flourishing in the window boxes of the shops on Clement Street, but mostly wanting to have the right answer if Scott asked that question.

His eyes brightened at my response and he said, "If you wait at the back door after class, I'll get the car and pick you up."

As Sinatra sang, "Dooby-dooby-doo," and Scott swung me into the final turn, I noticed some looks had settled on us. Usually any chatter between my partner and me was focused on brief instructions or corrections: lean into the step; pivot on your heel for that turn. But Scott and I, even with Bobby's musical substitution, were less strangers in the night and more cheek to cheek. Also whispering nonstop. That drew occasional, and I thought approving, glances from Tom Hepburn, and a lingering inquisitive stare from the Felchers. The last thing I needed was teacher's pet gossip circulating in this group.

"How about you leave first," I said, hitching my neck toward the others, who always exited, not out the main door to the boardwalk, but through the back door to the street. "I'll follow in a few minutes and, if you don't mind, stop for me in front of Ledo's Pizza." The opposite direction from the Turquoise Café, where this gang went for coffee after class.

He got it. "Copy that." Then, after a pause: "I've got to tell you, Nora, I didn't think you remembered our last conversation. The end of it anyway, when I asked you for a . . . well, I guess you could call this a date, right?"

Margo's invisible hand smacked my head into a nod.

"And if you did remember, I bet on no for an answer."

"Stay away from Atlantic City," I said. "You'd lose your shirt."

He reared back, off the beat, and gave out a hearty laugh. My cheekiness had caught him by surprise. Me too. Or maybe it was my dimple that emerged only with my widest smile. This was a Nora he hadn't seen before. I think he liked her.

At the Flying Jib, we were greeted by Scott's buddy with a half bow for me and a cuff on the shoulder for Scott, who'd phoned from the car to reserve a table. I got the once-over, twice. Scott got a discreet bob of the head. Affirmative, I guessed.

"I put you right on the water," the manager said, as he personally escorted us to the table set next to a panoramic sweep of window.

"May I present Teal Duck Creek, complete with a raft of green-winged teal and mallards, plus a few cranky geese and a couple of imported swans. It's beautiful in this twilight, isn't it?"

A flock of ducks, their tails shimmering iridescent, took off into a cloudless pewter sky. "Very," I said.

We peeled our gazes from the creek and took in the room, which was spacious and dressed in brass and mahogany with nautical touches. This late, it was only a quarter filled, with subdued chatter from other tables. He handed us the drinks menu. "Happy hour is over, but for you, mate, and the lady, of course, we'll make an exception. Our fried green tomatoes are the best on the shore."

After consulting with me, Scott ordered the mini crab cakes, calamari, and the tomatoes to share and a vodka martini with three olives for himself. I ordered something called a Mango-Peach Fizz, which sounded frilly even to me. When I told the server to go easy on the peach schnapps and asked to substitute seltzer water for the champagne, Scott raised an amused eyebrow. And when the server placed the drink in front of me, he commented, "It matches your dress."

It did. The dress was made of a silky fabric that defined my shape but didn't cling, and its creamy coral color was a flattering choice for a redhead. I'd added a gold chain and gold-and-coral earrings. "I guess I'm coordinated," I said.

"You won't get an argument from me on that. In my case, even when I had both my own feet, they were two left ones."

I laughed. "You've come a long way, Scott. I can say from recent personal experience, your lead is strong and confident."

"Well, that depends on who I'm leading." He turned away to gaze out the window, where a parade of geese waddled down the lantern-lit pier. I heard him inhale a deep breath before turning back to say, "I'm glad we—well, especially you—decided to do this, Nora. Lesson here. You never know what life has in store." He lifted his glass. "To . . ." He stalled out for a few seconds. "To surprises."

I lifted mine to the sentiment, though my record with surprises wasn't particularly reassuring.

We took our first sips.

"Ahhh. Fine martini. Dry as Blackbeard's bones. How's yours?"

"Nice, fruity. Blackbeard would have pitched it overboard. It's what my mother would have called a ladies' cocktail."

"Your mother." He leaned toward the just-arrived food, which was a small-plate feast, speared a ring of calamari, and handed me his fork.

The bite of squid was crisp outside, tender within. "You mentioned her in class a few times. She was some kind of professional dancer. Onstage, right? Broadway?"

"*The Fifties Follies* was her only show, and it closed after a week. But for ten years, she danced as a Rockette at Radio City Music Hall. That's where my dad met her. He was what they used to call a stage-door Johnny. Love at first sight."

"I hear that can happen," Scott remarked, stabbing a crab cake. "Sometimes it works out. Sometimes not." Ah, were we in the Bunny hutch here?

"It worked for my folks," I said. "They had the proverbial marriage made in heaven."

"Had? They're gone, your parents?"

"Dad passed away a few years ago. My mother died when I was seventeen. Lung cancer." I slugged my fizzy drink, hoping it would blur unwanted images of Mamma-mia's last days. Especially the one of me feeling so helpless, sitting at the edge of her bed, spoon-feeding her the only thing she wanted and was able to get down. Coffee ice cream. Since then, the thought of it turned my stomach.

"Seventeen is a lousy age to lose a parent," Scott murmured, and with that—no warning—my eyes filled. Which was ridiculous. My mother had been gone for thirty years. I was on a date with someone I liked. More than liked. Was incredibly attracted to. Had, in fact, made the subject of some very erotic, forbidden fantasies. And now the man of my dreams was a reality, sitting across from me while the table's candle shed pearly light on his strongly angled face, his sympathetic half smile, and I was digging up ancient memories?

We should have been joking, flirting. Or at least trading some edited personal history over the calamari before we moved into personal geography. But no, I'd detoured us to the Garden of Eternal Rest in Flatbush. What had I been thinking? Or had the bartender messed up the order

and flooded my drink with champagne, notorious loosener of tongue and
other body parts, the same de-inhibitor that got me in trouble with the
not-so-cutest boy at my twenty-fifth high school reunion? Was it the alcohol talking?

If it was, Margo's disembodied voice drowned it out: "Stop with the
'one foot in the grave' conversation. For heaven's sake, Nora, give the poor
grim reaper a break. Don't you read books? Watch TV? Vote? Even politics
is better than death for first-date chitchat."

Yet, that was when—and, I thought, why—Scott reached across the
table, lifted my hand, and pressed it to his lips.

Now, that was a surprise. I felt a rush of pleasure so fresh it made me
go woozy. God forbid, though, I should relish the moment for more than
five seconds. The pure pleasure was almost immediately followed by a
rolling fog of confusion.

"I'm sorry," I began. "I didn't mean to be a downer. It just . . ."

"Don't apologize. Please." He folded my hand into his. "People should
say what they feel as long as it doesn't hurt anyone. I learned that the
hard way much too late in life. Listen, if it makes you any more comfortable, I'll match you one for one. My dad took off when I was about the
same age you were when your mom died. The family hasn't heard from
him since. He was a Vietnam vet who self-medicated with scotch. The
thing is—we got through it. You and I got through a bunch of other stuff
too." The handsome, heroic, astonishing man across from me freed my
hand so he could hoist his glass. I hoisted mine.

"So here's to us," he said.

Our first "us." We clinked on it.

For the next hour or so we traded standard first-date talk. Schools
attended. Mostly Catholic for me, all public for him. College experiences. First jobs. Mine—in the summer between my bachelor's and grad

school—was, I liked to say, in advertising. I was a dancing corn dog on the boardwalk at Coney Island. Scott's was more dignified. Commissioned as a second lieutenant upon graduation from West Point, he'd immediately reported for duty at Fort Benning. I didn't dwell on Lon— only an outline—and Scott barely mentioned Bunny; Belinda, he called her now. Just that they maintained a civil relationship for the sake of the kids. "Who aren't kids anymore," he added.

Because Scott had skipped dinner and all I'd eaten was a slice of melon and a few strawberries to keep me light on my feet for class, we ordered another item from the happy hour menu, a pot of mussels. By the time we were down to the last few, he was dunking chunks of French bread in the broth and feeding them to me. As I slipped the final mussel out of its patent-leather-shiny shell, he asked, "Would you like anything else? Dessert?"

"I'm fine," I said, though dessert would stretch an evening that I didn't want to end.

He said, "Next time, we can try the Thai place near Patuxent Point. The *Coast Post* gave it three stars." So, there was going to be a next time. Whew.

In an ironic turn of events, Lieutenant Colonel Goddard, whose balance and stride I was supposed to be polishing, wound his arm around my waist to keep me steady on the cobblestones that led to the car park. I hoped there was more to the gesture than keeping me from falling.

"What a night," he murmured into the flower-scented darkness. The moon was a waning sliver of platinum, but a star-spangled sky was alive and flickering. "Perfect."

He stopped us in a pool of light under one of Tuckahoe's antique-style streetlamps and repeated "Perfect," only in a huskier voice. Then he leaned over and kissed me.

The kiss was warm and garlicky and, I thought—if what my brain was doing could be defined as thinking—perfect.

When he backed off and zapped me with those electric blue eyes, I swear I felt them piercing through the top layer that covered my feelings and into the crazy place below where my hidden emotions hung out, pole dancing, downing tequila shots, and getting into trouble.

"It's nearly eleven and I've got a big day tomorrow," I said. Actually, I had a very small day. No class to teach, only one meeting at We Got Rhythm in the late afternoon. Otherwise sun, beach, and books. But old, safe Nora couldn't deal with this ambush of sensations and she went after those wild things with a mallet, playing emotional whack-a-mole.

"Okay, Cinderella. We're on our way."

As we approached my street with all four car windows down, strains of dance music filtered in from half a mile away. The bandstand, a complex of stage, dance floor, and stadium chairs, was set so close to the beach that a couple could sway to "Beyond the Sea" against a backbeat of surf breaking on the shore. The band played Tuesday through Saturday from seven thirty to eleven thirty as long as the weather was good. On clear nights the music sailed through still air to Surf Avenue.

Scott pulled into a parking space in front of number eighteen and we both sat staring at the house.

After a moment, he said, "Big place. I'm counting six front windows."

Only one of them was lit. I'd left a lamp on in the breakfast room. My son's room upstairs was dark. He usually got in after eleven, so no surprise there.

"Probably too big for just Jack and me." I hoped Scott didn't think I was proffering an invitation. I clattered on. "But all that space lets you breathe deeply. And the interior is very open to the surroundings. You really can't see it now, but in the daytime . . ."

That's when he looked at his watch. Which probably read ten-after-boring. Or five-to-get-rid-of-this-woman.

But I was a runaway train. "And facing the water out back, there's a large balcony and a widow's walk off my bedroom. We've got a spectacular view."

"I'd like to see it sometime," he said, braking me to a full stop. "Soon." Now, that was an ending worthy of an officer and a gentleman. "But considering your big day tomorrow, I guess we'd better call it a night."

We were halfway up the wide path to the front door and I had my key out when the band swung from a rockin' "Déjà Vu" to the slow, longing "A Kiss to Build a Dream On." Louis Armstrong had sung and played it on one of my mother's favorite albums. I knew the words by heart.

Give me a kiss to build a dream on
And my imagination will thrive upon that kiss

The trumpet from up the beach unfurled a languorous, soulful vibe.

One minute I was standing in the diffused glow from the pathway lampposts, wondering how I was going to say good night to Scott Goddard—a prim handshake? a sisterly hug? a neutral peck on the cheek? After that first kiss, was I supposed to make the move?—when he swept me, and I'd thought that only happened in romance novels, but no, he actually swept me into his arms and drew me against him.

The band played on and we danced closer than I'd ever taught in class or dared to in public. Against him, I inhaled an intoxicating mix of what, I didn't know or care. I only cared that the scent of him stirred some sleeping beauty in me. His skin, under its eleven-o'clock shadow, was on fire, and the heat of him melted feelings that had been frozen solid for eight years.

He spun me out on the smooth flagstone, and when I double twirled the return, he reeled me in, laughing a strong baritone. Then he kissed me. How could a kiss be so gentle and so crushing all at once?

My memory sang the lyrics about a hungry heart and the kiss that would feed it.

My eyes were closed, so I only sensed a new bloom of light behind my lids. But I did catch the scratch of a window dragging open. The sound snapped my eyes open and sent them darting upward, my heart racing. Jack, his face clearly readable in the background brightness of his room, was grimacing as he stared at us. He shook his head in what looked an awful lot like disgust. Then he slammed the window shut with a bang so loud it set off barking in the neighborhood. Seconds later his bedroom went dark.

Scott let me go, backed away. We stared at each other.

He broke the silence. His mouth labored for a smile but couldn't quite make the twist. "Looks like I got you in trouble. I'm sorry, Nora."

"No, *I'm* sorry. Jack, my son. I didn't think he was home." I caught a breath, tried to untangle my thoughts, make some sense when I could form words again. It took a long, painful moment.

"The thing is, he's nineteen. At that age, seeing your mother kissing a man like . . ." Like *that*, was the unspoken implication. "It must have—I don't know—freaked him out." My attempt at a smile also failed. "Not that it's an excuse for his rudeness. He and I will have a talk."

Scott shrugged. "Nah, no big deal. At least not on my end. Except that I embarrassed you. I got carried away by the music, I guess. My apologies for that." I didn't have time to register a protest because he raced into, "Well, now it really *is* time to say good night."

Right. We exchanged nothing but mutual nods from the distance between us. A final backhand wave from him and he strode briskly, almost a march, down the path to the street.

I turned on a sigh to enter the house and confront my son. There was no sign of him on the ground floor. Upstairs, his door was open, but his room was empty. From the balcony off my bedroom, I saw that everything was quiet and ink black outside. *Jack may be walking the beach,* I told myself. He did that sometimes under a full moon or, when it was a sliver, carrying a lantern for light.

I was still upset, but a shadow of concern had crept in.

Downstairs in the kitchen, I poured some of Pete's wine and sipped it while peering through the sliding-glass door, scanning the beach for signs of life. That's when I caught a pinpoint flash of orange: one blink, long pause, second blink, shorter pause, coming from the deck. On the third, I flipped on the outside light and there he was, six feet plus of him, sprawled on the lounge chair. I walked out, glass in hand.

"What the hell do you think you're doing?" My voice was siren shrill.

Jack looked at me as if I were past due for a psych evaluation. Then he lifted his cigarette (*no, not this kid whose grandmother died of lung cancer, who'd had the perils of smoking hammered into him since toddlerhood*) and in an exaggerated gesture arced it to his mouth. He drew on it so the crystal tip sparked orange and then, eyes hooded, blew an impudent stream.

"Since when do you smoke?"

"Since when do you drink at midnight?" he shot back. He didn't seem to be trying too hard to suppress a smirk.

"Don't you dare give me mouth. Not after your performance at the window. Not ever." He was nineteen. Old enough to enlist. Old enough to drive. Old enough to vote. But I was still his mother. Respect, dammit.

He ducked the window reference. "It isn't a real cigarette. It's an e-cig, a vape. You can't die of cancer from it like Mamma-mia."

That made me so furious I lunged for the thing. Jack parried with an elbow block. "Hey, take it easy, Tiger Mom." He was laughing, which was even more infuriating. His father and I had never spanked him, didn't believe in it, but for the first time in Jack's life or mine, I wanted to slap him.

"Calm . . . down," he said, rising from the chaise. "Hey, seriously, you're gonna give yourself a stroke." He got in one patronizing pat on my shoulder before I jerked away.

"We'll deal with your vape later." My voice had gone to what Lon used to call a hisper, half whisper, half hiss. "What I want to talk about now is how you could insult my friend like that. How you could be so unspeakably rude?"

"Your friend? That's what he is? Do you liplock all your friends? Dance so freakin' close you look Krazy-Glued together? Did I really need to watch that inappropriate public display of affection? So I closed the window. How does that count as rude?" He was leaning against the railing, slouched like a gangster with the fake cigarette hanging off his lip.

"You did not close the window, Jack; you slammed it hard enough to wake the dead. You embarrassed me; you embarrassed Scott."

"Whoa. Come on, Mom. Like, who embarrassed who? I hear some guy laugh outside. Close by and loud. I open the window and see the two of you, at your age, getting it on within feet of me. You know, I think maybe *I* deserve the apology."

He jutted his lower lip in the pout he'd mastered at four, and later—when I thought of him as the poor half orphan—that pathetic expression invariably melted my anger and put me on the defensive.

This time, though, the tried-and-true switcheroo wouldn't work. He could serve the ball into my court, but for once I was ready to smack it back.

"You're right," I said. "I apologize. I'm sorry for not letting you know before this that I have a life. One that didn't stop when your dad's did." Well, it had, actually. But I was on my way to starting it again. "It's a life that may include men. Has included them. Does."

His lower lip slipped a notch lower. "What? You've been dating?"

"On and off." I didn't say very little *on* and lots *off* because I was trying to make a point. "And if you have problems with that . . ."

"Wait. Wait. You're dating this Scott guy? This was like a real date, not just a lift home that got a little crazy? And it wasn't the first date? Mom!"

I thought of Tiffanie and how many times I'd bitten my tongue keeping my advice to myself. I repeated, "If you had a problem with Scott and me, you could have discussed it with me later in private."

He shook his head incredulously. "Yeah, like you two were making out in private."

My words sizzled: "I didn't know you were home, Jack."

He took a deep breath of whatever crap was in that vape. "Okay," he said.

There was a pause while he just stared at me, examining my face as if I were a stranger, someone he'd met for the first time twenty minutes ago.

A snowy owl's chittering scream pierced the silence. I tipped the last of the wine from my glass and swallowed the bitter with the sweet. "Enough of this. I'm exhausted. I'm heading upstairs," I said. "I want you to think about what I said."

"Hold on one minute, okay, Mom?" He straightened up as if he were preparing for battle.

I waited.

"I know you went through hell when Dad died. And, believe it or not, I'm all for your finding someone to hang out with. I really don't want you to be alone for the rest of your life. But this Scott guy, he's not right for you. Maybe he's a nice person and, okay, a war hero and all, but he's damaged goods. You deserve better than a man who's got parts missing."

"Parts missing?" My voice rippled with rage. "Let me tell you: he's the most together man I know. He's not bitter or filled with self-pity, and God knows after what he's been through he'd have the right. He's smart and kind. And he thinks I'm wonderful."

In the silence that followed, I almost heard Margo cheering, "Go, Nora!" Even Sister Loretta was strumming a different tune, and their words and music were finally getting through to me. My life was far from over, and love, the kind I'd fantasized having with Scott, wasn't the be-all, end-all of happiness, but it could be a hefty chunk. I'd be damned if I'd give up on it this soon.

Jack, wide-eyed at my outburst, said, "All I'm asking is, don't make any quick decisions. You don't want to have buyer's remorse down the road if something better comes along."

Now it was my turn to gape. When I got my voice back, I said, "I'm not known for quick decisions, Jack, so you shouldn't worry about that. You *should* worry about your attitude, though. And if you want to talk remorse, how about some from you?"

He gave me a tentative smile, took in a lungful of the salt air sweeping in from the ocean, and exhaled what seemed to be a shrug of a breath.

"I guess I'll hang out here for a while," he said, ducking my nudge for an apology. If that wasn't cheeky enough, he extended his hand with the e-cigarette pinched between two fingers. "I was just trying it out anyway. I thought it might be fun. Not so much. You can trash it."

My simmering anger boiled over. "Since you're so good at trashing things," I snapped, "trash it yourself."

Yeah, that was a "gotcha," and had it been flung at anyone but my son, I would have swaggered off in triumph. But this was Jack. So there was no swaggering. Just slouching to the kitchen to drink what was left in the bottle of pinot noir, and trudging upstairs to my bed and a restless sleep.

chapter seventeen

Jack wasn't in the kitchen when I came down for coffee the next morning. He'd brewed a pot of Emine's best ground and laid out my mug, a spoon, and, on a napkin, the last black-and-white cookie from Margo's welcome gift, the one I'd tucked in the freezer as an upcoming surprise for him. And there was a note.

Hi, Mom. Walking the pups, then hanging out with Ethan. I may stay overnight. Don't wait up or worry. Cell is on. Love ya.

My reaction was mixed, relieved that I wouldn't have to face more questions, irritated that there wasn't even a hint of "I'm sorry" in his note for the acting out and the damaged-goods slur. His suck-up arrangement of coffee and cookie, while it amused me, didn't entirely appease me. So best we didn't run into each other until he'd had time to think it through.

The coffee tasted bitter. I poured it down the sink, tossed the cookie into the trash, slathered myself with sunscreen, wrapped a pareo around my swimsuit, grabbed my straw hat, pulled a book from the shelf in the great room, tossed it and a bottle of water, two towels, and my cell phone

into a bag, and exited the kitchen. As I crossed the deck to hook a folded
beach chair, I stopped at the chaise littered with Jack's discarded vape
and a magazine with the cover ripped off. *Playboy*? God forbid, *Hustler*? I
hesitated for a morally split second and snatched it up. It turned out to be
Rolling Stone, one of my own favorites at twenty. See, I told myself, he
really wasn't a bad kid.

I was the only person on Barefoot Beach, though it was beginning to
get spotty with blue rental umbrellas three blocks up where the boardwalk began. The sun was still low in the sky and I could have walked the
night-cooled sand without flip-flops. Local news had warned of an invasion of jellyfish on the Delaware coast, but according to the reporter, the
stingers hadn't crossed the state line yet.

Just as I sank into the beach chair, my cell started ringing. Scott, I
hoped, though I wasn't sure what we would say to each other after the
way the night before had ended.

It wasn't Scott, at least not from the name on the screen. Who was
Petersen with a Maryland area code?

I answered it, and on that warm beach my blood ran cold. "Hi,
Nora." I recognized her voice, the Vintage corporate administrator, but I
made her say her name anyway.

"It's Kimberly Kline. So sorry to bother you on your vacation." She
waited for my protest, which didn't come. "I promised I'd get in touch as
soon as I knew something. I'm afraid I've got bad news." As if she had to
tell me, as if her voice hadn't oozed pity from "Hi" on. "It went down to the
wire between you and pottery, but—"

I interrupted her, trying to stave off the inevitable speech. Seized by
the urge to shut her up, to bury my phone in the sand or toss it into the
ocean, I death-gripped it and bought ten seconds by saying, "You came
up Petersen on my cell."

"Right. I'm working from home. My cell phone is charging so I'm using the landline. Petersen's my married name. So . . ." She would not be diverted.

Digging in my beach bag for a tissue, I tuned out most of her long explanation rigged with financial terminology that supposedly explained why I was being—I heard her humming search for the right words, although she had to have rehearsed this speech before delivering it— "released."

"I'm beyond sorry, Nora. I did everything I could. But in the end, since it applied to more than one facility, this was a board decision." She sighed. "I really wanted to give you better news."

Yeah, I really wanted to hear better news. A part of me had read the headline during our meeting on the day I left for the beach: "Nora Farrell Fired. Life Falls Apart." But another part of me, the one that protected me against pain, was deliberately illiterate. That's why, how, I'd been able to shelve the issue of my Vintage contract in the attic of my mind for the past couple of weeks, assuring myself, as I shoved it behind rhyme and reason where cobwebs grew, that the executive committee would never opt for clay play over dance therapy. And that if they tried, my supporters would revolt like the peasants in *Les Mis*, only wielding their crutches and canes while chanting for justice.

Kimberly seemed to be reading my mind. "I have to tell you, lots of folks aren't happy about the outcome. In fact, Mr. Lewisohn circulated a petition to retain you. He filled two pages with signatures. Unfortunately, the budget has been officially approved, so it's a fait accompli. Still, I thought it might be a comfort to know how our residents feel about the decision. And about you, Nora."

It *was* a comfort, actually. I sniffed, I blew my nose, but I didn't cry. I shut my eyes and managed to say, "Mr. Lewisohn is a sweetie. They all are, the ones in my classes." Mr. Hancock, depressed after a stroke, whose participation in the weekly Dance Out Your Feelings exercise had strengthened his left side and occasionally teased out a laugh. Mrs. Morgan, totally blind, who sang along with the music in our stretching circles, and Estee Friedenham, our ninety-four-year-old Holocaust survivor. I'd set her poetry to movement so the group could express their fury and then the triumph of the human spirit. Even the nursing home patients with dementia, the violent charges who took swings at the nurses and hurled breakfast trays at the wall, calmed down when I played "Paper Doll" or "I Found a Million Dollar Baby" and laid my hands on their shoulders to sway them in their chairs.

At the moment, I felt a bit like taking a swing at someone myself. So much was slipping away.

"I'm going to miss them," I choked out. Oh God, miss my life with them, making a difference fifty minutes at a time.

"Well, the economy could take a turn next year and free up money for ancillary services," Kimberly said, her voice chirpy with false optimism. "One never knows."

One never did. And that was, to my mind, the crux of the problem.

As the conversation drew to a close, I opened my eyes and stared out at the everlasting sea, which looked smooth and glassy this morning. But I knew that was an illusion. The sea was always moving, with tides, with waves. Nothing stood still as the earth turned.

For a movement therapist, I was lousy at moving. Well, I'd better get good with it—moving on, and moving out too, I reminded myself. And ASAP, because, like it or not, those effin' everlasting waves carried you where and when *they* wanted to go.

When I'd received the phone call telling me they'd found Lon's body, and for weeks after that, I didn't cry. *Couldn't* really, and was convinced I was a crazy person because my grief was deep and wide, but dry. It made my bones ache and played havoc with my sleep, my appetite, my ability to work, because I'd lost my focus, and my legs hurt, but mostly because music, which was essential to my practice, made me itch. Not metaphorically—really, physically. Especially the theme music from old sitcoms, which was all I wanted to watch on TV. No news, no murders, no wars, no political debates, no drama—just *Everybody Loves Raymond, Frasier*, old familiar reruns. I sat huddled on the living room sofa or in bed with the blanket pulled to my chin, bingeing on TV Land, Lifetime, and Netflix. *The Golden Girls* was my favorite, but its theme music made me break out. "Thank you for being a friend," the chorus sang, and *boom!* hives blossomed on my arms and neck. I chuckled and I scratched but I still didn't cry.

And then one night, almost a month after we scattered my husband's ashes, I was in the shower, ready to soap up, and it occurred to me that I was tasting salt in the fresh spray. I moved from under it, touched my cheeks, and then brushed my fingers against my tongue: tears. I licked snot from my upper lip, and that was when I felt my chest heaving and knew I was crying. Uncontrollably, almost soundlessly, and, it seemed, endlessly. When I finally stopped, my fingers were pruny and there was a net of my hair lacing the drain, but I felt better. And I never cried again about Lon. Not consciously. Some mornings, I woke up with my cheek pressed against a damp pillow, but I couldn't connect the tears to Lon because the dream had already vanished.

That's why I was so surprised when after I said good-bye to Kimberly Kline I collapsed back into the flimsy plastic woven beach chair, stared at my toes, their blue polish peeling, and, with a long gasp to get me going, began to sob.

By the time Margo called that night, I could talk about it without those jagged hiccups you get post-hysterics. Besides, I rationalized, it was sufficiently shocking to sidetrack her desire to dissect my date with Scott.

She opened with, "Just checking in. Everything okay?"

And I said, "Actually, no. I've been fired. Correction, let go. Vintage canceled my contract with both residences. As of this morning, they said adios, au revoir, sayonara."

"No! The bastards. *Said* it? Oh my God, they canned you on the phone? How cold is that!"

I wasn't going to tell her I'd been given fair warning face-to-face but had ridiculously hoped against unrealistic hope that I'd beat out the pottery therapist, an attractive young guy with one earring who helped the residents make vases and other gifts for their adult kids. The odds had been stacked against me from the start. I also neglected to add that I'd held off telling her because I didn't want to deal with the drama prematurely.

"It's a business, Margo. They don't play by Miss Manners' rules. And they made it clear it wasn't personal. They were forced to make cutbacks because of the economy. A profit-making company with shareholders can't afford to be sentimental. Whatever, there goes one huge chunk of my life. And my income."

"Oh, baby, I am so sorry." I closed my eyes and could imagine her putting on her game face. Not the player's—the cheerleader's. She didn't disappoint. "Nora," she cooed, "you're wonderful at what you do. You'll find something."

"Maybe, but not contractual in this economy. Everyone's cutting back on nonessentials. If I land something, it will be full-time, probably base salaried, and year-round. To keep Jack at Duke and a roof over my head in Baltimore, it's good-bye, Tuckahoe. Good-bye, summers."

"Never," Margo said. "You can sell the Calvert Street house and take that money and . . . oh shit, you're still renting, right?"

We had been for decades, from Mr. Lieber, the same sweet man who'd drawn up the lease for Lon when he started to teach at Hopkins. The rent was still absurdly low.

We'd looked to buy once, but Lon's purchase of the beach house had taken the largest chunk of his royalties on the first book and the advance on the second and we were helping to support his mom in California. Money was tight.

Then Lon went to part-time at the university so he could write more and we were living mostly on what I brought in. When the taxes and upkeep on the aging Tuckahoe house skyrocketed, we'd abandoned the notion of buying a place in Baltimore.

"So you can't sell Calvert Street. But you have a portfolio, right?"

"No, darling," I said. "People like you have portfolios. I have investments. In my case, lousy ones." I'd put Lon's life insurance payout into what seemed like safe mutual funds, but nothing had been safe in the last downturn and I'd lost most of it.

"The only way Jack's been able to go to Duke is because my father started a college fund for him. Dad banked a year and a half's worth of tuition before he went into assisted living, which gobbled up whatever resources he had left. Still, I figured between what I earned from Vintage, the vet therapy gigs, the psych hospital, whatever savings I had, and what the dance studio brought in, with Jack's scholarship and loans, I could squeeze out the other two-plus years. But now—now I'd better land a job stat or I'm screwed. More important, come January when the college fund runs out, Jack's screwed."

I'd exhausted myself totaling all the work it took under normal circumstances to keep our heads above water. Without the Vintage contract or something to replace it, we'd go under.

From my seat on the sofa, I could see the ocean, which, under the last of the light, looked still, black, and—for the first time ever for me—dangerous. Light-headed, I sucked in air that suddenly seemed too thick to breathe. *So,* I thought, *so . . . this is what it feels like to drown, with your lungs fighting to gasp, your brain deprived of oxygen struggling to make sense, make plans.*

Margo was saying, "Nora, get a grip. There are options if you'll listen . . ." That hauled me back to the surface.

"No way," I said, knowing what was coming next. For a self-defined free spirit, Margo was predictably predictable and invariably generous. I was touched, but I was also intransigent. "I will not take a loan from you because that would be like sticking a Band-Aid on a hemorrhage and even more because it would ruin our friendship. Yes, it would"—I could see her lips trying to form a protest—"money always does."

I heard the huffed dragony breath. "Fine. Be that way. I'm not going to worry about you. You'll figure something out."

Oh yes, I wound up telling her about the date with Scott anyway because it was inevitable and it made sense to get all the catastrophic breaking news out in a single broadcast.

I did the BFF thing and detailed the evening, including the mussels, the kisses, the dancing on the path, and Jack's insulting reaction.

"He's a great kid, but you spoiled him rotten."

I forgave her. She'd never been a mother, didn't have the experience or the instinct.

"All that crazy guilt you concocted over Lon. And poor Jack, God forbid he should feel any more pain."

"I sent his father off to his death."

"And you think I'm dramatic. Lon was acting like a first-class putz that summer. Driving everyone crazy with his writer's block. No noise in the house. Jack couldn't have friends in to play. He was even short with you. So you told him to accept an invitation to speak at the conference. Doesn't sound like a death sentence to me. It sounds like a brilliant plan."

The annual Jack London Fanfare Conference in San Francisco. Lon had declined when the organizers first asked him in April. A week before the symposium, I pushed him to call them back and see if there might be room for him last minute. They were thrilled.

Margo was saying, "Lon would bask in the adulation of his fans, take time away from the book, and reboot his brain. It was a good idea, Norrie."

"An idea that killed him. He asked me to go with him. I told him no."

I hadn't wanted to pull Jack out of his day camp tennis program. And the truth was, I'd needed a breather from my husband. He'd been a bear to live with for two months.

"If I'd been there . . . ," I began.

"You might have saved him. Yes, I've heard it before. The man died of a heart attack in a hotel room, in bed, maybe in his sleep. But if you'd been by his side, it never would have happened. You do know that's delusional thinking."

There was something else. We'd been arguing on the morning of his flight to California. He was pissed at me for not going along. I was pissed at him for being pissed. At the door with his suitcase, he'd pecked my cheek, an ice cube of a kiss. I'd wished him safe travels, but no "I love you."

"You've been eating your heart out over this for eight years. And treating your son like glass because of it. That didn't do Jack any favors. And now you're learning that you reap what you sow. That window-slamming tantrum? With no apology? The kid should have been grounded till his first Social Security check came though."

"He's nineteen, Margo."

"Not when he's acting twelve."

After returning from his overnight with Ethan Winslet, Jack had stayed out of my way. The rare times we found ourselves together, we exchanged tight smiles and few words. It was uncomfortable, but for once I wasn't going to buckle. Maybe Margo wasn't that far off the mark.

Her final lines: "Hang in there, baby. You're like a cartoon cat shoved off a cliff. Right now, you're spinning around in midair, working on your eighth and a half life. I guarantee you'll land on your feet. You always have; you always will."

No one did best friend better than Margo. But for once, the woman who won a Rising Star nomination for an off-off-Broadway production of *As You Like It* and a Bancroft for her role in the Driftwood's *Three Sisters* sounded as if she was overacting.

chapter eighteen

Another day passed before I heard from Scott. He had my cell phone number. He could have called, but he texted: Enjoyed other nite. Hope U did 2. C U Tues. Happy 4th.

I reread it, trying to prod intent from the words. On my way back from the studio, I stopped off at the Manolises' to show it to Margo, who hustled me out to the veranda. Under a green-striped awning that protected her delicate skin, surrounded by air suffused with the vanilla fragrance of her favorite milkweed flowers and pepped up by the ginger-flavored iced tea she swore was better than Red Bull for a burst of brain power, we huddled together on a wicker swing for two, like CIA code breakers out to save the free world.

Margo inspected the text through one of the pairs of magnifying eyeglasses she bought in batches at the Tuckahoe flea market. She squinted. She bit her lip. She pushed her specs up on her nose. "Well, he got back to you, which says something."

I'd thought about that, but he really had to, I'd concluded, or it would have been awkward in class, especially since there he had to hold me in his arms. Then again, he could have quit class and he hadn't. So far. That was a promising sign.

"It's not exactly poetry," she said. "He's not gushing undying love. But remember, he's a military guy. They talk in stripped-down sentences.

Hooah. Bravo Zulu. High and tight. Pete uses that one. He won't tell me what it means. It sounds sexy, but it probably has something to do with marching in formation." She stroked Scott's text message with one lavender-polished fingernail. "Now, I like this part: 'Hope you enjoyed it too.' That sounds like he cares."

We should have been having this conversation in middle school, not in middle age.

"Scotty Goddard looked at you in English class."

"He did not."

"He did too. I saw him. And he kind of, like, smiled."

"OMG!"

"But," I said, "does 'see you Tuesday' mean just in class or is he reminding me of the Thai place on Patuxent Point he mentioned at dinner?"

"OMG, we're going to be late for third-period algebra. Don't you dare tell Scotty I have a crush on him."

"Well"—Margo handed me back the phone—"I'm not a Talmudic scholar, and even they spend centuries interpreting the word of God or some medieval rabbi, and he didn't give us much to work with, so it could go either way. I would have felt more confident if he'd phoned. Maybe he was afraid Jack would pick up."

"It's my cell number. Who picks up other people's cell calls?"

She ducked her head in mock shame.

"You pick up Pete's calls?"

"Sometimes. Sometimes I just check out the ID. Don't give me that look. It could be an emergency. I do it as a service when he and the phone are separated. He doesn't carry it with him everywhere."

"Which means he's not cheating on you or he'd be glued to it. It's impossible to conduct an illicit affair without electronic devices."

"Oh, please. Fred was cheating on Wilma with Betty back in the cave. It's gone on forever."

"I assume you check the previous phone numbers and names as well."

"Which he obviously deletes as soon as he hangs up. Along with any incriminating emails and texts. The girlfriend must have taught him how."

Incredulous, all I could do was shake my head.

"Hey, I'm trying to save my marriage here."

She took a sip of her iced tea and stared at her garden. The day was overcast and the winds were rough, the way I felt. Daylilies swayed on their stalks and hydrangeas shivered in the gusts. She put down the glass and stared at her hands, which she smeared before bedtime with age-spot-fading cream. Even back in college, she'd worried about growing old. "With men, it's all about fresh and new. And young."

"Not all men," I said. "Scott and I are only a year apart in age."

"Another thing that makes him a hero in my book. So he's a good kisser, huh?" Margo tossed off the question casually, but it was the only casual thing about her and it was false. The diamond stud earrings were real. The taupe silk slacks and cream-colored eyelet blouse were designer. That she could weave her fingers, with the six-carat engagement ring, the endless diamond wedding band, and two jeweled pinkie rings, into an expectant clasp defied anatomical limitations.

When I hesitated, staring at his text message on my phone, she snapped her fingers. "In the moment, please. Kiss. Tongue?"

"Oh, for heaven's sakes." I looked up. "Do I ask you about your sex life?"

"No, but that's different. Marriage is a sacrament. Isn't that what Catholics believe? So what goes on between a husband and wife in the bedroom is protected by the . . . I don't know, the pope or something. But dating is fair game. Besides, I'd tell you if I thought you were interested. In fact, I'll tell you anyway."

I cast a glance toward the house behind us.

"He's not home. As I was saying, my husband—who has not been performing his conjugal duties with the appropriate frequency, enthusiasm, or—what's a fancy word for hardness?—that same man actually woke up with a major woody and proceeded to ravish me this morning. I always wondered what 'ravish' meant, and, girl, did I find out."

I shot her a TMI look and tried to stop the torrent of images leaping like horny salmon over the privacy dams in my brain.

Margo had no brakes. "The man actually climbed on top of—"

"So now you know he's not getting it on with this imaginary girl-friend you've fixed him up with."

"Au contraire, *mon amie.* I don't remember the last time he's been that sturdy for that long. And this morning he did stuff he never . . ." She ignored the hands I clapped over my ears and raised her voice to get through. "Stuff he's never done before. Very acrobatic. Incredibly cre-ative, and"—she sniffed—"highly incriminating. I didn't teach him those moves. *She* must have. And he was practicing on me. Picturing her while practicing on me." Her eyes welled with tears.

"Oh, Margo," I said. She laid her head against my shoulder and I stroked her hair for comfort, the way her mother hadn't in her childhood. After a while, she shook herself to her feet.

She had a charity meeting to chair and I had a phone call to make to the NADMT to see if my professional association knew of any job open-ings in Baltimore.

Margo's words at the door: "Respond to his text. Pay no attention to what your mother told you about playing hard to get. Play hard, get nothing. This is like dealing with royalty. You don't initiate contact, but you should answer. Keep it light, bright, and breezy. You'll see him at the parade Monday, but he'll be on a float, so probably only from a distance. Definitely add good wishes for the holiday. Better run it by me before you send it."

The thought of Margo Wirth Manolis vetting my texts to Scott God-dard made me laugh. My conversation later with the receptionist at the National Association of Dance Movement Therapists, however, made me want to cry. She'd send me a list of opportunities in the area, she said, but the pickings were lean for part-timers. Good-bye and good luck.

The next mention of Lieutenant Colonel Goddard came from an unlikely source. After my Friday morning Zumba class, I hung around in my office making sure accounts were up-to-date and entering personnel scheduling. I was nearly finished when Sal Zito sauntered in and planted his hard ass— his glutes, he bragged, were like two raw potatoes, which was not an appetizing thought—on a corner of my desk to announce that a fifteen percent increase in rent for studio space was kicking in September first.

"Sal, my finances aren't in great shape right now. I'm not sure I can swing that."

"Gimme a break." He leaned in and I backed up. After his weekday schedule of two spinning classes, two lifting sessions, and no shower yet, he smelled more than ripe.

"I mean, really, come on." He splayed his fingers. "Your husband was a famous writer. I even read his books and I'm not a reader. And there's always some story on TV about Stephen King or Grisham getting multimillion-dollar contracts. Then they sell the book to the movies and more dough rolls in. You can't be hurting all that much with that mansion you got on the ocean."

"It's not a mansion. Lon bought it thirty years ago when Tuckahoe was a backwater, literally. Even when his books were selling, and they're not now, he never got those kinds of advances."

"Yeah, the poor widow. My heart bleeds. Hey, take it or leave it. I got two waiting on line. A Vietnamese massage lady, strictly on the up-and-up, no funny business; she's got a degree. And a kids' ballet school. Listen, you're a dependable pay and Carmela thinks you're okay and I trust her vibes, so I don't want to lose you, but there's no one that can't be replaced. You think about it. I gotta know mid-August and that's cutting you slack."

My mood, as I made my way out, was as sour as the odor of Sal's sweat. But as I passed the dance studio I got stopped by the lure of the recorded *darbuka* music, wild drum rhythms, spilling out of Emine's belly-dancing class. So I stopped in because her sessions always gave me a lift.

Margo once punned that in Em's classes the bulk of the women were really big. She was right, and even Margo, whose body dysmorphia was legend, admitted that the more zaftig bodies looked better than the skinny ones when doing the Turkish dances. "They've got a lot to shimmy. Plenty of belly to roll, and their cleavage looks fantastic in the tasseled bras. More bounce to the ounce."

Some of the women wore leotards with jingly hip scarves, but many had taken a cue from their teacher and suited up in authentic belly-dancing costumes, which Em bought wholesale from a manufacturer in Istanbul and sold at a small profit. The outfit she wore that day had been designed especially for her, a confection in lavender, the bra set with stones and hemmed with beaded fringe. In Western mode, Emine was pretty, but dressed and made up to dance, she was stunning. Her geography had all the right hills and valleys so that when she undulated or shimmied or hip snapped, everything came together to convey exotic and sensual. With her flat belly and her breasts pushed high, she definitely didn't come off as the mother of two kids, one a fifteen-year-old who kept her up at night worrying. She loved to dance and she loved to teach. She'd told me once, "The café, the baking, the catering, *that* I do for our bank account. The dance I do for my soul." The message came back to me now with Sal Zito's timeline ultimatum still fresh, and it tightened my chest. If I allowed We Got Rhythm to go under, what would I be doing to Emine's soul?

As I watched from my seat on the ledge of the studio's panoramic window, shades drawn to keep out the stares of the curious, I realized this class would be an especially painful loss if the studio went under. My Zumba and ballroom students could find other schools up and down the coast, but there wasn't a class like Emine's for fifty miles. And these women, yes, they benefited from the exercise—belly dancing burned a lot of calories. More important, I suspected, was their feeling beautiful because of, not despite, their extra pounds.

"And that is it, ladies," Emine was saying, winding down with a sinuous inward figure eight. "Good job. Thank you." She clapped for them and they applauded her and one another. A gloss of perspiration glowed on her cheeks. She swabbed her neck with a towel and sat down on the ledge next to me.

She said, "You know this is the biggest turnout we've had so far. Five more than last session."

"Word of mouth. Which says something about you." At that moment, I wished with all my heart I could offer her a raise.

"You look—I don't know—sad? Depressed? What is bothering you?" she asked.

Margo claimed Em had a third eye, like one of the Turkish anti-hex symbols, the *nazar boncuğu*, but planted in the middle of her forehead. "She knows when I'm constipated, for God's sake. I think she can read my entrails, like the witches in Macbeth."

Over the years, I'd been taught by experience that one person can't provide everything you need or want from a friendship. That people have different strengths, and if you're lucky they share them with you. For example, Margo was a cheerleader. Not in her own life. For herself, the score was usually 20–0, their favor, whoever *they* were. And if things happened to be going well, she was sure she'd strike out next time at bat. But for my games, she shook her pom-poms and rooted for me to hang in there because everything would turn out fine.

Em was my analyst. She liked to think problems through, slowly, methodically, usually aloud, and then suggest solutions. That worked sometimes, but I didn't think I could handle it today. I was juggling way too much: my work or lack of it now; my love life, probably ditto; my son, who was getting away from me; my perilous financial situation. Everything seemed ready to crash, and talking about it was only going to make it worse. Sometimes you simply had to focus on keeping it all up and in motion.

Except Em was waiting, her knowing eyes fixed on mine. I blinked first.

She worked for me, but she also worked *with* me and she deserved to know what was going on. It would affect her future. I told her about Sal's rent increase, my financial shortfall, and the reason for it.

"The loss of your job with the Vintage company, I'm sorry for that," she said. "But you will get another, I'm sure. Even so, you know I have thought for a while that the studio should be earning more money. We talked about it a year ago, remember? I had some ideas for increasing business, but you were in the middle of fixing up the house with Margo and you said one thing at a time and you weren't ready to hear them then."

That sounded like me. "I'm ready now," I said.

We batted possibilities around for the next fifteen minutes. I suggested more newspaper ads. Perhaps a radio campaign. A plane flying over the beach trailing an advertising banner.

Em had let me talk, but now she shook her head. "No, no. All that costs money. The trick is to make money without spending more to make it."

Her suggestions were much better than mine. Belly-dance demonstrations at the Gold Coast Mall that would lure whole families to watch. The Powells and the Felchers on the Tuckahoe bandstand to show off their ballroom skills. "We could schedule more classes for our present customers, and extra classes in the new dances. Like the hip-hop. I'll ask Larissa. She goes to the clubs and she can teach them. Very sexy for the younger clients."

"You're good at this," I said as I felt the stirrings of hope.

"Let's think up other ideas," Em said. "We can draw up a business plan over the winter and try them next summer. It will take time for these efforts to turn into more profit, but eventually . . ."

I didn't have eventually. Decisions were waiting to be made.

"Ah, your mouth is glum again." Em tugged down the edges of her lips to make a sad face. "There is a saying my father used to repeat. *Ağacı kurt, insanı dert yer.* Worry destroys a person the way that worms destroy a tree. Worry is not the answer, *arkadaşım.* Work is."

Dear friend, she'd called me. She was mine as well, so I nodded to make her believe that I believed, which I did a little. Then I did what good friends do. I switched the focus to her life, her problems. All of them starred Merry, of course.

Adnan had appealed to the owner of Clean on Board to reinstate his daughter after the scuffle last week, but the decision was firm. So no job and no references either. But to let her languish through the summer wasn't an option, Em said. Merry would fill empty time hanging out with her equally bored friends, a recipe for trouble. So Em made sure she was busy first thing in the morning, helping to make cupcakes and pastries and package the coffee and cakes for the café's takeaway. Two hours of that and the girl was off to the food bank, where she stocked shelves and assisted in preparing lunch for the homeless and destitute in the area.

"It's important for her to see that a reward for work is not always pay. She has great compassion for animals, the cats especially, but not so much for people." Em sighed as she slipped her bare feet into sandals. "And then, I think, she has started to go to the playhouse some afternoons." She gave me a slitted glance made narrower by the heavy black eyeliner. "Did Margo talk to you about this?"

She hadn't. Interesting how our triangular friendship sorted out. There were subjects we split among the three of us. Others never made their way beyond two. Still others took circumlocutious routes so eventually everyone was in the loop.

"Merry came home with paint on her T-shirt the other day. That shiny gold they used on the set of *The King and I*. And I found the script for the play in the hall bathroom along with a to-do list for a show called *The Gin Game*."

The theater put on three plays a season. While rehearsals for the elaborate musical took over the stage weekday afternoons, the Driftwood drew audiences weekend evenings with a simple-to-mount drama or a singer or comic in concert.

I said, "Margo is playing the female lead in *The Gin Game*." A two-act, two-actor play. "I guess Merry is helping her out over there." I shrugged. "If you're concerned, ask Margo."

"I'm not concerned, only curious. But perhaps this is better as a secret between them. Margo loves such things. The drama. Merry too." She laughed. "In some ways they are both teenagers. Secrets, secrets."

Then she said, "Adnan saw you Tuesday night. At the restaurant, the Flying Jib. With Scott."

That took a moment to sink in.

"We went out for a drink after class," I said, trying to keep my voice feathery. We were up and walking now toward the women's changing room. "What was Adnan doing at the Flying Jib so late on a weeknight?"

"Ah, making a delivery. They have my chocolate baklava and the Turkish Delight Torte on the dessert menu. The café slows down by eleven, so a night delivery doesn't interrupt the flow. On his way back to the van, he saw you coming out the front door and then walking outside. He said you two were very romantic. He wasn't spying. But he saw you kissing." She whirled, not the full barrel turn she'd taught in class, but a half turn that ended with a hug. "I'm happy for you, Nora."

The perfume Em ordered from Turkey that mixed patchouli with lemon flower was close up and calming. I needed calming.

I detached myself, forced a smile, and said, "You're a little premature. The kiss was a surprise, but no big deal. I don't think it will happen again." It had, on the path, but Adnan hadn't been lurking behind the cypress trees on my lawn, so I saw no need to mention it. And after the second kiss and the reaction from the window above, I had no expectations of another one.

"Oh, I hope it will happen. He is such a nice man. A true gentleman. You are two good people. I think you would be a fine match."

Me too. I just wished Jack thought so.

chapter nineteen

July Fourth is the make-it-or-break-it weekend for retail businesses in resort towns, and a year when Independence Day fell on a Monday brought record-breaking crowds to Tuckahoe.

Visitors began to trickle in late Wednesday and streamed in on Thursday. By Friday there was a gush of them. Up where the hotels clustered, the beach was chair to chair, blanket to blanket. On Friday night, Tuckahoe was one giant party, and the next morning those who didn't sleep in took a beach breather and wandered through the downtown, jamming the narrow alleys of the Mews. Merchants had added extra staff for the busiest days of the season, and Em had doubled her baking output at the Turquoise Café.

I started Saturday early, up at five forty-five, scanning the scene from my widow's walk. A yolk of sun skimmed an eggshell horizon, smooth and creamy. High above, ruffles of clouds were beginning to go sheer. Below, the water was a calm pale blue. The muted pastels that soothed my soul would last only a short time before the vivid colors, the primaries and the hots, took over. This early, the beach music was still pianissimo— the soft cawings and cooings of seabirds, the wind tickling arpeggios. In an hour, the stretch of sand I loved most—Barefoot Beach—would start to fill, not with the armies of tourists that invaded farther up, but with scattered sunbathers. Until then, I reckoned I could own a parcel of the finest sand on the Delmarva shore in relative solitude. That was a luxury, an irresistible one.

I was on the beach by six, sprayed with sunscreen and stretched out on an old quilt, one hand caressing a bottle of the apple tea Emine sold in six-packs, the other playing absently in the sand, sifting the fine grains through my fingers. The two weeks since my arrival had been full and complicated, and because I was a therapist, my mind was always set to analyze. But not that morning. This was not a day for deep thought, I told myself, and shifted my focus to a figure paragliding over the Atlantic, canopy billowing, and after a while my mind soared and I imagined riding the wind across the sky, savoring the freedom of weightlessness. As light as the air itself, bathed in cloud-filtered sunlight, I flew high above the earth and its problems.

Ten minutes later, shouts and laughter from hotel guests down the beach wakened me. I was hot and sticky. I peeled myself from the quilt to stand and took a swig of apple tea. The ocean was still smooth, and as if a trio of mythical sirens was singing to me, I found myself rushing toward it. I arabesqued over a sea turtle meandering across my path. I felt the sand under my soles go from brocade on the shore to satin underwater. I waded up to my neck and then I dove into a sea so calm, so polished to gleaming perfection, that my cleaving it was like cracking a mirror. The water was as cold as the dark side of hell and it was delicious. I carved my path with the front crawl, the way Miss Dorney in high school had taught me. I swam for twenty minutes, pushing toward that chemically induced Atlantis where endorphins were waiting to welcome me.

The sirens made me think I could swim forever. But I couldn't, of course. At some point, I crashed, chest aching and legs drawing and, for a split second of panic, I wondered if I'd miscalculated this time, like an addict shooting for bliss and overdosing.

When my shoulders started freezing up, I slowed my stroke. I forced myself to remember the instructions Miss Dorney had shouted from the side of the pool. "Exhale under water. Don't roll your head. Good work, Nora. You've got the rhythm." I'd had it then. I had it now. I washed up on the shore like a conch shell, my outside inert, but alive within.

I staggered to my quilt, toweled off, and decided that if I sat down I'd never get up. Shivering from muscle fatigue in the heat and still lightly panting, I gathered my things and made my way to the path and then to the house.

In the kitchen, a box of doughnuts on the counter had been left with its lid up. Crumbs were scattered on the table next to a container of milk, cap off. When I went to put it back in the fridge, I saw the door was open a slit. In the sink, an orange juice glass, unrinsed, was waiting for me.

Maybe it was my exhaustion from the swim. Maybe it was my conversation with Margo the day before, but something inside me snapped. *No. Enough.* I hated to even think the words, but we needed to talk, Jack and I.

In my bedroom, I was stopped by a sheet of paper tented on my dresser. I unfolded it. As soon as I saw the Duke logo and the date, July 1, my heart sank. We were exactly a month before tuition was due for the fall term. The university emailed reminders to the students with a link to the site accessing the bill. Jack had printed it out and scrawled over the list of fees and next to a smear of chocolate icing, "This came in yesterday. Thanks, Mom."

Just like that. *Thanks, Mom*, dashed off by a child of entitlement. Margo had been right. I had only myself to blame for his great expectations and casual assumption that they'd be met. The dirty glass in the sink to be washed and put away by me. The stuff he wanted for Christmas that magically appeared under the tree. I'd given him a touch-screen laptop for his going-off-to-college gift last year. God forbid my child should be deprived of anything. Not after the Great Deprivation of his father's death. Well, it might be too late to change things, but then again it might not be. I threw a robe on over my bathing suit. It was time for the talk. Now.

A female voice filtered into the hall from behind the closed door of Jack's room. My first thought was *Claire* and *What's going on in there?* I knocked and heard, "Yeah," which I took for permission to enter. Jack was at his desk Skyping, and the woman at the other end—he'd skewed the computer so I couldn't see her face—was monologuing at a clip. I knew immediately it was Tiffanie. She was griping about her summer job and how mean her boss was, and Jack waited for her to take a breath before he said, "Right. Sounds like it blows. Hey, my mom's here so I've got to go. Call you back later."

Without a good-bye for him or, of course, a hi for me, she severed the connection.

He turned, took a deep breath, looked me up and down, and gave me a squiggly smile. "Someone went for a swim. Nice out there, huh?" His gaze shifted from my disheveled state to the paper in my hand. "Another year, another fifty thousand bucks."

"Closer to sixty a year with room and board," I said. "But, yes, with your scholarship and loans, forty-three thousand." Per term, it was still a number big enough to make me choke, but I found voice to add, "You left the milk out on the counter."

"What?"

"The milk. In the kitchen. You left the container on the counter. And you didn't close the refrigerator door completely when you took it out. Cold air was leaking through."

"Jeez, I'm sorry. A call came in and I—"

"Jack, you can't do that kind of stuff. You know how much a gallon of milk costs these days? You've got to be more responsible."

He was nodding like a bobblehead doll. "I'm sorry. I'll work on it, Mom. This is about milk?"

"This is about my losing my job," I said.

Never underestimate shock value. It's worth the price for the attention it buys.

He rolled his chair halfway across the room. His eyes bugged when I told him that the ax had swung on my Vintage contract. That a solid chunk of our income was gone.

"Wow," he said. "I'm sorry, Mom."

"Yeah, me too. Your college fund that Grandpa started? The money runs out after this semester. Come January, I'd better have a new job to replace the missing Vintage paycheck. If I don't, we're going to have to make some sacrifices."

"Sacrifices," he repeated. "Okay. Like what?"

I knew I would have to get it out fast or I wouldn't get it out at all. "Like selling this house."

Jack stopped breathing for a few seconds. After his first intake he said, "What? No. No. You can't do that, Mom."

"Well, I might have to, sweetheart. I love this place as much as you do, but we might not be able to afford it anymore. I can't swing our living expenses and the cost of Duke on what I bring in from the other two jobs. Selling the house may be the only way." I reached out to pat his hand. He pulled it back.

"You can't sell it. Dad would turn over in his grave."

The sea was Lon's grave, but my son was right. His ashes would spin a tsunami at the thought of our giving up Surf Avenue. But ashes couldn't write checks.

Jack was up and pacing. "We'll think of something. There's got to be other options."

I'd thought of them all. Examined them from every angle. Dismissed them all.

"You could rent it out," he said.

"If I rented in season, we'd lose our summers here."

"Rent it out for a month. July. And we can be here for August."

"It's not that easy. Arranging rentals is a full-time job. I'd have to pay an agency to do it and they'd take a percentage. And you really have to be on top of the day-to-day problems that crop up. There are property managers who do it, but they charge high fees, so there goes your profit. Also, some of the people you rent to don't take care of the place like they should. It's not their own home and they don't treat it like it is."

I repeated landlord horror stories I'd heard from women in my Zumba class. The one about a young couple, two-week renters, who on their first night at the beach decided to dine alfresco and hauled the mahogany dining room table onto the deck. They left it out there, exposed to the elements, for their entire stay. A warped and peeling total loss.

There was the gas grill rolled onto an enclosed screen porch that set the house on fire. The stuffed toilet that stayed stuffed for a week while the tenants used the two other bathrooms. The pack of grad students who had fun with a sign the owner had posted downstairs. "We appreciate your NOT smoking." The "NOT" had been crossed out and replaced with "POT." It took weeks to rid the house of the smell of weed.

I sighed. "It would cost a ton to get this place in shape for renters. I'd have to buy enough dishes and glasses for at least twelve. Big-screen TVs for all the rooms. And most families want a pool, which we don't have."

"Okay," he conceded. "Strike renting. How about this? You could turn the house into a bed-and-breakfast."

I didn't want to hurt his feelings, but I had to laugh. "I'm not sure the neighborhood is zoned for that. But even so, a B and B requires upkeep. Doing other people's laundry. Making waffles. Making beds."

"I'd help," he said.

"Jack, I have to get on your case to make your own bed. And speaking of beds, how would you like some kid who isn't toilet trained sleeping in yours?"

The whole idea of strangers taking over our house gave me the creeps. It was an invasion of privacy, a disturbance of our personal space. Icky.

Jack, though, wasn't about to give up. He snapped his fingers. "Movie shoots. The people a few doors down from the Winslets rented out their house to a Hollywood production company for major money. It was a set for a horror movie about a serial killer who roamed the beach back in the olden days." The Winslets lived on a street lined with Victorian houses. Ours had been built in the sixties. "I'm thinking Jennifer Lawrence sleeping in my bed? Now, that would be cool."

He walked over and put his arm around my shoulder. "Don't worry, Mom. We'll figure something out." At that moment, I tucked away the self-doubt I'd been feeling since Margo trashed my parenting skills. Maybe I hadn't done such a bad job.

I was still clutching the bill from Duke, which figured as one of the possibilities. I shoved it in the pocket of my robe. Jack was too smart not to notice.

"Even with my scholarship, Duke costs a bundle," he said. "I'll bet Maryland would be half the cost."

He was right about the savings, and the University of Maryland was a fine school with a top-notch lacrosse team. But the campus was huge and the population overwhelming. On our college tour, Jack had been unnerved by its size. "Too big," he'd said, eyes darting to take it all in. "It's like a city. You could get lost here."

More than geographically, I'd thought, watching my not-mature-for-seventeen son nervously gnawing his knuckle. "That's a no," I'd said.

Which wasn't going to turn into a "yes" even under the current circumstances as long as I had options.

Jack was up for co-captain of the Duke lacrosse team in his sophomore year. He was doing well academically. Most of all, he loved the place. And yes, Durham had Tiffanie, but a photo of Jack horsing around with Claire at Coneheads was pinned to his bulletin board. *I* pinned my hopes on that.

"You're good with Maryland?" I wanted to gauge the look on his face when he answered.

"I'll do what I have to do," he said. Then, giving himself away, he added, "You know, I could probably get work at the school store at Duke. Pull in some more money that way in the fall. And I saw a sign in the window at Marty's Surf Shop saying they're hiring for part-time. I can apply for that today."

His staying at Duke was also personal for me. I'd been accepted to Bennington College. Its dance program was among the best in the country back then, and I was excited to live in Vermont. I loved my Brooklyn nest, but I was more than ready to fly off to someplace exotic like New England.

My mother had been overjoyed at the Bennington admission and proud of me. By then the lung cancer had robbed her of most of her breath, but tethered to an oxygen tank, she'd dragged the machine as she danced around the living room waving the acceptance letter. My father had also been in favor of the out-of-town school. "You'll get twice the education, Nora. One in the classroom, another on campus."

And then Mamma-mia's condition had taken an unexpected turn for the worse and she died two weeks before my high school graduation. When I saw how my dad was grieving, barely able to function, I made the wrenching decision to live at home instead and commute to NYU. When I eventually moved into a dorm room with Margo near the campus, I was close enough for a quick subway check on Dad. It had been the right choice for me at the time. I wouldn't have been able to live with the other one. For Jack, though, my sacrifice didn't bear repeating.

"We'll work something out," I said, followed immediately by the

FaceTime alert from the iPhone on his dresser. Now, *that* screen I could see. On the second trill, Jack glanced at it, then at me. "Just don't sell the house. Mom, promise me." He tried to stare me down, but when the phone chirped again, he couldn't resist and picked it up. Saved by the bell. And by Tiffanie. Go figure.

chapter twenty

The Fourth of July parade kicked off at nine a.m. with the Mount Pisgah Baptist Church marching band's ragtime rendition of "Yankee Doodle." After that came the floats sandwiched between church choirs and school bands blaring patriotic songs, heavy on the brass and drums.

In the past Jack and I had made sure to get there early enough to claim places in the curb row, but this year he had so many dogs to collect for his morning run he couldn't predict when he'd arrive. He told me to go ahead without him. Downtown was jammed, and by the time I got to Sawgrass Avenue, I had to settle for standing in the row behind a line of squirming Cub Scouts seated on the curb.

The heat climbed from steaming to blistering as the crowd got larger and tighter and the floats crept by. City council members, costumed as Mooncussers, the eighteenth-century pirates who lured ships to the spits and shoals around Tuckahoe to steal their booty, sailed through on a replica of a three-masted galleon. Local pols hurled campaign buttons into the crowd, real estate brokers pitched refrigerator magnets, and a procession of businesses showered the kids with candy, setting off scrambles all along the route. The Cub Scouts piled the stuff in their caps. Perched on the hood of a red Corvette, Edgar Whitman, my very own foxtrotting dentist, tossed pastel toothbrushes that the sugar-high kids mostly ignored.

The Coastal Medical Center gave away bumper stickers and chilled bottles of water. As the scouts rushed forward to scoop them up, a nearby hand shot out, wagging a bottle at me, and I turned to see Jack edging into the squeeze. "Hey, Mom. Been looking for you. I scored some water. Here you go."

He maneuvered so a ponytailed blonde could sidle in next to him. "Mom, Claire. Claire, Mom. Claire and I work together at Coneheads."

Ah, the cookie cutie, probably eighteen but she looked younger, sucking on a tricolor ice pop and checking me out with big brown eyes.

She waved hi with her free hand. I raised my water bottle and called out, "Nice to meet you."

She said, "Nice to meet *you*, Mrs. Farrell." Polite. Not Tiffanie. Then, as the music glided into a somber version of "America the Beautiful," a swell of applause and cheers rose in acknowledgment of the oncoming float. A swag of red, white, and blue along its side announced VFW Post 8105. I spotted Tom Hepburn on board from his shock of silver hair and, in the next breathtaking moment, Scott in his crisp dress blues.

I'd replied to his last text: Other nite was fun 4 me 2. C U soon. Margo saw it, but only after I'd fired it off into cyberspace. Nonetheless, she'd approved, after my explanation that I'd decided against adding "Happy 4th" because with his wartime experience, his memories, and his souvenir injury, I wasn't sure "happy" was appropriate. But he was smiling up on that float, a dazzling smile that upped the drumbeat of my pulse.

As the music swung into "It's a Grand Old Flag," he climbed down to hand out miniature U.S. flags. First he worked the opposite side of the street. Then he pivoted, and I knew the precise instant he saw me. One moment, he was grinning, glowing at the rousing reception from the Cub Scouts. The next, he spotted me with Jack. And he hesitated.

Beside me, Jack said, "Oh shit." We'd been pressed in the crowd, but now he shifted. He took a few steps back and brushed my arm as he began to turn. I knew—a mother knows—he was scoping a path out of Scott's target zone, mapping his escape. I reached back, grabbed his wrist, and gripped hard.

"Don't . . . you . . . dare!" I said.

"What's happening?" Claire asked.

Jack mumbled, "Nothing. We're getting flags."

Scott had braced his shoulders and resumed crossing the broad avenue to where we stood. Arriving in front of us, he fastened his gaze on the boys at our feet.

"Hey, guys, you pick up enough candy?" The scouts showed him their orange caps filled with sweets. "Oh yeah, the dentist is going to send his kids to college on your cavities. Who wants a flag?" He dealt them out to eager hands.

One of the boys piped up, "You got a lot of medals. You army?"

"Yes, sir," he said to the boy. "Army. But I'm not on active duty anymore. Do you know what 'retired' means?" A chorus of nods. They had grandfathers. "But once a soldier, always a solder." That's when he straightened up, held out a flag to me, and said, "Hi, Nora." And damn, damn, damn, it was only when he said my name, when he smiled a squiggle that betrayed his nervousness, that I got ambushed by a wave of warmth that had nothing to do with the sun's sizzle. Fondness, pride, admiration—a mix of perfectly respectable emotions—surged. I took the little flag and returned the smile.

His gaze was still fixed on me when Claire said, "Hey, Colonel." The look he tugged from me went to Jack, with a nod, before landing on the girl.

She said, "Claire? From Coneheads? You're double vanilla on a waffle cone. Or sometimes a hot fudge sundae."

His eyes sparked with recognition. "Claire, of course. Happy Fourth.

I didn't know you without your scoop. And the blue lipstick threw me off."

Her lips were stained by the blueberry ice stripe.

"Good parade this year, huh?" He was still keeping me in his wavering line of vision. I watched perspiration bead above his upper lip. "Flag, Claire?"

"Absolutely," she said. She pinched the teensy flagpole between two fingers and gave it a teensy wave. What I'd heard of her voice so far had been chirpy. But now it dropped an octave and went somber: "Thank you for your service. I mean, really. From the heart." She was one for hearts, Claire was.

"Right, thank you for your service," Jack echoed, startling me. Too little and late, but I was willing to give credit where due.

I took a deep breath. "My son," I said. "Jack." Pause. "Farrell."

They performed the male greeting ritual, shaking hands and taking each other's measure.

Scott snapped a backward glance as the band launched into "The Battle Hymn of the Republic," the traditional music that signaled the approaching end of this year's parade. On cue, the floats picked up speed for the last lap toward home, which was the parking lot of the West Woodruff Middle School.

"Looks like your ride is leaving," Jack said. Could have been rude, maybe not. Oversensitive, I wondered whether it sounded like he was hustling Scott along. I sent my son a warning look. He sent me back all innocence.

Scott answered good-naturedly, "Yeah, the photographers want us posed on the floats, so I guess I'd better hop on." He smacked his right thigh. So when he leaned in to me, I figured that, in spite of his easy climb down from the float, whatever he wanted to say privately had something to do with his leg. But what I got were a few hurried words. "I've been really busy, Nora. Hit by some unexpected stuff. I'm going to try to make class tomorrow, but right now everything's up in the air. It may be a last-minute call. I hope that's okay."

No, a part of me wanted to say from inside my hermit crab shell, where I'd been burrowing in for most of the last eight years. Life was so much safer hunkered down in my house on Surf Avenue, where even when waves broke hard at high tide or a nor'easter slammed the coast, you didn't get swept away.

The other, braver part nodded yes.

We were halfway through that hazy purplish hour before sunset, waiting for night to fall so we could watch the fireworks explode over the ocean. Margo had claimed territory for us by spreading an old blanket on the sand, her island among the hordes that occupied every square foot of beach. A Brooklyn girl, she loved those hordes. They reminded her, she told me, of the precious, rare summer nights of her childhood when, every other Tuesday, her favorite aunt, Tante Violet, her mother's twin and temperamental opposite, plucked little Margo from the dreary Wirth brownstone to watch the fireworks splash light and color over Coney Island. Memories that for Margo shone brighter than anything in her jewelry box.

She settled back against the towel draped to protect her delicate skin from the plastic beach chair (like the ones they'd carried on the subway to Brighton Beach), took a sip of her Diet Coke, rummaged in her beach bag, and dug out a bottle of sun block formulated from Tuscan herbs especially for exposure to twilight. Margo swore the most damaging rays ambushed you at dusk.

"You too," she said, pointing to my arms. "You're beginning to fry."

When I declined to smell like a Caesar salad, she went from casting a "you'll be sorry" glance at me to a longer look at her husband, who was stretched out in a lounge chair next to her, earbuds in place, sunglasses nested in his chest hair, eyes closed. I wondered if he really had "WWFG—The Shore's Home of Country Music" coming through, or if he'd dialed the volume low enough to pick up outside chatter. He looked blandly innocent, but was he tuned in to our conversation?

"Maybe it's your lack of sex paired with your lack of estrogen, Nora, because everything's shriveling up in you, including your brain. Cut Scott some slack. The man *does* have a life besides learning the cha-cha."

That was unfair and I fought back. "All I said was I was disappointed about maybe not getting to see him in class this week. You kept pushing me to expand my horizons. Okay, so I did, and now that I'm disappointed that they're shrinking, you're telling me I'm overreacting."

"I'm saying, roll with it. This is real life, honeybun, not some school-girl fantasy. Relationships take time. They need to be nurtured. They face obstacles. And you told me yourself, Scott and Jack shook hands at the parade, so you've made it over the first hurdle."

My gut warned me it wasn't as simple as a quick change of heart. I knew my kid. He'd played nice as a peace offering to me because he was tired of tiptoeing around Tiger Mom. It was also possible he had something brewing with Claire, who was obviously a fan of the vanilla-loving colonel, and Jack didn't want to mess that up.

"You know Pete thinks Scott's a great guy, right?" Margo was spritzing sun block. "When they were on the board of the retired veterans' home together, Scott had some good ideas about staffing. Pete was disappointed when he resigned. Scott said it was for personal reasons, no details, but now I think that must have been about the time of his divorce. Pete never did get the Bunny-Scott matchup. Like the time she came to the home's fund-raiser one year in a dress cut down to there." Margo pointed to her well-covered navel. "Everything, and I mean *everything*, was on display. Her skirt was so short you could almost see her whiskers.

Totally inappropriate, though Pete said it gave the old soldiers a lift. Well, not below the belt, considering they were the last of the World War II and Korea vets, but there were a lot of bushy white eyebrows raised. The woman has no class. Sleazy."

"But pretty," I answered.

Margo wrinkled her nose, probably not at the scent in the air, which was a blend of boardwalk hot dogs and that Caesar dressing sun block, but at the thought of Bunny.

"Pretty? I suppose. If you like the 'rode hard, put away wet' look. Trust me, Bunnicula will not be a tough act to follow."

"She must have had something." I sighed.

Margo clucked in obvious disapproval. "I hope you're not having a crisis of confidence, Nora. Back in college, you were the poster girl for breezy self-assurance. Which is probably why the boys fell for you like ten-pins. And Lon—he could have had anyone, but you just bowled him over."

She dropped the spray bottle of sun block in her beach bag and pulled out a jar of neck moisturizer. Margo had specific potions for each part of her body. Greased up like that, she should have slid through life. She hadn't.

"Your parents thought the world revolved around you, so of course you were confident. And confidence is very sexy."

"You were the sexy, confident one," I countered.

"In my case, it was an act. Well, not entirely. I have to admit that the ten years with the child psychiatrist helped. And the nose job. But you were genuine, natural man bait."

"Man bait? Me? That's crazy. I never—"

"I'm not saying you slept around, sweetie." Margo shot her husband a calculating glance. He expelled a light snore and she continued. "But let's face it—you weren't a vestal virgin either."

Oh, please—you could count on one hand the number of men I'd had sex with. Margo, on the other hand, and another other hand and at least one more hand, was into the double digits before she met Pete. It was part of her bohemian persona as a drama major, she'd proclaimed. Actually, when we were in our twenties it was part of most of our friends' personas. As long as you practiced safe sex and didn't mistake it for love, it was kind of a badge of honor that you could treat men the way they treated the women passing through their lives—not badly, but casually, compartmentally.

Five men, but no one really did it for me before Lon. No one after, either. He ruined me for anyone else, or so I thought until I laid eyes on Scott Goddard.

"Give the colonel the benefit of the doubt," advised Margo, who hardly ever gave anyone that benefit. She raised her hand, taking an oath. "I guarantee, he's not after anyone but you."

That's when Pete opened his eyes and gave me an appraising look. "Needed that nap," he groaned. Then, overdramatically, I thought, he sat up, checked his watch, unfolded to upright, and stretched.

"So," he said, "I don't know about you two, but all I had for dinner was a yogurt and a bag of baby carrots, and that was at five. I'm starved."

Margo cocked her head in my direction, sending me a not-so-cryptic message as he slipped on his "Orioles—Go Birds!" T-shirt. Neon orange and black. You couldn't help but notice it and the man wearing it. Which was the point, according to Margo. In his prime, he'd been mobbed on the beach. Now he had to advertise.

"Anybody want anything? You, sweetheart?"

"I'm fine." An ironic smile played around Margo's mouth. "I brought along a box of granola bars. Low-fat, high-fiber. It's in my bag. Help yourself."

I knew she was testing him, baiting him.

"No, thanks. I don't want anything sweet. But how about you, Nora? Candy apple, funnel cake, taffy? I can stop at Benny's." The shop that had been feeding Tuckahoe and the surrounding towns junk food for decades.

"I'm good," I said.

He patted his wife's head. She showed me the whites of her eyes.

"I'll be back before the show starts." And he was off.

"The annual hot dog run," I said.

After twenty years, I knew the menu by heart: hot dogs all around and the biggest tub of french fries Frybaby sold. Ditto on the onion rings. Lon and Pete used to polish off the high-cholesterol stuff by themselves. No wonder my husband's arteries had been as clogged as the Lincoln Tunnel at rush hour.

"Yeah, but now Pete's a vegetarian. This year it's more an excuse to get away and call the girlfriend." A shadow of pain, followed by disdain, skimmed her face. "Also, to press some older flesh. His fans await him. He just has to dig 'em up."

We watched Pete detour to the most crowded patch on the sand and slowly thread his way through the blankets and chairs. "Wanna make a bet how long it takes before someone stops him and asks—"

She didn't get to finish her sentence as Pete got waylaid by a gray-bearded man in an O's ball cap.

"Hit number one. They usually say, 'Aren't you . . . ?' They never used to ask, but he's been out of the spotlight so long, these days they double-check. Give them a minute and they'll be deep in a shallow conversation about the 1998 game between the Yankees and the Orioles where Pete made that once-in-a-lifetime catch off Rodrigo Ferez." She waved off a sand fly. "Oh my God, can you believe this? He's signing the guy's stomach."

Pete was indeed scrawling his autograph on an XX-large-T-shirt-covered potbelly.

She shook her head. "My husband carries a pen in his shorts pocket. Sad, isn't it?"

It was Pete who broke the news. Not immediately. First he mowed through the three ears of nonbuttered corn he'd brought back from his trip to the boardwalk. When finished, he pitched the bag holding the cobs into the trash can, which was at least ten feet away. A perfect shot, which prompted a smattering of applause from the neighboring blanket. Margo had endured enough.

"Pete Manolis, ladies and gentleman," she announced, and flourished a very smooth hand toward her husband. "Let's hear it for the Greek Icon."

"Hey." He extended a bare foot and kicked her ankle. "Cool it. You're being ridiculous."

"*I'm* being ridiculous? How many bellies did you sign? No, really. How many?"

She was smiling, maybe joking. Men get a certain fawn-in-the-high-beams look when they're dealing with the mysterious, fulminating volcanoes that are women on the rumble. They're not sure if it's laughter waiting to explode or something much worse. I saw Pete spin the wheel of reactions. He landed on playing along, but you could tell he wasn't sure if it was win or lose. The foot that had nudged his wife was now nervously stamping sand. Oh, he was really taking a chance.

"Three bellies, four shoulders, the back of a hand, and one very shapely tush."

"The shapely tush, now that I believe," Margo drawled.

"Marg, I'm joking. Come on. Lighten up." He strolled around to kiss the back of her neck. She didn't shake him off. He was smart enough to change the subject. Or try to. "You'll never guess who I ran into on the boardwalk."

"Kim Kardashian, and you just had to stop and sign her ass."

Outrageous was Margo's specialty, but we all laughed and the dangerous moment passed.

"Scott Goddard at the Korn Krib. You know him, Nora."

I nodded, working to keep my face expressionless.

"I haven't seen him since he quit the board of the vets' retirement home. Amazing guy," Pete enthused.

Margo flicked me a "calm down" glance and took over. "Scott's back in Nora's ballroom class this year. And he's a good dancer. Right, Nora?"

"On his way," I mumbled. Then offhandedly, though I was sure that Margo wouldn't buy the casual delivery, I added, "Maybe I'll stop by and say hi. You know where he's sitting?"

"About four rows almost directly behind us," Pete said. "Plaid blanket. He was with someone at the Krib. I think. She was in line ahead of him, paid, and handed him the bucket."

I scouted out the plaid blanket.

"Pretty?" Margo asked him, cutting to her version of the chase.

"I didn't see her face and he didn't introduce us. Redhead is all I know."

"It's a recessive gene. She could be his sister. Or his daughter, here for the holiday. Lots of people come in for the Fourth," Margo said for my benefit.

I saw only the back of the woman seated on the blanket and didn't recognize the hair. I was acquainted with the color, though, a heinous, carroty, do-it-yourself, whoops! dye job. But Scott seemed okay with it, with her. He was on his feet, hands moving, head nodding, chatting away. Hey, we'd only been out on one real date and it had ended awkwardly, canceling out the kisses, erasing any expectations, I thought with a twinge. I bit my lip as he reached down to grasp the redhead's hand. Okay, more than a twinge. A pang stabbed me. Damn if she didn't stumble against him getting to her feet. No, stronger than a pang. His hands were on her shoulders balancing her. A prick. That's what it was. That's what he was. A quake of anger rocked me. All that lovey-dovey stuff with me? Feeding me mussels and dancing me down the garden path—what did it mean if less than a week later he had another woman pressed against his chest? Even Margo was shocked. Her tsk-tsk cut through the noise all around us.

So much for me dropping in on Scott Goddard's blanket for a hello.

Oblivious, Pete said, "I think I'll walk with you, Nora. I'd like to talk to him about getting back on the board. Three years have passed, so maybe he'll reconsider."

"No, you don't. Sit," Margo commanded, and flashed him a "don't ask" look.

A few minutes later some kind of answer sauntered our way, heading toward the water. Hot pink halter dress and matching pink flip-flops, neon orange hair cut short. Now—I sat spellbound at the approach—she passed directly in front of Margo, who fanned away a reeking cloud of cigarette smoke. In a voice that would have easily reached tenth-row orchestra, my friend said, "There are rules against smoking on the beach. There are fines. It really stinks up the place. I can't believe how some people can be so inconsiderate."

Belinda aka Bunny Goddard, converted to redhead and skinnier than I remembered, glowered down at the source of the comment. She locked eyes with me for a split second, then nonchalantly flicked her ashes within a millimeter of Margo's painted toes. I swear I saw little sparks of fury shoot from my friend's bangs as she brushed them back from her forehead. Ominously, she began to shift to her feet. Which is when Pete, in a version of the quick saves that had inspired cheers in Camden Yards in his heyday, snatched his wife's hand and yanked her back into her chair. "Let it go," he said.

But, of course, Margo had to have the last word. She growled, "Bitch," after Bunny, then whirled on me. "Can you believe that chutzpah?"

I believed. Bunny wasn't short on nerve.

The three of us watched Bunny's progress as she turned, wound a path back to the plaid blanket, sashayed up to Scott, dropped her cigarette butt in the sand, then ground it out with the toe of her flip-flop. Scott bent to pick up the discarded inch of cigarette. The man who played by the rules. That's what I used to think anyway. I could read Margo's mind from the exasperated look she gave Pete—not me, Pete. *All men are liars.*

As the first of the fireworks detonated over the ocean, Scott sat. Then Bunny lowered herself to the blanket beside him. Was she leaning against Scott's legs—one flesh and blood, one carbon-fiber composite? I said yes, but the light was fading, the silhouettes were low and jumbled, and Margo, viewing the same pantomime, said absolutely not.

"Ugh. The evil one rises from the crypt. I thought he buried a stake through her heart. Didn't you tell me she moved to Florida?"

"That's what he said." But Bunnicula was baaaaack!

"Stop squinting, Nora. It's dark, so you won't see anything anyway. And your mind will play tricks. Jump to conclusions. I *said* don't look at them." She reached over and, with a single finger, lifted my chin so I was forced to focus on a purple spiral soaring, then spraying a thousand amethyst sequins overhead.

For the next half hour I sat glum and quiet, occasionally turning to catch an indecipherable flash of Scott and Bunny when the sky lit up. At the finale, stars of spangles and stripes of iridescence unfurled the American flag against a black velvet sky, giving way to splurges of color that erupted against a fusillade of cannon booms. From the bandstand at the end of Margate Avenue, a rousing rendition of Sousa's "Stars and Stripes Forever" thundered over the beach. And I found myself silently weeping. Over the beauty of it, the meaning of it. How we had to fight to preserve it. And how many had paid so much over the centuries. Their lives. Their legs. It was partly about Scott Goddard, of course. Which Margo, as a woman and a friend, knew. She reached into the pocket of her hoodie and handed me a balled-up, probably used tissue.

After the lamplights on the boardwalk reset from dim to bright, and the crowd was lit sufficiently to make its way safely off the beach, the three of us stood and, in synch, Margo and I swiveled to check out the plaid blanket. Bunny was gone. But Scott was standing there, staring at the ocean, or at us, or at me. I couldn't tell. Margo put her hand protectively around my shoulder and hugged me to her. Her tone was bitter. "I don't care if he is a wounded warrior. Screw him."

chapter twenty-one

There was some kind of summer respiratory virus going around. It started with a sore throat that turned to a cold that became a cough. Nasty bug. Larissa was down with it, so I taught her Tuesday morning Zumba class, made up mostly of young mothers who for an extra seven bucks could park their kids in the playroom, which Sal had fitted out with cribs, toys, and sitters.

By the time I finished with the cooldown, I'd run myself and the moms ragged but exhilarated. For me, the mood lasted as long as it took to spot the message light winking in the heap of stuff in my cubby, grab my iPhone, and punch up Scott Goddard—damn, I'd missed his call—telling me he was so sorry but he wouldn't be able to make it to class that night. I remembered his warning me that he might cancel last minute, but still it smarted when he said he was working on a project that had turned out to be more complicated than he'd anticipated. He was up to his neck in it. His words. I'd seen the project leaning against his legs on the beach the night before and I imagined he was up to something. He signed off with, "I'll explain when we have time to talk. Apologies again, Nora. Send my best to the gang."

The gang was down by three that evening: Larissa, Scott, and Tom Hepburn, who was home waiting for a return call from his doctor to see if his X-rays showed pneumonia. The atmosphere was subdued as everyone squirted hand sanitizer after each change of partners. I ended class early when Morty Felcher spun himself into a coughing fit doing the Lindy Hop and Marsha was concerned he might have cracked a rib.

I got home to find the door to Jack's room open and my son on his laptop Skyping.

"Hey, Mom," he called me in and over. "You're home early. I'm on with Jennifer." When I blanked on that, he ducked away to whisper, "Sixteen's daughter. Older one." He pulled me into the picture to introduce me.

I gave her a smile, which probably resembled the rictus on a death mask. She gave me back a flash of perfect teeth, and the hair toss that's reflexive with beautiful women. If the looks didn't seize your attention, that flipping of the hair, especially sun-streaked California blond, would hijack it.

"With Dirk coming in this weekend," Jack said, "Jen figured she'd better clue me in about her dad. You know, like how being a scientist type, he's kind of dorky."

Dorky Dr. Dirk DeHaven Donor Dude. Margo would relish that.

"I'm not going to pull out all the skeletons in the closet," Jennifer said. "Whoa, look at your face, Jack. Your mom's going to think you've got an ax murderer as an ancestor. Hey, every family's got their secrets, right? I'll let Dad tell you about"—she faltered here—"whatever he's ready to share, whenever."

I laughed lightly, dutifully, then said into the camera, "Well, I've got some reading to do. Have a good talk, you two." We finished with the standard amenities, and when I left, Jack jumped up to close the door behind me. In the hall, I heard the scrape of his chair, then laughter, hers and his.

The next few days were spent wondering, *What are we in for here?* My son was obviously nervous and euphoric simultaneously. He was whistling pretty much nonstop when he was home. The same song over and over. Lon had been a big Beatles fan and Jack was weaned on the *Abbey*

Road album. Now he was stuck like a phonograph needle on scratched vinyl playing "Here Comes the Sun."

He was happy—I got that. But how subliminal was his choice of tunes? Was this his theme for the Donor Dude's visit? "Here Comes the *Son*"?

Meet this afternoon to talk?

The text came in from Scott Thursday morning while I was loading the dishwasher. I stood for a mesmerized moment, snapped out of it, and typed, Sorry. Teaching classes this afternoon. I caught myself before I hit send and deleted "sorry" because women say sorry too often for things they shouldn't be and really aren't sorry for. I substituted the active, confident "Busy." Which was true.

Larissa was still down for the count with the virus hanging around her vocal cords so she couldn't bark, "Move, move, move. Lift the legs. Ach, *lenivaya!*" Which meant "lazy" in Russian and became a catchphrase among her masochistic devotees. *"Lenivaya!"* they'd shout at one another as they danced, laughing.

I was scheduled to teach her Zumba Toning class, a wipeout hour of cross-body workout with weights. That was at one. At three, I'd get a respite, her Golden Zumba class for the senior set. Low-level, low-impact, it provided a decent cardio workout and revved up the metabolism.

I could have fit the colonel in at two. Why was I postponing? Why didn't I meet him and get it over with? A few minutes of ending it and we could pick up where we'd left off a few years before. Just dancing.

There's a sacrament in the Catholic Church for penance and reconciliation, and my instinct said that's what Scott Goddard was setting me up for. First he'd report reconciliation—as in he and Belinda were back together. Then he'd ask for forgiveness for leading me on. I'd hand out penance, two Our Fathers and two Hail Marys, absolve him of his sins, and send him home to work out the details of his deal with the devil.

Except I wasn't in the mood to hear confession. Or maybe he just wanted to let me know he was dropping the Tuesday night class. I didn't want to hear that either.

A trill signaled his next incoming: Understood. We'll catch up soon.

I let him have the last word and was grateful for the distraction of Larissa's two classes so I didn't have to think about my past, present, and lack of future with Scott. Home by four thirty, exhausted, I rummaged through the bookshelf in the great room and picked up one of the two copies of the book Emine and Margo had each given me for Christmas. I finally decided I needed to read *Embrace Your Fabulous You*. I probably should have read it on New Year's Eve instead of drinking a split of champagne solo with my Lean Cuisine and falling asleep right after *Jeopardy!*

It was a gorgeous afternoon. I hit the deck, stretched out on the lounge chair, my ancient boom box on the table beside me playing my favorite tapes, while I slogged through the chapters entitled "Why Me and What Next?," "Self Sabotaging: How to Stop It," and "My Body Beautiful." I'd just turned the page to "My Magnificent Brain" when I thought I heard the doorbell gonging through Sarah Vaughan's "Tenderly." I muted the music and tuned in to the crunch of bushes parting and the crackle of twigs from the path that ran along the side of the house. Before my magnificent brain was able to register a visitor, he materialized.

"Nora?"

He might have shouted, "Surprise!" and thrown confetti for the way my pulse bounced with astonishment at seeing him. Scott Goddard had one foot planted on the bottom step of my deck and was leaning toward me, scanning my face.

"You okay? I didn't mean to scare you."

"You didn't," I lied. "You just surprised me."

"I rang the bell. A few times. No answer, so I figured you weren't home. And then I thought as long as I was here, I'd get a look at the beach view you raved about. When I heard music coming from this direction, not Jack's kind either, I made enough noise so you'd hear me— well, you'd hear *someone*—coming." He gestured toward the path with his water bottle. "That pyracantha could use a good trimming. And you might want to have someone clear out the underbrush. It's smothering your impatiens."

The first curl of a smile dared to form at the corners of his mouth. "Now, if you were the enemy, I would have approached in stealth mode. But we're friends." He paused the unscrolling of the smile. "We *are* still friends, right?"

The sun had caught him in a blinding spotlight. I let him bake in it for a moment. "That depends," I said.

"On?"

"On your definition of 'friends.'"

He thought about that for a moment. "Fair enough. Sounds like we're due for a talk."

Another talk. The recent ones had featured reports that had shaken up my life. These days, I seemed to have my own personal CNN, news twenty-four/seven. But Scott was another story. One I might not have wanted to, but needed to, hear out.

He darted a glance to the second floor, scouting for spies, I supposed. "We could walk on the beach . . ."

The sun was waning. A high-wind forecast for evening was already stirring. The stretch of sand fronting the private homes on Surf Avenue, from Mooncussers Rock to the gull rookery, was rarely crammed, but now it was almost deserted. Every slice of summer day here offered pleasure, but this hour was one of the most delicious.

Scott looked at me, hat in hand, a Greek fisherman's cap that he'd swept off politely when he first saw me and now nervously fingered around the braid.

"Sure," I said.

He slapped on his white cap and followed me down the steps and onto the narrow path. When we were on level sand, we walked side by side. He wanted to talk, he'd told me, but for a while we ambled in silence, just letting the scene happen around us.

Finally, Scott said, "I heard Belinda ran into you on the beach the other night."

I let that statement steep for a minute like green tea, and pulled it just before it turned bitter. "Not exactly ran into," I said. "We didn't say hello. She stopped just long enough to piss off my friend Margo."

He licked perspiration from his upper lip. "Pete Manolis's wife, right. Belinda doesn't like her. She thinks Margo's got a smart mouth."

I wasn't about to give Bunny's assessment a pass. "Margo's smart in a good way." I defended my friend.

He nodded. "Belinda didn't mention seeing you two until I was driving her to the airport this morning. That's when I started adding things up. Did Pete tell you we bumped into each other on the boardwalk? Yeah, of course he did. And then I find out you saw Belinda on the beach. I was concerned you may have put two and two together and come up with six."

"She outed you." My laugh was weak.

"Wrong. I haven't been hiding anything. There's nothing to hide." He stooped to pick up a sand dollar, brushed it off, and pocketed it. He was marking time, I thought, measuring out his words before he let them go. Once said, never unsaid. "It may be too late, Nora, but you should know the truth."

I crossed my arms in the universal signal of self-defense.

He was a soldier; he soldiered on. "You know my mother-in-law, late, ex, whatever, died a couple of years ago. Nice lady. Belinda's an only child and she inherited everything, including the house. It was on the market for a long time and it finally sold last month. Belinda came up from Florida to clear it out. She asked me to help, and the truth is, I try to keep the peace. It's easier and I have the kids to consider."

I knew about considering kids.

"In fact, my daughter drove in from Baltimore to lend a hand. She's good with her mother, but in small doses. So Liz stayed with me. Belinda slept at the old house." A factoid inserted for my benefit, I thought. "The three of us were supposed to go to the fireworks together. Then Liz opted out last minute. But we were already set up on the beach, so . . ."

"Yes, you looked pretty chummy on that blanket, you and Bunny." *Oh, what the hell? Did I really have anything to lose?*

"What?" He stopped, I stopped, and he spun to face me. "Nora, I don't know what you think you saw, but nothing 'chummy' happened. I don't do chummy with Belinda."

It *had* been dark. I *hadn't* been sure.

He went on. "Not that I wouldn't put it past her to try to make you jealous. You've been a thorn in her side since the day you two met. Which is understandable, given your, well, assets."

Or maybe Bunny was a mind reader, I thought as Sister Loretta nudged a cloud of guilt down from the pearly gates. It drifted off almost immediately.

"Listen," Scott said, "the thing is, I was trained to impart information on a need-to-know basis. But I think I miscalculated this time. I should have laid this out for you earlier. Before . . . before that last dance."

His blue eyes grew somber. "There's nothing between Belinda and me. Whatever it takes to make a relationship hasn't been there for years. Except for the legal connection—and that's ended—and the kids, of course, which never ends, there's been nothing. In either direction," he said pointedly. "That's all behind me. I thought—I *hoped*—you and I were ahead."

Okay, maybe only one Hail Mary and an act of charity.

"She's gone for good?" With vampire Bunniculas, you had to be sure they wouldn't rise again to suck the life out of you if the occasion called for it.

"For good. The house is cleaned out, the settlement's signed, and"—he checked his watch—"she arrived in Orlando at noon. I probably won't see her again until Liz's wedding, and that's a year from September. Her fiancé's an Annapolis alum so it's a big wedding in the Naval Academy chapel." And then, out of the wild blue yonder, Scott asked, "Wanna be my date?"

I flashed him a look to see if he was teasing. His eyes were twinkling. But maybe he was serious. Either way, I had to laugh. *Had* to, as in could not contain my laughter. Joke or genuine, the invitation deserved it, and with the release of all my bottled-up resentment and disappointment over Bunny on the beach, a crazy joy bubbled up and out. Scott reared back to watch me, one eyebrow raised, which struck me as hilarious, and I cracked up completely, which set him off, and we leaned against each other, laughing helplessly for at least a minute. After we quieted, he turned and nodded, ready to move on.

It was five o'clock, I could make out from his watch. The arsenic hour, we'd called it when Jack was a preschooler and got fussy. Everybody's sugar dips in late afternoon. But my dopamine, the happiness hormone, had to be off the charts, and I was suddenly starved. I had cheese in the fridge and crackers in the cupboard and an invitation of my own to issue. No wine tonight, though. The way I felt—way too reckless—wine was dangerous. I offered Scott lemonade, a simple gesture of hospitality. He accepted.

He took my hand as we walked back to the house and was reluctant to break the link as he settled in a chair on the deck. "I have to let you go so you can get the lemonade, right?" He was grinning. "Why don't we forget the lemonade?"

He was tugging me into his lap as Jack hollered from inside, "Mom, you home?" It sounded as if he was calling up from the bottom of the stairs. He must have spotted my handbag on the hall table.

Scott dropped my hand. "I'm on my way," he said, up and out of his chair. I had to laugh—I'd never seen anyone go vertical faster.

"It's okay." I decided my son would learn to deal. Finally something was nudging me to get back in the game.

"No need to rush," I said to Scott (and maybe to me). "Really. Stay."

He sat down, but gingerly, positioned to jump up and make a break for it if necessary.

"You sure you're okay with this?"

I answered by calling, "We're out here, Jack," and plunked myself down in the chair next to Scott's.

The screen door slid open with a creak that told me it needed a shot of WD-40.

Credit to my son, he didn't lose his cool when he emerged to see the two of us seated side by side. I turned to show him my eyebrows raised in a classic "don't mess with me" expression, one I used sparingly and, like my hisper, made the point.

"Hey, Mom." If he felt anything beyond mild surprise, he contained it. He bobbed an acknowledgment as he added, "Colonel."

"Make it Scott," my visitor said, establishing territory with familiarity.

"Sure. Scott. Just stopping by to grab my Coneheads apron. You want me to bring home a couple of gallons of rocky road?" he asked me. "We're almost out."

"One gallon of rocky road. And one vanilla." You never knew when someone vanilla might drop by.

Then Jack was gone with a wave. No scene. No attitude.

The next thing Scott said was generous, considering that the slam-bang of the window last week had been their introduction. "Good kid you have there."

I thought of those men and women who at nineteen had given, or were prepared to give, limb or life for their country, and I said, "Good, yes. But still a kid."

"I know what you mean. I've got one a year older. He's talking about joining the Marines. Maybe that will mature him. Nora . . ." Scott leaned in so I got a close-up of his dark, long, wasted-on-a-man eyelashes nervously flickering. "By any chance, would you happen to be free for dinner Saturday night? Or we could take in a movie. Cutting it close, I know, but I thought maybe . . ."

I wasn't about to go into Dirk DeHaven's upcoming visit, the reason for it, or why I felt I ought to be around and available on Saturday with no delay or excuses if Jack needed me. I wanted to be there for him if this meeting turned into a disappointment or, God forbid, a catastrophe. I'd already turned down a ticket to the Driftwood's first production of the season, *The Gin Game*, the two-actor drama starring Margo, so I could hang around the house, waiting to congratulate or, worst-case scenario, console my son.

Scott watched me grope for words. "You probably have a previous . . ."

"Commitment," I finished, careful to avoid the word "date." "I do. But some other time?"

He drew a single breath before asking me out for the following Saturday, a fund-raiser for the Veterans Food Pantry. "I'm vice commander of the post so I have to make a welcoming speech. They do kind of a USO show organized by the ladies' auxiliary. In the past they held it at the VFW hall, really casual, with ribs, fried chicken, my kind of food. But we had such a big turnout last year, this year's is being held at Upton Abbey, the new resort over in Pinella. The one with the casino. It's supposed to be five-star fancy. More your kind of place."

Did I come off as five-star fancy? I told him I loved ribs.

"I think you'll like the crowd. It's a diverse group in terms of age, race, and background. Most of them have been stationed or posted overseas. So they're pretty interesting. We can always duck out early if you get bored."

Did he think I was an elitist snob?

"I'm looking forward to meeting them," I said. "And"—because no risk, no reward—"to being with you."

"Me too." His voice pitched up with surprise, perhaps at my boldness, then dropped to husky. "Very much, Nora." An awkward silence was followed by a pat on my knee and him rising from the chair. "Okay, then. See you Tuesday in class. And slot me in for next weekend."

"Consider yourself slotted."

He bounded down the stairs back to the path. This time no crashing through the underbrush. He was right about stealth mode. When he didn't want to be heard, he wasn't. And when he wanted to be heard, he made sure he was.

Well, that was an interesting afternoon, I told myself as I leaned back in the deck chair. *Now, don't start dreaming an hour with Scott into a lifetime with him, because you'll freak yourself out. Read your damn book. Embrace your fabulous you.*

I got to the part about how women are their own worst enemies, holding on to their hurt, and how it doesn't have to be that way if you open yourself to opportunities. Like I needed a book to tell me this. I put it down to take in an especially glorious sunset, and dream a little.

chapter twenty-two

It was Dr. Dirk DeHaven, Donor Dude's Delivery Day. And it was a dreary one. Not a respectable rain, but a laconic drizzle grayed the sky and washed everything a dull monotone. I was out early Saturday on the side path with my pruning shears, clipping away, when Jack found me.

Poor kid was desolate. "Can you believe this weather?" he said. "I mean, sunny for the whole last week and today it's a mess." He took in the scene. "What are you doing out here?"

I'd decided that since I might have to sell the house, I'd best get it in order before I called in a Realtor to check it out. I didn't mention the Realtor idea to Jack. He had enough on his mind, and if I got a hit from the networking I planned on doing that morning, the last resort might never come to pass.

"Just trying to clear the path. It's wildly overgrown," I said. "Better to work in a light rain than with the sun beating down."

He nodded, backed off two steps, and, arms out, palms up, asked, "So, what do you think? Am I presentable?"

He was wearing an open-collar knit shirt with the Duke Blue Devils *D* embroidered in navy on its pocket. The chinos were recently purchased—I'd seen him ironing out the manufacturer's crease—and now I reached over to snip off the plastic thread that dangled its price tag.

His hair, even without the glint of sun, shone a streaky blond. My son. So handsome.

I knocked off the "so," which would have made him squirm. "Handsome," I said.

"Casual enough for crabs?"

"You're doing steamed crabs for lunch?" It was hard to imagine the doctor with a crust of Old Bay Seasoning lodged under those pristine fingernails.

"Yup. Dirk got hooked on them when he interned at Johns Hopkins. He even has them shipped from B'more to Frisco. San Francisco," Jack corrected himself. "But he wants the real thing today. The whole nine yards. Beer. Paper on the table."

Servers dumped the hot, crimson-shelled crustaceans leaking succulent juices on tables covered with sheets of tan butcher's paper that at the end of the feast looked like a battlefield strewn with the skeletons of the vanquished.

"I figured The Claw is authentic."

A local dive, not yuppied up, the real thing. On second thought, maybe crabs weren't an odd choice. Maybe Dirk realized the diversionary potential of steamed crabs. All that shell cracking and picking sweet meat from crevices and prying it from tunnels would give the men a task to focus on if their conversation lagged. Plus he was a surgeon; maybe this was designed to show off his skills. In any event, they'd both have something to do with their hands. Jack's were in constant motion now, flexing, drumming against his thigh. He caught me noticing him cracking his knuckles.

"I'm nervous," he admitted. His left eyelid was twitching. "Dumb, huh?"

"Understandable. It's a first meeting. No one knows what to expect." *Or what to want,* I thought but didn't say. Or maybe they did, both of them, and it was only me who was in the dark.

"Yeah. Well, I guess I'm on my way. Ugh, look at that sky."

Storm clouds were gathering. "You can't control the weather, buddy."

"I know. But I wanted to walk the boardwalk. And downtown. See the stores. Maybe go to the lighthouse. The nature preserve. Stuff to keep him interested."

"He's more interested in you than the scenery. And you can drive him around. Not through the Mews, but the other places."

"I guess. Okay, I'm heading out. Love you."

"Love you too. This is going to be good, Jack." That's all I ever wanted for him. But this time, God forgive me, I didn't want it to be *too* good.

True to her word, the receptionist at the National Association of Dance Movement Therapists had fired off six job openings. I'd emailed my updated résumé with a sane-sounding cover letter to each of them. So far only one had responded, and that position was full-time, year-round, and way up in Pennsylvania. Plan B: for the rest of the morning, hunkering over my bedroom laptop, I sent emails to former colleagues telling them of my job search, renewing acquaintances with people I'd worked with or conferenced with over the years. "It's been much too long," every message began. And ended, "Let's do lunch when I'm back in town, but in the meantime if you know or hear of anything, please keep me in mind."

Early afternoon, I propelled myself through a series of mindless tasks, rearranging closets, folding laundry, Windexing all the downstairs glass. When I caught myself decrumbing the toaster tray I concluded it was absurd hanging around the house. I could be home from almost anywhere in Tuckahoe in under ten minutes. And maybe Margo was right that I coddled Jack.

"Overwater or overfeed any living being and you know what happens," she'd said, hitching her neck toward the stringy orchid hanging its head in my kitchen window. "Everything withers from too much attention. Except Pete Manolis. Now there's a specimen that can't get enough. In Jack's case, I'm not saying you should neglect him. I know what a lack of parental interest can produce: me. Not that I'm chopped liver, but that's in spite of Paulette and Bernie and at least partly because of a parade of loving nannies and high-priced shrinks. But you don't want to go to the other extreme, Nora. Don't turn Jack into a mama's boy. Back off. Give him a chance to stand on his own two feet. It's what you've got your degree in."

So with the evening stretching empty ahead and no calls or texts from Jack, which I decided meant good news, I switched my cell phone ringer to the alarming *William Tell* Overture, notched up the volume to VERY LOUD, changed into sneakers, strapped on a Love Strong backpack, locked the door behind me, and trotted downtown, trying to get my heart pounding from something other than nerves.

Half an hour before, the weather had turned abruptly from a gloomy dampness to an atmosphere as crisp and pale yellow as a fine chablis. The sky above was a tender blue and the scent around me was flowery and freshly washed.

Usually the air-conditioned interior of Turquoise Café lured summer patrons inside, but on this suddenly exquisite day, the patio, with its bougainvillea-woven trellis and its cobblestones shaded by twin willows, made an alluring oasis. Three of its four tables were taken, and when Em saw me through the window, she lit up and pointed toward herself, then the patio, signaling me to claim the last one for us.

She was ready for a break, she told me, and unloaded her tray's clove-and-cinnamon chai and plate of *börek*, made with *yufka*, a hand-rolled dough thicker than phyllo and layered with spinach and cheese. Low on caffeine, light on sugar, this late-afternoon snack wouldn't ratchet up my jitter level. She sat down with a sigh and the newest entry from a menu of Merry stories.

Merry had been keeping a ginger cat stashed in her bedroom walk-in closet, a hideaway set up with food, water bowl, and litter box. Sarman's subsequent eviction had spurred a major tantrum and slammed doors.

Erol had taken the brunt of his sister's fury because he'd tattled. In retaliation, Merry had painted his toenails pink while he was sleeping.

Our mutual friend Margo also knew from retaliation. She was a maven at it. She'd banned Merry from the Driftwood until the girl pulled herself together. Once Merry apologized to the family, including Erol, she'd be welcomed back. On probation, though. She'd better watch her step. As a bonus, Margo—who sometimes amazed me with her generosity, and Em related this with an awed shake of the head—had taken in Sarman as a resident of the playhouse. She bought a case of cat food and Merry brought over the litter box with a vow to clean it twice a week. One crisis, if not averted, at least managed.

On our second round of chai, something warbled though Em's monologue to stop me mid-chew. A whistle. Jack's recently suspended whistle, more sprightly than ever. "Here Comes the Sun." Had my head been screwed on straight, I wouldn't have been tempted to turn it and see my son walking in tandem with Sixteen past the patio toward the door. And maybe he wouldn't have seen me and called out, "Mom? That you? This is so cool."

After we wound up pulling two more seats to the little bistro table and Em escaped to fetch coffee, there was the expected awkward silence, but only for a few seconds, because what I assumed was Dr. Dirk DeHaven's bedside manner, a twist of confidence and charm, seemed to transfer easily to social situations. He was sitting across from me, Jack between us. He leaned in.

"This is a nice surprise," were his first words. "Jack wasn't sure you and I would get to meet this weekend. He said you thought you might be intruding. Let me assure you, you wouldn't have been. Aren't."

I smiled my default smile, the one that said I had absolutely no idea how to respond. The one that didn't involve my eyes or my brain, or so Margo had once observed. Now, that was who we needed here: Margo, who was a pro at making small talk and in character. I could see her doing "Mother Courage": earthy, gutsy, and totally without fear.

"Jack's been looking forward to meeting you," was all I could come up with.

"And I him." The grammatically correct DD reached for the last *börek*. Ah, a privileged man. "I understand that Lon . . ." He paused, while I felt a furious flush rising. *Lon,* I thought. He called him Lon? As if this interloper had the right to address my late husband by his given name. "Jack's dad," he amended, so of course I felt guilty for prejudging, "died when Jack was eleven. You've done a fine job raising him."

"He's a good kid," I said, as Em brought over their coffee, fresh tea for me, and cherry baklava, warm from the oven.

"I'm not a kid anymore, Mom." Jack was drawing a smiley face with his finger on the teapot's steamy porcelain.

"To a mother, her kid is always a kid, Jack." The Donor Dude had the temerity to wink at me. "But you *are* an impressive young man."

Then the conversation fell into a black hole, and all hands reached for their cups.

After two or three sips Jack said, "Tell Mom what you do. About your work. He does heart surgery. Mostly on kids, right?"

I'd had a hard time taking my eyes off Dirk DeHaven from the moment he sat down across from me. Now I had an excuse to stare, as he explained in layman's terms the intricacies of his work with pediatric patients who'd been born with miswired circulatory systems. He rerouted veins and arteries and gave them normal lives and life spans. It sounded important, *he* sounded important, and I could sense Jack puffing up with pride next to me, but I was only half listening. My other half was calculating the role genes played in shaping looks and behavior.

The doctor resembled Jack less in person than in the emailed photo.

There must have been a time lag since he'd posed, because his hair had thinned and gone almost all white, so there was no longer a perfect color match, and the newly exposed scalp and a swaggy chin made his face longer, less Jack's strong square. The eyes were dead-on. But not the mouth, which Dirk wiped with care to remove a smear of cherry filling.

"Whatever you do," Margo had said about meeting DD, "don't think about how weird it is that his semen got shot up your wazoo."

"Yeah, thanks for reminding me not to think about it. And you should talk. You had plenty of strange men's little swimmers freestyling up your fallopian tubes. Well, at least until they crashed into your IUD."

She ignored my insult. "There's a difference. You carried his *baby*."

"Potential baby. When it became a real one, it became Lon's, not freaking Sixteen's."

But maybe now he was here to claim what he thought *was* his.

"Mom, you okay?" Jack asked.

"Why?" Had I been glowering? "Just listening. It's all so fascinating, the advances in surgical techniques."

"That's right. Jack told me you work with amputees, veterans. Now, that's a noble calling. And there are all kinds of new technologies emerging in your field. Prosthetics with microprocessors. Advances in stump maintenance."

Jack made a gagging sound. "Hearts, okay. But stump maintenance? Jeez. Maybe you two could talk about this one-on-one next time."

Dirk slid a glance toward me while I thought, *One-on-one? Next time?* He said, "Jack's obviously not heading to medical school after college."

"Right. Or at least not doing anything too bloody. Maybe ophthalmology," Jack said.

Ophthalmology? Until now, he'd wanted to be a professional lacrosse player or a college athletics coach.

"So, Mom, this is what we've done so far today." He counted off on his fingers: a stroll on the boardwalk, a climb to the top of the Dunmore Point Lighthouse, back to The Claw for crabs and beer. After lunch, they'd spent an hour or so on the beach. (I felt an electric warning buzz prickle my skin.) "And we sat on Mooncussers Rock, kind of catching up." And there it was. The jolt. *Zap!*

Mooncussers Rock! To the Farrells that rock was a mystical talisman like the Blarney Stone in Ireland. Sacred. Lon had carried Jack out there in his pj's during his kindergarten summers and spun stories of the pirates who had ravaged the coast of Maryland, the rascal Mooncussers. On later August afternoons, my son had helped my husband make the rock into a fort, dressing it with the toy soldiers and miniature artillery of Lon's childhood. That was Lon's rock. Lon's and Jack's damn rock, and on the first visit Jack had taken the Donor Dude to plant his ass on it.

I couldn't look at my son. Or at his sperm donor. Thank God Em had returned to check on us so I could stare helplessly at her.

"Anything I can get for you?" She swept her question to me, catching my desperation.

Yes, you can get me back my old life, I thought. Even the last eight years of it without Lon were better than what I suspected lay ahead. They'd stolen my rock. It was just a symbol, but that was the point of symbolism. It stood for something.

"Actually, you can help us out here, Mrs. Haydar." Jack slipped his iPhone from his shirt pocket. "Mom is lousy with a camera. Sorry, Mom, but you know it's true. It's the French Revolution with her. 'Off with their heads.'" I managed to nod. He held the phone out to Em. "Would you mind?"

He called the shots. First, the two men stood side by side, Dirk's hands clasped behind him like an English duke's, Jack's arms dangling purposelessly. For the next few, they moved closer together. Then Dirk clasped a hand on Jack's shoulder and my son's grin broadened.

I was nursing my tea, wishing it were bourbon, when Jack called out, "One with you, Mom."

Oh . . . dear . . . God.

There was no arrangement that didn't tick me off. With Jack in the middle we looked like the standard family portrait. Wrong. But left to right—Jack, Dirk, me—made me the outsider.

"Very nice," Emine said when she'd snapped at least five and she and I thought we were finished. Jack moved out of the last frame, saying, "Thanks, Mrs. Haydar. Appreciate it," and took back the iPhone.

"It's getting late," I murmured. "I really need to get home." *I have wine to drink, a shrink back in Baltimore to call, and his new prescription for Xanax to fill.* I didn't say it, but, oh, did I think it.

"One more," my son ordered. "A shot of just the two of you."

The parental unit. Was that what he was thinking? No panic, but something like numbness took hold of me. I glanced at Dirk, who finally looked as uncomfortable as I'd been feeling before I started feeling almost nothing at all. He raised an eyebrow to me and shrugged, and we inched together.

"I need more happy, you two," Jack called out. I bared my teeth and held a facsimile of a smile by gritting them. He and I would have a chat later about which pictures were banned for posting on Facebook.

Then it was over. Correction, not quite. We had an exit scene that Margo would have given an eyetooth to direct.

I was already on my feet, which were awake enough to move me. The numbness seemed to have drifted up and settled around my chest, under my rib cage, so I felt like I'd inhaled a cloud. A little moist, a little thick, a little fuzzy. I wanted to get myself home before it floated to the brain.

I allowed myself to be drawn into Jack's embrace. He whispered, "Thanks, Mom. Big surprise, right? But you did great."

I patted his cheek and the stubble of five-o'clock shadow.

Dirk and I shook hands. For a split second of panic, I felt, or thought

I did, a tug that could have ended in a hug. I held fast. "Very nice meeting you," I said, holding my ground. The formality of the farewell did sound bizarre, which would have been Margo's take.

"Same here. I hope we do again," Dirk said.

"Yeah, sure you will," Jack interceded. "Dirk's coming back in August."

"Really?" Someone's voice that sounded like mine rang in my ears.

"Looks that way," Dirk DeHaven Donor Dude said. "I'll be in Baltimore, in any event. I've got a follow-up meeting at Hopkins."

"They've invited him to be a visiting professor in the med school. But you'd be working in the OR too, right?"

"It's all up in the air right now. There's a multitude of factors to weigh."

"But you *are* going to meet with them again."

"I am."

"And maybe stop by here."

Dirk laid a hand on my son's shoulder. "Or you can drive into Baltimore. We can take in a game at Camden Yards. You a baseball fan?"

"Here is better," Jack insisted. "Baltimore's a sweat swamp in the summer."

While they were debating, I waved myself off. They didn't notice.

At home, my message light was flashing. Emine checking up on me.

I'd call her later. Em liked to probe beneath the surface (unlike Margo, whose *specialty* was the surface). I didn't think I could handle that. Not yet.

The fleecy cloud had, as I'd feared, invaded my head. A swim might chase it, I thought. I changed into my bathing suit, not a new slimming one either—a flimsy, stretched-out halter style five years old with no power to girdle boobs, belly, or bum. Great, because I'd already sucked up enough for one day.

The ocean was warmer than I expected for mid-July. I didn't bother to scope for jellyfish. Let them watch out for me. I was swimming with the current in calm waters when I caught the outline of Mooncussers

Rock. I'd avoided passing it on my walk to the ocean, but it was a rock; it stayed in one place. Sometimes silvery veins in the duller minerals flickered in the sun and memories flitted around it along with the sand flies. From where I was today, though, it looked lifeless and solid, and I wouldn't let myself get close enough to see if the magic had vanished.

chapter twenty-three

Class the following Tuesday evening, and Lieutenant Colonel Scott Goddard was holding me in a rather compromising position, pressed so close that I was sure the American flag pinned to his left pocket would leave a patriotic imprint on my right bazoom.

My left hand was placed properly on his upper arm, which was solid, the muscles toned under the summer-weight shirt, and his biceps tightened as I ran my thumb over it. This stroke was not approved by any dance system I knew of, but the scent of him, the tempting nearness of his flesh, his neck, his jaw—I just couldn't help myself. My right hand, which was lightly grasped in his, got a return squeeze. I heard him chuckle. At that moment, I wanted to dance with him into a clichéd sunset.

He may have been thinking the same thing, because Bobby had already announced, "Change partners," three times, but Scott wasn't having any of it. When I reminded him of the switch rule, he gazed down at me with a half-fond, half-ironic smile and held on tight. "So sue me. Take me to dance court. Even if I lose, I win."

A few minutes later we were jitterbugging to "Runaround Sue" when something went wrong, very wrong.

I heard before I saw. Sniper sharp, Scott saw before he heard, he told me later. Sight and sound were almost simultaneous, the blur of the drop and the *thunk* of a slack body hitting the polished wood floor. Morty Felcher's body. Then Marsha's bellow of shock, followed by her spiraling scream. Scott released me, sprinted to Morty, and dropped to kneel on the leg he'd been born with while barking behind him, "Call 911!"

George Powell phoned it in. It didn't look like Morty was breathing. Scott began CPR. Marsha thrashed in my arms in an effort to see what was happening. "Morty!" she cried. "Fifty-two years together. Don't leave me!" And what I thought, in the midst of the madness, with inexcusable self-absorption, was that she'd had him for fifty-two years and what a blessing.

He was breathing evenly by the time the EMTs arrived. Scott and I trailed the ambulance in his car.

"How was his pulse?" I asked him.

"Thready. Maybe a heart attack. Possible stroke. Or it could be something minor like dehydration or he's coming down with the flu." I leaned against Scott. As solid as a rock.

I said, "Now I suppose it's up to God and the docs. You did all you could."

"Maybe, but I've heard that before and it's not much consolation when 'all you could' wasn't enough."

One day, if whatever we were starting here took hold, we could go on a guilt trip, the two of us. I had baggage; he had baggage. We could schlep it together. There were worse reasons for an alliance than a common history of tough times. Then again, there were better ones. I thought how wonderful it would be to have this man by my side when I was on my feet and nearby to steady me when I got shaky—or ready to apply mouth-to-mouth when I needed it.

I decided, especially after what I'd seen tonight, I could rely on him. That was progress.

The entire class gathered in the ER waiting room. It was two hours before the nurse came out. "Who's here for Morton Felcher?" and everybody stood. The nurse laughed. A good sign. "He made it," Scott murmured.

"Mr. Felcher wants his wife," the nurse said, and Marsha dashed forward. "That's me. Fifty-two years."

"Congratulations, hon. Come on back with me." To all of us she added, "They're going to implant a pacemaker. He's doing fine so far. And he's got quite a sense of humor for a man just returned from the dead. He ought to do stand-up . . . once he's standing up."

Scott drove me home. But before we reached the house, he pulled into a space at the end of Surf Avenue at the margins of a drape of light shed by the streetlamp so it was mostly shadows that merged for our kiss. It was a different kiss from the previous ones, more tender. After all, we'd faced death together. But then one kiss merged with another and urgency replaced tenderness and one touch led to another and, in what I interpreted as an expression of love of country, his hand strayed to the spot on my skin that had carried the imprint of Old Glory. He also reconnoitered the surrounding territory.

When we came up for air Scott released me and flicked on the soft interior light.

"Honestly." His head was tipped back and I took in his profile, as brilliantly cut as a silhouette on a Roman coin. "I couldn't be happier that Morty's alive. But"—he shifted to face me—"I've got an evil side that would like to kill him myself for pulling this stunt tonight of all nights. Look at you. I never realized your eyes are so blue. The thing is, Nora, I had a special evening on deck for us. I thought we'd go to my condo after class and kick back. I bought champagne and . . . You really do have beautiful lips—you know that?"

It was late. I was suddenly tired. "Is it on ice, the champagne?" I blurted, mainly to divert him from my lips.

"It's in the fridge."

"Keep it chilled. Saturday's coming up fast."

"Not fast enough for me," he said.

And that's how we left it when he dropped me off in front of the house. The pathway lamp illuminated the sweet bay magnolia tree so its white flowers bloomed incandescent against the purple darkness, but the truth is, I could have found my way to the door by my own glow.

"Where have you been?" My son snapped his focus from the laptop screen and what appeared to be the Skyped image of . . . I moved in . . . Dirk. Back in San Francisco, I assumed.

"Hi," I said to Jack, who'd swiveled his chair to confront me.

"Hi." I ducked into the camera's eye to wave at DD in California.

"Hey, Nora. Good to see you. Jack, I'll let you go. Now you can relax, son. Bye, all." The image vanished.

Jack surveyed me for a long moment. "Do you know what time it is, Mom?" He squinted at the computer's date-time logo. "Past midnight. I've been crazy worried about you. I called you three times. No answer. It's Tuesday night, okay, maybe with class you're running late. So eleven. But midnight? Where've you been? Do I have to imagine why you didn't pick up your phone? Or my messages?"

He was getting awfully close to the line, and I flashed him a barbed-wire look. I pulled out my cell phone, and yup, the light was flashing, furiously, reproachfully, it seemed to me.

"Sorry. I was in the ER sitting under a sign that prohibited cell phone use because it interferes with diagnostic equipment."

He did a double take. "Holy crap, you okay?"

I told him about Morty Felcher.

"Wow. All right. But next time call me, like, as a courtesy. Please? So I don't worry."

"Agreed. Sorry again." *When did I become the teenager?* I wondered. But the bigger question was, when had Dirk DeHaven started to call my son *son*? And what the hell did that mean?

"He called him *son*." I'd rushed to phone Margo the next morning. "'Now you can relax, son,' is exactly what he said when they were Skyping."

"Oh, for heaven's sake, you get your knickers in a twist over the most trivial things. Son. The generic 'son.' As in 'buddy.' Or 'kid.' I call Merry 'kid' sometimes. Does that make her my daughter, God forbid? Sweet child, but so troubled. I mean, you met the Dude. No fangs or horns. You think he's trying to steal your baby boy? Come on. Even you said he was friendly and approachable and he treated you with respect. It doesn't sound like he played the entitlement card either, like, 'I'm a world-famous healer. Kiss my ring.'"

"No, but you could sense his effort to be a regular guy. Except he's not regular, Margo. He treats the children of emirs and princes. He probably has a room at home lined with autographed pictures of the grateful parents. A gallery of the rich and famous."

"Like in Pete's man cave, you mean?" Pete's prized possession was the signed photograph of him with President Reagan when he was named MVP in the Orioles' last World Series win. The prime minister of Japan was also up on that wall next to Bono and under Madonna.

"Regular guys are highly overrated in my book," Margo drawled. "You think Scott Goddard is standard issue with his Silver Star, his magic leg, and how he gave Morty Felcher the kiss of life or whatever? He's no regular guy." Her tone turned sly. "I'll bet he's extra-large all over. Well, you'll find out Saturday night."

"With you everything is about sex." I regretted it the instant I said it.

Now I was in for an update on Pete's performance in the bedroom, X-rated, no doubt.

But Margo surprised me. Her response was far from prurient. It was romantic, in fact. "And what's wrong with sex, may I ask? It's fabulous with the right person. And mine is suddenly his old self again. Young self."

So Pete was back in the saddle and his wife's good graces. No mention of the other—imaginary, I was sure—woman. "You just need to decide on your right person, Norrie. Now, you're certain it's not the world-renowned and, may I add, *divorced* doctor, who happens to be the provider of half of your son's chromosomes, which makes it very convenient?"

"If it were up to Jack . . . ," I began. "He just about lassoed us together." I described the photo shoot. She hooted.

"You can't blame the boy for trying. He's working out the emotional geometry. How the pieces fit. So of course he sees you as a prospective couple. I bet you'd make the *National Enquirer* as a touchy-feely story. Sperm man weds egg woman twenty years later. One big happy family. Personally, I wouldn't count the Dude out. He could be your in knight in shining armor come to rescue you. For one thing, you'd never have to worry about money again. The Surf Avenue house wouldn't have to go to market. He'd probably love a place in Tuckahoe, especially if he makes the job at Hopkins permanent. Think on it. You wouldn't even have to work. There's your answer. That would solve everything."

"No, it wouldn't. I love my work. I want to work," I protested.

"But you wouldn't *have to*. Money buys options."

"Whatever, it's a moot point. Dirk didn't show a scintilla of interest. Trust me, there's no chemistry on either side."

"Nonsense. It's much too early to tell. Or for him to make a move. All I'm saying is, don't shut any doors. Or"—I could almost see her wink through the phone—"open any too wide, too soon, if you know what I mean."

I didn't. I was dealing with a Jewish Confucius. I didn't know what the hell she was talking about and I was afraid to ask. What I did know was that my life was already a patchwork quilt of complications and I didn't need any new material.

As if I had any say about that. Incoming emails had pinged a few times during our conversation and I checked them as soon as I got off the phone. Two starred new ones. I'd been getting sweet notes from some of the people I'd emailed with my job hard-luck story, but nothing tangible or even promising. This response was from Tess Gaffigan, whom I knew from the psych hospital a decade back. She was now the social services honcho at the National Care and Rehabilitation Centers of America.

Tess had written:

We may have something for you. I'd like to meet with you sooner rather than later. How does next Tuesday at ten sound? My office is at corporate HQ in Bethesda.

The second email was from Nate Greenberg, Lon's New York agent, burbling that he'd found the perfect writer, someone named Hector Fuentes, to finish *Thunder Hill Road*. From Nate:

Short notice, but just heard Hector will be in Washington for a writers conference from the eighteenth through the twenty-first. I could take the train down and we could meet for lunch. Monday's good for him. You?

I went to Hector Fuentes's Web page and read the list of his credits—magazine articles, short fiction, two moderately successful novels under his own name. And Nate said he'd been writing unacknowledged for a famous mystery author, doing the real work while the big name swiped the glory.

Suddenly the week ahead had turned complicated. Good complicated, or so it appeared at the starting line. Problem was—and I knew this from too much experience—life had a way of moving the finish line. I made a note to pack my running shoes.

chapter twenty-four

The Upton Abbey Resort and Casino, site of the vets' food pantry fund-raiser, was a cathedral whose developers prayed to the god of excess, British style. Twin doormen were dressed as Beefeaters, costumed Tudor gentry roamed the lobby, and the décor was late Balmoral Castle with accents of brass, crossed swords, and hunting prints hung on oak-paneled walls. According to a plaque near the door, the VFW event was being held in the Mary Queen of Scots Room, which, considering how the lady ended up, struck me as hilarious.

Our entrance into Queen Mary's chamber caused a noticeable dip in the decibel level. One moment it was a whirlwind of chatter, laughter, and clinking crystal; then the crowd caught Scott entering with me and the noise lowered to a buzz as elbows poked and whispers were traded. *Scott Goddard's with a date. Who?* You could almost hear the question hum through the crowd.

"Looks like we got their attention," Scott said as he took my hand to lead the way to the bar. "This is going to be an interesting evening. I'm having a martini and I highly recommend you do the same."

Tom Hepburn, drained of his usual sparkle, came to greet us. He was still on antibiotics for pneumonia and wasn't allowed alcohol, which must have cramped his style.

When Scott clapped him on the shoulder, he lit up. "You two should work the room. Your fans await. More than that, they're dying of curiosity about this lovely young lady. You are looking especially fetching tonight, Nora." Tom was on automatic flirt, but you could see his heart wasn't in it.

We left him nursing his glass of ginger ale and threaded our way among the guests, Scott presenting me as his friend Nora. The men swept swift recon glances, but the women, some wives, some retired military, took their sweet time checking me out. I didn't blame them. I was an unknown quantity, an outsider, and their regard for Scott was evident in every handshake, hug, and backslap. Would any woman be good enough for the local hero? Then again, I piled up points just by not being Bunny. As Scott introduced me, I turned on the low-level charm.

"Listen to Mother Margo," my girlfriend had advised. "I know the drill. These people are military. Remember I played Nellie Forbush in *South Pacific*. Off the field, this bunch doesn't go for flash and bang. You're aiming for understated. Pretty, not bowl 'em over. Pearls, not diamonds." She'd meant more than my wardrobe.

As for my wardrobe, she had one stipulation and it wasn't for the fund-raiser but for what she'd named with a wink the après-party party. Access to the essential me had to be via a stripper zipper.

"It's a strange phenomenon," she'd mused. "A man who can repair a car engine and untangle the guts of a computer can't deal with anything complicated on a woman. Take that as a metaphor if you wish, but I'm talking buttons and hooks and eyes. Trust me, dearest, you don't want him having to do engineering mid-hard-on."

When I started to protest her assumption that Scott and I . . . that we would be . . . she overrode me. "Oh, come on, Little Miss Innocence. Do you want to get laid, or don't you?"

"Well, if you put it that way." I caught a breath. "No, I'd rather make love."

She'd flashed me a contemptuous look. "Idiot. Love takes time. Laid is instant gratification. Get 'em while they're hot."

She had a point, but not necessarily mine.

While the roast beef was being served, Scott excused himself and moved to a platform up front. As if he'd snapped an order for silence, the crowd hushed. He took a breath, then launched into his keynote speech. It was extemporaneous, straight from the heart, and brief. He talked about the plight of unemployed or underemployed veterans and how some families would have broken apart or wound up in shelters without help from the food pantry. He concluded, "This is our tenth year and our work is needed more than ever. So please open your hearts and your checkbooks. We have to take care of our own."

After dinner, there was a show billed as a USO tribute featuring entertainment from earlier periods when America was at war. A vaudeville routine from World War I. The VFW Women's Auxiliary Silver Slippers tapping to "Chattanooga Choo Choo." A Marine gunner singing a beautiful rendition of "I'll Be Seeing You." When he crooned the line, "I'll be looking at the moon, but I'll be seeing you," Scott's hand, nesting mine, squeezed it. Finally, we all stood to sing "God Bless America."

Then, just as everyone thought the party was over, there was a surprise. Max Cassidy, the developer of Upton Abbey, took center stage. He wasn't going to miss this opportunity to welcome Tuckahoe's warriors to the resort, he announced. He wanted to personally thank each and every one of us for our service, and that included spouses who kept the home fires burning. He wanted us to know that Upton Abbey would offer priority employment to all veterans and—here, he took a dramatic pause—he was proud to present Lieutenant Colonel Goddard with a check for ten thousand dollars to support the food pantry. Scott strode up to grasp the other end of a large poster-board check. The resort's official photographer snapped a series of grip-and-grins, one of which would no doubt make the front page of the *Coast Post* with a headline proclaiming something like "Local Resort Gives Back to the Community. Casino Helps Poor Vets." And then, good deed accomplished, commercial plug done,

Max Cassidy sailed off on a tide of applause. Margo was right. The man had style.

In the wake of the cheers, Tom Hepburn edged to my side and said, "Now, that was a very nice ending to a very nice evening. Scott's got to be walking on air, and you, my dear, are a hit. That's the intel I'm picking up."

I thought Tom might have defied doctor's orders, because now his glass of ginger ale wafted the smoky scent of scotch and for a few seconds the old twinkle returned to his eyes. But it dimmed quickly.

"While we have a moment alone, I'd like a word."

"Of course, Tom."

"I'm a man for straight talk and I think you can take it. You know I never had any sons, and Scott's like a son to me, and he would bayonet me if he knew I was telling tales out of school. I like you very much, Nora, and I can see Scott's gaga over you. But I don't want anyone to get hurt here." He paused for a wheeze. "That man, one in a million, has been through hell."

"I know," I said.

"What do you know? Or think you know?"

"I read his medical chart during intake at the studio two years ago. I saw the newspaper stories. He came close to being shipped home in a casket. With his level of injury, it was touch-and-go. He could have bled out before a medic got to him."

"He saved a buddy. Did you know that?" Tom poked a finger in my direction. "Dragged him to safety and did it on an almost severed leg. Hence the Silver Star. But that's one thing. Every soldier is aware of the possibility of death or injury in combat. It's always lurking out there and Scott's entire career until Iraq prepared him for it, so it never had a chance of breaking him. It was afterward that almost did that."

"PTSD?" That tumbled out of me, from the therapist, not the woman.

Tom's smile was indulgent. "Sweetheart, anyone who's been on the front lines comes out a different person. Anxious, pissed off, at least for a while. You'd have to be crazy not to be changed by what you do and see in combat. But no, from all I know about it and him, the colonel is remarkably free of what they used to call combat fatigue when I was in Vietnam. What he has is a serious case of PTBD."

"I never heard—"

"Post Traumatic Belinda Disorder. That bimbo Bunny? She almost did him in. I'm not going into the gory details, but he came close to losing everything." Tom inhaled a raspy breath. "So, however you two wind up, for better or worse, I'm asking—no, I'm *begging*—you to be kind to him." He took a slug of what I was now sure was scotch, although it wasn't just the alcohol talking. "Even the strongest man can be undone by a woman. And he cares for you more than you know. You be good to him, y'hear?"

I was stunned by the fervor of his entreaty. "Copy that," I said.

Reassured, Tom nodded, and then he vanished.

Five minutes later, Scott and I took advantage of the announcement of door prize winners to slip away.

As we exited into the hall, he said, "I am so ready to put my feet up and taste that champagne I promised you." He stopped to give me a tentative look. "You up for that? My place?"

I'd given thought to some version of that question since our first kiss under the streetlamp. And I'd been tugged by an impossible attraction to Scott Goddard long before then. But now impossible had become possible. We were twenty-one-plus, of reasonably sound mind (though the rush of pleasure that bubbled up as I gazed at him made me wonder), and we were both free. There was nothing holding us back. Even I, who'd banked my precious guilt as if it earned interest, knew that. And *felt* it.

Beyond Scott, on the brass plaque, I'd have sworn I saw the likeness of Queen Mary wink at me.

"Sounds good," I said, and, at least for the evening, I sealed my fate. The way Mary did when she said whatever it took to lose *her* head.

We didn't talk much on the way home. We reviewed the entertainment and replayed Max Cassidy's presentation of the check and then lapsed into a gentle quiet. That's when I noticed how hard Scott was gripping the steering wheel, which made me wonder if this was a white-knuckle drive for him. Occasionally, though, he reached over to squeeze my embarrassingly clammy hand. At one point, I felt a rivulet of sweat trickle into my lacy bra. *Relax,* I told myself. *Just go with the flow.* It works for the ocean.

His condo was a villa surrounded by trees and bathed in the glow of a full moon. As he turned the key in the lock, a couple of short yelps greeted us. "That's Sarge's welcome-home bark. He knows you're one of the good guys. Believe me, you don't want to be one of the bad guys."

The shepherd bounded over as we entered. "Hey, boy. You remember Nora. The pretty lady." Sarge gave me a quick once-over, then swung and butted his head against Scott's right shin. "Smart dog. He knows he'll give himself a concussion if he hits the wrong leg," he joked.

Sarge had peed, pooped, and played Frisbee from nine to nine thirty, according to the note propped on the hall table by the neighborhood teen who'd been hired to walk him. But now it was past eleven.

"I need to take him out for a quick walk, but it will be his last outing for the night," Scott explained. "Then he'll trot into his crate and we'll have the place to ourselves."

He shot me a significant look. I felt heat splash my cheeks. The shepherd turned questioning eyes on me. I crouched down to hide my giveaway blush and stroked his smooth coat. "Better safe than sorry, right, boy? Ready for a walk?" Sarge whined assent high in his throat.

"You can come along if you want, Nora." Scott removed the leash from a hook on the wall. "Or you can stay and make yourself to home, as my mom liked to say. Settle in. Try the chocolates. They're Swiss. I ordered them online. I hear women like chocolate, and you said at dinner you prefer the dark kind."

Now, that was sweet. The gesture as well the truffles from Teuscher. More confirmation that he was just starting out on the dating road and this was as new to him as it was to me. He'd mentioned that his experience with women since the divorce had been limited. And how could he extrapolate from twenty-five years with the wife from hell? *Mean,* I scolded myself, as the worst part of me snickered silently.

My feet were killing me. The shoes were not hooker stilettos, but they were higher than my usual sandals or sneakers and not broken in. I wasn't broken in either, and my official debut evening had exhausted me. The sofa looked plump and soft and the coffee table held a remote tagged "Stereo." It was too inviting to turn down.

"I'll stay in and kick back, thanks."

But after the door closed behind him, I didn't collapse into the cushions. I snatched a cube of dark chocolate for energy and made my way barefoot around the living room, taking advantage of the opportunity to see how Scott Goddard lived and what he surrounded himself with, what brought him pleasure and comfort, picking up clues about the man himself.

The sofa was tweed, a good choice with a dog that shed. Common sense. Two chairs: one brown leather, probably from his late mother-in-law's house, old and worn to a glossy patina. Bunny wouldn't have appreciated its beauty. She would have ceded this chair to him with good riddance. Or maybe it wasn't from a place they'd lived in together; he may have chosen to leave that marriage with as few reminders as possible.

I walked over to inspect the contents of his bookshelves. Tom Clancy, of course, and Sun Tzu's *The Art of War*, Machiavelli, and Daniel Silva, all expected. But also Jane Austen and Flannery O'Connor. I flipped open the cover to find a bookplate imprinted with Scott's name. Interesting man. Then. There. No, couldn't be. Between *The Sun Also Rises* and *The Sea-Wolf.* Yes. Yes, with a jolt of heartbeat so strong I had to grab the shelf to steady myself: *Wild Mountain.* The spine confirmed it. Lon Farrell. I laughed without reason, withdrew the book, and turned to the title page. Beneath the tiny stylized fish, the visual icon of the book, there was my husband's handwriting. Blurred. Again there was no real reason for my tears, which made a watercolor of a still life. I blinked twice, clearing my vision enough to read, "For Scott, There are fictional heroes and real ones. With admiration for the latter and my personal good wishes," followed by my husband's familiar signature.

The inscription was undated, but I could pinpoint the time. The spring *Wild Mountain* was released, Lon had done a flurry of signings at bookstores up and down the shore. Scott must have been between deployments that year. Someone stateside could have had the book signed and shipped it to his base, but an eerie tickle told me the two men had met.

Maybe that should have freaked me out, but it did just the opposite. I like seeing connections. Links. Patterns disguised as coincidences. After the first smack of shock subsided, I replaced *Wild Mountain* in its slot between two greats, gave the Hemingway a fond pat, and picked up the remote on the way to the sofa.

I clicked. Rachmaninoff's Prelude in C-sharp Minor surged through the room. One of Lon's favorites. Finally weirded out, I moved on. Past Christopher Cross and "Sailing," Santana and Sheryl Crow. Lon had played "Sailing" ad nauseam the first summer I spent at the beach house and he had a thing for Sheryl Crow. I finally landed on Lady Antebellum's "Need You Now." Lon was no longer around when that hit the charts. I leaned back against the cushions and, lids lowered, drifted with the music, rousing only when I heard the rasp of a throat being cleared nearby. I opened my eyes slowly to find Scott grinning down at me. "Got in a snooze, huh? Good for you. Sorry we were out so long. Nature took a while to call. You did okay?"

"Fine."

"Let me get him bedded down. It will be quick."

He stopped in the kitchen on his way back. I heard the fridge door slam and he materialized with a dark green bottle and two wine glasses. "It's California, not French. I try to buy American."

"As long as it's bubbly, it could be from Brooklyn," I said.

"You're from Brooklyn, right?" He set the glasses on the coffee table.

"Born and raised."

"Then Brooklyn champagne would be vintage."

He popped the cork and poured. He watched intently as I took my first sip. "Very Flatbush," I proclaimed. "Assertive and bold with an undertone of bus exhaust and a hint of kosher hot dog in the finish."

He laughed. "You're witty. Besides being beautiful."

"Beautiful? Me? Now? My hair is messed up and I've got hardly any lipstick left."

"You don't need lipstick. In fact, I think we should get rid of the last of it. And let's mess your hair a little more."

The first kiss was bubbly. The second carried its own fizz, which shot straight to my brain, causing all the unnecessary muscles to relax, but my skin, which he stroked with a look of astonishment, came to life under his touch. I traced a finger along the angle of his jaw and he groaned. He brushed his lips along the inside of my elbow. Who knew that was an erogenous zone? *Oh God.*

We made out like the teenagers of our generation. Then we grew up. Scott stood and backed off to unbutton his shirt, removed it and his undershirt, and folded and stacked them neatly at the end of the sofa. I figured that was his military training kicking in.

He offered me a hand, a lift to my feet, pulled me against him, and went for the stripper zipper on my dress, the one Margo had said was essential for easy entrée. She'd been right about the zipper, wrong about the bra. The man who knew how to load a Beretta M9 didn't fumble with a Bali 34D.

He put space between us so we could take each other in. I folded my arms under my chest, supporting what had never, from their first blossoming, been perky. It didn't seem to matter to him. His pupils fired. "Incredible," he said with a sexy twist to his smile.

I nodded, my throat tightening. His arms and upper torso were well muscled, and I was happy to see just enough hair grassing his pecs so he didn't look airbrushed to glossy like a hero on the cover of a romance novel. He was a real man, and from three feet, then one foot, and up against him—measured any way—Scott was hot. A rhyme that entered my lexicon the moment I thought it.

As I went for *his* zipper, he said, "Not here," and hitched his neck toward the hallway.

I don't remember who led as we staggered into the bedroom.

We faced each other in the moonlight that poured through the window.

As I moved to unbuckle his belt he murmured, "Damn, I want you," but then he broke away. He walked across the room and turned off the lamp on one of the night tables. Then he closed the bedroom door. I wondered why; Sarge was crated. Now the door blocked even a sliver of light from the hall. When he came back, he lowered the shades.

That plunged us into total darkness and me into disappointment. I liked to make love with my eyes open. Seeing the action was another turn-on for me. As I felt around empty space for him, I wanted to assure him that he didn't need to hide the techno leg, and if he removed it, that was okay too. I'd seen my share of prostheses on and off.

Not his, though. I remembered how, just before we concluded his intake interview at the dance studio and after we'd gone through his medical history and his objectives for the class, he'd suddenly shifted his gaze from my eyes to his hands, which were capped over his knees. His eyebrows had knitted as he said, "I suppose you want to see the prosthesis. The fit." But he'd made no move to bend over, to roll up his trouser leg. In fact, he'd tightened the grip on his left knee.

Body language was my second language. I had no problem reading those gestures. He didn't want me to see his leg.

Some do. Proud of the technology that gave them back their mobility, the craftsmanship that fabricated their state-of-the-art prostheses, they want to show them off. Or they're interested in my professional assessment of the socket fitting. Or they're just comfortable with how it's turned out.

Some don't. It's not usually shame that holds them back. They're just private by nature.

My sense back then had been that the colonel was private. Of course, I'd respect his boundaries.

Maybe I should have brought it up then, because I couldn't now. We were in a different place, and in this place, his bedroom, we didn't know each other that well. And how ironic was that, considering where we were heading—if I didn't crash into furniture on the way.

Suddenly he was next to me. I knew because I heard his breath catch and inhaled the scent of him, not his piney cologne, but a primitive mix of healthy sweat and alcohol that made me reach for his fly. He caught my wrist midway and brought it to his lips; then, hands splayed against my shivering back, he steered me to what I discovered as he laid me down on it was the bed. He sat down on the edge, peeled off his trousers—I heard the belt buckle hit the hardwood floor—and I supposed his jockeys came off too. No folding this time. He was moving fast and we were at a point where rules didn't apply. I pitched my Victoria's Secret bikini like a pro. For all I knew, it hooked onto a blade of the ceiling fan, a lacy flag of surrender. Or victory.

Scott lay down next to me, and we began operating entirely by braille. The smooth coolness of the sheet under my skin. The roughness of midnight shadow on his cheek. The sinewy, sinuous probing of tongues. Our breathing was hushed, the space between us thick and steamy. I slid my hand over his chest, his taut nipples, then rode the muscles of his belly to his hardness. He broke the silence with a groan, then a baritone laugh when he found me soft and wet.

All was going well. Then accidently, while stroking him, my hand strayed to the flesh of his left thigh where it joined the prosthesis. His startle reflex rocked the mattress.

"Sorry," I whispered. "Pain?"

"Not at all." He shifted toward me.

Ah, I thought, he was sensitive there. Heightened nerve response, probably stimulating for him, and traced my finger downward. A mistake I discovered when he grabbed my hand and moved it to his right side. "Better," he said.

But it wasn't. For a while he was all over me. Hands and tongue, attentive, inventive, and incredibly exciting, but when I wanted to touch him, pleasure him, he deflected me and distracted me with overwhelming sensation. His practiced trigger finger found a ready target. When he allowed me to find him again, he was soft.

I did everything I could think of to arouse him. Another mistake. He was a sharp guy and he must have sensed I was working (not good) frantically (even worse). Finally, he tugged me up, drew me close, and cupped my chin in his hand. "Enough. Don't knock yourself out. It's useless. I am. Useless." Such a sad, sad word.

"Scott."

"Listen—" He cut me off and rolled to face me. I felt his breath on my cheek. "You know I'm attracted to you, Nora. Frankly, attracted doesn't begin to describe what I feel. And if you have any doubts about that because of"—he groped for the word—"because of tonight, don't. Please. It's just that I get going, and at some point, a switch in me turns off."

So I wasn't the first. Had there been previous dates? Or just his wife?

After a sigh that drilled through the darkness, he said, "I don't know what's going on. Maybe I'm not ready yet. Maybe I never will be because I'm terminally screwed up. I don't know. Right now all I know is . . . I'm sorry."

I answered too quickly, too chirpily, "No need. And no big deal. First date. Well, first real date. Both of us overanxious. Plus the champagne. That can interfere. Look, this happens." I continued to blurt, clumsily trying to make things better, making them worse. "If you want, we can take a break. I'm not Cinderella tonight. It's not like I have a curfew."

He didn't answer that either. Or he did, but not with words.

He flicked on the bedside lamp, and before my eyes could adjust to the light, he was off like a shot to the bathroom. After a few minutes he emerged tying the belt of a terry robe.

"Let's get ourselves dressed and get you home," he said.

He drove with the radio on. No music. Nothing that would evoke love, consummated or un. He tuned in the shore's all-news station, but when the report changed from a flood in Mississippi to the latest casualties in the Middle East, he switched to ESPN's local outlet. The night game between the archrival Orioles and Yankees had ended with a spectacular catch by a rookie, a Cuban kid, all of nineteen. Jack's age. The announcer crowed, "What we saw tonight in Camden Yards was the best second baseman in the Orioles' lineup since Pete Manolis. Castillo hasn't got the Greek Icon's power at the plate yet, but he's on his way."

Pete was out of town and Margo was probably sleeping soundly, storing up strength to interrogate me about the après-party party. I'd duck her tomorrow and be out of town on Monday, which would give me time to invent something to satisfy her. She'd never get the truth from me.

When we pulled up to the spot in front of my house, Scott fixed his gaze on the windshield and said, "I really appreciate your accompanying me to the reception tonight." The tone was dress-uniform, white-glove formal, as if his bare fingers hadn't been billeted in the most private part of me less than an hour before.

"I had a good time," I answered.

"Right. Me too." His tone was unconvincing.

He didn't mention seeing me Tuesday. Or ever again.

The sky through the window was cloudless. Inside the car, the barometer was high. I could feel the pressure of Scott's desire to get me out of my seat and out of his sight as soon as possible. We traded good-byes on a handshake-turned-squeeze that I initiated.

Ever the officer and the gentleman, he waited while I walked up the path lit by the garden lamp. That's when it really hit me, hard, that we were over, because that was a path we'd once danced so hopefully and should be dancing together and I was trudging it slowly and alone.

At the door, my fingers trembling as I inserted my key in the lock, I heard him gun the motor. By the time I turned for a final, futile glance, he was gone.

chapter twenty-five

After a sleepless night, I pulled myself together and left for Washington at nine Monday morning for my lunch meeting with Lon's agent and the prospective ghostwriter. The plan was for the three of us to meet at a restaurant off Pennsylvania Avenue, Maison Madison, which was almost as old and venerated as the White House. I followed the maître d' to a table near the window where two men were chatting. At the sight of me, Nate sprang to his feet and Hector Fuentes laid his napkin on the gold charger and shifted his chair back so it scraped the hardwood.

"Nora. You made it. I was worried about traffic on the Bay Bridge," Nate said.

We didn't kiss in the double-peck continental style. Nate wasn't that kind of guy. He hugged me decorously.

"You look well."

Thank God he hadn't said beautiful or wonderful or any of the exaggerations that would have come off with my makeup at the end of the day. I'd swiped on extra to cover the bags under my eyes and the worry lines crossing the bridge of my nose. I'd had a bitch of a Sunday, thinking about Scott and the night before, ruminating on my romantically blighted future, my lousy luck, my selfish perspective on what I'd named "the incident." Not my fault, I reminded myself. It had nothing to do with me. I'd tried to smother my obsessing with the Sunday *Times*, the magazine section, the crossword, but it refused to die because nudges conspired to revive it. Margo called twice—I let her ring—and Jack crashed my afternoon with questions.

He caught me in the kitchen. "How did your date go?" His thin layer of innocence didn't fool me. He was probing about the status of Scott and me as a couple.

"Fine. The VFW put on a good show," was my evasive answer.

"You going to see him again?" Offhandedly.

I shrugged. "Time will tell."

That was the truth. I had no idea if Scott would turn up Tuesday for ballroom. He might catch a convenient cold. He might make an appearance in body only, emotion checked at the door. Who knew what he might do? Or me? Who knew what I'd do if and when I saw him?

"You know," my son said, keeping his eyes on the knife he was using to spread peanut butter, "he's not the only fish in the sea."

Ah, now we were getting somewhere. I answered, more pointedly, "Did you have a specific fish in mind?" knowing exactly which one he'd hooked for me. He shrugged and tossed the knife into the sink with a resounding clang. End of discussion.

This meeting with Nate about *Thunder Hill Road* was a welcome distraction. Nate was saying, "Hector and I were talking about the state of publishing these days." By then, the ghostwriter was on his feet and I realized we had the odd couple here. Nate was six-three and this fellow couldn't have been more than five-two. Nate had a deliberately shaved head. Hector's was jumbo-sized and overgrown with a thicket of pitch-black hair. A black unibrow perched like a balcony on his domed forehead. His skin was a stark white and he wore a black shirt and black-and-white polka dot bow tie whose horizontal lines accentuated the breadth of his barrel chest. He gave off the impression of a bulldog, compact, strong, and, from the brisk double nod and the knuckles rapping impatiently on the tablecloth, ready to pounce. He flashed me a gap-toothed smile and ducked a quick bow on the introduction.

I sat, the men sat, and Nate filled in the first few awkward minutes with an update on his other literary projects. He was a senior VP now, having climbed the ladder on rungs of charm and talent at one of the most prestigious agencies in the country. When he ran down a list of his current clients, I recognized every name from the *New York Times* bestseller list. Yet with all these live wires, he'd made room for a dead man. Nonetheless, a dead man with the potential for profit. If *Thunder Hill Road* turned out to be a hit, the agent got fifteen percent of the action. And if Hector Fuentes copped even partial author credit, Nate had a rising star in his galaxy.

Hector was Nate's choice. He made that clear over manhattans for the men and a glass of Riesling for me. I waited to be convinced. I'd skimmed Hector's two credited novels, the second having absorbed most of my non-obsessing hours the night before. It was well crafted but not genius, not particularly original. Then again, we had original here already; Lon had done that work. All the book needed was six or seven chapters to tie up the story line and finish up or off the characters. After speaking with Nate the week before, I'd thumbed through two recent releases Hector had helped produce in the factory operated by one of the world's best-known suspense writers. It was hard to tell where the old lion left off and the young cub took over, and that counted in the ghostwriter's favor. He'd captured the essence of his master, and that's what I wanted for *Thunder Hill Road*. It was essential that Lon's work and the ending chapters meld seamlessly.

Nate worked through his spinach ravioli and peach tart to convince me. Hector mostly listened as he chomped through a Kobe burger on brioche. Then, as the conversation moved to a discussion of writing styles, he spoke up. "I understand Lon Farrell," he said, wiping béarnaise sauce from his chin. "I can channel him."

I wondered how this small, pale man could contain my large and ruddy late husband. Lon's protagonist in this book was a crabber on Maryland's Eastern Shore. I asked Hector if he'd ever been on a crab skiff, seen one, captained any kind of boat, could swim.

"In here." He tapped his temple. Which was poetic and clever, but I wasn't persuaded that imagination would be enough.

That's when the agent, who was something of a magician, as many are, plucked a large, thick manila envelope from his briefcase and extracted a manuscript. He waved the fan of paper over the table.

"Read at your leisure, but not too much leisure, because I'm eager to get going. Hector's done three chapters that pick up after the house-fire scene. They've got Miles, Fran, and Seth, which should give you a good idea of how he handles that triangle. And Bones, of course." Bones was the Chesapeake Bay Retriever who in an earlier chapter had snatched a five-year-old from a riptide. "I want you to see how he moves the plot along and how he captures Lon's tone." He slid the pages back in the envelope and extended the package.

An unexpected gift, John Updike had written, was the only one worth giving. I wasn't so sure. This was too much of a surprise. The promise of something with Scott had nudged Lon from my real life, but reading this would summon my husband back, either howling with fury at being surrogated once again (the Donor Dude Redux) or crooning gratitude for hauling him back into the limelight, even posthumously. Saturday night had left me feeling pretty fragile. I wasn't sure I could handle Lon's specter bounding back.

I accepted the manuscript as its author observed me with twitching eyelids. He'd written sixty pages purely on spec at Nate's urging. It was the only way, Nate said as he fiddled with the bill, to show me, really show me, how right for the job Hector was. I had to be absolutely on board with the choice. My comfort was his first concern. He concentrated on adding numbers while telling me that.

We said our good-byes. Hector gave me his paw, a short-fingered square of padded flesh, for a gentle handshake. I got another, warmer hug from Nate with instructions to reread Lon's last two chapters of the unfinished manuscript before starting the new material so I could judge continuity.

"I'll call you Thursday to see what you think," he said.

"No, no," I protested. "Not before next week. I'll try to get to it over the weekend. Seriously," I added as he gazed at me with eyebrows askew in a half-forlorn, half-chastising expression. "I'm up against the wall with the rest of my life."

"Seriously, aren't we all?" he said, as he flourished his signature on the American Express receipt.

The two men stood politely to watch me leave. When I glanced back, which had been the habit of my life, a habit I would have done well to break, I saw maybe a third, maybe Lon. But he was very faint, just about transparent, and I decided to ignore him.

The Baltimore house was empty when I arrived at six. No ghosts. No birds, bats, or snakes, which occasionally invaded in summer. Not even a live mosquito, though I'd never gotten around to having the screens repaired beyond taping the holes myself. Only one problem, but it was major. Before leaving for the beach, I'd set the thermostat to switch on the air-conditioning at eighty-five degrees, as Lon had always done. But something must have gone kerflooey with the cooling system. We hadn't lost power. The lights worked; the TV news blared; the fridge held a chilled bottle of wine. But it had to be at least ninety-five inside the house.

Under previous circumstances, I would have called my landlord, Mr. Lieber, to let him know, since the service contract was in his name. But Mr. Lieber Jr. had hijacked his father, shipped him to a nursing home, and taken over the business, which included the row house that Senior had first rented to Lon the summer before he started teaching.

Mr. Lieber had been honored to have a famous author occupy the house on Calvert Street. As a token of his great respect, he had set the rent ridiculously low and raised it with small increases only five times over the next two and a half decades. When we expressed concern that we were taking advantage, he said to Lon, "Look, I'm a rich man and any extra from you wouldn't make me so much richer. Also I can tell my friends at the country club that great books are being written in the first piece of real estate I ever bought for investment. Maybe one day I'll put up a plaque."

And although Lon and I had periodically talked about buying a house in the city, the advantage of home equity and the tax benefits, we kept falling back on the lure of the low rent and how it would break Mr. Lieber's heart if we moved out, especially after Jack came along. "Like a grandson to me. I don't have any grandchildren of my own." Mr. Lieber dropped by even more often to check the plumbing, the state of the furnace. Sometimes on an evening visit, he had a glass of schnapps with Lon and the two of them would help Jack build bridges with LEGOs.

After Lon died, Mr. Lieber wouldn't think of an increase for the widow of a once famous author with a half-orphaned child. I was grateful for the break. But if we'd bought a house in the early days, there would have been something to sell now, money to support the Tuckahoe place so our summers wouldn't be in jeopardy.

The house was stifling. It was after six and BGE was closed for anything but an emergency like a gas leak. I went from room to room, opening the windows to let in air, which declined the invitation. It wasn't just the temperature that was intolerable; it was the vast emptiness of the house, which seemed to me a desert on two floors. I swiped and polished, which took care of the fine sift of dust, but I couldn't wipe away the musty odor of neglect or a feeling of loneliness that went way beneath the surface.

In another month, Jack would be returning to school, and by September I'd be back here alone, but with a possible new twist that made me uneasy. If things kept chugging along on the current track, I might have to share my son with his Donor Dude on the holidays. Thanksgiving in California—could Jack resist? Winter break in San Francisco? The thought, plus the house—musty and gummy—made it hard to take a full breath. So I grabbed a pillow and headed to the back porch, where I made a bed on the glider, churned for a while, and finally got lulled to sleep by the familiar grinding and honking music of the city.

You would have thought that out there in the oppressive dark, I'd dream of the night beach, icy waves, cooling breezes, but I didn't. What I remembered on waking the next morning was that I'd danced in my dreams, the cha-cha, the salsa, the Lindy Hop, dances that didn't involve the embrace of a partner's arms.

My schedule for Tuesday got screwed early with a seven a.m. call from Tess Gaffigan, the woman who might have a job for me. A situation had cropped up at headquarters that forced her to shift our appointment from ten a.m. to five p.m., her only available spot that day. She hoped I could make it and the change wouldn't inconvenience me too much.

Well, yes, to the first, and no, to the second.

I left a message for Jack, telling him I was spending another night in the city. I texted Bobby that there was no way I'd be back in time for class, so he and Larissa would have to cover for me. And I asked him to announce that I'd gotten tied up in Baltimore. I didn't want Scott, if he showed up, to think I was ducking him. Damn. I didn't want to do anything that made him feel worse than he already did.

Then I called BGE and reported the air-conditioning situation and instructed them to phone Lieber Jr. to schedule the fix. No need to stay in the house any longer than necessary.

Scott wasn't on my mind—Jack was—when I drove over to Poplar Grove, the psychiatric hospital where I held Motion and Emotion sessions three times a week, September to June. This morning's destination was the office of Josh Zimmerman, my professional colleague, unofficial shrink and mentor who'd come through for me before with advice about my son. Josh's self-deprecating assessment of the quality of this service was, "Just a reminder, kiddo, you get what you pay for." But he sold himself short. Josh was good.

Poplar Grove was situated at the end of a graveled, treelined driveway that opened to a view of a sprawling three-story building dating from the 1920s. An interior refurbishing in the eighties had installed larger windows and lighter colors so the atmosphere was cheerful and airy and smelled like eternal springtime—the scent of promise manufactured by Glade. Poplar Grove maintained a locked ward for a few of the determinedly destructive, *self*-destructive mostly, but the majority of patients roamed freely through the halls and into the lounge with its high-def TV (though the programs were monitored for depressing or violent themes), the computer room (though some sites like porno and pro-anorexia forums were blocked), and the library, with shelves of books vetted for optimism and positivity. The humor section got a lot of space, as did biographies of subjects who had overcome adversity. Nonfiction was benign. Stephen King was persona non grata, as were vampires, shapeshifters, and aliens—many of the readers were already sufficiently haunted by phantom creatures of their own creation. Blood and gore were outlawed. I wouldn't have been surprised if they'd excised war from *War and Peace*. All was calm, all was bright.

Of course, some residents walked the halls with no destination in mind. The constant ambling was a hallmark of those grappling with depression or high anxiety, and it worked for much the same reason that dance therapy did—activity elevates endorphins and lowers stress hormones. The strollers, the staff called them, were aimlessly on the move all day and at night until their sleepy-time drugs kicked in.

That morning, as I made my way down the second-floor corridor, I spotted a patient I'd worked with the season before, a young man who'd snarled at our final meeting that I was contributing to his abandonment issues by taking off for the summer. Now he shuffled past, obviously recognizing but ignoring me. I smiled and called out, "Hey, Jared. How's it going?" He called back, "Fuck you." His diagnosis had been something catchy like rage-management deficiency. The work must have been going slowly.

I got a more welcome reception at Josh Zimmerman's office. The sign hanging on his inner door had been turned from "Session in Progress" to "Available. Please knock." I tapped, heard him bellow, "Enterrrrr," and stepped over the threshold. He'd been transcribing notes, but now he swiveled to greet me, his face lighting with a smile.

"Well, well, look who's here. Miracles do happen. Nora. What a nice surprise. Good to see you." He was a hugger and he hugged with gusto, then danced a two-step back and pointed me to the patient chair. "So sit. Relax. I've got coffee, iced or hot. Iced, yes?"

After we'd settled in with our drinks and caught up on the gossip around the Grove, his grandkids, my Zumba classes, he said, "This is a social call because you just happened to be in the neighborhood?" The glance he raised behind his half spectacles oozed skepticism.

"Pretty much," I said.

"But not entirely. Something's obviously important enough to interrupt your sacred summer. I've got twenty minutes before my next appointment. The meter is running. Shoot."

He'd been on my email list for the begging letter so he knew my employment situation, though not its ramifications. I told him. He shrugged. "You'll work it out. This is a good thing, sweetheart, though it doesn't seem like it now. Remember what I always say about change."

"It's the mother of opportunity. But I gotta tell you, Josh, it's also the father of anxiety." Which elicited a laugh.

"Your interview later could produce the perfect fit. Or not. But something will turn up. You're losing sleep over this?"

"Sure, I lose sleep over everything. But at least I have a handle on how to deal with it. I've done job searches before. I'll continue to network. Actually, I'd like to discuss another situation."

He knew about the circumstances surrounding Jack's conception. I'd filled him in when I was struggling with my eleven-year-old's sorrow after Lon died. I'd wondered to Josh if it made a difference in the intensity of his grief that his dead father was not his biological progenitor.

He'd told me then, "Lon raised him. Lon loved him. Lon *was* his dad. So Jack will go through the same shit as any boy who loses a father. You haven't hidden how much you wanted him, what steps you took to bring him into the world. And Lon was the one who shared that with him. Which was brilliant. No, you're the primary force in his life now and his biologic link. You're the reality. To an eleven-year-old, the sperm donor, Mr. 1659, is just a number."

Well, he wasn't anymore, I told Josh. Dirk DeHaven was a living, breathing human being with a name and a life that looked like it was going to include Jack. He'd visited once already and he planned to return in August and I was scared of what might be coming next.

We talked about that for a while. How I shouldn't anticipate problems. That if they arose, I needed to act out of love and not fear. "What does Jack call him, by the way? How does he refer to him?"

"Dirk to him. Usually the Donor Dude or just the Dude to me."

"Good. And if he has any fantasies about the Dude being Superman or LeBron James, time and contact will shrink them."

This was when I took a deep breath and plunged ahead. "I don't know about Superman, but he's dropped hints about a fantasy that concerns me."

Josh leaned forward, hands steepled, nodding empathically.

"I think he sees us as a couple, the Dude and me. Dirk is divorced and age appropriate, so Jack's got the idea that we'd be a good match."

Josh stroked his beard. "He said that?"

"Implied it."

"Tell me," Josh urged, and I heard an undercurrent in his voice. Alarm? Amusement?

I gave him Jack's "other fish in the sea" advice. I rehashed Margo's geometry theory.

"I go with your friend. Jack sees the puzzle pieces fitting, the two sources of his DNA. The human instinct always moves us toward order and against entropy. 'Let's get it together' is the motto of our species. So does he have any basis in reality for this? For instance, did Dirk come on to you during the visit?"

I shook my head so vigorously I dislodged one of my earrings.

"And you, do you find the Dude attractive?"

"He's fine. I mean, nice looking, pleasant, kind of charming. But no, not the way you mean. No chemistry for me. Besides, he lives in California, though he may do a visiting year at Hopkins, which would bring him to Baltimore."

"Interesting, the Baltimore move. That's fueling Jack's fantasy. Not that I'm insinuating he has a point, but is there someone else in your life?"

I thought of mentioning Scott, but what was there to mention? I'd heard him call himself useless in his bedroom the other night. It was clear that *he* didn't see a future, or even a present, for us, so how could *I*?

I might have taken a second too long to answer Josh, but when I spoke, my voice was strong. "No, no one else."

"Then let it ride," my shrink friend said. "There's nothing pathological about Jack's thinking. In fact, it's logical from his perspective. Address it if it gets worse, or if it bothers you. If you do bring it up, treat it with respect. And if *no one else* turns into *someone else*, be aware you might get some initial resistance from him." He paused for a sip of his iced coffee. "That's it?"

Josh's other credo, besides the one about change, was, "If you don't have something to say, shut up."

"Okay," he said. "In any event, you want any more of my priceless advice, you have my number." He rose. "And I have yours." My time was up. At the door, he switched the placard and pecked my cheek. "As the song says, see you in September."

Which suddenly seemed not so far away. I had to get moving.

chapter twenty-six

I should have passed Go and headed directly to Bethesda. But I had five hours left before my appointment with Tess Gaffigan, and I couldn't skip a once-a-summer opportunity to stop at the Woodberry Kitchen for a plate of their best-anywhere oysters. It was when I was on my way again after lunch, stopped at the first red light off Clipper Mill Road, that my stomach suddenly churned. It wasn't the oysters.

I was within a few blocks of TV Hill, where four television stations clustered at the highest point in the city, so it wasn't that bizarre to see Dana Montagne, WBJ's news anchor, on this street. Her face, instantly recognizable, as familiar to me as my own, was beamed in high definition three times every weekday.

If she'd been stunning when she'd started out in her twenties—her features sculpted to just short of beautiful in a medium where beautiful would have been overkill—now, in her late thirties, she'd achieved tele-genic perfection. She projected warmth and an earned confidence that inspired trust and brand loyalty among all demographics. Beloved by Baltimore, and as I watched, my heart beating in my throat, it seemed she was particularly beloved by someone I knew—the man at her side.

Because I wanted to be sure, when the light turned green, I slid into a parking space a few slots back from the jewelry store from which Dana

Montagne and Pete Manolis had just exited. The Svengali and Trilby Studio produced one-of-a-kind handcrafted jewelry in platinum, gold, and precious gems. I'd salivated over its ads in *Baltimore* magazine. As the couple moved toward the sidewalk, I began to pray, *No, no, God no,* then, *Oh shit,* as my amen. It *was* Pete Manolis, Pete freaking Manolis.

His signature gorilla-length arms were very much occupied, the left one draped around the newscaster's shoulders, the right swinging a tiny lavender shopping bag with the jeweler's *ST* swirl-patterned logo. Gallant as ever, he was carrying the gift he'd just purchased for a woman who was definitely not his sixtyish secretary, Janet Buxbaum, or one of the groupies in Margo's paranoid fantasies.

They'd known each other for at least a decade, Pete and Dana. In the first few years after his retirement from the O's, he'd occasionally subbed for the weeknight sportscaster at WBJ. I'd seen her a few times at the Manolises' dinner parties, single, then married, recently divorced. I had to wonder how long this had been going on.

Just before I decided to get the hell out of there, she leaned over and said something to him that caused him to laugh large but without any detectable sound, not his standard roar. It was a laugh that kept their secret. Her return smile gave it away. Dazzling, even more dazzling than the one that cast a spell over her TV audience.

Poor Margo.

Tess Gaffigan kept me waiting a full twenty minutes before she appeared on the run in the hall outside her locked office.

"You're here," she said. No apologies. Just a jerk of the head to follow her. She was a small woman, but her heels—I noticed as I clipped behind her—were inappropriately in-your-face-for-work four inches high.

From the looks of her digs, a large corner triangle done up in chrome, glass, and a view overlooking downtown Bethesda, she'd come a long way since we'd hung out together at Poplar Grove years ago. She'd been a social worker then, doing clinical work that was a bad fit for her personality. Hardly a paragon of empathy, Tess was too judgmental, strident, always in overdrive, unapologetically ambitious, with no place to move and therefore frequently frustrated, which led to testy. But she was witty and bright and fun to be with for drinks after work or gossip cackled over restroom stalls. When she got the offer from National Care, she took off like a shot and never looked back. Correction: she looked back long enough to hit me with invitations to the company's fund-raising events or contributions to its nonprofit arm. I didn't attend but wrote token checks. So now it was payback time. I hoped she knew that.

As I stared at the desk nameplate and her title, "Director of Social Services," I wondered if the open position would require working under her. Not an enticing prospect.

She motioned me to the only seat across her skating-rink-sized desk, sat, and pulled a tablet from some niche onto her desk. She typed something into it, then stared. My file probably.

She looked up. "So." There was no offer of coffee, no cozy reminiscences. Her meter obviously ran at a faster speed than Josh Zimmerman's.

"I know who you are and I know what you can do. Did, anyway. The dance-and-movement program. Has anything changed?"

"Well, there have been numerous studies in the past decade that demonstrate the benefits—"

"Yes, yes." She actually waved to cut me off. "There are studies for everything. Given enough bullshit, you can prove the world's flat. I'm talking about your routines. The stretching, the expression, the individual journey material, the poetic expression—we've never done anything like that before at Nat Care. It would be an innovation here. And you're the best at it I know."

Her phone rang. She checked caller ID, said, "Screw him," and let it go to voice mail. "I was sorry to hear about your husband, by the way. I read the obit in the *Post* online, but I was in London for a conference. I hope I sent flowers."

She hadn't. "I was kind of in shock. I don't remember who did what. But thanks."

That produced a nod and a half smile. "Listen, this is the deal, Nora. Four days a week. Two sessions in the morning—that's when our older folks are fresh. The ones with dementia start going downhill after ten. And then—bear with me here—I want another session around four or even five. It sounds counterintuitive because of the sundown effect in Alzheimer's, but our medical team thinks activity late in the day mitigates it. Also, group gatherings tend to reduce depression for our guests with mood disorders. Especially in winter."

I took a moment to digest that. Something in the monologue had caught in my throat and I needed to clear it. "By morning sessions, what time do you mean?"

"We start early here. Maybe eight thirty. Breakfast is over and we'll get them on their feet. I remember you do fifty-minute sessions. So maybe another group at nine thirty? Then again at four, five, something like that."

"Wait. I have sessions in the morning? Then I leave. But I'm back in the afternoon?"

"The rest of the day is full. We give these people an enriched program. They go to PT, OT, group and individual psychotherapy. Art. Guest lectures. Cooking demos. We tried out pottery last year and it was a huge success." It had certainly been a hit with the Vintage board. "So yes, you'd be in morning and afternoon."

I could manage that. It would take a little zipping around Baltimore, but it was doable. I hadn't mentioned my summer-free requirement in my email, because I wanted to get my foot in the door, but we were down to details, so it was now or never.

"You remember I always had summers at the beach," I began.

"Right, when you were playing super-mommy with Jack. My God, he must be shaving by now. And that house of yours hasn't been swept out to sea?"

"Jack just finished his freshman year at Duke and the house will last for centuries." I felt myself hesitate at the edge of a cliff. Then I jumped. "I'm still doing summers in Tuckahoe."

"You've got to be kidding. You're still taking two months off?" She rolled her eyes, as light as a cat's but more readable. They spelled out, *"Give me a break."*

"Two and a half months and they're not off. I'm working." I told her about the dance studio. How we were five years in and holding our own, but I had plans to build the business. How that time away was non-negotiable.

I'd figured back when I'd jumped at the chance to interview that Tess would never go for my ten-month plan, but I was hoping that our history and my charm—not that either was of particularly high quality—might inspire her to work something out. Maybe we could negotiate a compromise, though Tess had never been the compromising type. As she blank-stared me, I slipped my handbag from my lap and slung the strap over my shoulder, preparing to stand for good-byes, expecting hers to be a snarl of "Why did you waste my time?" Instead, after what seemed like a full minute with her eyes closed, she popped them open and announced, "Okay. I'm good with that."

"You are?" I sounded far too incredulous. I wasn't much of a negotiator myself.

"I am, believe it or not." She tapped a stack of promotional brochures next to her laptop, then slid one across the desk to me. "We got to be number one in the country because of our creative approach to organization. We hire the best, and we hold on to them by keeping them happy. As for our program, though we have a full and varied array of activities, quality takes precedence over quantity around here. Summer has a different emphasis anyway. We have more outdoor activities like tai chi and sun salutations yoga. Also more water work. All of our facilities have pools. Our outdoor one here is on the rooftop. Gorgeous. Wait till you see it. And when we're finished here, I'll show you the studio that would be perfect for dance."

It took me a minute to register.

"Here? The studio is here? Is the Baltimore studio the same?"

"Baltimore? Did I say Baltimore in my return email?"

She hadn't. I'd assumed. "I thought Baltimore. You have a branch in Baltimore, near me."

"Off Roland Avenue. Much smaller than this one. Near you, huh? You still live in that place on Calvert Street. My God, I've moved five times since we worked together. No, you'd be here. We always try out our new programs at headquarters so I can keep an eye on how they're going."

I processed that for less than twenty seconds. "The thing is," I said, "my other clients are Baltimore based and my sessions with them are scattered through the week. You want morning and afternoon. That would mean driving back and forth between Baltimore and Bethesda five times on some days. And rush-hour traffic could turn an hour's drive into two. I don't see how I can do that."

She looked unimpressed by my problem. "You're a smart cookie; you'll work something out. And we'd make it worth your while. *I* would. I budgeted your project from my discretionary fund so I could leap policy. See what you think of this." She scribbled something on her memo pad, ripped it, and handed it over. We were close to the National Security Agency, but this was a rehab facility. Was her office bugged? Was that a security camera mounted on the picture frame on the wall across from me? Was that the reason she didn't just say the compensation figure out loud?

"My AA researched the going rate. But I want the best and I'm willing to pay for it."

When my gaze rolled down, it stayed there. On the number she'd written. With my two other gigs—the vets' center and Josh and company at Poplar Grove—I'd have enough to ensure the preservation of my summers and keep Jack at Duke and in lacrosse sticks. I'd be more than okay. Then again, I'd also need to put something aside for the long-term therapy I'd need as a result of driving a hundred and fifty miles a day.

"I think it's generous," Tess said. "You?"

I peeled my stare away from the scrap of paper and nodded. "Generous, yes. Very. Thanks." I sucked in a deep breath. "And I report to?"

"Me." She tapped the title plaque. "I'm director of social services. Oh yeah, you look thrilled. What, you want warm and fuzzy? Work for Build-A-Bear. Seriously, I'll leave you alone unless you piss me off, and I can't imagine what you could do to piss me off. Unless, of course, someone dies in one of your sessions. Then again, the old folks have to die sometime. Better with music than with tubes."

"The stumbling block is the back-and-forth between Baltimore and Bethesda. That would be a killer," I said. I didn't say that the idea of having her as my supervisor was almost as off-putting as the drive. Almost, because I liked Tess. She had a sailor's mouth and a bull's balls, but at least you knew what you were dealing with. Maybe it wouldn't be so awful. I waved the paper with the salary on it. "Nice. But couldn't we stack the classes on the same—"

"No." She led with her sharp chin and jutted her jaw. I remembered the shovel jaw. It meant she was digging in. "Maybe we can pick up your travel expenses. I'll think about it. Why the hell don't you move, anyway?"

"I'm going through enough changes in my life right now. Besides, I'll never get a deal like the house in Baltimore."

"You'll never get a deal like the one I just offered you."

Tess tipped her chair toward me. She reached out across the desk and patted my hand still holding the paper. "Also, it would be fun, us working together again."

I'd be working *for* her. Which wasn't the same as working together. I didn't say that. Fun? I was considering that when her phone rang again.

She looked and sighed. "Different asshole, but this one has an MD attached to it, so I'd better pick up." For the next minute she fired off a barrage of verbal bullets. "Impossible." "Sorry, but no." "It won't work." "No, I can't explore the options because there are none." "Report me to whomever you please. You won't win this, sweetheart." Sweetheart! "Why? Because your argument is laughable, that's why. Listen, I'm in the middle of an interview here." She winked at me, enjoying the sport. "I'm hanging up now." She clicked off.

My mouth was open. I closed it. She gave me a beatific—or was that amused? satisfied? triumphant?—smile. "Now, what was I saying? Oh yes, think about it. You don't have to make a decision immediately. The job doesn't start until November first, which is when the gal who runs the horticulture therapy program begins her maternity leave, which, I have a feeling—she's having twins—will go on forever. Betsy makes a lot less than that figure." She tipped her chin at the paper with the numbers on it. "But to reiterate, this whole dance-movement thing is my wild idea and it comes from my budget so I call the shots. I want to hear from you by September first so we can get our ducks in a row, orient you to the National Care brand. That gives you two months to rearrange what you need to rearrange and get back to me."

I couldn't imagine making it work. But if I didn't take it—I grimaced as I watched my beautiful beach house slide into the sea of oblivion.

Then I went off with her to check out the studio where she hoped I'd conduct my sessions. It was beyond luxurious, tricked out with a state-of-the-art speaker system, baby grand piano, multilevel bars, nonskid chairs for seated exercise, and a wall-mounted defibrillator. Everything deep pockets could buy.

I'd be an idiot to turn it down. Or a masochist to take it. Rock or hard place, my choice.

chapter twenty-seven

The rest of the week was a necklace of diamond-bright days. Not a cloud in sight, sun high and white, giving way to a waning sickle moon in an ink black sky. There was even a shiver-making meteor shower exploding above the ocean Thursday night. After the shake-up trip to the beltway cities, all I wanted was to bond with my house and my beach and extract every last drop of pleasure from my ocean. I taught my classes and took care of the studio's administrative details; then I hurried home to sit under an umbrella on the beach, listening to Andrea Bocelli and reading decades-old *New Yorker* magazines I'd found in Lon's office. My idea of heaven.

You'd think that after thirty years, my love for the house and the summers spent there, the infatuation of the early days, would have turned into a yawningly comfy T-shirt-to-bed, kiss-on-the-cheek marriage. But, no, just the opposite. The passion for the place and my time there was stronger than ever, maybe because I faced the threat of losing my precious Tuckahoe summers. I knew what those nearly three months did for my soul—how after cramped, rushed winters, they slowed my rhythm and lifted my mood, and that the endless sky over the vast ocean was there to provide perspective (should I choose to use it) for my own puny problems.

I still couldn't get over it: me, city born and raised, living steps from the beach, surrounded by so much natural beauty. My waking breath was of briny sea air. I fell asleep to the lullaby of the surf. I was constantly reminded of my blessings and, believe me, I didn't take a single grain of sand for granted. And then there was my friendship with Em and Margo, which flourished like honeysuckle in these hot months. I was incredibly grateful for that too. Now all of it was at risk.

Margo. I heard only one peep from her that week. She always became laser focused on rehearsals as opening night approached. She kvetched to me about costume flaws, slow pacing, unexpected changes, then tossed off a question about how I was doing. I said, "Fine," which seemed enough for her in her distracted state. We'd catch up on my trip when she had some time. She was sure it had been interesting, but she'd skipped breakfast and her lunch had just arrived. Merry was unpacking her salad so she'd better get some food into herself. Bye.

Em was caught up in high season at the café, so I faced the new reality alone. Well, not quite. The following afternoon Philippa Tarlow stopped over. Flip Tarlow and her husband were among the Manolises' closest friends and members of Margo's maven squad. The couple ran the most successful real estate agency on the Maryland shore. When I had called Flip to tell her, choking the words out, that I was considering— only considering, mind you—putting the house on the market and invited her over for a first look, I'd also asked her to keep it confidential. Not that my concerns would have interfered with Margo's current self-absorption, but just in case her focus slipped into a wider orbit, I wasn't up to her meddling.

"This is an absolutely knockout house," Flip drawled as I led her on a tour. "Good bones. Elegant proportions. Super traffic flow. Incredible light." And she loved what I'd done with it. I told her Margo had helped with the interior. "Of course, I see her signature style. It's stunning. However . . ."

I'd known the "however" was coming. A list of howevers was mounting on Flip's legal pad. The guest room looked dated and needed a complete overhaul. While I was at it, I might want to spiff up Jack's bathroom, which had taken a boy's beating over time. The kitchen was lovely, but the downstairs powder room needed all new fixtures. The entrance hall begged (her word) for a redo.

I was cruising along with her suggestions, tallying the costs of the improvements as we canvassed the rooms. Where was I going to get the thirty thou I figured it would take . . . so far? Then Flip redirected the conversation to a whole new level of pain, from stratospheric financial to deep down in the emotional center of my world.

"You do know it's a buyer's market out there now."

I hadn't known, but I shouldn't have been surprised. Over the last few weeks, I'd felt like a target of what my superstitious mother had called the *malocchio*. It was as if God himself had been giving me the evil eye.

"The thing is, you're competing in the second-homes category in general and in your price range and location in particular." Flip's smile, so inalterable I thought it might be tattooed on, flipped into an arch of sympathy. "There are three other homes comparable to yours available on the beach between Bethany and Ocean City. And yes, Tuckahoe has panache, but so does Rehoboth. Even Delaware being the land of low taxes hasn't helped move two listings that have been on the market there for almost a year." She let that sink in and hit me again. Hard this time. "What I think would make this house infinitely more marketable, because people like to plan for the future, is a first-floor bedroom."

"Which it doesn't have," I said.

"But it could."

All we needed to do was overhaul Lon's office. It was certainly large enough, and a few steps from a full bathroom. We'd strip the bookshelves, fill in that space with a wall-to-wall closet. "And voilà! A first-floor bedroom."

And voilà! A sacrilege.

Or maybe not. Could be this was just what I needed for my breakthrough. Maybe I could get rid of Lon's shrine if I knew his literary legacy was safe.

I got back to work reading the ghostwritten chapters, which, if they passed my test, would allow me the dream of a bestseller, a critical success, and money enough to keep the Surf Avenue house afloat.

Nate knew his stuff. Hector could write. He'd captured Lon at his best, the vivid river rush of prose of the early years. My late husband, who'd struggled so against the current in the later ones, would probably have been jealous of this fresh talent. But he would also have calculated the sales, predicted the reviews and the revival of his reputation. "Giddyup," I could hear him saying, one of my California cowboy's favorite expressions.

I sent Nate a businesslike email. "Essential: my approval of cover type size for Hector's author credit. Also I have final say on completed manuscript."

The return response flew at the speed of light. Hardly businesslike. "Yes and yes and yippee!" Nate's words virtually danced on my screen. "We're on our way."

Suddenly it was Tuesday again, and I was worrying about how Scott would handle our first encounter since our bungled bedroom scene. He handled it by texting me a barebones message late that afternoon. Can't make class tonight. Sorry.

During my mandatory foxtrot with Tom Hepburn, I asked offhandedly, "Scott's all right?"

"Far as I know," he said. And that was all he said before handing me over to George Powell for the final waltz.

I gave myself a pep talk on my solitary walk home. Our bedroom misadventure, plus the tone of Scott's afternoon text, plus his nonappearance in class . . . I did the math and it added up to over and out. I understood we were just getting started, and I got the reason he was backing off. Still, it was unfair, damned unfair, that when I finally found a man who made me feel something other than indifference, it fell apart for technical reasons. But that was nothing I could fix, so, I told myself, I'd just better suck it up, move back into the no-cry zone, and resume my regularly scheduled life—the one that had served me reasonably well for the past eight years, familiar and safe, with no rewards but also no risk. In the thick humid air, that logic hung pretty well.

At one fifteen a.m., after I'd thrashed about in bed since midnight, it all came tumbling down. So good-bye, logic. Hello, feeling, and the feeling was *ouch*. I toughed it out for ten minutes, staring at the ceiling before picking up the unfinished *Embrace Your Fabulous You*, but its uplifting platitudes only made me feel sadder. In a last-ditch effort to pull it together, I paced the widow's walk, tracing the supposedly mood-elevating pattern of an exercise I used in my Motion and Emotion sessions. It didn't work. Was I a charlatan on top of everything else? Eventually, I crawled back to bed, where I snatched snippets of sleep until dawn.

I had a Wednesday class, but there was no way I could Zumba! with an exclamation point after my raggedy night. I made a call to Larissa, who agreed to sub for me.

By ten, I was cocooned under a striped umbrella with a cup of coffee and a book featuring a brave heroine. The sky was overcast, with occasional spritzes of drizzle, and the beach was almost empty. Also quiet, until my cell phone let loose a shrill cry from Margo. Depression must have addled my brain, because I picked up.

She didn't bother to say hello. "Get over here. Now. I need you."

"I can't," I said. "I'm having my own problems."

"That's an incredibly self-absorbed response, Nora. Mine are worse. Besides, it will be good for you to focus on someone besides yourself. Therapeutic."

I groaned. "Can't you come here? My therapy is reading the latest Nicholas Sparks and the heroine is about to—"

Margo interrupted. "My life is not a romance novel, Nora. It is real and it is crashing down on me and I don't trust myself to drive. Not in my current condition. I'm serious."

"It had better be a matter of life or death," I warned.

"Matter of death or death. Suicide or homicide."

"Okay, then," I sighed, "but I'm not dressed. Give me fifteen."

Twenty minutes later I let myself in her front door, heard her call out, "Upstairs," and found her sitting yoga style on the bed, still in her leopard-print silk pajamas, eyes red rimmed and shooting furious sparks. An open, picked-through box of See's chocolates seductively nuzzled her left thigh.

Her first words were not a greeting. In fact, hearing them, I almost pivoted to exit. She looked up from her iPhone to ask, "It reeks of sex in here, doesn't it?"

"Excuse me?"

"You can't smell it?"

I drew the quickest, shallowest breath that would sustain me. It did carry the tang of spent passion.

"Ugh, Margo, have you no boundaries? I'll never be able to look at Pete again. Honestly, if I didn't have to inhale, I wouldn't."

"Well, don't hold your breath. You're going to be here for a while. Think Eugene O'Neill. Think *Long Day's Journey into Night*. Only morning."

I begged, literally, for as few details as possible, so what she settled on was that this latest crisis had begun with Pete waking at dawn to hit the bathroom—the commode flush roused her for only seconds—and sometime later nudging her awake. He'd been eager, willing, and more than ready for a sunrise romp on their California king.

"Six o'clock, top of the morning, and he's on top of me rock-hard nearly nonstop for more than ten minutes." She managed a weak smile. "That was the main course. The hors d'oeuvres included some new stuff, inspired by the girlfriend. I guess. Well, thank you, Brianna or Kendra or whoever. My husband went through his entire repertoire to please me and, dammit, he succeeded. Give the gentleman two cigars, as my agent Lou Beigleman, of blessed memory, used to say."

We then fast-forwarded to Pete heading to the shower and a wiped-out Margo collapsing back to sleep. When she woke he was gone, having left a note on her pillow. "Tomorrow. Same time, same station."

"That's when I panicked." She popped a truffle pacifier into her mouth and said between sucks, "I'm thinking the girlfriend can be no more than thirty, thirty-five at a stretch, and if I have any chance of holding my own, and Pete's, it's time to step up my game. But how?"

I could feel a grand "uh-oh" coming on.

"Then the lightbulb. Pete takes these vitamins called Super Silver designed for fifty-plussers. Okay, so I'm three years short of fifty, but I thought I'd give myself a head start. I read the dosage info. One pill a day. If one is good, two should be better, especially the first day, like a booster shot to get me started. Drastic times call for drastic measures, right?"

She waited for a sign of agreement, didn't get it, and pressed on. "I read the label. The ingredients were only vitamins and serotonin in megadoses. That seemed harmless enough. So I shook two out"—she took a pregnant pause—"and got not Super Silver. I got Super Low-Down Dirty Liar, Super Cheating SOB." Chocolate spittle gathered in the corners of her mouth.

She opened her hand, finger by finger, for dramatic effect. On the cushion of her palm rested two diamond-shaped blue pills. "Read 'em and weep. You read. I weep."

I read the stamped name aloud, "Pfizer."

"Wrong side. Flip it over."

"Viagra."

The word hung in the air like a red flag. Margo gave off an about-to-charge snort. "Vi-freaking-agra. Sneaky Pete's been hiding Viagra in his vitamin bottle."

I sighed, waited a beat to choose my words, then responded, "It's one of the best-selling drugs in the country. Many men his age resort—"

"Noo-no-no. Didn't I tell you Dr. Fleckleman warned Pete that taking those erectile-dysfunction meds was dangerous with his low blood pressure? He could die from it." Her voice lowered to a Madame Frankenstein timbre. "*I* almost did."

"Died? You? From Pete's taking Viagra?"

"Not by injection. But yes, I was still groggy, and if I hadn't spotted the name, I would have swallowed those two blue pills thinking they were vitamins. Then I could have come up with a hard-on who knows where. Like my tongue maybe. Or my nipples. Or I could have died from a massive erection of the left ventricle."

"Margo . . . ," I began again, knowing it was as futile as standing on the tracks in front of a bullet train. She was picking up speed, heading for the crazy station.

Or maybe not so crazy. The image of Pete swinging the bag with the bauble he'd just bought for Dana Montagne and the goofy-cum-smug smiles they'd exchanged while leaving the jeweler's popped into my memory bank. I tried to cash it out. It wasn't going anywhere. I tried to rationalize it away. "But he's still having sex with you. That doesn't add up."

"It adds up to brilliant. Have sex with me and he deflects any suspicion of another woman. He hides the Viagra so I'll think it's me who's the big turn-on. But the pecker-picker-upper is really to keep the mistress happy. The tramp he's risking his life for."

This was the time I could have commented that his hiding the Viagra might have had to do with male pride, not wanting his wife to believe he needed pharmaceutical assistance in the bedroom. Or maybe I should have reported what I'd seen in Baltimore.

I was Margo's best friend. Didn't best friends support and protect? But I wasn't certain beyond an unreasonable doubt. Coward that I was, I went for common sense, which never struck a chord with Margo.

I said, "The time has come to talk to your husband. You're past due."

"The hell it is. The hell I am. We've been through that before, you and your Sister Loretta pious advice. And I've been through it with Pete and his fake explanations. Talk is cheap, Nora. Divorce is expensive. What's Maryland's state motto? *Fatti maschii, parole femine.* Men act, women talk. Well, screw the founding fathers. Am I not an actor? Actors act."

"Oh God, what did you do, Margo?"

"Calm yourself. Nothing that will land me in jail on a felony charge. I just put things back where they belong. The Viagra is currently stashed in my jewelry vault. The bottle in the medicine cabinet now holds its original contents, Super Silver. And wouldn't I love to see Pete's face when he sleep-walks into our bathroom to fortify himself with his little blue pill and finds little white ones that promise nothing more than a bunch of nutrients for, as the label says, 'the most important parts of you' and not what he thinks is his most important part."

"He'll know you did it."

"Damn right he will. I want him to. Let him bring it up. I'm dying to hear his bullshit explanation." At which point her chocolate high crashed and her gaze turned bittersweet. "Look, Pete's going to leave me. I don't know the for-who or the when, but my gut and his weird behavior tell me he's already halfway out the door. I can't stop him, but I'll be damned if I'm going to let him go quietly. I've got a plan."

Of course she did.

"First I'm going to hire the best private detective on the East Coast to follow my wandering husband. I'll give the guy the key to the Baltimore house and have him check the medicine cabinets for Pete's extracurricular Viagra. I'll have him take photos of the happy couple in compromising positions. Then, after I stack up the evidence, I'll get the most low-down lawyer, the most vicious matrimonial shark money can buy, and when the time is ripe, there will be an attack that will make *Jaws* look like feeding time at the National Aquarium. If this marriage is going to be shipwrecked, count on only one survivor." She stabbed herself in the chest with a perfectly manicured fingernail. "One. Yours truly. *Moi.* The Margonator."

Then she toppled forward into my arms and sobbed like a baby.

She pulled herself together by opening night of *The King and I.* After the breakdown on the bed, after my "show must go on, get your ass to rehearsal" lecture, she'd hauled herself to the theater, where, according to Emine, who'd heard about it from a stunned Merry, Margo had taken out her pent-up fury on the cast, whipping them into shape with no mercy. The result was a flawless, flamboyant production that commanded three curtain calls and the lead actress summoning "our brilliant New York director, Margo Wirth Manolis," to the stage for a bow. She dipped her head once in modest acknowledgment. Then, with the applause still ringing, she darted offstage left and (this next generous gesture was as much Margo as her self-indulgence, her need for attention; this was what had always tipped the scales in our friendship and my loyalty to her) returned tugging a dazed Merry. I knew the girl had painted scenery, scoured for props, done the cast's makeup, and most of all kept Margo on track as she threatened to go off her emotional rails.

Margo had even gifted her with a new Android to replace the old cell phone Adnan had handed down to his daughter. This one had all the bells and whistles so Merry could record rehearsal glitches for Margo's review, send her photos of scenery construction in progress, and remain available during the boring hours playing Plants vs. Zombies and Candy Crush, among the apps Jack, playing big brother, had loaded for her.

Meryem Haydar was credited in the program as "Assistant to the Director." Now she joined the cast in an ensemble hand-linked bow, grinning on the upsweep, looking like the kid next door. No black lipstick, no blue hair, just jeans, a white shirt, and that exultant smile.

Emine, sitting next to me third-row center, swiped her eyes. "She's a good woman, Margo. Merry will never forget this night. I will never forget this night. Her father have should been here."

He should have, I thought. He should have seen what the troupe thought of Merry and how hard she'd worked. He should have heard the applause for her.

In the theater lobby, I said to Em, "Margo tells me Merry's a great help and everyone loves her. So I assume she's doing much better."

"Yes. *Maşallah, nazar değmesin.* May the evil eye not touch her. Except there are problems with Adnan. A storm between them yesterday."

My heart sank.

"Ramadan starts in a few days and we received an invitation from the Turkish-American Association of Maryland to their Iftar dinner, which breaks the daily fast. An important event. A United States senator will be there. Other influential people, Turkish people in business. A family had canceled so they only just called us. The problem is the dinner is a week from this Saturday and Merry was counting on being here for the final performance. Especially for the cast party afterward. But Adnan is insisting she go with us. So of course they clashed."

Emine replayed the scene for me. Merry had been standing next to her brother, her fists clenched, as Adnan announced the invitation and added, "To attend such an event honors our family."

"Family means except for me, right?" Merry had said. "Because you and I made a deal."

"This was unexpected, but of course you and Erol must come."

"Yeah, well, you can't do this. I'm assistant to the director. After the last performance, they strike the set. I have to be at the theater to help."

Adnan jabbed the air near her, but without touching, "You have to be where I tell you to be."

"What? No." She reared back. "I can't believe this. You don't get it, do you? You do know we're not in Turkey anymore, right? This is America. Here men and women are created equal."

"But you are not a woman, Meryem. You are a child, *my* child, and you will obey me. You are part of our family and you will go to the Iftar."

Merry curled one side of her lip in disgust. "So you're like some dictator or something? Well, we'll see." She was seething. "And you." She'd whirled on Em. "You let him get away with all this crap. You never stand up to him." Her pupils flared. "You're both so . . ." She'd stomped from the room, rumbling an avalanche of unsaid curses.

"A daughter talks like that to her father," Adnan had muttered after her. "This is what they do in America?"

When Emine tried to pour soothing waters on the fire, he switched into Turkish. "Don't take her side on this one. Do not cross me."

Em said to me now, "He and I haven't spoken since. He's furious. She's furious, and I'm caught in the middle."

"You think she'll go with you Saturday night?"

She shrugged and pulled her shawl around her shoulders as if she were cold. We were in the street, walking through a hot, thickly humid night, heading for our cars. "You saw her face on the stage. She loves this so much. I don't know what she'll do. Or him." She gave me a wan smile.

"There is a Turkish saying that translates, 'If you spit downward, it hits the beard; if you spit upward it hits the mustache.' In other words, either way, the situation sucks, as my fresh-mouthed daughter would say. I can tell you this: if she defies him, there is no telling what he'll do. He said he will take steps. That's the phrase he used, 'take steps.'"

"Which means?"

"Only God knows. Pulling her away from the theater. Sending her off to boarding school in the fall. Shipping her to Istanbul. All would be disaster." Her voice quavered when she repeated, "Disaster. And I don't know how to stop it."

chapter twenty-eight

The following Tuesday night I was in front of the room demonstrating the salsa with Bobby when Scott waltzed in. He was seven minutes late according to the clock on the far wall and I had just emerged from a double turn into a low dip—that was Bobby showing off—when I saw him walk through the door. Maybe the spin had left me dizzy, but I jerked so hard in surprise that Bobby looked down at me and said, "You okay, honey?"

"Don't drop me," I said. And if *that* wasn't Freudian.

Scott and I danced only one dance together that night. As the class scrambled for partners, I didn't approach him and he made no move toward me. Our pairing was accidental. Or that's the way it seemed, anyway, but he was an expert at military strategy, so maybe not. When everyone sorted themselves out for the final foxtrot, the two of us were left for each other, with each other. Of course, the music had to be something so romantic, so ironic—"Let's Face the Music and Dance"—that I broke out in a sweat flash even before he touched his fingertips to mine.

I moved robotically through the first chorus. During the second, he spun me out, unwinding me gently, slowly, and in perfect rhythm. On the return, I felt the flat of his hand trembling against my waist. I heard him clear his throat twice before he said in a hushed voice, "Uh, Nora, I was wondering if you had time tomorrow, maybe we could grab lunch."

My brain said, *Wait, what? I thought you'd gone MIA on me. You've been out of sight for more than two weeks and suddenly you're reporting for . . . Wait, what?*

"Lunch?" I repeated stupidly.

He nodded. The look he cast me was appraising, doubtful.

I forced myself to take a calming breath, then hummed something that must have come through as assent, because he went on. "I was thinking someplace outdoors where I could bring Sarge along, if that's okay. I'd like to keep an eye on him for the next few days. He tore his paw on a scallop shell. That kind of wound can go septic and he's on meds."

Dog talk. We were back on safe territory. "Of course, bring him."

"And someplace quiet, so we can hear ourselves talk."

Aha, talk. I managed to string together a few words myself. "How about my deck?" I asked, thinking if this was the official announcement of the end of us, he could take those steps down and away in seconds without looking back and I could head to the TV for reruns of *Rhoda*. But maybe what I'd thought was the evil eye had been God getting ready to wink at me.

"Your deck would be great. I'll pick up a couple of crab cakes at Loonies. Around one, okay?" He smiled. It was a little wiggly at the edges, but enough to get my heart pumping. God, I'd missed him.

He showed up at my front door at precisely thirteen hundred hours military time with a loaded shopping bag and a limping canine companion.

"Hey, fella. You doing okay?" It had been a while, but the shepherd seemed to remember me. His greeting was a happy growl and a rough-tongued lick.

"He's doing better," Scott said. "The antibiotics are kicking in."

Sarge limped the perimeter of the deck twice, sniffing, then settled under the table in an umbrella-shaded spot where I'd set up a bowl filled with ice water. "Thanks for that," Scott said as he unpacked a bag with the Loonies logo, a six-pack of beer sweating condensation and two chilled bottles of wine, one red, one white.

"I didn't know what you'd want, or even if you drink in the daytime, but *I'm* sure as hell going to."

"The cabernet," I said. "Fill her up."

We ate and drank our way through small talk. About Morty Felcher back on his feet doing a spirited mambo the night before. About Scott's daughter starting to teach in the fall. We talked about Scott's work. He had prospects for a job in his specialty, something to do with defense strategy. It looked like a good fit. He could work from home, wherever home was, and he wanted it not to be Tuckahoe. "In winter anyway. This town hibernates in the off-season and by February it's terminally depressing. The job is near D.C. and there are tons of condos in the area. So we'll see. They haven't made me a solid offer yet, but I've been back twice, I've got top security clearance, and they get credit for hiring a disabled vet, so I figure I've got a shot."

I didn't tell him about my offer. I was still thinking it through, still on the fence. I'd surveyed my two closest friends. Each had responded in character. Em had said only, "You need to weigh very carefully the pros and the cons."

Margo was unfamiliar with carefully. She'd said, "What decision? Snap it up! It's fabulous."

I'd replied, "The job is. I'm not sure about Tess. You should have heard her on the phone with one of the physicians. Hell on wheels. This woman is tough to get along with."

"Oh, for heaven's sake, Nora, if you can get along with me, you can get along with anyone."

"You're not my boss."

"Wanna bet?"

There had been no follow-up from National Care. Typical Tess. She wasn't going to make love to me. She'd done as much foreplay as she intended to. The top-level salary. Summers on my terms. Her telling me I was worth it. Now it was up to me. Take it or leave it. I was still inclined to leave it, because no one in her right mind would drive from Baltimore to Bethesda and back twice a day four times a week. I'd lose my mind doing that. But I was hoping I could adjust my Baltimore schedule. If I could jam my sessions at the psych hospital into a single day and negotiate something similar at the VA medical center, then it might work out. I had a call in to Josh at Poplar Grove. He was on vacation with his wife in Tuscany, so that conversation was on hold.

When I tugged my focus back from the brink of my own life, Scott was pouring himself a second glass of wine. "You?" He held up the bottle to refill my glass.

"Not yet," I said. I was saving it for when I might really need it. For when my lieutenant colonel would bark, "Dis-missed!" or murmur, "Fall in."

"Okay." He seemed to be talking to himself more than to me, getting ready to plunge, like a diver on the high board. I had a feeling his toes were gripping the edge. "I'm probably going to feed you TMI, but after my failure to launch in the bedroom I owe that to you."

That last took a lot. He was nervously rolling the wine cork between his palms.

"You don't owe me a thing, Scott. No one's running a tab here."

"Copy that and correct it. I owe it to myself to tell you. But please, shut me up when you want to run screaming from the table."

And so it came to pass that I heard about his marriage.

We didn't go back to the begats. We started at Exodus. Bunny's from her marriage vows.

"I'm not saying it's easy on the spouse left behind during a military deployment," Scott said. "It's hell. I assume some responsibility for all this, or the U.S. Army does. My absences, the multiple missions. She had the kids to raise by herself; then her mom was diagnosed. Belinda had a lot to manage. On the other hand, she didn't take advantage of the programs set up for dependents. You know, she's never been a people person."

I barely kept my eyes from rolling on that one.

Bunny had managed to get through her husband's first deployment without falling into another man's bed. Or at least she never confessed to screwing around during Scott's initial round in Iraq. But after he returned from the second one, this time minus a leg, she seemed to be a different person. *An alternative dearly to be wished for,* I thought. Scott hadn't seen it that way.

"She was cold, distant." To my raised eyebrow, he added, "More than usual. It was like she was disappointed in me for getting blown up. But, hey, your husband is away for two years and comes back half a man—"

"That's crazy!" I couldn't help myself. I smacked the glass table, startling Sarge underneath, who yelped and shot to standing.

"Whoa, woman. Easy there, boy." One of Scott's hands slid over to cover mine; the other reached down to calm the dog. "I didn't say that's what I am. But if you hear it over and over, you come to believe it. Bunny"— he'd slipped into the vernacular—"doesn't fight fair. Never did. And she wanted out. She had other interests. She'd hooked up with a radio DJ in Miami. It had been going on for more than a year by the time I got back. And it didn't stop even after that. She made some trips to Florida supposedly to see a high school girlfriend who was going through a tough time. More lies. The so-called friend was the guy she'd met at Foolaround .com, Moe of *Joe and Moe's Drive-Time Team for Music and Mayhem,* WTON-1050 on your AM dial."

"You had no idea?" I motioned for a refill of my wine glass.

"Not at the time. She played the dutiful wife in public. We made the front page of the *Coast Post,* a story in the *Baltimore Sun,* a piece on WJX, the happy couple. Local hero, Silver Star for bravery under fire, back from the war minus a leg, doting wife. She loved people thinking that, loved the press while it lasted, but it was all a sham. The truth was, the marriage was ashes. It was dead cold in that bedroom. Not me. Well, not at first. In the beginning, I was eager, willing, and, I swear to you, Nora, able. But someone tells you what she told me, in some ways that's worse than any IED. It eats away at you, and after a while . . ." He shrugged and leaned back in his seat. "So now you know." He scanned my face and asked, "Too much, too soon?"

"No. I'm glad you trusted me enough to bring me in."

"I do. Trust you. I'm beginning to trust myself again too. I got to a point where I decided—you helped me decide—hell no to who she said I was. That's not me. And I'm tired of being alone in the dark. Tired of stumbling around with all the lights out. Tired of wanting you but hiding out from you. So . . ." He stretched his left leg in front of him and pulled his chinos up from the cuff. "Here I am. No, dammit, my leg is not me. Here *it* is. In full freakin' sunlight."

I bent over. I felt the smooth space-age silicone and touched the seamless sleeve where the prosthesis met the stump. "It's a beauty," I said.

He laughed. "My shrink got it right. I've got a shrink now, by the way, and my appointment was why I missed class Tuesday. I'm two weeks in and last session we talked about you. He said if I told you, you'd say something like that. You really are an amazing woman, Nora."

He steered me up then, one finger under my chin and, when I smiled, drew me to him. He kissed me. Hard and soft. I longed to explore other parts of him, hard and soft. Did this mean we were back on track to who knew where, who knew when? All I knew is it was better than it had ever been because there were no secrets between us. After I came up for air I said, "You're pretty amazing yourself."

"I'm working on it. But I've got to tell you, it might take time."

To that I said what soldiers' women have been saying since the Trojan War, probably since the first man ever went off to battle. "I'll wait for you."

At the door, Scott gave me a brush of a kiss. "To be continued," he murmured, though he didn't say when. His walk down the path was jaunty, which could have been the spring mechanism in the revised prosthetic foot, but I didn't think so.

It didn't take long before I was wishing I could order a new foot for myself. The last one was stuck in my mouth, making it hard to breathe. Seriously, I asked myself, what had I been thinking? As the wine fog cleared, the impact of what I'd just promised hit me. I'd said I'd wait indefinitely for someone I barely knew except by reputation and the first thrilling rush of feeling, which in my experience were never the most reliable measures of anything. I'd just made a promise I wasn't sure I was ready for, wasn't sure I could keep.

As if Scott Goddard hadn't had enough of broken vows.

chapter twenty-nine

I slipped into the director's reserved last-row center seat for the final few minutes of *The King and I.* It was closing night, which called for an encore of "Shall We Dance?" and Margo's traditional thank-you speech that included the crew by name and such notables as Tuckahoe's mayor (present) and her parents (dead), who would have spun in their graves had they known she was frittering away her life on such stage nonsense. No mention of Pete, sitting up front.

Only once in my memory had Margo included Pete in one of these closing-night salutes. That was a decade ago, after the run of *Damn Yankees.* Otherwise she claimed he was a distraction. "Everybody cranes to see him and suddenly it's all about the Greek Icon and the cast gets lost in the shuffle." In the interim, his star had faded, so I doubted there would have been a major buzz and she could have thanked a generic husband, but Margo wasn't inclined to make nice to the Big Cheat these days.

After the final curtain and a stop at the restroom, I ducked outside for a breath of unconditioned air and was inhaling the intoxicating fragrance of gardenias when Emine's SUV pulled up, the passenger door flew open, and Merry leapt out.

She dashed past me, calling on the run, "Hi, Aunt Norrie. Party started yet?"

"Not yet but about to," I said.

"Made it. Yesss!"

Em flipped on the inside light and waved me over. She zipped down the driver's-side window and I leaned in.

"Congratulations." I hitched my neck toward the stage door. "How'd you manage that?"

"It was like working out the Treaty of Versailles, but I came up with a compromise. Merry agreed to go to the Iftar, which started at sundown. Adnan agreed that she and I could leave right after dinner before the speeches started."

"And everyone was happy?"

"Of course not. No one was happy. Merry sulked through dinner and hardly touched the food, which she whispered to me was gross. In fact, it was delicious. But she needed a reason to pull a long face." Em drew her mouth down with two fingers at the edges. "The father and the daughter glared at each other. She complains he disses her. But she disses too. Before dinner, he introduced us to these people he was trying to impress. Erol shook hands. Merry never even smiled."

I laughed a little. "Payback is hell."

Emine's kohl-lined eyes flashed. "Payback is not one-sided and it is not over. Adnan is burning up at her. 'The tree branch should be bent while it is young,' he tells me. Soon it will be too late to bend her. For this, he brings in someone who will try to break her."

"Oh God, oh Em," I said, not necessarily in that order. "His mother?"

My friend heaved a giant sigh.

"He's sending Merry there?"

"His first choice, but I wouldn't allow it. Selda's coming here. I think Margo would call it caving. But that was my compromise."

"Your sacrifice," I said, remembering her mother-in-law's last visit.

"A mother makes sacrifices. Selda will tell you all about hers when she sees you." Em made a wry face.

"And when is that?"

"Adnan was calling her when we left the dinner. But I have a feeling they have talked before. I think he's been planning this for a while."

Suddenly a swell of music followed by a collective whoop of laughter surged from the theater.

"The party," I said. "I'm heading in. I'll keep an eye on Merry."

"I hope she has fun, my daughter. If her grandmother has her way—and Selda always does—it will be Merry's last fun for a long, long time."

Everyone was having fun. The set was still up. It would be stripped after the party in a twenty-minute flurry of activity, then stored for possible future use. Margo was seated on King Mongkut's throne, singing along with the rest to her pianist's rendition of "There Is Nothing Like a Dame" from *South Pacific*. Pete, sitting on one of the stools at a makeshift bar, called me over. "Hey, Nora." He removed a Trader Joe's shopping bag from the next stool and patted its seat. I popped a Guinness and planted myself.

"So how are you doing?" He never moved his gaze from his wife.

"We're all fine," I said. "It's been a busy season so far. Some new sign-ups at the dance studio. Summer people. The weather has been . . ."

Pete didn't want to talk about the weather. He cut me off. "Margo told me a while back you and the war hero were seeing each other. That still going strong? Because if not I've got someone you might hit it off with. This guy owns the new resort up the coast. Upton Abbey. Name is Max Cassidy."

"Right. Margo mentioned him. The gazillionaire." I didn't say I'd seen him in action and had been pleasantly surprised.

"Don't blame him for his money. He came by it honestly. He's a smart guy, lots of irons in the fire, big giver to charity. No airs. I mentioned you and he's interested. Can I give him your number? He's a hot commodity."

As if I were a hot commodity, I said, "Let me think about it."

Pete gave me a bemused look. "Well, uh, sure. But not too long. I know someone who'd jump at the chance to date him, but if I bump you for Dana, my wife will hand me my head on a platter."

"Dana Montagne?"

"One and the same."

Interesting. If he was thinking about fixing the anchorwoman up with Max, where did that leave my Pete-beds-Dana theory? "Hold on," he was saying, "here comes the gift presentation."

Another tradition. After the annual musical, the cast and crew presented Margo with a remembrance gift. She had a collection of these cherished souvenirs. An Empire State Building snow globe for *On the Town*, a gold baseball charm for *Damn Yankees*, a merry-go-round music box for *Carousel*. None of them was outlandishly expensive, but they always evoked genuine feeling. Now Merry walked onstage hugging an elaborately wrapped box while the pianist switched to "The March of the Siamese Children." Owen, the lead actor, made the speech on behalf of all the Driftwood Players out front and behind the scenes, and with a "We love you, Margo," he laid the box in her lap. The circle closed around her as she tossed tissue paper. She held up for display a silk robe with the mythical half-man, half-bird Garuda symbol of Thailand embroidered on the back. Stunning, it deserved her gasp. "Wow! Thank you, all. You love me? I love you more!" She meant it.

As the applause died down, she said, "Okay, people, all hands on deck. Time to—" She never got to finish, as the baritone of Pete Manolis resonated through the theater. "Whoa, Team Driftwood. If I can have your attention for a minute, please."

Pete loped to center stage, carrying a small bag he'd taken from the larger one. I knew that logo.

His speech began with congrats on a great run and segued into Margo's dedication to the theater dating back to when they first met. "And now we're celebrating the twenty-fifth anniversary of her degree in theater arts."

If Margo had arms his length, she would have reached over to strangle him. She didn't appreciate allusions to the passage of time, especially her time. "As you can see, my lovely wife is still going strong, stronger than ever." His lovely wife was furiously tapping a foot. "To mark that occasion and to celebrate the success of *The King and I*, I have a gift for her as well."

Pete went to her, took her hand, and tugged her to stand next to him as he removed from the signature Svengali and Trilby Jewelers bag a satin quilted jewelry box. He pressed it into her hand. The circle tightened around them. Margo seemed to weigh the box, and then she raised the lid.

A bracelet, brushed gold wrought into an Oriental cobra design centered with a ruby the size of a cherry.

"That's a Chanthaburi star ruby from Thailand. Violet red with a six-point asterism." Pete must have memorized Trilby's description. "Top quality. And the gold's twenty-two karat. That's almost pure." It didn't sound like bragging, I'd have to argue with Margo later, since I could tell from the set of her jaw, she thought it did. To me it sounded like a man who wanted to score points with his wife, thought she was the best, and wanted her to have the best.

Margo eyed the bracelet and Pete suspiciously. Merry was the first to kick off the chant, "Try it on, try it on." Margo slipped the snake of a bracelet onto her sparrow-sized wrist. Perfect fit. She held her arm up so everyone could see it.

When the oohs and aahs died down, she said, "It's lovely. Thank you, sweetheart," in a tone much too flat for at least three carats of gem and twenty-two-karat gold.

As he picked up on her mood, Pete's expression became a mudslide of disappointment.

"You do like it, right? Because it's one of a kind. Trilby designed it herself."

"I do," Margo said, grinding out the phrase as if she wished she hadn't said it in the wedding vows twenty-plus years before. She pecked her husband's cheek with what struck me as a dry dismissal of a kiss. "Here I'm supposed to say, 'You shouldn't have,' right? Well, that ain't gonna happen." Now I could see she was playing to the crowd. "Because I'm glad you did." Which sounded to me like a Noël Coward exit line, witty but lifeless. I didn't hear the beat of a heart behind it. Still, it drew the laughter she was going for.

She checked her other wrist, a moon-faced watch with giant numbers that she'd bought for thirty bucks in the Ocean City flea market. "Company, it's late; we're running way over time here. So while we still have some willing and able left, let's get this show on the road. Strike the set."

Pete stood, broad shoulders slumped, as Margo bustled off to supervise the deconstruction. Then he walked over to the bar and poured himself a glass of vodka. He carried it as he took the four steps into the orchestra seats and sipped it as he walked up the aisle.

I took off after him and trotted to keep up. "That was great, Pete. The speech and the gift."

"You think so? I think it was a washout." Sip, swallow, stride.

"No, really. Margo's tired; that's all. It's always a brutal two weeks when she does the musicals. And you know how she is at closings. She gets something like postpartum depression. Tomorrow she'll be all smiles and flaunting the bracelet to the world. It's absolutely stunning." My thinking cleared to an aha. "You picked it out yourself?"

He stopped then, at row QQ, and faced me. "You have got to be kidding," he said. "Ask Margo about my gift history. It's a running joke between us. But this time, I got smart. I brought along a jewelry maven. Dana."

Right, okay . . . so Dana Montagne helped him choose the bracelet. That explained the giddy conspirators. A breath of relief whooshed from me. "Dana Montagne," I repeated.

"Yeah, but don't tell Margo, okay? I'd like her to think I did it on my own. I could use a little spousal-caring credit. Not that she was impressed. Shit, we thought we had a hit on our hands. Something that would knock her on her ass. Obviously it flopped big-time." He gulped the last inch of vodka. "I just don't get it."

You had to think like Margo to get it, and no one thought like Margo. I had no idea what was fulminating in that bizarrely wired brain of hers, but for Pete's sake, I was going to find out.

"What just happened out there?" I asked, grabbing her elbow to slow her down as she sailed past me carrying a bouquet of tools and a roll of duct tape.

"What?"

"Your reaction to the bracelet. Your attitude. Pete's devastated."

She whirled on me then, nearly impaling me with a Phillips screwdriver.

"Poor Pete. Well, fuck him and his bracelet. It's a guilt gift. I knew it and I wasn't fooled for a minute. If that devastates him, too bloody bad."

"Oh, Margo . . ."

"Oh, Nora," she mimicked my exasperation. "That's the simple explanation. How about the manipulative one? This was a look-how-much-I-love-you-so-how-could-I-possibly-be-bonking-anyone-else gift."

"Really, sweetie, you need to see someone." I'd thought this for the last fifteen years. But she'd been in therapy through adolescence, and in college she'd declared herself finished. "All therapized out," was the way she put it. Now as an actress and director, she was afraid that a shrink playing around in her head would mess with her creative process.

"See someone? Like Laura Wasser?" She got a blank stare from me. "Don't you read the *National Enquirer*? Not even on the Piggly Wiggly checkout line? Laura is the divorce lawyer to the stars, and if she's good enough for Britney Spears, she's good enough for me."

"I was thinking someone like Josh." Not Josh, though; he'd heard too much about Margo from me. "Someone who specializes in"—time for a splash of cold water—"paranoid fantasies."

A stunned silence followed. Then: "That's what you think, huh? That I'm off the deep end. Let me tell you, I've barely navigated the shallows. Secrets swim under the surface, my dear. And not just in spy novels and Lifetime movies. Half the people we know probably lead double lives. Because we don't *really* know them. We only think we do."

As in Bunny Goddard screwing around in Florida while collecting accolades as the devoted, faithful military wife. Maybe Margo was right.

She was saying, "Soon, very soon, I'll haul Pete out of the closet and let him bask in the sunlight of truth. Because the truth—along with a multimillion-dollar divorce settlement—will set him free. And now"—she sniffed—"if you'll excuse me, I have a fake world to destroy."

chapter thirty

The next Saturday night, and we three—Em, Margo, and I—were huddled like chicks on the corner cushion of an elaborately carved tapestry-
upholstered sofa in the Haydars' apartment above the café. A gilt-framed
wedding photo dominated the living room wall across from us. The bride
and groom—he in tails, she in beaded white satin—stared with complicated smiles directly into the camera. Selda had pushed for a different girl
for her son—by Em's telling, a scrawny seventeen-year-old with a shadow
of a mustache and compliant respect for her elders. Most important: she
was from a moneyed family. But for once, Adnan had rebelled. He'd
fought on two fronts for Emine. Won over her parents, who detested his
family, and went up against his mother, who'd never lost a battle. His
eyes in the picture were brazen with victory, and I saw a hint of triumph
in the bride's tipped-up chin too.

Em followed my focus and said, "It was the last time he went against
her. To him she is the *valide*, the mother of a sultan. Four sultans. All of
her sons are spoiled and my sisters-in-law are terrified of her. She arrived
two days ago, and already she's taken over my kitchen. Today, even the
oven downstairs to bake the *pide* bread for tonight. As for Merry, I am
waiting for a murder. The question is, which one will strike first?"

"And on Ramadan you can't even have a shot of raki to deal with it,
right?" That was from Margo, who I knew was craving something to take

the edge off. Pete had called late afternoon to tell her he had to stay in Baltimore overnight. Apologies to Emine for missing the dinner, but this was business. Yes, on Saturday. The Orioles were playing a home game tonight. He didn't have time to explain, but Margo would find out soon enough.

She'd called me immediately after. "Business on a Saturday night. Funny business. Monkey business." Pete had already added one entry this week to what she called her "Gotcha List." Prowling through his cell phone, she'd found a message from the plastic surgeon's office postponing an appointment. "My husband has major cojones thinking he can get tucked behind my back. If Dr. Wu isn't doing a balls reduction on him, believe me, I will." Now she sat fuming.

"I'm not a drinker anyway," Em was saying, "but this may drive me to it. Allah will forgive me. He is all understanding."

With that, the front door opened and Selda bustled in with Merry dragging behind her. Selda carried her handbag. Merry lugged two loaded shopping bags. Her face was a portrait of misery.

"Take them to the kitchen so I can greet your mother's friends," Selda instructed.

Merry blinked what I interpreted as *"SOS"* in Morse code. Her scrunched eyebrows read, *"Rescue me."*

"You didn't hear me, Meryem? There is yogurt that needs to be in a cool place. Go!" She watched the girl trudge off; then, satisfied, she turned first to her daughter-in-law. "I got perfect tomatoes." An hour before dinner, she'd decided Em's tomatoes were overripe. "And Meryem I gave a lesson in how to shop. How to pick the best fruit. The child knows nothing about fruit." Her glance swept the sofa. "Full house," she announced, not all that hospitably.

"Anne," Em said, using the Turkish word for "mother," "you remember Nora and Margo."

"Of course." Selda pointed to me. "You are the picky eater, yes?"

"Right," I said. "No eggplant."

She touched her temple as if to say "It's all in your head" or maybe "crazy lady."

"And you've met Margo Manolis," Em said.

"Last time once. You are the Greek, yes?" She sniffed.

"My husband is."

"You look different." She moved until she was far into Margo's personal space. "Ahh. You had the eyes done. The lids." As Margo sucked in an incredulous breath at her nerve, Selda said, "Me too. Last year. Why look tired and old when you don't have to?" Then she turned her back on us, calling, "Merry, you will take out the serving platters," and barreled off through to the dining room, where she lifted a goblet to check for smudges, then whipped the swinging door to the kitchen so hard it hit the wall.

As day faded to night, Adnan came upstairs to wash. An app on his iPhone chimed the official end of the fast and he made a brief welcoming speech and explained the meaning of the holiday. Then we took sips of water and ate Medjool dates and olives to begin the Iftar break-the-fast dinner, as was the custom in Turkey.

"You will sit next to me," Selda said to Merry, who had pulled Erol to stand in front of her like a shield. "I will teach you to eat properly. Americans make a dance with their knives and forks. You will follow what I do. It is much more cultured." Her barbarian granddaughter's eyes glazed over. "You watch too, *kuzucuğum*," Selda said to Erol.

"Yeah, little lamb, you too." Merry punched her brother's arm.

"Margo, take the chair on Merry's other side, please," Em announced. I caught Merry's soft, "Thank God."

Em began to head for the kitchen. Selda blocked her. "Sit. All is in good hands." Adnan tried to follow his mother. She waved him away. "Sit, my sweet boy. You worked hard all day."

With a slam of the swinging door that shook the silverware, dinner was under way.

There were olives, soft white cheese, and pastirma, cured beef.

"It doesn't taste like the pastrami at Schwartz's," Merry said, referring to the famous deli in Ocean City. "The kosher is better."

"What means 'kosher'?" Selda asked.

"Jewish halal," Margo answered.

Selda fanned herself.

After the red lentil soup ("Meryem, don't blow breath on the spoon. This is very crude."), Selda plated everyone's food. As she served the stuffed zucchini, she said to me, "*Kabak dolması*, it is called. Made like the eggplant, only you won't die from it."

The "lady's thigh" meatballs and roasted lamb shank were delicious. Then a stew of nameless meat that made Merry gag on her first taste. "OMG, what *is* this?"

"*Arnavut Ciğeri*. What? You don't know this dish? Your mother never cooks it?"

"It *is* pretty gross," Erol ventured.

"What is this 'gross'? It is liver with onions."

"Liver? Like from an animal?" Merry looked horrified.

"Yes, of course. Your father used to love it when he was your age. He likes the taste of the sumac in it. Makes it sour like lemon." Adnan, who had high cholesterol, helped himself to a hefty second portion under his wife's glare.

The meal was well spiced, but over-peppered with comments from Selda: Merry must not salt her food before she eats it. She should sit up straight or she will freeze hunched over. And she can skip dessert because she is built like her mother. Here Selda held her hands spread wide to indicate big hips.

"But I love *güllaç*," Merry protested. It was one of my favorites too, a pudding made with milk and rosewater, dusted with pistachios and pomegranate seeds.

"*Anne*, please," Em jumped in, too furious not to. "Merry, you can have as much *güllaç* as you want."

"Fine." Selda sighed. "Since only once a year. But tomorrow I want to see what dress size you are."

"Uh. Tomorrow, what's tomorrow?" Panic soared in Merry's voice.

"We go to the outlet stores. The Ralph Lauren, the Donna Karan." Discount malls lined the highway to the beach. "Your father is driving us."

Two voices rose at once. Em's: "Adnan!" Merry's: "But I'm supposed to go to the sand castle contest. Aunt Margo, Mrs. Manolis, I'm on her crew. . . ."

Selda waved for silence. "This is more important than the sand. I looked in your closet today, Meryem—"

"You did what?" Fire exploded on Merry's cheeks.

"Just a look. This is a bad thing? To your grandmother, you show such a mean face?"

"Her room is private," Em said. I could tell that my most patient friend was barely maintaining control.

"At her age, nothing is private," Selda snapped. "I looked. I saw only one dress. The rest in there are dungarees and the shorts. You are a girl. I will buy you some dresses."

"You could go sometime during the week, Selda." Margo was playing a new role for her: the voice of reason.

"Adnan can take time off only tomorrow—yes, Adnan?"

He nodded.

Em said, "I could drive."

Selda shook her head, dislodging a hairpin from her French twist. "You don't understand why you have such problems? I can tell you. A child should not rule a house."

Merry turned to Margo. "Kill me," she muttered. "Kill me now."

Margo squeezed her hand under the table. I heard her whisper, "Let her buy. We'll return." Over a double portion of *güllaç* spooned out by her mother, Merry snickered; then she sobered. "But the sand castle contest."

"Ah, there are contests and then there are contests," Margo said. "Some you win; some you lose. Some you lose to win."

Selda drafted Em to help her with the dishes, which was Margo's and my cue to leave, and we grabbed it. Walking through the café, we traded "horribles" and *kaltak* comments about Selda; we worried about Em and Merry, felt helpless. At the car park, Margo was reminding me to be at the beach no later than ten the next morning when her cell pinged. "Pete. He must have come up for air with the girlfriend." She read the text. Watch eleven p.m. news WJX

Whazzup? she texted back.

You'll see. Don't miss it.

She said to me, "Who knows what—or who—he's gotten himself into? Don't you dare miss it, Nora."

At home at eleven, I watched reports of a fire in Towson and a flood in Hamden, the predictably hot and humid forecast for all the Mid-Atlantic, and the venerable anchor announcing, "Now subbing for Jack Schine, who has the night off, one of Baltimore's true greats, here with sports, Pete Manolis."

"Thanks, Mike." Pete stared into the camera, loving it. Being adored in return. "So how do you like them Birds? They trounced the Tigers 11–2 in Camden Yards tonight."

Margo called when it was over. She was buoyant. "This was a test. They're seriously considering him for some kind of sportscaster job. He could use a tightening under the chin and maybe some filler between the eyes, but, God, wasn't he fabulous?"

chapter thirty-one

"So now you know he's not playing around behind your back, right? You're finally convinced the man is innocent?" I asked Margo at eleven Sunday morning as we toted buckets of water from the ocean. They'd help fill the huge hole that Pete, along with Margo's theater crew, had dug in the sand, the first step in building the medieval castle representing *Camelot*, next year's musical production at the Driftwood.

"He left Baltimore at six this morning to return here in time to start the dig. I give him points for that," she allowed. "On the major crime—adultery's still a crime in Maryland, believe it or not, with a laughable ten-dollar fine—or his desire for it, jury's still out. Though we did have the Viagra talk."

I stepped on a starfish but didn't stop. With Margo you had to keep up.

"He was in our bathroom when he went for the Viagra and found the vitamins instead. He came out shaking the bottle. I explained and he explained. He said what you said. That he was embarrassed to admit he had a soft-serve problem with, in his words, his beautiful, sexy wife. He was afraid I'd take it as a personal insult."

"How could he *possibly* think that?" My tone was on the wrong side of snide.

She ignored me. "I suppose the rest of the evidence was circumstantial. Now I know that the nonstop texting was from the managing editor, the news director, and the lawyers at the station to work out possible terms of a contract. Also that some of them were from Max Cassidy about a possible commercial starring Pete for the casino at Upton Abbey. And the appointments with Dr. Wu were about Pete's possibly getting his face in shape for high-def TV."

"Lots of possibles," I said.

"According to Pete that's why he didn't tell me before. Nothing was set in place and he didn't want me to noodge him. Drive him crazy, was the way he so diplomatically put it. He says I get too involved and emotional before I have all the facts, and since he didn't have them . . ." She shrugged, sloshing water on both of us.

"And now he does?"

"After last night, the station got a bunch of positive posts on their fan page. They're ready for him to sign. Now it's up to Pete to make the decision. Or me. Bottom line, it's up to me, he says. We're a team, or at least that's his slick sales pitch." Her opinion of it was a cynical twist to her mouth. "But I'm not sure how I feel."

Her expression went flat as Pete dashed over. "Sweetheart, let me take those." He relieved her of the two buckets. "And I set up your music." The sound track from *Camelot*. "The Merry Month of May" was wafting through The Grilling Month of August air. "It's really pulling them in. You're collecting a crowd. I'll take yours too, Nora." He scooped up my buckets.

We watched him swing the water, as light as air to him, as he took giant strides back to the Driftwood dig. "Big suck-up," Margo grumbled, which was better than Big Cheat. "Can you tell he wants this gig bad? Really bad. But there are issues to consider."

"Oh, Margo, I can't believe you're still worried about the extracurricular activities."

"Possible ones, possibly," she said, pensively. "I've been thinking."

She was always thinking. When it came to Pete, usually the worst.

"On TV, he'd build a new fan base, not just the old-timers who remember him from the field." She twisted her wedding band, a diamond eternity ring, around her finger. "Dana Montagne has a theory." The newscaster who helped Pete choose the ruby bracelet. "She says TV blurs the lines between image and reality. You come into people's homes. You enter dark bedrooms bringing light. You report the eleven o'clock news, and it's pillow talk. All that makes for a false intimacy."

According to Margo, Dana left her husband for a fan who fell in love with her beautiful talking head and made sure he got to know the rest of her. The affair in three dimensions had fizzled, but only after Dana had divorced the nice husband.

"Dana's a Catholic-school girl, first in her class at Mercy High, and she fell off the marital wagon. On the other hand, Pete Manolis is no altar boy, so what are the odds there? And when he travels with the team for away games? Ugh. That's party time. There will be temptations."

"Margala!" I used the name her tante Violet called her, standing in for the one voice Margo believed in. "There are always temptations. You've got to trust him. And if you can't trust him, trust yourself."

"Me? I trust me to work my ass off to protect my marriage."

"I'm talking about if Pete . . ." She waved me off as the man in question, her big question, came loping back with our empty pails to refill. "Not now," she whispered. "But we'll talk."

Of course we would. We always did. Well, she always did. Me, not all the time.

For example, Scott Goddard and our incomplete and inconclusive love affair had not been a recent topic of conversation. Like Pete, I was not about to share with Margo before all the facts were in. She, for a change, was too caught up in her own angst to bug me about mine.

I would have had nothing earthshaking to report, anyway. Scott and I had gone to Coneheads for ice cream after class Tuesday, where we came face-to-face with Jack. In a rare instance of advance planning, he'd traded work shifts with Stewie in order to be free on the Saturday night when Dirk would be in town.

The conversation between Jack and Scott had been limited to:

"Toppings?"

"M&M'S for me. And for your mom . . ."

"Heath Bar bits and double whipped cream. That never changes."

Jack handed over the order with his standard smile and parting line, "Enjoy, folks."

As we spooned our ice cream, Scott said, "Do you get the feeling we're being scoped?" My son's eyes flitted like fireflies from his customers to us.

I smirked. "You think?"

Later, as we pulled into the parking space at my house, I said, "Jack's on until midnight. Would you like to come in for coffee?" Innocent, I swear. No intent to seduce. But Scott may have thought otherwise because he said, "Tempting, but I think I'll take a rain check. I saw my psychologist again yesterday and I've got some homework to do before I'm allowed to . . . Uh, I'm not sure how to explain this without sounding like a doofus, but it's kind of like the peasant having to overcome obstacles before he can win the hand of the princess. Well, I don't necessarily mean peasant, or your hand, but whatever." He started laughing. "Oh jeez, I'm making this worse."

"No, I've got it. You've got to slay dragons to claim my whatever." I was laughing too. When we trailed off, he leaned over and we kissed. One deep, loaded-with-meaning-and-pleasure kiss.

"Going now," I said when we separated.

"I'll watch you in," Scott said.

I was maybe three steps down the lantern-lit path when he called softly out the car window. "Nora, I'm making progress. I just wanted you to know."

There was no right answer for that, so I just nodded and kept walking.

Sunday at three o'clock, and we were finishing up King Arthur's castle an hour before the judging. I was on my knees in the sand carving a turret when Margo trilled, "Norrie, you've got a visitor."

I raised my head and zip-lined from Margo's wide-eyed gaze to Scott. I felt my heart leap, then crack a little at the sight of him. Because what I noticed first, what everyone would, was his prosthetic leg. He was wearing shorts—not a pair of knee-length walking shorts that might have softened the image, but high-cut athletic shorts that shouted, *"Look at me, look at me!"* And the part of him that had been added wasn't one of those artistically molded limbs, silicone sheathed to look like the real thing. I'd worked with a woman at the VA hospital who had a wardrobe of prostheses, pale for the winter, tan for the summer, shapely duplicates of her other leg down to the freckles. She even had one with an arched foot for dancing in high heels, and one for sandals, its toes painted with a French pedicure

What Scott was wearing wasn't the one he'd uncovered on my deck. That had been a more elegant design. This was your basic stripped-down, in-your-face version, everything exposed: the carbon-fiber socket, the shank—looking like a cadaverous metal bone—the screws attaching that pylon to his sneakered foot. His shirt wasn't going to make any excuses either: no army motto or camo print so you'd link the leg to the service and nod respectfully. I knew, of course, that this was a test, one of the obstacles contrived by the psychologist to haul Scott and his leg out of the dark closet. I could imagine some cartoon commanding officer barking, "*Show the damn thing; you earned it. Nothing to be ashamed of. A leg short is not a shortcoming. Get over it, soldier.*"

I could also imagine the guts it took to do what he was doing, feeling the way he felt after getting clobbered in his marriage, and my instantly repaired heart swelled with pride for him, in him.

Pete, who'd been wetting down the sculpture for a final polish, brushed sand from his hand before offering it. "Hey, Scott. Looking good, man." I loved Pete for that "looking good, man." It covered everything.

Margo was on her feet, also dusting off sand in a palm-against-palm sweep. But she was playing Helen Keller in *The Miracle Worker*. Her focus never drifted below Scott's waist.

"You remember the colonel," Pete said.

"Sure. The veterans' home board. Pleasure," she said.

The four of us talked. Three did anyway. I just watched and listened, not wanting to give away who I became when Scott was around. Whatever that was, I knew Margo would make something of it.

As the talk trailed off, Scott backed up to survey the sculpture. "Your castle is first-rate. It should definitely cop a trophy."

Pete said, "That was from someone who knows his battlements, Marg."

She yawned out, "Sure, good," but she was just about electrified with curiosity and plans to make my life a misery of questions when Scott said, "My next stop is the Coneheads dig. I promised Claire"—to the Manolises—"who works the soft serve on Tuesdays, I'd stop by."

I could see Margo doing the math behind a frantic series of blinks: Tuesday plus Coneheads equals an after-class ice-cream date with Nora. Oh, yum.

He touched my elbow.

Blink, blink. Margo recalculated the total with that addition.

"Want to go see the Coneheads' banana split, Nora?"

"Sure. I think I've done my job here. Right, Margo?" She nodded vigorously. "And I was heading over there in a few minutes anyway," I said.

Scott took my hand. The last I saw of my girlfriend, she was swallowed in sun shimmer. The only bit left of her was a smile hung in the molten air, the Cheshire cat delightedly licking its lips.

Scott and I walked the packed sand of the shoreline toward the Coneheads dig and the next challenge. I knew we were heading for test two as well as I knew my son's name. Claire must have said Jack was going to be out there this afternoon. Now the kid who thought Scott was damaged goods would see his left leg in all its uncovered glory.

I shuffled through my list of saints for intercession. Saint Giles, patron of the disabled. Rejected. Scott wouldn't even apply for a handicap tag for his car. Saint Anthony of Padua recovered lost items. *Parts of limbs?* I wondered. How about Saint George, who protected warriors? Retired.

Forget the middlemen. *Dear God,* I prayed, *please protect this man from stares, sneers, and signs of pity. I ask you this in Jesus' name. Amen.*

Claire spotted us first and flew to meet us. "Hey, Colonel, no, Scott. You said call you Scott. Right. And Mrs. Farrell. Uh . . ."

"Nora," I filled in.

"Nora. Glad you guys made it." She was her usual hummingbird self in a colorful bikini that I, who tended to modesty, cheered for. *Go after my son,* I rooted her on. *Hook him with cookies; reel him in with cleavage.* Anything to get him off Tiffanie's line.

Scott said, "I told you I was going to check your banana split for accuracy. I'm an expert."

She ticked off, "Your three flavors. Black raspberry. Mint chocolate chip, and, of course, vanilla. Can't forget that. Here we're working all in one color, sand, but it's still incredible. Come see what we've done."

The sculpture was huge, much bigger than Margo's, and swarming with packers, carvers, and smoothers. "Jack's heading to the top to straighten out the cherry. It's kind of lopsided. Jack," she called up, "look who's here."

My son, with one foot on the sculpted dish, was attempting a toehold on the scoop of ice cream above it. He looked down and called, "Hey," and I called, "Watch what you're doing," which probably mortified him. He hoisted himself to stand within reach of a sand cherry ball perched gingerly on a puff of sand whipped cream. He nudged the maraschino to one side, then another, repeating, "Straight yet?" until it was. "Perfect," Claire shouted, and applause broke from the Coneheads gang and the surrounding crowd that had gathered to watch. Then Jack scrambled down and bounded over to us, all grin and cockiness.

"Definitely first place," Scott said.

Jack nodded, almost breathless, managing, "Yeah, I think we've got a chance. Though we stopped by earlier and Aunt Margo's Camelot is awesome. Hi, Mom." He planted a kiss on my cheek. "I noticed one thing while I was up there that I need to fix. Gimme a sec."

He raced to the dish, patted and smoothed part of its surface, and trotted back. And on the way, from mid-distance, he saw Scott's leg, really registered it. I knew that because I read it on his face, from his catching the metallic flash of it, to the *bam!* and *jeez!* of recognition, to being transfixed. Then he snapped out of his trance and searched until he glommed onto Claire. Which was my confirmation that beneath the flutter of this girl was a woman as bright and guiding as a lighthouse.

"Can't have a cracked dish," Jack blurted as he returned to our group. Then with a jerk of his head that told me he'd heard himself, he corrected to: "Not that anything's perfect." Which was so sweet, so lame and sweet, I wanted to hug him.

"My sentiments exactly," Scott said, with a twinkling glance at me.

Claire might have seen that glint or she just plucked something brilliant from the air midflight because she said, "I love your leg, Colonel. It looks like it got swiped from a sci-fi movie."

Which gave Jack permission to take a longer, closer look. I watched his eyebrows draw up a doubtful curve. His mouth, a duplicate of my mother's, soft with generous lips, congealed into a thin line. *Don't,* I thought. *Please don't. You were doing so well.*

Scott went on. "This is your basic titanium and carbon-fiber, but I've got a fancier one at home that looks more like the real thing." The one I'd seen. "But it's waiting for a . . . uh . . . new part," Scott said, skipping over my arched eyebrow. My son's Adam's apple bobbled ominously.

Scott went on. "They make them super-high-tech now with microprocessors that adjust to the terrain and kinematic sensors that keep you stable. And I'm sure you've seen the ones with running blades. They're so fast the Olympics banned them. They said they gave the blade runners an unfair advantage."

"Well, I think yours is totally cool," Claire enthused.

The colonel didn't miss a beat. "Yeah, I kind of like it myself. Keeps me from falling on my face."

Everyone laughed, Jack's voice rumbling in with the rest, but I checked out his eyes. Their amber light was trained on me, signaling caution.

Then, suddenly, the wind picked up, a salty, gusty surprise lashing in from the ocean, begging me to throw caution to it.

Right there in front of my son, I took Scott's hand and weaved our fingers together. I said to him, "Hey, we better get going. I've got stuff to do." I called out to the Coneheads crew, "Good luck, you guys. You did a great job." To my son, "The judging's in less than an hour. Text me the results, okay?"

"Sure," he said, his voice a slouch.

"I'll remind him," Claire said. "His head's crowded. He thinks a lot." True. He had a lot to think about these days.

She gave us a teeny wave good-bye. Jack only stared at his toes digging into the sand and mumbled, "Bye."

Two blocks down the beach and out of their sight, Scott said, "Well, that went over like a lead balloon."

"Nah." I gripped the lie, then couldn't hold on, didn't want to with Scott, and slid to the truth. "It went as well as could be expected."

"I freaked him out, right? The leg?"

"It's not you. Claire nailed it. His head is crowded right now." It was time to tell Scott Jack's story, beginning with the circumstances surrounding his conception and ending—no, not ending, beginning again—with Dirk DeHaven Donor Dude, who was coming in for his second visit Saturday, which made everything more intense.

"We need to talk." I, who dreaded those words, actually pronounced them and watched Scott rear back an inch.

"Of course. My place, yours, or"—he flared his eyebrows salaciously—"under the boardwalk?" he asked, hitching his neck to an empty stretch of sand shadowed by the planks above.

"Under the boardwalk first."

"I was kidding. You're not, are you?"

I broke free and raced into the dim and cool, giggling with giddiness, while wondering how he'd react to this free-spirited version of me. He followed more slowly, wearing a puzzled smile. As he walked toward me, I gave him an answer: my arms outstretched to enfold him. He was astonished, but not so much that he couldn't kiss me back.

"This is what you had to say?" he asked, laughing when we came up for air.

"This, yes. But there's more."

"Oh, there's more, is there? Well, I suggest my place for more—" He paused, then added, "Talk."

We did that with Sarge curling up on the sofa between us. We buried our hands in the dog's fur, stroking him, our fingers sometimes brushing, as

I recounted the story of Lon and me and Dirk and Jack and me, and where the lines intersected. When I was finished, Scott said, "You've lived a complicated life."

"Doesn't everybody, beneath the surface?"

"Some more than others." He was running his thumb over the back of my hand. "Jack must miss his dad a lot."

I nodded. "They were really close, and Lon's ending"—a better word than "death," especially for an author—"was sudden." I skipped past that awful final chapter as fast as my memory cells could carry me. "Jack hasn't had a male role model for eight years, pretty much all of his adolescence. And that's one of those times you especially need your dad."

"Yup." I saw a lightning flash of pain cross Scott's face. I remembered then, he'd said his father, the Vietnam vet, had taken off when he was eighteen. After a moment of silence, which he didn't fill in, I said, "And now with Dirk in the picture . . . Well, my son may be in college, but at that age they're not much more than kids. I think there's still that empty spot he hopes the Donor Dude will move into. Maybe I'm wrong. Jack says that I am, that he gets it that Dirk's not his dad and Dirk gets it too." I scratched the shepherd behind his ears, eliciting a growl of pleasure. "I'll have a better handle on what everyone's up to after this weekend." I didn't mention Jack's matchmaking fantasy. Scott thought I lived a complicated life. No need to let on it was more complicated than he could imagine— and more crowded. He might conclude there was no room for him. I did say, to head off any plans he might have had, "We're all going out to dinner Saturday night. It's amazing what you can learn about people over onion soup."

"And mussels," he said, eyes bright.

"Oh yeah. Definitely mussels."

I thought for an idiotic moment that Sarge had been trained to respond to the word "mussels" because the dog snapped to sit up at the mention of it. His ears were perked, but his stare, on alert, never wavered from its fix on his master. Then I heard what animal sense, innate and trained, had picked up seconds earlier: footsteps on the front path. The doorbell sounded.

Scott checked his watch. "That's for you, boy." To me: "His walk is here." He jerked a nod and the dog bounded from the sofa and, tail wagging furiously, raced for the door.

I strolled onto the patio. From there, surrounded by privet hedges and crepe myrtle trees freighted with clusters of pink flowers, I heard Scott say, "Keep him out for a couple of hours, okay, Dylan? He's been cooped up all day. He could use a good run in the dog park. Maybe he'll meet up with that girlfriend of his, the sheltie he's crazy about."

I heard the door close, then Scott humming on his way back. "Strangers in the Night." Had that become our song? He came up behind me and wound his arms around my waist. The fragrance of roses perfumed the air. My head was swimming with it and my skin prickled with excitement. "Alone at last," he murmured. I leaned back against him. He was solid on his feet as he bent to kiss my neck. Then he executed a perfect tuck turn, one we'd practiced probably a hundred times in class, and folded me in his arms.

In the bedroom, first thing, he made sure the window shades were fully drawn up to let in every last molecule of brightness. To underline his point, which was touchingly obvious, he turned on every lamp in the room.

"Now," he said, "we're in full-disclosure mode. No secrets."

"Not even from the neighbors?"

"Marty's in New Jersey visiting his grandkids. Anyway, he has cataracts. We're covered."

But Scott had plans for uncovered. He traced a finger from the hollow of my neck to the first button of my shirt and stalled. He took a reverse step. His voice was smoky. "You do it. I want to watch you do it."

It should have sounded romantic and sexy, and I tried to produce a smile to disguise my panic. The last time we'd undressed I'd been wearing one of my fancier bras, satin with lace insets, on orders from Margo. Now, though, as I thought about the layer that separated me from full frontal and backtal nudity, my mouth went dry. I wasn't wearing the Victoria's Secret black bikini panty my personal fashion consultant had insisted I buy for the après-party party. I wasn't even wearing one of my standard T.J.Maxx three-for-seven-bucks pastels. That morning I'd snatched from the bottom dresser drawer a pair of basic-issue parochial school white cotton Fruit of the Looms and a bra stretched to its limit by too many washings. Because what I'd expected to get into my underwear that day was sand and grit and not, in my wildest dreams, Scott Goddard.

I didn't give him the slow, provocative striptease he yearned for. I flicked hooks, snapped elastic, tugged, and tossed at warp speed. Then I stepped over the shabby pile and watched as he—standing in a shaft of sunlight—removed his shirt and, fingers trembling, worked to unbuckle his belt. The therapy sessions, the assignments and tests, had all led to this moment. I closed my eyes, silently cheering him on. When I opened them, I saw he'd made it through. It took only a single glance at what was outstandingly evident, and a magnetic force drew me toward him. "No." He halted me, palms out. "Stand your ground. Please. Stop and look." His voice was gentle but commanding. "Slowly. So you know what you're getting. There's still time to change your mind. Caveat emptor."

With my heart drumming a nervous tattoo I skimmed his body, pausing at the techno leg, while he watched me, a sentry fine-tuned to pick up signs of trouble. But he had to have seen what I felt. Which was as far from pity or disdain as I could get without falling off the edge of this brand-new world.

Love? With Lon, it had been almost instantaneous. With Scott I'd felt attraction approaching for years and pushed back against it. But now it was okay, good, wonderful, and on its way to . . . who knew? But, oh, I wanted to find out.

He was waiting for my answer. I ended my sweeping appraisal with a deep breath and a husky, "Done. Now will you make love to me, please?"

And so we moved in an improvised dance to the bed. Where for the next timeless hour we discovered each other as new lovers do. We were very busy.

We did stop once, when, tangled in the sheets, I banged my knee against the shell of his prosthesis socket. "Hey," he said. "You okay?"

"Fine. I just have to remember you've got extra hard parts."

"Ah, you noticed." He chuckled and I heard relief behind the laugher. "Seriously"—he smacked his left leg—"on or off."

"Your call."

"Off, then. The last thing I want to do is hurt you. Plus, it's more weight to haul around. And"—in the glaring light, I saw a smile curl—"we don't want one long, hard shaft getting in the way of another long, hard shaft."

Cocky? No, confident.

He pivoted so I wouldn't witness the mechanics of the final reveal. The peeling back of the sleeve, the roll of the sock liners, the release of the vacuum lock, the detaching. It would take him time to realize that none of this shocked me or turned me off. But that was for later. He didn't look at me as he reached for his robe at the foot of the bed and draped it over what had been a vital part of him and now lay on the floor, covered like a lifeless thing.

Swiveling, he was back with me, the all of him that really mattered.

We explored sweet spots and hot spots, new territory for both of us, getting lost in each other. When he entered me it didn't feel like invasion; it felt like liberation. My emotions, kept in check for a very long time, exploded when he did. My release came with a shudder.

Afterward, we lay thigh to thigh, exhausted and exhilarated in a pool of purple dusk. We'd outlasted the sun.

chapter thirty-two

"You do know we're being watched, right? Marsha Felcher hasn't taken her eyes off us since the cha-cha," Scott whispered in my ear Tuesday night. "She claims to be retired from some federal agency—I think she said the Department of Agriculture. But I detect the pungent odor of horse manure and a cover for the CIA." He grinned, and as Marsha spun off in another direction, Scott pulled me closer than was appropriate for the American Smooth dance style I taught. "You, on the other hand, smell delicious."

We were waltzing to "Rainbow Connection," sung by Kermit the Frog, our time-honored choice for the last dance of the last class of the summer session, a get-together at the Turquoise Café to follow. For this finale evening I'd chosen, all by myself with no input from my fashion maven, a pale green halter dress that brought out the Irish in me. My hair, brushed loose to the shoulders, was freshly colored copper and as shiny as a newly minted penny. I must have been wearing a smitten look, because it wasn't only Marsha picking up vibes. Tom Hepburn was sending us sly, fond glances. The old roué knew a romance in session when he saw it.

At least I was trying to keep it under wraps. Scott didn't bother to suppress his smile. "Don't sit next to me at the party," I said. "Seriously. You're going to give us away."

"You're just afraid to play footsie with my power leg. And 'seriously' back at you, why do we need to hide?"

"Because this is my business and I don't think it's good practice to mix business with pleasure."

Which was probably a moot point anyway, because there might not be a business after tonight. On my way into Hot Bods, I'd picked up the mail in my cubby and found a manila envelope with "Now or Never" scrawled on top. Sal Zito. I'd been ducking my landlord for the last week, but he'd outsmarted me. The envelope was heavy. I didn't open it then. Didn't want to foul my mood. I knew next year's contract was inside and I had no idea if I was going to sign.

Scott, a welcome distraction, was saying, "Pleasure. You are that and so much more to me."

So much more. I felt that, too, as Kermit sang about lovers and dreamers and Scott drew me closer. Closer was different now. Sunday in bed had taught us things about each other that only the best sex can teach. Such as my lover was generous. Also adventurous. Which brought out a long-suppressed daring in me. I'd forgotten how much pagan a good Catholic girl could store beneath the surface. I'd never been a wild child, though in my marriage I'd followed a sensual lead. But I was all grown-up and on my own now, and what we'd seen without the artifice—and liked—had created a new intimacy between Scott and me. It showed up in the way we moved together. Perfectly, and with soul.

Kermit sang about the Rainbow Connection, and I thought maybe—please God, one day I would be miraculously cured of this plague of maybes—just maybe, I'd found it.

And then Kermit paused the lyrics, our background was all music, and Scott backed up an inch to say, "Okay, I was going to wait to tell you at the café, but since I'm being exiled, I'd better do it now. I got some good news today." He waited two beats for my prompting nod. "I landed that job I've been interviewing for. Consultant to a defense contractor in Bethesda." He was beaming. "It's a great fit. Full-time, though I can work at home on certain projects that aren't top security. And they gave me a signing bonus."

"That's fantastic. I'm so happy for you." I thought I was, but there were implications. Would that mean he wouldn't be back in Tuckahoe next summer? Then again, would I?

"Thanks. I'm pretty excited about it. We should celebrate."

"We're going to. At the café."

"That's a good-bye party. I'm talking about a new beginning here. You know how you christen a ship? You bang it with champagne." The double entendre made me giggle. "I love your laugh." His blue eyes went to velvet. "I've a bottle of Dom in the fridge and"—pause for dramatic effect—"I've left all the lights on."

Ah, another après-party party. The invitation was not entirely unexpected, and this time I was dressed for it on all layers. Whoever invented the thong should be strung up by it. Uncomfortable as hell, a vine climbing into a crack. But sexy. Somehow, inexplicably, and incredibly, sexy.

The Turquoise Café was especially beautiful at night with its swags of gauze drifting like iridescent clouds from the ceiling and the misty light from the patio lanterns casting soft shadows on the walls. It was late on a weekday and the place was only half full. Em, working the espresso machine behind the service counter, looked haggard. When she spotted me at the head of our little parade spilling through the door, she gave her head a slow, mournful shake and slid her gaze toward the force of nature barreling toward us. Selda, the mother-in-law from hell—corset trussed in a stylish black dress at least one size too small, pearl necklace swinging—flourished a hand in greeting. "Welcome to the Turquoise Café. We've been expecting you." She should have been. I'd booked our party with Em a month before.

Selda herded us to the restaurant's largest table. Scott slipped into the seat directly across from mine. His wink was discreet, though I heard what I thought was a whisper of *aha* coming from Marsha on my right.

Selda handed out laminated menus decorated with line drawings of Turkish specialties. The menus with a professional polish were an innovation. Customers had always relied on the big board, chalked with the day's features, or the carry-out trifold Adnan printed out himself.

When the buzz of settling in didn't quiet immediately, Selda clapped us into silence. "You are ready to hear tonight's specials," she informed us. I'd been scanning the menu. It listed some items I'd never seen before: *tavuk adana*, skewered ground chicken, and a grilled mixed-meat kebab. At least no calf's liver with sumac. "Tonight's special is *sucuklu pide*, pita bread stuffed with Turkish sausage. The sausage is homemade." Selda touched a finger to her enormous brooch and dipped what was supposed to be a modest bow. "By me." She pointed to the door behind the service counter. No wonder Emine was looking as frayed as an antique Turkish carpet. Selda had taken over her kitchen.

Suddenly, its swinging door flew open and Meryem Haydar flashed an outraged glance at her mother before charging through the dining area like a rogue elephant. You could almost see steam rising from her as she worked to juggle a sponge, a trash bag, a roll of paper towels, and a spray bottle.

"And you, the picky one, what will you have?" Selda pulled me back to the menu. She'd made the rounds of the rectangular table and I was the last holdout, unable to decide between custard and cake. She drummed a pencil impatiently against the order pad.

I chose the *künefe*, a cheese pastry made with shredded phyllo. "With extra whipped cream," I said. It was an "I dare you" addition. I waited for a comment on the width of my hips, but she shrugged and wrote, then couldn't resist a minor jab. "Extra, extra everything," she said. "Only in America." She pronounced it dismissively, as if we were a country of savages.

The woman had 360-degree vision and now she hissed, "First the sponge and then the paper, Meryem." Merry was cleaning the table behind us. Teeth clenched, the girl wrung the sponge with extra fervor, as if it was her grandmother's neck. I tried to catch her eye, but her head was down, chin resting on her chest.

Selda gave Merry a sharp look and muttered, "'One who does not slap his children will slap his knees.' True Turkish saying."

"Who or what was that?" Marsha asked, when the battleship had sailed, leaving a froth of astonished chatter in her wake.

"That," I said, "was Emine's mother-in-law."

"She's the spitting image of a sergeant I had when I first joined the Marines," Tom Hepburn said.

"And the cleaner is the granddaughter?" Yolanda Powell said. "Poor thing."

That's when I decided it was time for an intervention or two. On my way to Em, I stopped at Merry's table. "Sweetheart." I put my hands on her shoulders and leaned in. "What's going on? You okay?"

"I'm Cinderfuckingrella, so, like, how can I be okay?" She was spritzing and scrubbing. "Is she watching me?"

"No, she just went into the kitchen."

She put the bottle down. "Look at me, Aunt Norrie. I'm a freak of nature, thanks to her. How do you like the hair?" Her creative spiky do, back to its natural brown and highlighted by Margo's hairstylist at Margo's expense, was slicked back and reined in with a headband. "She wanted me to wear something called a hairnet, but my wuss of a mother finally put her foot down on that. And this penguin getup?" Long-sleeved white blouse, black skirt that fell below her knees. "This is what Adnan calls a compromise? Selda actually wanted me to wear a uniform. An all-white dress, like a nurse or something. She has me working three nights a week. Plus two afternoons. And I get paid squat. Less than the minimum wage. I Googled it. Now she's talking weekends. Like Saturday nights. If she thinks she's going to take away my Saturday nights . . ."

Merry's breath had become shallow and punctuated with quick little gasps.

"Hey. Slow down," I tried to soothe her.

"I'm . . . not . . . allowed to . . . slow down," she said. "I don't know how much more of this I can take. And my mom. I don't blame her for everything. I really don't. Selda's worse to her than to me, even. It's my dad. He's, like, bought into all this shit. He thinks his mother is some kind of god. And now she's talking about staying forever. I swear I'd rather go to Turkey and stay with Mom's mom, my *anneanne*, who doesn't even wear lipstick. I'd rather be anywhere than here."

The last time I'd seen Merry cry, she was six years old and fell off a swing, skinning both knees. This wound was deeper. Twin rivulets of tears trailed her cheeks. She swiped them away.

Selda, wearing a prune face, swept by us on her way to our table with a *meze* plate. "Wasting time, Merry." The wicked witch and I traded glares.

"As soon as I can get your mom alone, I'll talk to her," I said.

"Thanks, Aunt Norrie, but it won't do any good. She's a lowly *gelin*, a daughter-in-law. The only person Selda listens to is my dad. And he's drunk the Kool-Aid. I'm doomed."

I finally cornered Em on our way out.

"I know, I know," she said. "Merry's right. She calls me a wimp. But I have tried. I have even confronted. It does no good. Selda has the last word. Her son gives her that. On a platter."

The espresso machine hissed disapproval in the background.

"The plan was she'd be leaving right after Ramadan, and then we are back to normal. I told Merry, it's only two weeks more. The light at the end of the tunnel. But now the tunnel is dark and stretches to eternity. Last night Selda announced she needs more time to whip Merry into shape. Whip? She says whip about your child, I tell Adnan. He says he will talk to her but that one has to handle these things carefully, with respect. She's his mother, after all. And where's the respect for me, your wife, and for our child, I ask. Be patient, he tells me. Well, my patience is at an end. Tonight I watched her—look now, how she is shaking a finger at Merry. What? My daughter didn't wipe off the napkin caddy to suit her?"

She pitched her towel onto the countertop. "That's it. I just made a decision. If she stays, I go. And I take both kids with me."

"Em," I started, but she talked over me.

"What is the saying? Women and children first. This is who I have to save. No, my mind is made up. Adnan has one week to make up his. He tells me he will consult with the imam. He says he needs advice as to how to proceed to make everyone happy. Of course such a thing can't be done. Perhaps the imam will bring him to his senses. If not, my husband will have made the choice. And if he chooses wrong, the next choice will be mine."

Outside, I took a deep breath of the salt-tanged air to clear my head. Scott was waiting for me under the streetlamp where we'd made last-minute whispered plans to reconnoiter.

"Not good, huh? You look upset," he said as I moved into the haloed light. "Mother-in-law problem?"

I nodded. "Bad. And it could get worse. I wish there was something I could do, but I don't see what."

"You're there for your friend. Sometimes that's the only thing friends can do for friends, be there for them. To listen. And, though I hope it doesn't come to that, if it falls apart, to help pick up the pieces." He took my hand and we started walking. "Now, what can I do for you?"

I knew exactly what he could do for me. I told him part of it. "I could use some of that Dom Pérignon therapy you mentioned." The other part he didn't have to hear, the wanting to be held by him that turned into an aching need as soon as I thought it.

Later, back at his place, we moved from champagne in the living room to something even more intoxicating in the bedroom. For at least a few hours, Scott and what we did together outblazed the crises flaring all over my life. Afterward, as I lay in his arms, my raging heat ebbed to a glowing warmth, I thought that fighting fire with fire really did work, even if it's just for the moment.

To make it last and because all the desire I had left was not to move from the spot, I sent my promised "don't worry" text to Jack, telling him all was fine but I wouldn't be home that night. He'd texted back: K. No rounded, generous *O* before it. Just the spiky, spindly, single *K.*

He was pissed.

chapter thirty-three

I left Scott's warm bed and arms at seven thirty.

"Why so early? What's the rush?" he murmured, lassoing me back from my reluctant crawl to the far edge of the mattress. He drew me close so that our bodies spooned under the light cover. His words were cottony, his longing clear from the way his hand traced the curve of my hips. "I'll make you breakfast."

"Right, well, I know what you want for breakfast."

He laughed. "And lunch and dinner. Do you blame me? You're wonderful. But afterward, pancakes. Or an omelet. I flip a mean omelet. And I have farmers' market blueberries for dessert. Stay."

"Oh, I wish I could." I turned toward him to stroke his cheek, prickly with overnight stubble, and my heart began to pick up its beat. I tuned it out and untangled myself from his gentle grasp. "But I really need to get back. I have an appointment. People coming over."

I didn't give him details. My face said I wasn't inviting questions. We dressed. Slugged orange juice. He drove me to my car with jazz tuned on the radio. I took a rain check for an invitation to Sunday breakfast. I reminded him that the Donor Dude was visiting over the upcoming weekend, but I was looking forward to trying the incredible omelet à la Goddard.

"When?" he asked.

"Soon," I promised.

"Not soon enough."

The reason for my rushing off was a call that had come in as I'd headed to class the night before. Flip Tarlow, Margo's Realtor maven, was thrilled to tell me she had a possible buyer for the place.

Yes, of course, she remembered that I hadn't made a decision to sell yet, and she was really sorry about how last-minute this all was, but some prospective buyers had just stopped in her office. It was a walk-in, a "whim-in," she cutesily called it. A "darling young couple from Philly," they'd been thinking, just beginning to think, about beachfront property. Something with an existing house, if possible. When Flip told them about Surf Avenue, they were verrrrry interested, they had verrrrry deep pockets, and that combination might not occur again for a loooong time. "Worst case, your beautiful home isn't right for them."

Best case, I'd thought as I nervously chewed a hangnail. I was painfully ambivalent about showing the house.

"But at least we'll have their reaction to help us make adjustments when you *are* ready to move ahead," Flip had pressed. She hoped a walk-through at ten tomorrow would be convenient.

"Tomorrow?" My voice had sounded hollow. The way I felt.

Yes, they were on a tight schedule. No, I didn't have to be there. She didn't *want* me there. I couldn't imagine the comments people made about other people's homes. It wasn't for the faint of heart.

Good thing Jack wasn't going to be around. Ethan was going to walk the dogs with him in the morning and then they were going out for the day on the Winslets' boat.

While Flip had yammered on, I'd wandered through the house in my head. Through my beautiful great room with the high ceilings and a view of the sea and the *shush* of the waves lulling me to nap on the white sofa.

Through the bedroom with my widow's walk and the French windows through which a gauzy Lon had drifted in. Though not lately.

I ripped the hangnail free.

Flip must have heard me bleeding because she'd crooned, "Darling, you're not committing to anything. This is a trial run, though I've personally experienced buyers making an offer on the spot. Love at first sight. That's rare, though."

She'd emailed me a checklist for the final straightening up. Windex mirrors. Mop the tile floor in entryway. Don't worry about closets. They looked fine on last visit. As for Jack's room, just make sure all stray food is picked up. These two were probably young enough to laugh off the standard mess of a college kid. Fresh flowers on the dining room table would be a nice touch. Bathrooms, very important. Nothing on the sink, lots of pastel towels.

"Also, you could bake something chocolate in the morning. Makes a home smell homey. Or get the spray that smells like cookies in the oven." She'd said that in an email that arrived while Scott and I were making love.

Sorry again this was such short notice. But I couldn't afford to pass anything up, right?

Oh damn. Right.

Margo was surprised when I called to ask for refuge on my way home from Scott's. I didn't put it that way, of course. I said, "How would you like company this morning?" It was opening day of the annual Tuckahoe Outdoor Craft Show. Margo was a fan of wearable art, handmade quilts, and quirky bead-and-wire sculptures.

"*You* are the company?" She sounded properly incredulous. "It's at Weymouth Farm again, Nora. Last year, you kvetched the whole time about how you hated walking in the dirt, and when you got stung by the wasp hanging out in the macramé birdhouse, you swore you'd never go again."

"I'll wear bug spray. I need earrings. Silver ones to go with my fuchsia dress. From that guy you know who makes the swoopy kind that look like waves?"

"John, of Long John's Silver."

"Him. I like his stuff."

"Since when? What fuchsia dress? What redhead wears fuchsia?"

"Meet you in front of the fried-dough stand at ten."

I was late. I'd squeezed in a quick run to Piggly Wiggly for the cookie spray and swung back to the house to spritz the fake-bake scent around my kitchen. By the time I arrived at the fried-dough stand, Margo was tapping a sandal, raising dust. A gigantic mosquito flitted around her head but didn't land. Must have been the nontoxic insect repellent distilled from organic French lavender she'd dabbed on her neck. The bug landed on my arm and, before I could slap it off, stabbed me. "Well, we're off to a good start," she said sarcastically.

We walked in and out of the tent-topped displays. I bought a pair of overpriced handcrafted earrings I didn't need for a fuchsia dress I didn't own. Margo stared at them dubiously. "With your ballerina's long neck, the shoulder-duster styles would be fabulous. But these are more subdued. They'll work with Scott's VFW crowd." Then, all innocence, "How *is* the colonel? You two were awfully chummy at the beach Sunday."

Pete was right about Margo's propensity for drawing snap—and frequently wrong—conclusions from scanty information. But after Sunday at Scott's and again last night, it was time to share. On my terms, of course, which were minus the juicy X-rated details she lusted after.

I started off blandly. "Scott's fine." And slid to provocative. "He snores, though."

She braked to a stop in front of a tent lined with African wood carvings and clapped a hand over her mouth. But not for long.

"Oh my God. You finally slept with him. Wait, you said snore? I assume you don't mean the two of you falling asleep on your deck holding hands. This *is* sex we're talking about, right?" I nodded, which pulled the pin on her grenade. Shrapnel flew: "Where? His place? Decent or some grungy bachelor pad? No, save the décor for later. Oh my God. You should see your eyes. Glowing like hot coals. Okay, hot. Back to the sex. How many times? Was it good? And the leg, how did you deal with that?" I ducked the most pointed questions, but the woman was relentless. She ended by asking if we'd made plans to see each other after the summer. No, we hadn't discussed that.

"Well, you should, Nora. Exactly two weeks from today you'll be on your way back to Baltimore."

Two weeks! Too soon! Time is running out! The same siren that went off every year mid-August when I realized the end was near. The Manolises and the Farrells always left the Wednesday before Labor Day to get ahead of the final swarm of locusts, as Margo called the holiday crowd descending on Tuckahoe.

"You don't want this to be a summer romance." She purred a long *hmmmm.* "Doesn't Jack leave for Duke next week?"

"Wednesday."

"So you'll have the house to yourself. But not necessarily *by* yourself. Days of hot, steamy weather predicted. Indoors, anyway. But come up for air long enough to make plans."

Three stops later—Margo had collected a mixed-media collage and a tie-dyed kaftan while I had only a pair of unnecessary earrings tucked in my handbag—we entered the Irish tent, where weaver Kate Donnegan, whose brogue was as thick as oatmeal, greeted us. She'd taken my ballroom class a few years back, but after her husband died she didn't have the heart for it. I understood.

Kate sold garments she fashioned from wool she wove herself and also carried some pieces from a weaving co-op in Killarney. Margo tried on sweaters and shawls, but it was only when she wrapped herself in an Irish wool cape that she broke out in a smile.

"Oh, look at you," Kate crooned as Margo preened in a mirror propped against a tent pole. "The violet is so flattering for your coloring. And the cape is a perfect weight. It will take you right through fall."

"Fall," Margo repeated, slipping the cape off as she sent me a look that said, *"Plan for it. With Scott."* Unfortunately, my plans were stratospheric on many fronts—up in the air.

Margo handed the purple cape to Kate. "It's gorgeous. I'll take it."

With the large green bag slung over her arm, she was on the move again, hauling me along. "Come," she said. "There's a guy, Mark Blumenstein, who does the most amazing sculptures with cooking utensils. It would be perfect for . . ."

The kitchen I probably wouldn't have next summer. Which, if said aloud, Margo would have taken for whining, so I mumbled, "I've been thinking about your friend Philippa Tarlow. I may want to feel her out about whether the house is salable."

Margo whirled on me, sounding the alarm. "Premature, premature! You will not have to sell the house. And if by some catastrophic turn of fate you find yourself down to your last shekel and have no alternatives, you ask me for recommendations for an agent. Definitely do not call that awful woman. I haven't spoken to her in three years since I caught her cheating at bridge. Really, if you can't trust a person at the bridge table, can you trust her with your house?"

Which was probably why, during my first conversation with Flip, when I'd asked her to keep our call confidential, she'd replied, "Real estate agents are like doctors and lawyers. We observe a professional code of confidentiality. I don't tell Margo Manolis and you don't tell her. Deal?"

A thank-God deal. Margo would have eviscerated me on the spot had she known about Flip and me. But she didn't know, would never know.

We parted ways—with a double kiss on the cheek from her—at the sculptor's tent. Just in time, too. I was alone, approaching my car, when my cell phone rang. It was Flip to tell me the darling couple thought the house was adorable, absolutely charming, but with only three bedrooms and no pool, not quite for them.

That was, without a doubt, the whitewashed version of their reaction. They'd probably thrown up over the deck into my hydrangea bush and had a good laugh about the twenty-year-old wallpaper in the second-floor bathroom, which was mustard color and flocked with fleur-de-lis.

I'd never hired her, but that afternoon, I fired Flip Tarlow.

chapter thirty-four

In the days before Dirk's second visit, Jack had been incessantly whistling his anthem, "Here Comes the Sun/Son," and, as obedient as one of his Sea Spot Run canine clients, a golden disk rose in a cloudless sky on Saturday morning.

Jack bounded down the stairs and into the kitchen, reading aloud from his iPhone. "Head-high SSE medium period swell with occasional one- to two-foot overhead high sets. Oh yeah. Perfect conditions."

He and Dirk had plans to surf off the beach at Rehoboth. I wasn't thrilled with the idea. I whisked eggs in a bowl. "You're not pushing him to do this, right?" I asked.

"Me? No way!" Jack swigged orange juice straight from the container. "It was his idea."

I could see Dirk in the white doc's jacket, the rep tie, the fancy watch, but not so much in palm-tree-printed board shorts. "It just seems strange," I said. "A forty-eight-year-old man riding the waves. Late forties are already heart attack territory."

"Mom, there's a guy down at the Spindrift who's gotta be eighty and he's still going strong. If you're in decent shape you can go on forever."

The pan was hot, butter sizzling. I poured the eggs and started to scramble.

"Besides, Dirk's a cardiologist so he knows that territory. He wouldn't risk his life. Jen says he's a fitness fanatic. He's a runner and he goes to the gym before work. On weekends he cycles the mountains. He'll probably make me look like a measly wimp."

I stopped scrambling to wave a spatula at him, "Listen, I want you to be careful. No showing off for him, you understand?"

Jack swiped his mouth with the bottom of his T-shirt. "I'm not into hotdogging. That's just dumb." He ambled over to pat my arm. "Come on, Mom, relax. I'm nineteen, and I started lessons when I was seven. Remember what Dad used to say? 'First in his class at boarding school.'"

Lon loved the daredevil in his son. When I'd expressed fear at Jack's lack of fear, Lon had shot back, "I'd rather the kid break his neck than we break his spirit." I hadn't liked the choices.

"Dirk's really experienced," Jack said, reassuring me. "He says that South Beach near San Francisco is incredible in the fall. They get these crazy currents from the Golden Gate Bridge that make for some wild rides. November is the best month."

Also Thanksgiving vacation. Would there be an invitation for a trip out west to get to know the DeHaven sisters over turkey and stuffing? Would all those genetically linked Californians—Jack carrying the daring chromosomes—be off to the beach to ride unpredictable waves to who knew what shore?

Twenty minutes later, I heard Jack yell from the front hall, "Mom, I'm leaving. We'll be home around five."

I answered, sounding so laid-back I gave myself a gold star for good mother. Josh would have been pleased. "Give my regards to Dirk. And have a super day. Oh, and what time are dinner reservations?"

Jack had made them. "Six thirty at a new place, the Flying Jib. It's on Teal Duck Creek. I thought it would be a change for him from the ocean view, and the food's supposed to be great. Heavy on the seafood."

I hadn't told him I'd already been there. With Scott. Eating mussels, calamari, and crab cakes. And I didn't mention it now. Good thing, too, or my front door would have slammed harder than it did.

I also spent the afternoon riding waves. Metaphorically.

My destination had been the opposite—total calm. Marely's Cove, an elbow of beach, was off the tourist track. The dunes were high and they slanted deep shadows, so the area didn't attract sun worshippers. Brambles, craggy rocks, driftwood obstacles, and shell-paved sand made the place inhospitable to kids and tender adults. In high summer, algae that collected in the tidal pools gave off a stink. I liked the marshy smell. The cove was perfect for what I had in mind. Which was nothing. Absolutely nothing. I carried an oversized towel and a plastic bottle of what had started out as ice water. No books. No music. It was pretty much me and my mantra. Though I hardly meditated anymore, I knew I could reach back for it when I needed a sweet piece of peace.

Margo and I had met in a college class called Meditation and the Soul of Performance. The first token of our friendship had been sharing our mantras. Mine was *sita ram*, which was supposed to open the heart to love. Hers was *so hum*, a phrase she'd chosen because it sounded like a Jewish mother's affectionate instruction. "As in," she liked to say, "so hum already, darling."

I laughed as I walked down the path to the beach. A man seated nearby didn't lift his eyes from the *Wall Street Journal*. A crab skittering toward the water ignored me, and a great egret, its elegant head turned away, stood motionless on a half-submerged rock, intent upon searching out a fish dinner. I cleared a spot on the sand, spread my towel, lay back, closed my eyes, and synchronized my breathing to the pulse of the surf, and soon everything washed away—the past, the future, even the moment. I drifted down into my own internal ocean. I didn't know or care how long I was under. At some point, a secret signal prompted what should have been a gradual rise to the surface. But halfway there, the cell phone I thought I'd turned to silent before leaning it against the water bottle vibrated with a *clickety-click*, jolting me up. I gasped and grabbed for it. I could have turned it off. Then I saw the ID, Nate Greenberg, and I couldn't.

"Hey, Nora. Sorry to disturb you on a Saturday. I hope I'm not interrupting anything important."

"Just an afternoon on the beach."

"Lucky you. Okay, I'll make this quick. Yesterday I had lunch with a fiction editor at Marquis and Company, one of the big five publishers. We were meeting to discuss a totally different project and in passing I happened to mention *Thunder Hill Road*. Honestly, I was bowled over by Zach's reaction. Growing up, he'd read *Canyon of Time* and he'd been hooked, a major Lon Farrell fan, though he found the last two books disappointing. Especially *Wild Mountain*. He thought the pace was slow and the plot somewhat stale. I hope you don't take this personally."

"No," I said. "That was the consensus among the reviewers, the pace part."

"Right, so I didn't argue the point. And the 'stale' comment was a perfect opening for relating how we brought this new young talent on board and how Hector's freshness and vibrant approach to telling this powerful story fused with Lon's mastery of the genre. That got Zach's attention. Bottom line, he'd like to take a look at what we have so far. I gave you my word that I'd run everything by you." There was a nervous tapping on the other end. "So, are you okay with this?"

"Yes. Fine. Sure," I said, trying to keep my enthusiasm tamped down, but Nate picked up on it.

"Nora, I don't want you to make too much of this. It's a nibble, that's all. Even if the Marquis people pick it up, I don't see it as a blockbuster. It's a prestige thing for them, having Lon Farrell as one of their authors. So no big bucks in sight. But you're not doing this for the money, anyway."

No, I thought, but I wouldn't have turned it away had it come flooding in.

"What we're going for here is to honor one of the outstanding writers of his generation. Reacquaint the American reader with his writing. That would be the marketing angle. Resurrecting Lon—sorry, bad choice of words—cementing his legacy is a great story. The problem is that doing book tours, interviews, TV appearances without the author is going to be a push. Lon was a media darling with the Irish twinkle and the quick wit. Imagine him with Jimmy Kimmel." He sighed. "Even if they'll have Hector, he's no Lon. He doesn't have the looks or the charm to play well on the small screen. Anyway, we'll cross that bridge when, God willing, we come to it. Meanwhile, I'll get that manuscript to Zach. And keep you in the loop, of course. What's the weather like there?"

Suddenly sunny. The dunes hadn't shifted, but I had. I latched onto the possibility of a new book that would reach a new audience and I held on to it for dear life. Mine. Because if I could help create this living memorial to Lon, I might be able to move on. As Nate and I chatted about the weather, I walked to the water's edge, which was bathed in a noon glow. The wind was picking up. Over in Dewey Beach, Jack and Dirk must have been riding high. Everyplace I looked, the horizon was bright.

After Nate signed off, I had maybe twenty seconds to bask in his announcement before Margo rang with her news. Whatever Pete was doing for the Orioles—PR, player relations—he was obviously knocking it out of the park. Yesterday, the O's had matched the TV station's offer, and when Pete asked for time to consider, they upped it and added a re-sign bonus. Pete was out surf fishing at the moment, which was his version of meditating. He wanted to talk his decision through with her tomorrow.

First I'd heard about it, but Margo had a project of her own, a secret (even from me) dream she'd put on hold, and now, with the raise and the bonus, there was money to make it happen. She knew Pete was going to tell her to go full speed ahead. He really was a wonderful man. They really had a wonderful marriage. Life. He'd stay where he was, in the O's front office where the testosterone was so pure and potent that a woman could grow hair on her chest just breathing the air. Margo would stay where she was too. She'd cancel the private investigator's retainer and the meeting with her lawyer the shark. Case closed.

It never would be, I thought. Not for her. Not as long as Pete and women existed on the same planet. But for now, at least, she was happy.

By ten past six, I was fretting at the time—we had dinner reservations for six thirty—and over what looked like the beginnings of a storm stirring the sky out my kitchen window. Where the hell were they—still on the water? Was that thunder? Or maybe it was the garage door I heard, rumbling open and shut. After a moment, the side door slammed and Jack called, "We're here."

I put my pen down. I'd just signed Sal Zito's contract renewing my studio lease with the increase. Sal's terms included a ninety-day kick-out clause, and I knew I could come up with three months' rent, and we'd see after that. Emine and I were still exchanging emails about our plan for drumming up business, which looked promising. Besides, I couldn't let the masseuse Sal had waiting in the wings muscle me out of the space. Probably most of what we were operating on was hope, but there were worse things to keep you going.

"Mom, where are you?"

"Kitchen," I called back.

Jack rock and rolled in on a swagger, with Dirk behind him, marching to his own quick step.

I gave them an approving once-over. "You're all cleaned up." I'd stacked towels in the guest bathroom upstairs just in case.

"We showered at the Spindrift," my son informed me. "Tony says hi, by the way." His favorite teacher at his old "boarding" school.

Jack looked as scrubbed, peeled, and ruddy as a carrot in his chinos and Hawaiian shirt. Dirk was obviously freshly washed and combed, his platinum hair carved into trails revealing the pink of his scalp. Pale tracings of his sunglasses stood out against skin grilled to medium rare.

"You had fun?" I flicked the question at Dirk, but it was meant for Jack, who mattered more.

Jack said, "Fun doesn't describe it," and proceeded to describe it. Dirk looked on, smiling throughout. Nodding when asked to confirm some detail. Laughing at Jack's funny remarks. Occasionally, he added a comment when called upon. He liked my son. That was obvious. As for me, I'd been worried at first about being taken in, but now I was, simply and surprisingly, taken.

I'd always been a sucker for Celtic charm, my dad's and Lon's, but there was something appealing about the sturdy Dutch personality. And I had to admit Dirk was good-looking. Tall, broad shouldered, and though not film-star handsome, he carried enough eye-stopping features to make him interesting looking. His expression gave off intelligence. There were the lupine irises and the eyebrows, dashes of gold. The hair on his arms, thick and pale, like the pelt of a rare blond monkey. Oddly, his legs below the retro madras Bermuda shorts were hairless, glossy, and knotted with muscle. I wondered if he shaved or waxed. Some surfers did.

Jack caught me staring and detoured his monologue to say, "Incredible legs, huh? He runs ten miles most days. Or swims laps. How many, Dirk?" Who didn't answer, just dispatched a mildly embarrassed smile to me. "Whatever. And that's after a full day at the hospital, where he's on his feet most of the time. Like in the OR. And teaching." Jack shook his head in disbelieving admiration. "You should see him on the board. Perfect balance. It's in the quadriceps."

It occurred to me then, as I studiously avoided looking at Dirk's thighs, that Jack was going on a little too long about legs. Was this some kind of limb-comparison game? Was I supposed to think, wow, this guy has two really incredible legs and, hmmm, whom do I know who only has one? The owner of that techno leg had called late afternoon to say hi and wish me a good time that night even if it wasn't with him.

I attempted to cut Jack off by tapping my watch face. "Getting late. If we're going to make our reservation, we'd better hustle."

Dirk laid a halting hand on Jack's shoulder. "Let's talk about dinner and see if your mom's on board with the new plans."

Jack explained that indoors, with waiters and all, seemed so formal after a day on the waves. Plus, the Flying Jib specialized in seafood and they'd demolished two dozen crabs at lunch, so that was also a turnoff.

They'd stopped off on the way home and picked up some steaks (which, Dirk interjected, they'd stashed in the garage fridge on their way in and could be frozen for some other time if I preferred to stick with the original agenda). I, Jack resumed, wouldn't have to do a thing. The men would grill. They'd stopped at a roadside stand for local Sugar Queen corn, which he could throw on the grill. "And we have Coneheads ice cream in the freezer for dessert. All you have to do is take it easy. How does that sound?"

I said, "Like a good idea," though the restaurant with its hustle and bustle might have filled any lulls in the conversation.

"Great. Okay, I'll fire up the grill and you two can have drinks in the living room and relax."

Uneasiness clouded Dirk's eyes. Then the left lid twitched. He and I must have been thinking the same thing. That Jack was playing Noah again, matching us up as if we were a twosome made by biblical injunction.

"Scotch, gin, vodka," I offered him. "Bourbon. Beer?"

Beer was his choice. I wanted something stronger. I splashed vodka over ice. Jack, refusing help with the grill, promised to call Dirk if he needed a consult. He grabbed a Coke and headed out to the deck with a full tray. A few seconds later, he discreetly closed the sliding glass door behind him.

Dirk and I carried our drinks into the great room. I sat on the chaise end of the sofa, expecting him to plant himself in a far corner, but he put only about a foot between us on the cushion and then he leaned in.

"I need your help," he said.

Whoa. I tried to rein in what Josh called my tendency for catastrophic thinking. As in Dirk was having second thoughts about his connection with Jack. I couldn't hear Jack with the sliding glass door between us, but I saw him wrapping corn for the grill and his head rocking a rhythm, lips pursed. I'd have bet he was whistling, and put money on the song: Here comes the you-know-what. Maybe he'd overdone the son part today and spooked Dirk into retreat.

"I've got some news to deliver that Jack probably won't like. I hate to disappoint him."

My heart lurched, but my brain, for once, didn't lose its balance. I made myself listen to Dirk saying, "He's a smart kid. He told me about dean's list. But as important, maybe more so, he's got an engaging person-ality. Very open. He's a natural storyteller. Over lunch, he shook the fam-ily tree. I heard all about his grandfather, his grandmother the Broadway dancer, and his uncle Mick. Jack London. Someone named Claire and another girl back at Duke."

I'd love to know that story, I thought. But for now, I said, "The gift of gab he gets from my dad."

"And from his own dad, of course," Dirk said kindly. "Certainly not from my gene pool. I was an introverted kid, then a geek before it became fashionable, and I'm a private man. To be honest, when the fertility clinic phoned, I was pleased at the prospect of meeting Jack. But also concerned about how I should deal with it. With him. And you. I didn't want to get it wrong."

Here we go, I thought.

"I knew what I could give. But I wasn't sure what he wanted. Or how you felt." He shifted nervously on the cushion. "I think it's worked out well. What do you think?"

I nodded dumbly. Worked, he'd said. Past tense.

"I'm afraid, though, I haven't given him the complete picture. I didn't want to flood him with a lot of information at first. But now it's definitely time. It's become clear from some of his comments, and his actions . . . He wants to . . . He has this fantasy of . . . us. You and me, getting together in a romantic way." He paused, licked his lips. "I can understand it. You're a very attractive woman, Nora. Your son says you're a great catch."

I felt a blush surge. "Subtlety isn't Jack's strong suit," I said. Was this a come-on? Now, that could complicate things, depending upon how it was handled. I reached for charming but, I hoped, not encouraging. "And you're a very nice man," I responded. "Any woman would be lucky to . . . you know . . ."

"But." We said it simultaneously. Mutually startled at our duet, and as if it had punctured a bubble of anxiety, we simultaneously expelled a gust of relieved laughter.

"I guess that's settled, then," I said, thanking God that was all it was, and thinking it was just as well it was out in the open and Jack could stop with the matchmaking craziness.

"Not quite settled," Dirk said, and I sucked in a fresh breath of disquiet.

He took a long draught of beer. "There's a wonderful woman in my life and has been for a while. I knew Victoria was special almost immediately, but the scientist in me—well, I tend to overdissect things. My ex-wife and I divorced four years ago. It wasn't a pleasant experience and I didn't want to repeat it. I wanted to be sure as I could be about Victoria and me."

"And now you are."

"The talks with Johns Hopkins gave me the push I needed. Victoria's an ophthalmologist with a well-established practice. She loves her work and her patients. She can't take a year off to move to Baltimore, and the thought of all that time away from her, of how much I'd miss her, made it clear to me. I want us together. Permanently. So"—he hoisted his bottle of Sam Adams in a toast—"as of last week, we're engaged. Ring and all."

I lifted my glass. "Congratulations. That's wonderful news." Better than what I'd anticipated.

"Hopkins suggested a compromise. I'll lecture four times a year at the medical school, but I'm staying out in California. And now it's past time to tell Jack. You'll help me if I get in trouble?"

"I have your back. But he'll be fine with it."

"I hope so. He was looking forward to me being in Baltimore. In closer proximity to you. Preferably, side by side walking down the aisle." We both laughed at that.

Over steak, corn, and Brownie Bash ice cream—the Dude was a chocolate kind of guy—Dirk talked about the Johns Hopkins compromise, about Victoria, and handed around her photo on his iPhone. Jack sat quietly taking it in, his face a kaleidoscope of emotions.

When Dirk had finished with the announcement of the engagement, my son, so much like his father—Lon's disappointment wouldn't have interfered with his natural graciousness—said, "Hey, congratulations. I'm happy for you. Really." Then a pause before a question. "Does she know about me?"

"Of course. Victoria's looking forward to meeting you. You come with good references. The girls think you're very cool."

"I think *they* are." A pause. "You and Victoria going to have more kids?"

Dirk darted me an amused smile. "She's four years older than I am with a son at Cal Tech. She's finished. And I've done my part, don't you think?"

"Yeah, thanks for that," Jack said.

"Right," I chimed in. "More than you know."

Then Jack asked the question that I couldn't—wouldn't—allow myself to ask, though I was burning with curiosity. "Why did you do it? The donor thing. That's a big deal."

"Well, son," and I didn't flinch this time—Dirk knew who he was and we knew who he was—"I was up to my neck in medical school bills and I figured that money would help me pay them off. I'm a practical man."

Jack's smile began to fade.

"But I'm also am idealist," Dirk continued. "Those two motives sound mutually exclusive, but they're not. I guess the same thing that drove me toward being a doctor played the biggest part in this decision. I wanted to help people. I figured folks who went to a sperm bank really wanted a baby. They'd do what it took to have a child. If I could make that happen, it seemed the right thing to do. And I have no regrets, especially now that I know you, Jack. And your mom. And though he's not with us, I think I've come to know your dad as well, rest his soul."

Which was a great exit line.

Dirk had originally planned on staying in Tuckahoe another night, having Sunday brunch with Jack, and heading back to San Francisco that afternoon. But tomorrow's forecast had been updated from cloudy to dicey. Thundershowers were predicted all along the East Coast starting midmorning, with high-wind warnings and heavy rain for the beach area on their tail. Dirk wanted to get out of town before the storm hit. He changed into slacks and a sport shirt in the downstairs bathroom and grabbed his suitcase from the back of Jack's car.

Jack had wanted to, but Dirk wouldn't hear of him driving the long trip to the airport. So this was good-bye, but just for now. He wasn't sure yet of his lecture schedule at Hopkins, but maybe when he knew, they could arrange a meet for dinner between Durham and Baltimore. The girls and Victoria agreed the Farrells had to come west for a visit. "And, of course, we'll stay in touch by email and Skype. Everyone will be busier than we were over the summer, so it might not be as often, but Jen is counting on you to help her get through statistics, and you and I need to talk about the Blue Devils versus the Denver Pioneers on defense."

The limo driver honked from the curb. I got an arm around my shoulder with a final squeeze and then Jack and Dirk maneuvered a handshake that swiveled into one of those backslap hugs men choreographed.

Jack and I stood at the door and watched the Donor Dude walk down the path and hand his bag to the driver. He got in and waved from the backseat. The wave was more a salute, as if we'd all fought a battle for the same cause—Jack's happiness—and we'd all won.

What welled up in me at that moment wasn't relief that the man I'd thought of as an intruder was on his way home, but gratitude, a flood of it that brought a surprising blink-back of tears. Gratitude to Lon, who'd gone with the donor-bank plan twenty years ago and had, from all the donor dudes, pushed for this particular one—my husband had always displayed impeccable taste and a novelist's eye for character. And back then, when I'd wondered aloud if in the future we should support Jack's meeting his sperm donor, Lon had let me know he'd have it no other way. *So thank you, my lost love, wherever you are.* And there was more than enough gratitude for Dirk, who turned out to be both more than I'd anticipated and less than I'd feared. And for Jack, who had done us all proud.

The visit could have gone so badly. It went so well.

"He's a good guy," my son—Lon's son—said, as the cab pulled away. "We're really lucky."

"We really are," I said.

An hour later, I was upstairs answering emails on my laptop when Scott unexpectedly Skyped me from Bethesda. He was checking in to arrange our lunch date in Tuckahoe for the following day. But first, he wanted me to see an apartment there he was considering. He walked his smartphone through a highlight tour of the place: nice-sized kitchen, walk-in shower with multiple body jets, great view of the downtown Row with its art theaters and outdoor cafés, and, he made sure to note, the rooms were flooded with light. He was telling me that he'd leave Bethesda early morning and swing by for me around noon when I looked up to see my son at the door, ready, I thought, to say good night. Then I realized, no, something more. He had trouble peeling his stare from the screen even after Scott had signed off.

He finally made eye contact. "Mom, I know Dirk is out of the picture, but please don't rush into anything else. This is probably not politically correct, but I'm going to say it anyway because you're my mother and I love you and I don't want you to make a major mistake." He hitched his neck toward the blank screen. "You can do better. You know what I mean, right?"

Anger percolating, I began to inform him what I thought about what he meant. He backed away, hands up, palms splayed. "Okay, okay. Just saying."

"No, you're not just saying, Jack. You really *believe* it. And you're wrong. I wish there were something Scott could do to show you what he's made of."

"He's made of titanium, at least in part," my son muttered, then added, "That wasn't a dig. It's the truth."

"What you don't see is that he's perfectly capable." I was barely containing my frustration.

"No, Mom, what you refuse to see is he's not perfectly capable. Not perfectly anything. You're crushed on him. I get it. You're all impressed by the hero stuff, but check out this scenario. I'll bet he goes to sleep without the leg on. No, don't tell me if I'm right." He shuddered. "Really. I don't want to know. But say he does. So there's a fire in the middle of the night. He can't rescue you. He can't even rescue himself on one leg. *You've* got to drag *him* out, because what's he going to do, hop down the stairs?"

"He keeps a crutch on the side of his bed."

"TMI. Jeez, Mom. Way TMI."

"Jack . . . ," I began, then faltered as he shook his head sadly and said, "I worry about you."

I'd been his only parent for eight years. I was all he had left in that department. Of course he worried.

When he was a kid and about to throw a tantrum I'd tell him to use his words. Now he said, "I've used all my words. I'm done," and, shoulders slumped, left the room.

Still at my computer, I turned back to the laptop screen where Scott's image, like one more ghost, lingered on my Skype page. I leaned away in my desk chair; then I hunched forward, but I couldn't get comfortable in any position. Something painful was going on in my rib cage. *What happens,* I asked myself, *when your heart is pulled in two directions? Does it stretch or does it break?*

I should ask WebMD. I laughed, but laughing was painful too. I clicked off.

chapter thirty-five

Sunday dawned weepy, a melancholy drizzle drifting down through ominous skies. The morning weather forecast predicted a squall hitting the beach midafternoon, so Scott had brought Sarge along for our lunch date. If the storm rolled in with thunder, he didn't want the dog to be alone.

Sarge had returned from Iraq with a mild case of PTSD. "Yes, dogs get it too, believe it or not," Scott told me in the car on our way downtown. "In Sarge's case, he was spooked by loud noises. Understandable since he was in the thick of it over in Iraq. You can't imagine the noise level in firefights, and when explosive devices detonate it sounds like the end of the world. The exchange that killed his handler and wounded Sarge lasted a full five minutes.

"Back here, he went spazzy over thunder booms and freaked out over the Fourth of July fireworks, which are way up the beach. Even a car backfiring sent him running for cover. It killed me to watch him whimper. So last year, I signed us up for a session of retraining with a search-and-rescue police team in Philadelphia and they got him used to it by randomly firing blanks while he was doing other tasks. Eventually, he could tolerate the noise."

"Aversion therapy," I said.

"That's right." Scott gave me an impressed nod. "He's pretty cool with noise now. But I still like to be around during thunderstorms, just in case. I hope you don't mind an extra guest at lunch."

I was always glad to have Sarge along. From the beginning, he'd picked up on Scott's emotions and adopted the only evaluation he trusted, that of his alpha man: I was one of the good guys. And he became more comfortable with me as Scott and I drew closer. Now on the dog-friendly patio of the Turquoise Café, its outdoor space sheltered from the elements by a paisley awning, the shepherd sprawled under the table, resting his chin on my shoe. We were pals.

But his instincts and training always hovered beneath the surface. He gave off a growl as Selda strode over to take our order, then quieted at the brisk baritone "Stop" command from above. Selda squeezed out what passed for a pleasant expression for Scott. I was served a smile approximately the thickness of the flatbreads of the Turkish pizzas she'd just added to the menu. She slid a look at Sarge, her forehead working hard to suppress a scowl. According to Emine, Selda detested cats and dogs, but business was business. "And for the hound," she said, "we have grilled Turkish sausage. Called *sucukizgara*."

We ordered a couple of appetizer platters to share and were on dessert when Em approached the table. She looked like hell. The worry lines Merry had etched in her face over the last few years had deepened into grooves since her mother-in-law's arrival, and today she was deathly pale, as if a vampire had feasted on her blood.

"She only just told me you were here." I knew that "she" was the vampire in question. "You enjoyed your lunch? And your dessert is good, yes, Colonel?" Em mustered a smile.

Scott looked up from spooning *kazandibi*, a vanilla-infused flan. "Mmm," he concurred. To me, she twitched a hitch toward the door that led into the dining room. "You might like the chocolate pudding, Nora. It's just made and cooling in the kitchen. Come inside for a little taste." I had a bad feeling when she added, "Please."

Scott was appraising the weather beyond the patio. The drizzle had become teardrop rain and a briny wind ballooned the awning.

"I won't be long," I told him as I pushed back my chair.

"Take your time. Far be it from me to come between you and your chocolate. And the sound of the rain is soothing. Listen to him." Sarge was snoring musically. "If it gets worse, though, we'll wait for you in the car."

I grabbed my quilted bag, the one commodious enough to hold two takeaway packages of Em's baklava. Jack was at Ethan's this morning, but when he got home we needed to have a calm conversation about his prejudices. A peace offering might help us get off to a good start. Peace, not at any price, but at $10.99 a pound, was a bargain.

Inside, Em transferred her tension hand to hand as she steered me past the kitchen and toward the steps leading to the Haydars' apartment.

When we were beyond hearing range of the customers in the dining room, she said, "Merry and Selda got into a big fight last night while we were getting ready for the baking. So stupid it was. Over how much filling to put in the *börek*. Merry was putting too much, Selda said. Merry answered with a fresh mouth. Selda grabbed her spoon. Merry pulled it back. I ran over. Merry was hysterical and shouting terrible insults at her grandmother. Adnan was out front so he heard, but by the time he saw, it was Merry yelling and running upstairs. That was last night. This morning her shift begins at eight, but she didn't show up. Still not. Erol thinks he heard a noise like someone on the stairs as the sun was coming up, but he could have been dreaming. I want you to see upstairs, the way she left it. Maybe you can tell me what I am supposed to do now."

On the second floor, Em led me into the bathroom her children shared. Erol had discovered the message. In lipstick on the mirror, Merry had drawn two versions of the iconic happy face, neither of them smiling. The sad circle had an oval open mouth of pain and its eyes dripped a trail of tears. The mouth on the angry face was a downward curve lined with triangles, shark teeth. Underneath, Merry had scrawled, "No More!!!" Underlined three times. She drew it like she felt it. Selda had gone too far.

"At least she can express her feelings," I said, as my stomach churned at the display.

"She has no problem with that. Follow me."

At fifteen, my son had pinned up posters in his bedroom of star athletes, especially baseball and lacrosse players. Merry's crimson walls— she'd insisted on painting over the childhood pink—framed posters of the most popular rapper, grunge, and hip-hop groups. Not that rare for a teenage rebel, I supposed. The shock for me lay stretched out on her bed.

The quasi uniform Selda had insisted she wear made a chilling collage against the chartreuse bedspread. The black skirt had been cut from belt to hem up the front and split like a lobster. Merry had also taken scissors to the prim white blouse, sheared it to ribbons, and, in what may have been a final burst of fury, torn what was left to shreds.

"This is a message for me. For Adnan, for Selda."

"Have those two seen it?"

"He has. He wanted to clean the mirror and throw away the cut-up clothes. But I wouldn't let him. If she becomes a missing person"—Em's lower lip quivered—"they, the police, may want to examine this. And Selda, who started it all, my husband protects. God forbid she should feel responsible. She wouldn't feel such a thing anyway. She would go into another tirade about my—always mine, when Merry does something to displease her—my ungrateful, uncontrolled daughter. If something happens to Merry because of Selda . . ."

I'd had practice fighting my own catastrophic thinking. I tried to head hers off. "First, you don't know that Merry has run away. She could be with friends. Or at a movie. Or shopping. Half a day off the premises is not a missing person. Second, let's say she has taken off. She has a history of running, but she always comes back on her own. You remember the last time after the fight with the girl at the cleaning service. She turned up then, and the times before."

"You saw the mirror and the bed, Nora." Em wrapped her arms across her chest and rocked on her heels. "This is different."

She was right. That arrangement in black and white was a sign of desperation, and with Merry you could expect desperate measures. I wasn't sure if I believed my consolation, but I said, "This could be a ploy to get your attention, to scare her father into getting rid of Selda. Merry has her say. She lets you stew. She returns to negotiate her terms."

"That's what Adnan believes. I hope you're both right. He's out looking for her. He's not scared like I am. He's boiling with anger. Oh God, look at what's happening out there."

The trees outside Merry's window were taking a thrashing from whips of wind. Rain battered the windows. "It's getting worse."

"Did Merry pack a bag?" If we could find out her intention, we might be able to determine her destination.

"Her big beach bag is still here. Her backpack, this she always carries with her. It is gone."

"Pajamas? A change of underwear? A jacket?" It had been cool at sunrise with the storm brewing. If Merry expected to be out at night, she would have taken a jacket.

"Who can tell what she took?" Em opened the door to the walk-in closet. Its floor was heaped with a mountain of clothing.

"More venting?" I asked, wondering if Merry had tossed her closet in a rage.

"No, this is the usual mess," Em said. "At least since the cat, Sarman, and his litter box moved out."

"Money. She'd need money for a long run."

"What she earned from us and from Margo, Adnan insisted she

divide it three ways, some to her savings account, some to charity, and the rest she could spend on herself. Where she keeps the last part, I don't know."

Adnan had riffled through emails on the computer the family shared. It looked like Merry reserved messaging for her new phone. She hadn't posted on Facebook in two days, though her last post was a rant against her grandmother accompanied by a photo of Oz's green-faced Wicked Witch of the West.

"She might have gone to the Driftwood. Have you called Margo?"

"She hasn't seen her, but she promised to get back to me if Merry turns up there or if she hears anything. That was a few hours ago. Merry doesn't answer her cell, of course. I left a message. I haven't called her friends yet. Do you think I should?"

"Let me talk to Scott," I said. "He's had experience in search-and-rescue strategy, also at finding people in hiding. If Merry really has taken off, it would probably be to a familiar place. Email me a list of her hang-outs and we'll check them out."

At that moment, a lightning strike blazed the dark sky, immediately followed by a crack of thunder that seemed to shake the house on its foundation. The wind howled a wild alarm. I shivered. A chill had seeped in from the rage outside. Or maybe it was inside me. Whatever I'd told Emine to comfort her, the truth was, I was frightened.

Em rummaged through the pile in the closet and pulled out a wind-breaker. "She could be out there in this weather without a jacket." She handed it over. Her voice broke when she added, "In case you find her."

I snatched a plastic bag holding one of Merry's sweaters, dumped the sweater, and stuffed and ziplocked the heavier jacket. "So it doesn't get wet if I get soaked in this deluge." I shoved the plastic bag in my quilted tote. As I tamped it down, my cell phone rang. Em and I both jumped. Not Merry. Scott calling to let me know that when the rain started pelting, he and Sarge had taken refuge in the car. But he didn't like how the storm was building and wanted to get me home. Us. He'd help secure my house. "Batten down the hatches," he called it. He was parked out front. We'd really better get a move on.

Downstairs, I gave Em a quick hug. "You stay in the café so she doesn't come back to find only Selda here. And yes, I think, start to make a few calls. Her closest friends. Try not to drive yourself crazy with worry," I said, knowing the futility of such a sentiment. "I'll stay in touch."

I pushed against the door to the street, not making headway, feeling the power of a ferocious wind pushing back. I braced and pushed again, so it opened an inch before snapping shut. "Wait," Em said, last minute. She unlatched the gold chain she wore around her neck. It carried the *nazar boncuğu*, the amulet against the evil eye. She slipped it into my pocket. "For luck," she said.

We're going to need it, I thought. Then I summoned all my will and muscle, gave the door a final furious push, and staggered out into the maelstrom.

I was in my kitchen peeling off soaked sneakers and socks when Jack appeared. I'd texted him on the way home. You still at Ethan's? All okay? and received the briefest reply he could manage. Yes. Fine. Seven letters that spelled out his mood of the moment.

He scoped the room and finding me alone allowed me a half smile.

I couldn't manage even that. "I thought you'd be waiting this out at the Winslets'. What are you doing here?"

"What you shouldn't be doing. Tying up the deck, making sure everything's in shape for the storm." He gave me the once-over. "I gotta tell you, you look like a drowned rat."

He spotted my slicker, still glossy, hanging from a hook near the slider, then peered out to the deck, where anything that could fly had been strapped down and the rest covered and huddled against the siding. "It wasn't smart of you to haul around that stuff. You're not twenty-five anymore, Mom."

He was heading for the counter. "I'll double-check in a minute. Just want a chance to warm up. God, it's crappy out there. Coffee. I need coffee. You too? Mom, I can't believe you turned over the table by yourself. It's got to weigh more than you do."

"Well . . ."

I started to tell him that I only helped flip it, because that took four hands, when Scott called in from the front hall, "All set. You're ready for anything short of a category three hurricane. I'm keeping the boots on. That okay?"

Jack held on to his glower for a full sixty seconds until Scott, dripping, materialized in the kitchen. Then it notched up to a glare.

For Scott's work under the pummeling rain, I'd dug through the closet in the mudroom and come up with a pair of steel-toed boots Lon used to wear when mucking around outside. They were a half size too small, but Scott jammed into them. I'd also unearthed a long-buried Oakland Raiders rain poncho. It was a goofy-looking thing in silver plastic with the team logo, but Lon had loved it and it had kept him dry in the stadium seats. Jack registered that signature poncho in a heartbeat and shot Scott a bullet of a look that ricocheted to me. I felt his sting at the sight of the intruder in his father's rain gear, on his deck, in his kitchen, in my life. Scott, unaware, gave him a cheerful, "Hey, Jack."

Nostrils flared, chin jutted, Jack bobbed his head. He could barely lift his hand for a wordless hi. Scott grabbed a paper towel and blotted his face. He spotted the coffee and poured himself a mug. "Ah, better," he said after the second swallow. "Nora, just so you know, I walked the perimeter of the house. I lashed down a few of the bushes on the left side and covered your strawberries. That wind is brutal. I leashed Sarge in your mud-room. I hope it's okay. It's only for a few minutes because we ought to get started." He hadn't bothered to shed the poncho. "Has Emine's email come in yet?"

"Hold on." I checked. "Just in. She listed some places Merry frequents." I ran down the roster. "Six are businesses and she phoned the ones she had names for. They haven't seen Merry. The other three we'll have to check out in person. Some makeup shop in the Gold Coast Mall. A bowling alley in Ocean City, and one of the arcades on the boardwalk. Em doesn't know any of their names. She also sent a recent photo of Merry." A selfie, mugging, with her eyes crossed, but good enough for an ID.

Jack had been staring intently into his coffee cup, but now he jerked his head up. "This is about Merry? What's she into now?"

I explained the situation and that Mrs. Haydar was frantic with worry.

Jack said, "I don't know about the makeup place or which arcade. I know the only bowling alley in OC is Ocean Lanes." He leaned back and slid an inclusive look at Scott and me. "But you don't have to guess where she is. I can tell you."

"What? Where?" I said.

Scott, who'd been an engineering major at the Point, asked, "How?"

"Mom asked me to load some programs and some apps on Merry's new Android. Aunt Margo didn't spare the bucks for that one and Mer-ry's always losing her phone. So along with Fried Zombies and Makeup Mania and maybe twenty more apps, I loaded Lost and Phoned."

"Ahh," Scott said. "Yes, good idea."

"Talk to me," I said. "What's Lost and Phoned?"

"You lose your phone, this app locates it," Jack said. "I've got it on my cell too. It's like a GPS. As long as Merry is carrying her phone with her, when you find the phone, you find her. Here, I'll show you."

He pulled his tablet from his duffel bag. His mood had shifted. Now he was the leader of the pack. "Okay, when I loaded the app into her phone, I also registered her number at the Lost and Phoned website. And I got a password for me because she's a little ditzy, so I figured backup wouldn't hurt."

"Smart," Scott said.

Jack raised an eyebrow in acknowledgment, then typed something into the virtual keyboard. The Lost and Phoned info center surfaced, Jack slotted in a password, and a list appeared. "My personal directory. See, there's Merry's number. I'll highlight it. One stroke and we know where she is. Or where her phone is. She could have dropped it somewhere or ditched it on purpose to screw around with anyone looking for her. I don't think she'd ditch it, though. She loves that phone."

"She knows the app's on there?" Scott asked, leaning over Jack's shoulders to get a better view.

"I told her. But it's buried among all the others and she's a goth, not a geek. If she thinks about it at all, she figures it's tracking her phone, not her. And here it comes." A map surfaced. "See. Like a GPS, right? Those little red dots called pings mark her trail over the last half hour or so. And . . ." He magnified the screen. "Our girl hasn't moved for all that time. She's at . . . 55 Churchyard Lane."

"Churchyard Lane?"

Jack said, "I walk the Brinkers' dog and they're at 40 Churchyard. It's kind of back in the woods. Off Miller's Creek and near the wetlands, a twenty-minute walk from downtown. Mrs. Brinker said it used to be a nice community, with a church and all. The church is closed now, and a lot of the original houses have been torn down. Some developer's talking about building out there, but just talking. These days, you've got maybe four houses along the path. Fifty-five Churchyard." My son thought for a moment. "I'll bet that's the old Henlopen house."

"Hazel Henlopen," I whispered. "The Cat Lady. But she passed away this spring."

"Mrs. Brinker told me they came to take away the cats. But a few hang around anyway."

"Animals have long memories," Scott said.

"Wasn't that house condemned? It's probably not safe," I said. "I'm going to phone the Haydars."

"Hey, Mom, not yet, okay? It could just be where her phone is. You don't want to get Mrs. Haydar's hopes up, and also that's a bad place to be and if she knows about it, she might worry more."

"I agree," Scott said. "So what are we waiting for? I'll go get the real expert." He turned to Jack. "My German Shepherd, Sarge. He's trained for search and rescue, among other missions. You don't mind sitting in the back with him?"

"Hell, no. I'm a dog person." I saw my son working to keep a grin suppressed. "You're saying you want me along?"

Scott's voice deepened to one I'd heard him use with Sarge when issuing commands. It was a voice you listened to, trusted, respected. "We're going to need you. If we're going through a condemned house, we'll need all hands on deck."

Which triggered my clairvoyant flash. I could hear Jack thinking, *Damn right he's going to need me with only one good leg.*

"And tools," Scott said. "I've got some in my trunk, but I'll need a pry bar and maybe a saw."

"My dad has all kinds in the garage. You can take what you need."

"Great." Scott rinsed out his mug in the sink. "Come on. I'll introduce you to my sidekick."

After they left, I sank into the chair, staring at the tablet Jack had left on the table. The red dots hadn't moved.

I got moving, though, when I heard my son say in the high squeaky voice he told me dogs liked, "Hey, Sarge. Hey, boy, how you doing? You're a handsome fella." And Scott, his voice deeper, but rich with reassurance, telling Sarge that Jack was a good guy. The dog growled blissfully, a hum of gratitude for someone brushing his coat or scratching his neck.

Minutes later, back in my slicker and carrying my tote with four bottles of water nesting in Merry's jacket, I was ready to go. With Sarge leading the pack, we were on our way.

chapter thirty-six

The Henlopen place was a beaten house off the beaten path. The skinny dirt road leading to it was lined on one side with elms and oaks. On the other were wetlands, an amoeba of a marsh clogged with cattails, sedges, and rushes. Above it hung an eerie mist.

As we drove up we took in the shambles of a house. "I've seen worse," Scott said, "but not in this country."

Once, it must have been beautiful. Like a has-been film star, it displayed the souvenirs of youth in its bone structure—the elegant sweep of the roof, the exotic cutwork of the gables, the fanciful scroll trim. But time and neglect had eroded its skin. Peeling paint exposed layers of former colors. Absent shingles like missing teeth ruined its expression, and the chimney was crumbling. One of the porch pillars, detached from its overhead mooring, leaned drunkenly against what had once been a swing for two and was now suspended vertically from a single rusty chain. The entry had been sealed with a massive lock and the front door was plastered with a "Condemned" placard washed by rain and bleached by sun to an anemic pink.

Throughout the drive I'd heard Jack softly sweet-talking Sarge, who maintained a quiet demeanor, emitting an occasional low growl, mostly keeping his cool. But when we parked in the driveway and Scott opened the door for the backseat passengers, the dog bounded out, tail wagging.

Scott, Sarge at his side, moved around the car to the trunk and removed a coil of rope, which he slung over his shoulder, and the large canvas bag loaded with his tools and Lon's. Since he was working with Sarge, he asked Jack to carry the bag.

Scott kept a judicious silence as he scoped the front of the property. Pulling up the poncho hood against the battering rain, he climbed two decaying stone steps to read the faded sign nailed to the door. "The city authorities declared this house structurally unsound, so we're going to have to be really careful in there," he said.

Two of the windows had been boarded up, but then maybe someone had seen the interior and concluded there was nothing for vandals to steal and, since the house had been scheduled for demolition, had stopped at that.

Scott stepped down, backed off, and looked around. "There's got to be access. Merry got in," he said.

"Maybe not," Jack answered. "I mean, the pings tell us she's in the vicinity, but they don't tell us if she's inside or outside the house. She could be anywhere around here."

If Merry hadn't been able to break into shelter, she might have thought to hole up in the woods, where the trees were natural targets for lightning bolts, and where snakes and muskrats lurked in darkness under the leaf canopy. A dangerous place. I tried to shoo off a more disturbing possibility. If she'd opted to make her way back to the scattering of homes where the Brinkers lived and taken a shortcut around the marsh, whose margins were blurry, she could have easily lost her footing.

Scott seemed to have his dog's ability to read human emotion. He chased away my worst-case scenarios with an upbeat, "Look at Sarge. Already on the job. See him sniffing. All canines have an ability to pick up human scent. Two hundred million scent receptors make for one big, wet nose. In Sarge's case, he's been trained to use it to save human lives."

The dog, tethered to Scott by a loose leash, had started his perimeter search, trotting over the spongy earth. We followed.

"I thought he was a bomb sniffer," Jack said.

"He's what we call a multifunction dog, cross-trained by the military to detect IEDs and other weapons and as a combat tracker. Combat trackers alert to generic human presence. But when I got him back to the States, I decided the best way for us to bond was to go through training together, the experienced dog and the new handler. Nothing works better to forge a relationship. We hooked up with law enforcement to qualify him as a SAR, a search-and-rescue dog. These trailing animals can home in on a specific live human scent. Like the Belgian Shepherd on the Osama bin Laden mission."

"Cool," Jack said.

"Yup. Sarge learned how to follow that personal mix of microscopic flakes of skin we're constantly shedding, along with sweat, perfume, shampoo, urine, and blood, if the subject is injured."

Sarge, moving at a canter, stopped to sniff, then reject, pieces of litter along the path.

"Damn, I wish we had something of Merry's to give him," Scott said.

I halted. "I have her jacket."

Scott wheeled on me. "You have her . . . ," he began.

"Jacket," I repeated, thinking that I'd struck gold because the colonel's eyes were as bright as nuggets of the precious stuff.

As the men watched, speechless, I reached below the water bottles in my tote and pulled up the windbreaker. "Her mother was worried she'd be cold when we found her."

Scott shook his head in wonderment as I handed it over. "A mother's love, you can't beat it." He motioned us under an overhang where we'd be protected from the worst lashings of rain. He unzipped the plastic bag and held it out open to Sarge, who was immediately on it. We could see his nostrils rippling as he captured Merry's scent.

"Oh yeah, that's a good one, isn't it, fella? Yeah, you got it now, don't you?" Scott burbled in a cloying tenor. For the next minute or so, he gave the dog a pep talk in that syrupy tone. "Yeah, you're excited, boy. Yeah, we're going to work. You love to work." He unclipped the shepherd's lead and in a deeper, authoritative voice, issued the command, "Find this!"

Sarge set the pace, trotting, it seemed to me, with a new sense of purpose while managing to avoid obstacles in the path, mostly brambles and blown shingles. He detoured around a couple of broken two-by-fours. "Grab the longer one of those, will you, Nora?" Scott called back. "Once we're in the house, we'll use it to sound the floor ahead to make sure we're not walking on a surface that will give way under our weight. Falling through a floor sucks."

"Copy that," I said as I picked it up, eliciting a turn of his head and a smile.

Our parade had just rounded the second turn when something seized the shepherd's attention and he picked up speed. When he stopped, it was at a side window. He huffed, gave a short bark, then sat statue still, ears perked, nose drawing deep drafts of air. "He's found a scent cone," Scott explained. "He's picking up a match to the jacket. This is where she got in."

As we moved closer we could see the window had been knocked out. "Probably with this." Scott motioned to a denuded tree limb lying off to one side.

He examined the jagged glass. "She smashed the window, reached inside, and unlocked the door. Smart girl, our Merry."

We took a step to the adjacent door. He turned the handle and pushed it open. He gave us, two humans and a dog, the command, "Stay."

Above us, the sky was a shroud. We peered inside, where it was even darker.

"We need light," Scott said.

I groped around the doorjamb and found the light switch on the inside wall. I flipped it. Nothing.

"Mom, first thing they do is cut off utilities," Jack said. Of course. He unlatched the tool bag, fished out a headlamp, and handed it to Scott, who strapped it on and switched it to broad beam. Jack pulled out two flashlights, handed me one, and shone his torch ahead on Miss Henlopen's kitchen, then down on the linoleum littered with glass.

"We can walk around most of the larger fragments," Scott said, "but be aware there may be smaller scattered pieces, spikes that can pierce your shoes." He looked down at Sarge. "His paws are sensitive, but we didn't have time to stop for his booties." He fastened Sarge's lead. His tone turned deadly serious. "Before we go in there, you need to know the first rule for any rescuer is not to become a victim. We can't help Merry if the search has to be diverted to help you, and this place could be like a minefield, with all kinds of stuff falling apart. I've got to keep my dog safe. And I'm responsible for you two. I'm open to suggestions, but I've done this before, so inside I'm in charge. Get it?"

"Got it," I said.

Jack gave an almost imperceptible nod. I caught his expression in the light from my torch. Not happy. I thought I understood why. In his mind, he was under the protection of a leader who'd previously managed to get blown apart and who, in Jack's eyes, wasn't fit for duty.

The dog startled. He looked up at Scott.

"He's onto something," Scott said.

Jack said, "I heard it too. There. Again. You guys didn't hear it?"

I did then. Mewling cries. Soprano. Feeble. Merry.

"Let's go," Scott said. Once inside, he began to uncoil the rope. "Our safety line," he said, as he secured it to a post near the kitchen door. "If all hell breaks loose and we can't see our way to the exit, we'll follow it out." We moved, deliberately, delicately, Scott yelling Merry's name. No answer. He touched my shoulder. "She knows you. Call for her and ID yourself."

I used all the voice I had. "Merry, it's Aunt Norrie. Are you here, Merry? Merry, answer me!" I heard only scratching nearby. Jack said, "Field mice probably. No big deal."

Sarge droned a low growl. Instinct goaded him to chase small prey, and he acknowledged their presence, but he'd been trained to overcome his natural impulse.

"Listen," Scott commanded, and the dog slackened on the lead.

Faint baby cries, the same sounds we'd heard at the door, filtered through the din. "Merry!" I shouted her name. Silence, then the scratching noise, and "Ugh!" I felt something scurry over my boot. I leapt aside and swung my light to catch a scampering shadow. "A mouse." I was panting. "No. Bigger. A rat." My dancer's reflex lifted me to my toes and I hopped from foot to foot, stifling the urge to run. My teeth chattered a revolted rattle. Scott reached over and squeezed my hand.

Jack swept an arc of light over Miss Henlopen's kitchen. The cries became howls.

"Not rats," he said. "Cats! Oh shit."

The place was teeming with them. Most had taken cover. Escaping the strange voices and smells, they'd concealed themselves under tables or on tops of cabinets. From dark places their feral eyes glowed green and gold. Two of the braver ones roamed from the kitchen to the hall, tails up. Sarge was shuddering with suppressed ecstasy. "Easy, boy," Scott calmed him.

"How did they get in?" I asked.

"Every house has chinks and tunnels, narrow spaces in the basement or attic that open to the outdoors," Scott said. "See how thin these critters are. They can slip out to hunt, come back for shelter. And you said the Henlopen woman ran a hotel for strays. She must have pulled five stars on Expedia. Word obviously got around."

"Merry loves cats," I said. "Especially the homeless ones. I'll bet right now that's the way she sees herself. She's got to be here."

Scott asked Jack to check the Lost and Phoned app to keep up with Merry's location.

It was a long minute of playing with his iPad before Jack said, "No signal. Mom, try your cell." Also down. "The storm must have knocked everything out. We're on our own."

"No, we're not," Scott replied. He bent down, ruffled Sarge's coat, and gave the command: "Wander."

We followed as Sarge did just that, ignoring the cats' cries, loping through the first floor, pausing here and there to sniff. He covered the living area, a small bathroom, a nook housing an old-fashioned sewing machine and bolts of fabric, but showed no special interest until he got to the staircase. There he stood at the bottom, nostrils twitching, ears flicking. "That's indicating, not alerting," Scott explained. "We're on track, but not there yet." When Sarge placed his front paws on the second step and tugged to go up, Scott motioned us closer. "He cleared this floor. From his reaction, Merry's been around, but he's catching a draft from upstairs that's interesting him." He held up the flat of his hand. "Feel that?" A whoosh of cooler air from above. "That's where he wants to go, which means so do we. But stay to the sides of the steps. They're stronger there than in the middle."

He reinforced the "Find" command. Sarge began to climb, and we followed, Scott tapping each step before we mounted it. Some were warped so badly they bowed. Halfway up, Jack lost balance and grabbed the handrail. I saw it waggle and heard his "oomph" as he steadied himself. I nearly tripped over a cat toy. But Scott, handling the lead, trailing the safety line, never faltered. His gait was perfectly balanced, no sway, no wobble, no hesitation.

As soon as the shepherd's paws touched down on the second-floor landing, he bristled with excitement. His tail went into wild spasms. He barked exclamation points. Scott unclipped the lead and gave him consent to go.

As he swept down the hall, his nose worked constantly. He charged through two rooms, in and out, and I swear I saw him shake his head "no" after each foray. We hustled after him in the corridor that had become a wind tunnel.

"Only one more room left," Scott shouted over the gusts. The dog dashed a frantic approach.

"Be careful," Scott called out as we entered. For the first few seconds inside, I was blind. I could only feel the needles of rain and darts of debris pricking my skin, and the slap of wet wind against my face. Shielding my eyes, I opened them. There was light from above. I looked up at a massive hole in the ceiling. Part of the roof had collapsed. Falling, it had built a mountain of rubble, a jumble of plaster, broken timber, plywood, and shingles, crowned by a heap of books and a few shelves from a huge oak bookcase that had toppled over on the mound. For a split second, my brain allowed entry to the certainty that no one could have survived under that avalanche of debris.

Sarge was high-stepping around its perimeter, emitting a series of quick, sharp barks. "He's alerting," Scott said. "Merry's in there. Under all that." He quieted Sarge and stepped back to assess the site. "Okay," he said finally. "I think I've got this figured. Nora, you call her name."

I did and I swear my heart stopped for the endless moment of silence that followed. Then—a cardiac jolt—as we heard a muffled response, a word that might have been "Help" in a voice I thought could have been Merry's. Not just thought. It had been a long time since this strayed sheep had been part of the fold, but now I prayed, begged, *Let it be her,* and added, my inner voice cracking, *And please, let "help" not be her last word.*

"We've got to get this thing upright," Scott broke through before I got to "amen." "Jack, I need you here."

While the dog paced half circles, the men worked to shift the bookcase. Scott lifted his share with arms built in boot camp, combat, and physical therapy. These days he worked out to keep those muscles. My son was strong, but I heard him groaning and, as he struggled to lift his side of the load, I saw him buckle.

"Nora. Over here, with Jack!"

"We're good," I called as I helped my son stabilize the weight. Then I got hit. I had both arms braced against my side of the heavy Victorian oak cabinet, when shards of shingles along with a shower of clotted plaster came shooting down. One of the broken shingles grazed my jaw. My head jerked in surprise and I staggered back, but held tight.

Jack called, "Mom!" And Scott yelled, "Nora!" at the same instant.

"I'm all right, but the sky is falling," I said. "For God's sake, let's go."

"On three," Scott commanded. On one, I sucked in my gut. On two, I started a Hail Mary. On three, we heaved the bookcase erect. Then, following instructions, we shifted it away and leaned it against a far wall. "Done," Scott said. "Good job, gang."

We turned our attention back to the debris pile. For a moment, nothing moved. Then there was an almost imperceptible shift in the mass.

"Stay still, Merry," Scott called out. "You are Meryem Haydar, right?"

"Uh-huh."

"Merry, are you hurt?" Scott asked her.

"Can't . . . breathe."

"Can you wiggle your toes? Don't move your legs yet." To us he said softly, "We don't want the pile to shift and block her air pocket." But shift it did, and that must have opened a new air tunnel, because her next words were clearer.

"Toes wiggle. Just my wrist. Hurts bad."

Then, in an undertone, he to me, "Talk to her. Keep her calm."

"Merry." I got as close to the debris pile as Scott would allow. "It's Aunt Norrie. We're going to get you out."

"Please." Her voice was weak, but it was *her* voice. "Hurry."

Sarge, quivering with excitement, stared at Scott expectantly, waiting for the command to make a soft walk up the pile and dig.

"Stay, boy," Scott ordered. "He's too excited. Besides, this calls for human judgment and fingers, not paws. Especially not a paw that's still recovering from an injury."

"I'm lighter than you. I'll climb up and move stuff bit by bit," Jack offered.

"It doesn't work that way. Watch me first. And somebody see if you can reach 911."

While I talked soothingly to Merry, Scott gently, very gently for a big, tough guy, laid himself on the pile. "To distribute my weight evenly," he said. Crablike, he crawled his way up the mound, precisely choosing bits to pick away as Merry whimpered, which broke my heart but also helped him zero in on her location.

"Communications up," Jack said, waving his iPhone. He gave the emergency operator our location. "They're on their way."

Finally, I heard Scott shout, "We've got her," and there she was, neck up, covered with white plaster dust, gasping for air. When she got a gulp of it, she began to sob. It was like watching a newborn emerge. Eyelids glued shut, then the first cry that blared, *"Alive."*

Tears washed Merry's eyes open. Now she was crying in earnest.

"You're okay, baby," I said, wanting to reach out to her, but before we went further, Scott needed to assess her condition. When she was calmer, he asked her the name of her parents, the school she attended, her favorite TV show. I nodded at her answers. No obvious signs of concussion. She could move her legs, so he felt there was no acute spinal injury. "Good to go," he said, and as debris rained from the ceiling, he methodically tweezed her free, shoulders, torso, and, with extra care, the arm that had been trapped under a jagged piece of roof timber. Her right wrist hung at an odd angle.

Out, but wobbly, she propped herself against me. I wanted so much to fold her into a hug and comfort her, but as I reached around her waist Scott said, "Careful, Nora. There might be more bones broken or internal injuries." Instead, as Merry rested her head on my shoulder, I stroked her cheek and crooned an Irish lullaby I'd sung to Jack in his crib. It seemed to soothe her. Her breathing evened, her skin warmed, and after I half sang, half whispered the last line, "May angels guard over thee," she murmured, "I want my mother."

We called Em so she could hear her daughter's voice. Merry was too weak to say much, just, "I'm okay, Mom. Please stop crying," and when I took the phone Em was sobbing her thanks in two languages. I told her to meet us at the hospital.

Downstairs, in the car and away from the crumbling house, we waited for the ambulance fighting through the storm. Shivering in the jacket that had led us to her, and wrapped in a blanket from the trunk, Merry told us the story of how she'd bashed her way into the kitchen, fed the cats with some of Sarman's cat chow she'd brought along, and finally, exhausted— she'd been up before dawn and had walked miles—went down for a nap in the late owner's bed. She was asleep when "all this crap came crashing down. I didn't know what hit me, but it was totally wet and gross and when I tried to move, it, like, smothered me." Her beautiful new cell phone had wound up somewhere in the junk pile, beyond her reach.

She was, of course, not the usual mouthy Merry, though she dropped the F-bomb three times as Scott stabilized her wrist with a SAM splint from the tool bag. Jack intently watched the colonel shape and tie it. I watched Jack.

"How do you know what to do?" my son asked.

"Military. Amazing what you pick up on the fly. Like never pee on a snakebite. Doesn't work. Pee on the snake. But at your own risk."

Jack laughed appreciatively, then moved in to observe Scott clean and apply antiseptic ointment to the slight abrasion on my jaw. When he was finished, Scott turned to Merry. "How you doing, sweetheart?"

"Thirsty again," Merry said. Jack fed her more swigs from a bottle in my tote. As she drank, he wiped plaster dust from her face with a mealy tissue he'd excavated from his pocket.

"Actually you look good as a blonde," he said. Which made her smile.

"Jerk," she said.

"That jerk helped dig you out of this mess," Scott said. "Listen to the man."

Jack flashed a look at Scott that told me there had been some kind of conversion under fire. I thought I saw respect, maybe even admiration behind it. Finally, Jack had witnessed some of what I'd seen in Scott from the beginning. My mood, already high from finding Merry alive and healthy enough to trade jabs with Jack, went soaring.

"Okay, Ms. Merry, that should hold you for now," Scott said. "The EMTs will redo it. Or the docs at the hospital. Or maybe they'll think I did a brilliant job and send you home."

"Where I'm not going, as long as the grandmother from hell is still in residence."

It looked like the old, irrepressible, totally impossible, and mostly lovable Merry was back. Given her history and given Selda, for how long was another issue.

chapter thirty-seven

We followed the ambulance to the hospital through the tail end of the storm, which was now more fog than rain, but lost it at an accident on the highway that held us up for half an hour. By the time we got to the emergency entrance, Sarge was making gotta-pee sounds and Scott asked Jack to walk him.

"No problem. Come on, boy, we're going to let you empty your tank," my son crooned as he clipped on the lead. Scott and I looked after them as they sprinted off.

"Bonding," I said.

"I hope so. Jack did a good job today. Never hesitated. Jumped right in."

"He would have climbed right on and collapsed the debris pile if you hadn't stopped him."

"I knew the technique and he didn't, but he showed initiative, guts. Points for that."

Scott curled an arm around my waist. "And you were great back there, too. Cool under fire. Arms of steel. You're a woman of many talents."

"You ain't seen nothin' yet," I answered, evoking a smoky glance from him.

In the ER waiting room, Adnan was sitting hunched over, running a *tesbih*, a chain of worry beads, through his fingers. His eyes brightened when he saw us, and he rose to shake Scott's hand and embrace me. I'd known Adnan for more than ten years, and this was the first time he'd come close enough to touch me, let alone pull me into a hug. "Thanks God," he kept repeating. "And thanks to you. I am so grateful."

He told us Merry was in an exam room being checked out. Em was with her.

Adnan wanted details of the scene at the Henlopen place and Scott had just started relating an edited version—no need to paint that heart-stopping picture—when Em emerged from behind the double doors.

"She's fine, she's fine. The X-ray showed only the wrist is broken, not the arm. They had to remove your very good splint, Colonel, to look at the injury, but they said it was like a doctor's work. They're putting on a cast now." She exhaled relief. "So, please, tell me what happened."

After Scott finished, a paler Adnan, worry beads in motion, said, "Nora, your son, he is a hero for putting in the finding app in Meryem's phone. You are all heroes to us."

"The dog too," Emine said. "So amazing, this dog. He gets lamb from me the next time he comes to the café." I noticed her accent was thicker, her sentences more arabesque than usual. Stress did that.

"This cannot happen again," Adnan said. "Meryem was lucky this time. But her luck will run down one day. Steps must be taken."

Emine drew her lush eyebrows into an arrow pointed directly at her husband.

"Steps *have* been taken," she shot back. "The wrong ones. What must be taken now is an airplane. Back to Istanbul. With your mother on it."

Which was our cue to get out of there.

An email from Merry to Jack arrived during the drive home. He read it aloud: "'Wrist broken. No big deal. Could have died in that crap pile. You guys saved me. Tell all thanks a heap. Get it, bro? Heap?'"

"She's crazy." He laughed and read as he typed, "'Next time no one's going to dig you out, so there better not be a next time.'"

"We'll see," she fired back. "It all depends."

There's a strange beauty that takes over a beach the day after a storm, a kind of breath catching all around. I walked the shore at dawn. The air was clean and quiet. No wind at all. Hardly any people. A few gawkers had come out to see the damage and an elderly couple with metal detectors swept for treasure, but if there was glitter it was buried. Nothing shone or shimmered under the washed-out sun. The waves were tame, as if they'd knocked themselves out and needed time to recover. The sand was ironed to a matte finish and littered with driftwood and empty shells, overturned trash cans and their spilled litter, and abandoned towels, as if their owners had stayed until the very last minute before surrendering to the storm and literally throwing in the towel.

As I walked the quiet beach, I remembered praying yesterday when it was touch-and-go. *So,* I told myself, *it wouldn't be hypocritical of me to give official thanks for answered prayers.* It had been eight years since I'd set foot inside a church for anything but weddings and funerals. Now I felt the need. I Googled the weekday mass schedule of Saint Martha Star of the Sea up the road in Bethany. Eight thirty. If I hurried, I might be able to slide into the pew on my knees.

The service at Saint Martha's, with what my father used to call "all the smells and bells," was like turning the pages of a family photo album and looking at your used-to-be self. You recognized the person, you remembered the surroundings, but nothing was what it had been. Yet it was still comforting, a mix of nostalgia and surprising regret. I said my thanks, prayed not for the house I loved or the job I wanted, or even for my son's happiness, but like the spiritual sailor I was, like the sailors we all are, for guidance on choppy seas.

After church I headed to the Haydars' to check on Merry. Downtown was relatively untouched by the storm; a few fallen tree limbs, a traffic light out.

The Mews Merchant Association had its cleaning crew sweeping the alleys of strewn flower petals—beautiful potpourris of them piled in drifts against the curb—and shopkeepers were stripping protective tape from the windows and replacing merchandise on outdoor kiosks. At the Turquoise Café, Adnan, wielding a broom, moved to the picket fence that separated the patio from the street to greet me and thank me again. No hugging this time.

Inside, Emine waved from behind the counter. Merry was sitting at a corner table, playing with a smartphone that looked familiar.

"Hi," I said.

She looked up and gave me a smile lit to a level of incandescence I hadn't seen since she'd accepted the glory from Margo onstage.

"Oh God, Aunt Norrie. Can you believe it?" She held up the phone with her left arm. "It's like a miracle. You want to hear something insane? This phone was still charged when the lieutenant from the fire department dropped it off this morning. I'm so relieved. Aunt Margo would have killed me if I lost it."

Nah, Margo would have replaced it, but not without a stern lecture and a barrage of warnings for Merry to get her act together. Merry gestured to the empty chair across from her and I sat. She accorded me the honor of her full attention, slipping the phone into the pocket of her blouse. Not a prissy white one. A crop top printed with colorful butterflies that skimmed the waistline of her jeans. She was also wearing sandals. "Thanks again for saving my sorry butt."

I was about to ask if she was as sorry as her butt when Selda appeared like the anti-genie. I gave her my order. "A decaf grande with milk and two packets of sweetener on the side." I wanted to hold on to my church mellow.

She wrinkled her nose at the abomination that decaf was to every proud carrier of Turkish blood. "Volkan is your server today. I'll tell him." She turned to Merry. "I need you in the kitchen to box the baklava."

"Excuse me?" Merry held up her arm to display the cast.

Selda snorted. "You have another hand."

"But I'm right-handed," Merry volleyed. "And I'm not supposed to bend those fingers."

"You have been tap-tapping the words on your phone with your left hand, so you can box baklava with your left hand. Everybody works here. Your mother since six o'clock and she needs some time to talk to . . ." She pointed at me. I wondered if she remembered my name. I was the eggplant hater. "So for a little time at the counter I am taking over."

"You're good at that," Merry said sweetly.

"Is this an insult?" Selda's nostrils went to full flare.

"No, *Babaanne*, a compliment."

"Nice, then. Come. *Now*."

Merry sighed herself to her feet and waited a beat before following her grandmother. Behind Selda's back, she held up three straight fingers on her injured hand and all five of the other. She whispered, "Eight more days. I almost died, but it was worth it."

I was still laughing when Em slipped into her empty seat.

"Eight more days?" I asked.

"Selda? Yes, she stays through Eid." Eid al-Fitr, the elaborate dinner marking the end of the month of Ramadan. "She leaves next Tuesday."

"Adnan is all right with that?"

"He booked her flight. She wasn't happy when he broke the news, but the mother of a sultan still defers to the sultan. And he did it on his own, without my having to threaten him, without even the imam's advice."

"Good for Adnan," I said, as Volkan placed a mug of steaming coffee in front of me.

"He was scared. He realized Merry could have died in that old house. At the end, his heart told him his children come first. Which reminds me, I didn't get to thank Jack for yesterday. He leaves for school when?"

"Day after tomorrow." I took a scalding swallow of coffee, and its heat spread from my throat to my chest. Perhaps it wasn't only the coffee that burned too close to my heart.

"Well, if I don't see him in person, I'll make up a package of treats for him to take back to college. Not a reward. I could never reward him enough. Him or any of you. Just a gift."

She stared out the window at the pallid late-August sun. "So soon the summer is over."

I nodded, surprising myself by choking up. "Too soon."

"Yes, but it will come again." She reached for my hand. "It always does."

If I hadn't wanted to keep her sympathetic touch I would have told her there is no such thing as "always." That was a lesson I should have learned at my mother's bedside when I was in high school and in my own personal graduate course when Lon died. But I was still flunking reality. Some spark within may still have believed in Saint Martha and the possibility of forever. For summers. For love.

The next afternoon, a call came in from Josh Zimmerman, who'd just returned from Italy. I explained the job offer from National Care (which elicited a "Mazel tov!") and how the nonstop commuting was the deal breaker. However, I said cheerily, if I could jam my sessions at Poplar Grove into a single day, I might be able to swing it. The silence at the other end lasted, even for a shrink, ominously long. It ended with a groan. "I'll do my best, Nora," Josh said, "but juggling staff scheduling is always logistically complicated and emotionally charged. You're asking for four days of adjustments. I'd be messing around with a lot of people's lives. I'll see what I can do, but I've got to tell you, I don't have high hopes."

Five minutes later, while I was Googling "Employment dance therapist Baltimore," my email chimed incoming. It was Tess Gaffigan.

Long time no hear. Have relevant news to share. Betsy the preggie plant lady is quitting in her fifth month instead of sixth. The woman knows how to plant seeds. She just found out she's carrying triplets. I thought baby elephant myself from the Everest size of the baby bump, but it's a trio. One was hiding out behind the twins. So, start time for you would be pushed up from November to beginning of October. To sweeten the pot, I'll pay you for the entire month of September. Such a deal. Need to know your decision by next week. Really, Nora, we'll have lots of fun and you'd be making a big difference in some valuable lives. What say you?

We'd worked together. Tess knew my professional hot buttons, like the "making a big difference" appeal. But it occurred to me suddenly that I also knew hers. She couldn't have changed that much since back in the day. That kind of stuff is hardwired. I knew the lineup of her instrument panel—what turned her on, what set her off. The power surged in both directions. Two could play.

She'd given me a week and I responded that she'd hear from me by deadline. It had been more than a month since we'd met at her office, and my internal knee-jerk reaction—and now my calculated one—was *Don't rush me*, my theme song.

But time is a workaholic and it rushes. The following day I was standing with Jack in our driveway next to his car packed for the return trip to Durham. Registration at Duke started tomorrow and he wanted to get settled in.

I tossed his tennis racquet on top of a pile of clothes on the backseat. The car smelled like a bakery. The takeaway box with two pounds of baklava Emine had sent over was sitting on the front seat next to a bag of homemade chocolate chip cookies Claire had dropped off yesterday on her way to freshman orientation at the University of Virginia. I hadn't been home, but she'd also left a foil-covered paper plate of them for me, with a note: "Glad we got to meet this summer, Mrs. F. Hope to see you again next year. Bye for now." Signed with the inevitable, endearing heart, "Claire."

"So," I said, wanting to postpone Jack's leaving, reaching for small talk and, if I got up the courage, big talk. "Plans to see Claire before next summer?"

"Sure. UVA isn't that far from Duke. I Mapquested the drive from Durham to Charlottesville and it's only three hours. She's a freshman. College is a big change. I think I should keep an eye on her."

"Like a big brother? Or like a boyfriend?"

His mouth curled in an amused smile. "Wow, you really cut to the chase, don't you, Mom? Okay, not like a brother."

"Ahhh. What about Tiffanie?"

"We'll see. I'm keeping my options open."

"So I can do the same?" It was a leading question. I was fishing and he snapped at the bait.

"Give me a break. You have *so* shut down your options. And I'm okay with that. Not that you need my permission for who you date."

"No, but I care what you think."

"Well, for what it's worth, I think Scott's a good guy. He carries his weight. More than. He was freaking amazing digging Merry out. You've got to give him credit."

"Right, but not extra credit. He doesn't want that."

"For the leg. I get it."

I leaned against him. "I'm going to miss you."

"Yeah, well, I'll be back. Me and my laundry. In October. Columbus Day is a long weekend. Here, right?" He gave the house a lingering, longing look. It meant as much to him as it meant to me.

"Yes, here."

Whatever happened, we'd still have the Surf Avenue house in October. Tuckahoe was gorgeous in the fall. Crisp air, crisp leaves, the sea a liquid bronze under a burnished sun. Nearly empty beaches for twilight walks in lengthening shadows. Dogs were allowed on the beach off-season, so there was always lots of romping and fetching. And Jack could hang out (maybe with Scott—nice thought), eyeballing the hot rods, classics, and muscle cars down the pike at the annual Cruisin' Ocean City show.

"I'm thinking Thanksgiving in San Francisco," my son said. "You and me and Dirk's clan?"

I sorted through the puzzle pieces. Scott would want to spend the holiday with his kids. Though maybe that was Bunny's time. Or they'd all be together. Dear God, life got tricky past thirty. I looked at Jack's face, his eyebrows raised to expectant. Tricky below thirty too.

"It's possible," I said. "We'll see what works out."

"If you're worried about airfare, Dirk said he'd take care of mine. Like a pre-Christmas present."

"You told him about our financial situation?" The last thing I wanted from Dirk DeHaven was to see Jack as an obligation. Also, the Dude was still a stranger. To me, at least. He didn't need to know the state of our bank account.

"No, Mom, of course not. You haven't mentioned it lately, so I assume we're still in the toilet moneywise."

I hadn't told Jack about Tess and the job because my decision whether to take her offer had been up in the air from the beginning. Since the downer phone call with Josh, the probability of it was plunging to crash and burn. Jack didn't need to know any of that. I wanted him to make the shift from summer to school as seamlessly as possible.

"Honey, I'm job hunting. I polished my résumé." My tone was optimistic. "And I've had a few leads." Not exactly a lie.

His amber eyes darkened with concern. "You know, if we get into real trouble, I can take a year off from school and get a full-time job. That way I could earn money toward the next year's tuition. Kids do it all the time."

They did. And some grew from the experience. But many never returned to college, and if I allowed that to happen, my husband's ghost, which seemed to have finally shuffled off its mortal coil, would descend from heaven to perch forever at the end of my bed, its finger wagging eternal outrage. *Rest in peace, Lon.* Jack would leave Duke over *my* dead body.

I'd loved my son "to infinity," I'd told him when he was a toddler, stretching my arms as wide as they could go. Now, listening to how he was trying to make things better, I loved him beyond that, and those arms drew him into a hug.

After I reluctantly released him, I said, "Honestly, Jack, we'll be fine. I'll land a job. You have my word. Everything will work out." Which, in the moment, I believed.

"Sure, but, Mom"—he rode over my reassurances, his voice earnest— "please, please don't take something you hate just for the money. I could go to BCCC for a few semesters. Their fees are super-reasonable."

Baltimore City Community College had a hotshot basketball program, but no lacrosse.

I glanced at my watch. "You'd better go to Duke. I mean *now*, so you'll get into Durham before the rain hits. They're expecting thunderstorms." Of course, I'd checked the weather online.

"Yeah. I'll text you when I get there."

"Don't forget."

He towered over me, my son, my kid, but nobody's child anymore. *He* kissed the top of *my* head. "Take care of yourself, Mamma-mia."

"You too, Bambino. And drive carefully." I didn't say live carefully. I didn't think it anymore. Not for him. And, very lately, not for me. "Work hard, but have fun."

I closed my eyes because I couldn't bear to see him turn away. When I opened them, he was behind the wheel feeding a disc into the CD player. He'd slid all the windows down and the sunroof open and the music of "Brown Eyed Girl" flooded the neighborhood. That was our traditional end-of-summer driving-back song. Lon's and mine, then, with Jack, ours. Now his and, in a week, mine.

I waved until he turned the corner, and then, already feeling the hollow of his absence, I walked down the front path with the rosy-pink Autumn Joy sedum blooming along its margins and into the house. It was too early for wine so I scooped myself a dish—okay, a bowl—of ice cream, Cone-heads' butter pecan, and turned on Carly Simon's "We Just Got Here." When the song was over, the bowl was empty. I wiped away my tears, changed into my bathing suit, and headed for the beach.

I left my flip-flops and towel on Mooncussers Rock and waded into the water. August water, warm and syrupy and healing. I flipped over to float. I'd always been good at that.

chapter thirty-eight

On a foggy, moonless night a week later, Margo, Em, and I gathered at the shore, the three of us dazzled like prehistoric women by newly discovered fire. Our bonfire lit a patch of beach behind my house, and its glow bathed wavelets curling against the craggy profiles of ageless rocks. A haze of sea smoke hovered above the water. It was an eerie scene that sent shivers up my spine.

"Curtain going down," Margo said, as the sky deepened to blue-black with just a scattering of stars. "Talk about a finale."

I tossed a piece of driftwood on the fire she'd built below the high-tide line with kindling from Home Depot and crumpled newspaper from a stack of *Coast Post*s I'd collected in my garage for the last few weeks.

Although summer would officially hang on for another three weeks, I was leaving for Baltimore the following morning, the Manolises would be gone in the afternoon, and by next week, after Labor Day, the tourist season would be over for Em at the café. For us, this was the end, and I pronounced it softly, sadly, into the smoke. "So long, summer."

The driftwood echoed the hiss of my sibilants before catching flame and sending a flare to light up our faces. We all looked wistful.

"I feel like you just arrived," Emine said.

"I feel like we just *sur*vived," Margo said. We all laughed.

"Look at it positively," Em said. "You will be back next year."

I was about to respond when I heard Margo clear her throat, an alert that she had the next line and I'd better not step on it. I lay back in my beach chair.

She said, "I'll certainly be here. In fact, you'll see more of me than you did this summer." She paused for effect. "Less of Pete."

Ah, she had a tale to tell. She was just waiting for her cue.

I fed it to her. "Because?"

"Because Pete will be on the road covering the Orioles' away games. And/or back in Baltimore doing color commentary for the home games."

That sat me up. "Oh my God. He's taken the TV job? Mazel tov!"

Em said, "Good for you. You finally made the decision."

Margo shook her head no, splayed a hand on her chest, and said dramatically, and grammatically, "Not I."

"Pete did?" I said. "You actually let him plan his own life?" Which was totally out of character for her.

She edged her chair nearer to the fire. "Come closer, ladies," she said, her voice going spooky. "It's time for a ghost story." A foghorn moaned in the distance, as if she'd ordered "creepy" from the sound man.

Em flashed me an unhappy glance and fished her necklace from under her sweater.

"Whoa," I said. "Maybe this isn't the time or place . . ." Em was rubbing the amulet against the evil eye.

"Nonsense. It's the perfect time and place. This is what you do around a fire at night. It's what we did at Camp Tikvah around the campfire."

Camp Tikvah was Margo's childhood summer camp, where she'd learned skills her parents believed were more important than weaving lariats and playing tennis. In a peaceful lake nestled in the Catskill Mountains, the counselors taught their charges to swim underwater in case they ever had to cross a river with storm troopers firing bullets from the shore. At Camp Tikvah, Margo had learned how to build a fire, so if what happened with Hitler ever happened again, she could at least make light and heat in her forest hideout. In spite of her parents' obsession, which never took a vacation, Margo had loved Camp Tikvah.

She was smiling now. "It's okay, Em," she soothed in a warm voice. "This one has a happy ending. Though I admit, it's a bit odd." A bit? Margo didn't do things by bits. "Last night my aunt came to me in a dream."

"Tante Violet?" I asked.

"Who else would I allow into my subconscious? Not my awful aunt Yetta with the tuna-fish breath. Of course, Tante Violet."

"She's been dead for thirty years."

"Like the grandmother in *Fiddler on the Roof*," Em said. She'd seen the Driftwood's production of the musical three years before.

"Yes, dear," Margo said. "Only Tante Violet didn't wear a *sheitel*, a wig. Her hair was beautifully highlighted and she was dressed in a Versace dress with the gold earrings I should have inherited that my cousin Cindy stole from the bank vault. But that's another story."

I hoped the firelight allowed Margo to see my eye roll.

"Tante Violet brought me a message from beyond. She told me Pete had learned his lesson, he was older and wiser, and that I needed to trust him because"—here she took a deep breath—"a tavern can't corrupt a good man, and a synagogue can't reform a bad one. It's a Yiddish expression."

"I don't understand it even in English," Em said.

"It means a good man is a good man no matter where he is, whatever temptations surround him. So I should trust him. And I should trust myself. And this is a direct quote. 'You'll survive no matter what, Margala. This you should know in your heart.'"

My girlfriend shot me a look that said, yes, I'd told her the same thing, but without the Versace and the thirty years in the grave it didn't carry as much weight.

"So at breakfast I told Pete to give WJX a call and he starts there in two weeks. He'll be covering the pennant race. And next summer he'll be broadcasting his tush off from God knows where. He's so excited. He really wants this."

"And you? You're good with it?" I asked. In fact, Margo looked more than good. She looked, in the light of the fire, radiant.

"I'll be too busy to miss him. I have plans of my own. You've heard me mention my secret project." Em and I, relieved the ghost story was over, nodded fervently. "Secret because I never thought it would come to pass, but now I'm going for it."

A dog barked somewhere behind us. I saw Margo's brows knit quizzically.

"Talk," I said, trying to steer her back.

"I'm talking. Last year, I took an option on some property near Teal Duck Creek and next summer that's where I'm going to open a theater camp for kids. I'm thinking six-year-olds to sixteen-year-olds, maybe up to eighteen. We'll do all the regular camp activities, but we'll also have acting and music classes, and lessons in the behind-the-scenes arts. Makeup and props, scenery and costumes. And we'll award scholarships for any child who can't afford the fee. Also, a quarter of the profits will go to charity. Pete gets to pick which." She stretched an arm to grasp Emine's hand. "One more thing. I'd like Merry to be on the staff. With your permission, of course. And on the condition she doesn't screw up during the school year. She keeps up her grades, she watches her step with the boys, she doesn't torment her brother, she's respectful to you and Adnan, and, most of all, she promises to never run away again. That should keep her in line."

For a moment, there was silence. Just the crickets chirping applause. Then the dog barked again and Em came back to us. "That is so beautiful and so kind," she said. "You are such dear friends. Not only to me but to my family. You, Nora, you saved my daughter's life during the storm."

I waved it away. "Scott and Jack did the major—"

"Oh, please." Margo's voice dripped sarcasm. "Let's defer to the men, why don't we? Modesty is a virtue, but false modesty is a mortal sin. Check with Sister Loretta. I heard you did more than your share of heavy lifting. Merry told me how you shouldered that bookcase."

Scott had said as we drove through the tail end of the storm trailing the ambulance carrying Merry, "You never know how you're going to act under fire until you're tested. Well, now you know, Nora. You passed."

"I did what had to be done," I said now.

"You always do," Margo fired back, with not the slightest whiff of sarcasm. That might have been the nicest thing my best friend ever said to me. It took a lot to earn praise from Margo, so when she came through, it really meant something. It meant the world to me.

Em nodded. Then she said, "And you, Margo, with the theater and the camp, taking Merry under your wings. You also are saving my child. You have such a good heart."

"Along with my big mouth," Margo cracked, but she was reaching into her pocket for a tissue.

"How can I ever thank you both?"

I suddenly noticed Margo wasn't wearing her usual three layers of mascara. She'd planned to cry along with Em, and cry they did. Me too.

After we mopped up, I said to Margo, "Paulette and Bernie would be proud of you, sweetheart. You're doing a . . . ? What do you call a good deed?"

"A mitzvah," Em answered. "It's called a mitzvah. Each one changes the entire world. Margo taught me."

We three had never been closer.

"Just one favor, Em," Margo said, as she delicately wiped her runny nose on the sleeve of her sweatshirt. "Let your mother-in-law know about the camp and Merry's part in it. I would have told the *kaltak* myself before she left yesterday, but I was afraid if she heard I was in the picture, she'd cancel her flight." Margo checked her watch. "She should be back in Istanbul by now. Write about it in your next email to her."

"It will be my pleasure," Em said. "I can't tell you how much pleasure."

"Good news needs to be celebrated," I announced. I'd brought along a bag of marshmallows, a box of graham crackers, and a few chocolate bars.

"S'mores," Margo burbled, as excited as a kid. "Just like Camp Tikvah." She passed out twigs from the pile of kindling. We toasted marshmallows and made sweet sandwiches. We dished about the fall TV schedule and the fashions at the most recent awards show, junk food chatter, marshmallow light.

We were debating *People* magazine's choices of the world's most beautiful when a ruffle of loud woofs detonated in the still air. We looked toward the sound.

"That's a big dog's bark," Margo said. "And really close. He wouldn't happen to be attached to a certain handsome lieutenant colonel who's been known to frequent your premises?"

Dog's out of the bag, I thought. Good timing.

"Yes, that's probably Sarge," I said. "He likes being out on the deck."

"Sarge stays over?" Margo asked slyly.

"In his crate in the mudroom."

"Well, at least he's not stretched out at the end of the bed, watching you two . . ." She caught herself. "So you and Scott are into sleepovers now, are you?"

I had to laugh. This time I had enough answers to satisfy my personal Grand Inquisitor, the woman I thought of as Torquemada in Prada. I'd made more life-changing decisions in the last week than I had in the previous eight years. Maybe the vitamin D in the summer sun had strengthened my bones. I felt stronger yet lighter.

"With Jack back at school, Scott and I go with the flow. I've stayed over with him twice. He does make a mean cheese omelet for breakfast. Tonight it's already late." It was almost ten. "By the time he and I finish . . . uh . . . talking, he'll probably want to stay."

"Uh, talking. Right." Margo was blowing the flame on a toasted marshmallow. "So the summer is over, but the . . . you know . . . isn't?"

"The 'you know'"—and I knew as much as anyone could after less than three months—"continues."

"Long-distance is difficult," Em said. "When I lived in Marmaris on the Turquoise Coast and Adnan was in Istanbul, it was so hard to keep the feelings going."

"It won't be that much of a stretch for us," I said. Even the crickets had gone quiet, listening. I talked about Scott's new job in Bethesda. His buying a condo there. My upcoming job with National Care and Rehab.

Margo's mouth was plugged with marshmallow or Em could never have raced past her to the finish line. She said, "You took the job with the awful boss? I thought you didn't want to work for her."

Margo swallowed the marshmallow and broke into poetry. "Gaffigan, Gaffigan, will Nora ever laugh again?" No alcoholic beverages were permitted on the beach, but the bonfire and the s'mores had worked their pixilating magic. She'd been transformed into a twelve-year-old on a sugar high.

I laughed, to prove I could. But also because I was happy, a new feeling for me on the last summer night in Tuckahoe.

"Working for Tess will be a challenge," I said. "Or maybe not. She could surprise me. But whatever, I'll handle it. Josh Zimmerman thinks I can." Josh had done his bit, reshaping the schedule so my commute would work before and after I'd relocated. "And even if it sucks, he believes that what doesn't kill you makes you more alive."

Margo curled her lip dismissively. "Whatever. And Jack. What does he say?"

"I called him right before I phoned in my yes to Tess. He told me to go for it. Absolutely." I preempted the next question. "Scott too. He'd given me a Bravo Zulu for action during the storm and he's convinced if Tess and I ever put on the gloves, I could take her in the first round." I flexed a biceps. "What really sold him is the job's location. He and I will be working only five miles apart and living even closer."

"You're moving in with him?" Margo's eyes, even without the mascara, were huge.

"I'll be moving out of Baltimore and looking for my own place in Bethesda. That's the preliminary plan. But let's see where the road takes me. Or," I corrected the passive to active, "what road I take."

It had been a busy summer. I'd saved a kid or two, a house, maybe Lon's legacy. With my call to Tess (and when I'd given her my "yes," she'd said in her sweetest, most sincere voice, "You won't be sorry"), with that leap of faith, I might have kept the summers I loved with the friends I loved.

And now it was time to pack it up. On my feet, staring at the ocean, I said, "High tide is due in about fifteen minutes. We need to have the fire out and the place cleaned up before the tide sweeps everything out to sea. Town council rules. Let's get going."

We got to work. Once finished, we slung our chairs over our shoulders. Trust the tide to come in on time. As we walked the sand, it vacuumed our footprints behind us, the only sign we'd been there.

I'd left the deck light on. Behind its panoramic window, the great room shone golden, and someone—guess who—had turned on all the lamps in the master bedroom. The house that I hoped would be mine for *my* forever, and Jack's after that, was a softly glowing beacon in the dark.

The small white string lights draped on the fence lining the beach path suddenly came to life. That had to be Scott's doing. He must have heard our laughter drawing near and flicked them on by remote. We passed early signs of fall along the trail: big bluestem grass, silvery in summer, beginning to shade into autumn purple; a few clumps of star asters getting a head start; and yellowing Northwind switch grass poking through the fence posts. As the lane narrowed, we edged into single file. Me first, then Em, then Margo. The path was clear and smooth enough for us to put one foot in front of the other without losing our balance. It was an easy passage. We just followed the lights.

ACKNOWLEDGMENTS

First, thank you to my multitalented agent, Elaine English, who has believed in me and my work through three novels under her care. Her guidance and encouragement have been invaluable and her friendship is cherished.

I'm grateful to my Penguin Random House team more than I can express, especially Ellen Edwards, who played a major role in shaping the narrative from its inception, and Tracy Bernstein, my amazing editor, who gets my sensibility and my writing at every level; she has perfect pitch and a keen eye that monitors details but never fails to see the greater vision.

This story required considerable research, and I, like Margo in *Barefoot Beach*, was fortunate to have a wide variety of experts backing me up. On the subject of dance/movement therapy, I am indebted to Sharon Chaiklin, a major figure in the field, and to Judith Fischer, one of its most notable practitioners, both of whom submitted to my interview process with patience and grace. Thank you, too, Fern Eisner, who knows the immediate world and shares her sources.

And then there are my theater people: Erica Ress-Martin of the Royal Palm Players and Rich Madzel of the Try It Out Theatre, who gave me insight into the workings on- and backstage. Toba Dobkin Barth also contributed her behind-the-scenes experiences and did double duty as one of my two main beach mavens. She and Malynda Hawes Madzel led me on productive (and fun!) explorations of Maryland and Delaware beach towns. We watched sunsets and storms together, prowled craft festivals, and visited restaurants, shops, and secluded beaches. I used material from these excursions to weave the scrim of atmosphere for *Barefoot Beach*.

I thank my experts in all things Turkish: Hasan Ilk; Ali Ozgur Erdoğan; and Semra Tekmen. They were very generous in sharing details about their native country and culture.

For military, technical, and medical information, I am indebted to Mack Allemande, Sid Golden, Laurel Z. Ginsburg, Bernard Icore, and Benjamin Icore; and to A. E. Dees, whose unique perspective on the book and heartfelt belief in its author propelled the project from start to finish.

To those men and women of the United States Armed Forces, active and retired, who shared their stories with me in person and in online forums for wounded and amputee veterans (many of whom wished to remain anonymous): I hope I honored you in my portrayals.

I'm particularly grateful to Jon Faust for his expertise and willingness to share the skills he employs as a volunteer firefighter. He and his colleagues do remarkable lifesaving work. And I'm grateful to Baltimore's legendary TV reporter Andy Barth, my go-to guy for baseball information and material related to broadcasting.

Essential to my work are longtime writer friends who are memorable characters themselves. Among those who have dispensed advice unsparingly: Nancy Baggett; Randi DuFresne; Cronshi Englander; Ruth Glick; Connie Hay; Kathryn Kimball Johnson; Chassie West; Linda Williams; and Alan Zendell.

I must single out for their ongoing counsel and, as meaningful to me, for their cheerleading skills—they never lost faith in the story—Binnie Syril Braunstein and Joanne Settel.

Finally, but always primarily, I'm grateful to my family, who continue to provide support, love, and inspiration. Especially to my daughter, Amanda Schwartz Kennedy, who speaks her mind, lives her heart, and proves by the life she leads that she will always be my greatest creative production and most definitely her own person. It is to Amanda that this book is dedicated.

barefoot beach

TOBY DEVENS

*This Conversation Guide is intended to enrich the
individual reading experience, as well as encourage us
to explore these topics together—because books,
and life, are meant for sharing.*

A CONVERSATION
WITH TOBY DEVENS

Q. What does a typical writing day look like for you?

A. My day starts early because I tend to wake up raring to go. I'm a morning person, although once I'm well into the story I write whenever and wherever. For me, it's all about momentum. Once I've started, the endorphins kick in, and it's like a runner's high. I'll be at it for hours at a stretch, rousing myself only when I realize my tush has fallen asleep or I've skipped breakfast *and* lunch. And when I'm finished for the day, I play a trick on myself (and fall for it every time). I don't stop at the end of a chapter. I pause at an exciting point along the way so that I get a jump-start when I next pick up the narrative thread.

I do try to fit in time with friends for a power walk or a cup of coffee. Writing is an isolating experience and my theory is you need to get out in the world if you're going to write about it. Then again, I'm always writing, either on a keyboard or in my head—playing with the characters, nudging the plot along. When I'm working on a novel, I feel as if I'm living in two worlds. Half of me resides in a brick-and-mortar home in Maryland, while the other half is hanging out in a never-never land of my own making, in this case a lovely shore town named Tuckahoe Beach.

Q. Is Tuckahoe a real place, or based on a real town?

A. It's real to me and I hope to my readers, but, in truth, it's as imaginary as Shangri-La. There is no town named Tuckahoe in Maryland, though there is a Tuckahoe River and a Tuckahoe State Park on the state's Eastern Shore. Many sites in the area carry the names of Native American tribes. I chose Tuckahoe because I liked the rhythm of the word, which some scholars think is from the Algonquin language. My fantasy Tuckahoe Beach isn't based on any single place but was inspired by the resort towns along the Delmarva coast, where I spent a lot of time (poor me!) soaking in the atmosphere. Sufficiently soaked, I constructed a setting tailored to the needs of the story. And I had a wonderful time designing that beach town of my dreams. As I created it, I fell in love with it.

Q. Did the idea of the book begin with the setting or with the character?

A. I was standing on the balcony of a friend's condo. The sky was golden and the sea was mirror smooth. Ten minutes later, storm clouds rolled in. I watched transfixed as the first spatters pocked the sand below. By the time the wind had picked up and lashes of rain chased the sunbathers, I was thinking, *I want to write this.* The beach itself was already a fabulous character in my mind—beautiful, seductive, temperamental, and able to cause all kinds of havoc—and it became a character in the book. So to answer the question: both.

Q. Do you model your characters on people you know, on your own experiences? You write in first person, so how much of your protagonist is you?

A. I love a T-shirt my daughter gave me that warns, "Be careful what you say around me. You might appear in my next novel." Funny. But not really true. I wish I were talented enough to replicate in two dimensions some of the characters I know in three. Of course, if I *could* do that, I'd never confess to it. As for my own experiences, there's probably some of me in all of my characters, because to bring them to life I have to practically inhabit them. So, in my novels, I've been: a surgeon whose husband left her for a man, a Korean-Jewish cellist who suffers from stage fright, and now a dance therapist and owner of a ballroom and Zumba studio. Mind you, these are just the leads. Figure in the supporting players and I've been both genders, all ages, and I've worked at occupations as varied as molecular biologist and fish salesman. What an interesting life—lives!—I lead.

Q. In Barefoot Beach *you write about dance-and-movement therapy, operating a repertory theater, owning a coffee shop, artificial insemination, wounded warriors, and military working dogs, among other topics. How do you research all these subjects?*

A. The story may be fiction, the characters invented, but I firmly believe the facts should be authentic. That is a matter of respect—for the reader, for the work, for myself. When you write fiction you're casting a spell (the poet Samuel Taylor Coleridge called this compact between poet or novelist and reader "the willing suspension of disbelief"), but one false note, one breach of trust, and the spell can be broken. If the eye stops on what may be a teensy mistake but appears to the reader as a glaring blunder, she's tugged from the world I created. It's important to get it right, and research helps do that.

On a more personal level, research is a learning experience for an author and I relish it. In my first novel, Kat Greenfield, a fiber artist, employs a technique I knew nothing about. Luckily there was a talented weaver nearby willing to talk to me. More than just talk. Carol sat me down at her loom and led me through the basics. Such fun! So much information!

In *Happy Any Day Now*, my protagonist is a cellist. I don't play a note, but I learned how an orchestra operates. I interviewed musicians, gathered info on their online forums, then had performing cellists review the manuscript for accuracy. And the book, with insider details, was richer for it.

Nora Farrell is a dance therapist and teaches Zumba and ballroom because I took tap and ballet as a kid, Zumba as an adult, and have always loved to dance. But what I thought of as recreation became Nora's profession after I spoke to someone whose fine-motor coordination, damaged by a neurodegenerative disease, was being improved by dance therapy sessions. Also, in a dizzying twist of fate, I discovered—only after I'd chosen Nora's career and begun my research—that an iconic figure in the dance movement community lived a mile from my home and the national organization was located around the corner. How could I *not* have taken that for a sign? I spent hours interviewing the literal movers and shakers in the field, who shared their knowledge and experience.

Sometimes landing a great resource takes searching and a bit of persuading. Sometimes it's as quick as clipping a coupon. For the ballroom scenes, I snapped up a discount offered by a national chain of dance studios, took lessons, interviewed the instructors and the manager . . . and polished my tango.

On my research quest, I rely on the kindness of strangers, a number of whom have become friends. I'm grateful to all who generously shared with me.

Q. Readers often like to connect with authors via social media. Is that something you enjoy?

A. I do enjoy it, because I so appreciate hearing what they think and feel about my books, and about other topics. Maybe I'm slightly biased, but they seem to be a particularly bright group. Of course, communicating in person, at appearances, signings, or book club meetings, is ideal. We can talk face-to-face and in some depth about all kinds of issues, some of which I address in my novels. But social media gives me a chance to reach out to huge numbers of readers, current and prospective, and have an immediate, sometimes instant exchange on Facebook or Twitter. I can converse one-on-one with a reader, and the world—*virtually* the world—can watch or join in. Here's to modern technology!

Q. You've written many articles. Which do you prefer, fiction or nonfiction?

A. These days, my heart belongs to fiction. In the long form, it's more challenging to bring off than a factual article or an opinion piece. The novelist has to create a universe from scratch, then keep the planets in motion and carefully track them for hundreds of pages. And yet what luxury to have the space to develop fully realized characters, play the themes throughout, and wind a plot from problematic start to satisfying ending. Besides, I get to write dialogue, which is a pleasure. Dialogue emerges more spontaneously than narrative for me, so some of my favorite lines in all novels, mine included, are uttered by characters. In *Barefoot Beach*, I'm thinking of Margo's witty and cutting ripostes, Merry's rebellious teenage slang, Jack's verbal duels with his mother.

And how's this for a fringe benefit? Because of its intricacy, its length, and its demand for the author's undivided attention, a novel, whether you're reading it or writing it, allows you to escape from your familiar environment. (Even if there's no place like home, it's fun to travel.) What other profession, with the possible exception of acting, allows its practitioners the opportunity to exist, for most of their waking hours, in a world completely different from the one that actually surrounds them? And mine, unlike the actor's, is of my own making. I write the lines. I design the sets. I invent adventures and determine the outcomes. I run the show. Not a bad way to spend a day . . . or the greater part of a life.

Q. What are you working on now?

A. Two projects. I'm halfway through a novel about a family that welcomes an immigrant cousin into their home and the ways in which the search for his missing sister reverberates through their lives. Two settings—Brooklyn and Budapest—provide the background, and the story incorporates some of my favorite themes: mother-daughter relationships, romantic and sexual complications, the powerful bonds of female friendship, the immigrant experience, and how the past invades the present with unexpected consequences. The book is part history, part mystery, a tale of love, loss, and redemption, and, most of all, secrets—many secrets. And surprises.

But then there's the beach, which is so alluring, so sultry, whether it's Fire Island, Malibu, or Cannes. Another story currently percolating unfolds on beaches around the world as it follows my protagonist's adventures and misadventures. She . . . No, I'll stop there. I don't want to talk it out; I want to write it out.

QUESTIONS FOR DISCUSSION

1. A major theme of *Barefoot Beach* is the marvelous power of female friendship. Has there been a time when a woman friend or a group of friends helped get you through a life-changing or extraordinarily difficult situation? Also, compare the nature of female friendship with the bonds men build with one another.

2. Margo tells Nora, "I'm not supposed to be kind. I'm your best friend. I'm supposed to be honest." Do you agree or disagree?

3. How might the story be different if Jack was a girl instead of a boy?

4. How do you feel about children of sperm donors, or adopted children, contacting their biological parents?

5. Nora, Margo, and Emine are close friends despite very different backgrounds. Have you ever experienced obstacles to friendship because of different ethnicities, religions, or upbringing?

6. Do you believe that Margo will be able to let go of the episodes in her past that haunt her and regain the trust she once had in her marriage? Is

it possible to trust fully again—in friendship, family, work, or love—after you have felt betrayed?

7. Is there someplace in your world where the surroundings impart a sense of peace and happiness in the way Nora finds joy and relaxation at Barefoot Beach? If your access to it were threatened, what might your reaction be?

Toby Devens has been an editor, public information specialist, and author of short fiction and articles for national magazines. She has lectured worldwide about writing and women's issues and has led writing workshops. Her first published book was a humorous and poignant collection of poetry that was excerpted in *McCall's* and *Reader's Digest*. She is also the author of *My Favorite Midlife Crisis (Yet)*, her debut novel. *Happy Any Day Now*, her second novel, was published by Penguin Random House to excellent reviews. Toby lives halfway between Baltimore, Maryland, and Washington, D.C.

CONNECT ONLINE

tobydevens.com
facebook.com/tobydevensauthor